"I must t_____ in a voice so low it was nearly a whisper, "...and in confidence. Nothing's definite yet, but it may be possible for me to buy Le Palais-Royal. That's why this lunch is so important. You see, all the ones who really matter will be here today. And...I'm counting on you."

Claude was stunned. "That would be a fine thing, Armand." The words sounded inadequate, but he could think of no others.

"Fine," said Armand. "If it should happen, though, I just want you to know there'll be a place for you. A special place."

Claude felt torn between enjoying Armand's praise and wondering if he was being manipulated. He replayed Armand's words. Had they amounted to a kind of bribe? "Thank you, Armand." He managed a smile. "But now I must get on with the sauce."

Armand smiled. "Of course. Bonne chance, Claude..."

# Appetites

## TOM MURPHY

ST. MARTIN'S PRESS/NEW YORK

APPETITES

Copyright © 1987 by Tom Murphy.

Library of Congress Catalog Card Number: 87-4392

ISBN: 0-312-91383-4   Can. ISBN: 0-312-91384-2

Printed in the United States of America

St. Martin's Press hardcover edition published 1987
First St. Martin's Press mass market edition/February 1989

10  9  8  7  6  5  4  3  2  1

*This book is for Frank Cucci:*
*Bon appétit!*

## Acknowledgments

Many kind people helped me to research this book. I am especially grateful to Richard Flaste and Pierre Franey of *The New York Times,* to Sirio Maccioni and his then chef Alain Sailhac of Le Cirque, who graciously allowed me to spend many informative hours in that wonderful kitchen, to Johannes and Avery Lichtenstein, whose insights into the world of haute viniculture are both illuminating and delicious, and to Phyllis Block, who conjured up the title.

Tom Murphy
Brooklyn, New York, 1987

# 1

ELISE STOOD AT the kitchen counter and forced herself to concentrate on the onion she was cutting into small, regular cubes. Maybe he'd think the tears were from the onion. Damn him!

Chop, chop.

At least now she didn't have to look at him. If she did, she'd get sidetracked. He'd take away the anger with a smile. Touch her gently, and she'd melt. It was plain unfair, the power Jared had over her.

"You just don't understand," he said, his voice so even she could feel the touch of cold steel in it. "We're so much in the hole right now, a few thousand more won't make any difference. But a new furnace will make a hell of a difference."

Chop, chop.

Elise knew she was flushing pink. She wanted to throw her chopped onions right in his face. Maybe the knife, too. Where had she read that half of all murders happened in kitchens? Jared was pigheaded. His ideas about money had no foundation in anything real. But if I say that he'll think I'm making some kind of slur on his family. Hell, maybe he's right. Maybe it doesn't matter. In a hundred years, who'll give a damn, anyway?

Chop, chop.

What would Daddy do in a situation like this? She hated herself for thinking about her father now. For needing him so badly. No. No point in wondering what Daddy would do, she told herself with a sinking feeling. He'd never get into a fix like this to begin with. But God, how she longed for just a little of his strength. His determination.

No, she thought, I left on my own and I got into this on my own. And I won't go to him for money or anything else.

Chop, chop.

"Jared," she said quietly, feeling a little silly, almost as though she were a mother having to spell it out to a six-year-old, "we have exactly two hundred fourteen dollars and six cents in the bank, and the mortgage is due in two weeks and I haven't paid the phone bill yet." The words came out in a rush, and as she spoke them Elise knew she was setting a trap for herself. Any challenge was catnip to Jared—the tougher the challenge, the more it turned him on. He'd convince her the two hundred in the bank was two thousand. He can convince me of anything, just about.

She remembered the night she'd first seen Jared, five beautiful years ago, right here in Stowe. He'd bought her dinner with fifty cents in his pocket, charmed the guy who owned the place into giving him credit, had the old man laughing and Elise, too. At the easy daring, the magic in him. Jared was a high wire act performing without a net, and he'd reached out to her with his strong hands and taken her with him over the dizzy heights. And it hadn't mattered then that Daddy and Kate didn't approve.

Now she could feel herself getting tired of their argument. Was it hopelessness she felt? She stopped chopping and put the onions in a bowl.

"They'll foreclose if we get behind with the mortgage. They're very tough about that. Last week there were five foreclosures in Stowe alone." Elise felt out of character as a Cassandra, but it had to be said. Somebody had to keep a toehold on reality.

"Hell, honey," Jared said, suddenly contrite, "we can scrap the whole thing if it gets to you that bad. I can get plenty of wood for the cutting like last year. We'll save up and maybe get the new furnace next year."

Elise felt a weight lifting from her heart. Amazing, how he could change everything in the space of a heartbeat. Now she could look at him, sitting there caught in a beam of clear morning sunshine, glowing. Wearing faded jeans and a lumberjack's shirt with a grace that surpassed any movie star she'd ever seen. Damn him.

"Yes," she said, "it does get to me, spending our last penny. Maybe it shouldn't, but it does." Inwardly she cringed. "I guess I'm just not used to handling money—to worrying about it."

Did he hear the guilt in her voice, the feeling that it had been wrong, somehow, to grow up in a house where every comfort was provided and money never mentioned?

He laughed.

That had once been the happiest sound she'd ever heard. Now it could hurt. And his words cut deeper. "Just charge it, please, and send the bills to dear old Daddy?"

She looked away, hoping he wouldn't see her pain. Why is there always this between us, his need to make fun of all the people he thinks of as rich tourists? That's how he first saw me. How proud she'd been that he'd accepted her. That she'd crossed over.

"Cheap shot. Who chooses their father?" She smiled, a quick bitter smile. "But let's face it. I never did think about money until I met you. Daddy would always rather invent a new sauce than teach his dumb daughter about finances."

Jared slid off the old table where he'd been sitting. "And I'd rather kiss his daughter than fight," he said, doing it. Lightly at first. Then not so lightly.

Elise knew there was no way to shield herself from the effect he had on her. It was like flicking on a light switch, her response was that deep, that immediate. He only had to touch her. Or look at her in a certain way. At first it had

3

been pure adventure, liberating. Now she sensed that her need for him was like an addict's need. Beyond reason.

"You taste good," he said huskily. Urgently.

"If you like raw onions." She felt herself smiling for real now.

And they were moving together with a motion so fluid that to Elise it felt almost like a dream. As though she were suddenly powerless and distanced, watching a film of herself and the golden young man at her side.

Yes. An addiction.

Then they were in the little bedroom at the back. She felt the gentleness of his hands as they touched her shoulders, then the buttons on her old denim shirt. Unbuttoning. How astonishingly tender Jared could be when you considered he was six foot two of concentrated muscle.

Contrasts, she thought, Jared is all about contrasts. The scholarship boy who chucked it all to spend a year in Aspen. The cynic who'll climb Mount Mansfield just to pick me wildflowers. The sexual pirate who always comes back to me. So far. Elise felt an extra edge of recklessness with him, now and always, a sense that anything might happen. Of skating fast over thin ice. Skimming across the bad parts.

Thank God for the good parts, she thought as he continued undressing her, making a ritual out of it, as though she were a very small child. Elise loved it.

She looked up at him through a mist of anticipation. Jared was concentrating, gravely wiggling out of his cowboy boots. Elise liked to watch him doing anything at all. An instinctive animal grace underlined every motion: Jared skiing, Jared smiling, Jared making love.

Especially making love.

He touched her cheek. Almost reverently, she thought. Then he changed again, suddenly fierce and urgent. Quicksilver Jared, kissing her hungrily. Lifting her as though she had no weight at all. He buried his head in her breasts and entered her standing, in one silken rush. Gentle thunder.

4

Elise felt herself soaring with him. Heard herself moan softly. Louder.

He lowered her to their bed and Elise could feel the sweet reality of their old worn quilt. Cotton turned to silk by passing time. By other lovers. She kissed his neck and felt the vein throbbing there, a drumbeat. He whispered her name and entered her again and she felt all the tender rage of him igniting.

The phone rang.

"Let it ring," he whispered.

"Let it ring," she answered in the same breath.

The phone rang and rang and somehow it lent piquancy to their lovemaking. Elise felt a pleasant guilty rush, a sense of mischief. The nice feeling of having gotten away with something. That was Vermont to her: getting away from something. From Daddy and his expectations for her, hopes that he radiated somehow, even in silence.

To her father, Elise wasn't much more than a ski bum. In the cool, appraising eyes of her friends from Harvard, Jared might be seen as a hick. *They all think I've betrayed my potential somehow, but they'll never know what I got in exchange.*

She stroked his hair, and it seemed made from sunlight. Glints of gold on dark copper. They lay on their old cannonball bed he'd liberated from the town dump, entwined and silent now in the afterglow. She thought, *I could stay right here, just like this, forever.* She touched his cheek. He opened his eyes and kissed her. The loving began again, slowly at first and then faster. Deeper. Better, if that were possible. Elise sighed, and with a new dimension of pleasure she thought, *Right now I'm happy.*

The phone rang again, somehow louder now, clanging like the Stowe fire alarm, raucous and jangling. Shattering the mood. "Damn and damn," she said, untwining herself. Elise was across the small room in seconds.

"Chez Elise, good morning," she said, not bothering to hide her annoyance.

"Elise?"

Was that Kate? Elise was used to the crispness and control of her stepmother's voice: Kate was British, and a general's daughter at that. But now there was something wrong, a hesitation. An odd quaver. She geared herself to be pleasant. Kate meant well. *She tries harder than I do,* thought Elise with a renewal of guilt.

"Kate? Hi. How are you? How's Daddy?" She talked fast, trying to skim over her uneasiness.

There was a pause. Elise could sense trouble gathering. Kate at last found the words: "Elise, darling . . . It's terrible. He . . . this morning—oh, Elise, your father's dead."

Impossible.

Elise felt trapped, stuck fast to the floor as though she'd grown roots. Her heart was an ice-cold lump. She couldn't move, couldn't think. She felt as though an avalanche was roaring down on top of her, unstoppable, flattening her to the ground.

She looked across the room at Jared. He was up now, getting dressed. He might have been a thousand miles away.

Elise fought for words, struggling against the avalanche that was crushing her down. Filling her head. Roaring in her ears. But her throat was frozen, too. She forced the muscles to move, but the breath had gone right out of her. "Oh," she managed at last. "Oh Kate. No. No!"

"It was his heart, darling."

*Christ, what right has Kate to call me darling?* Elise seized on her resentment of Kate as though it were some priceless treasure. Something to cling to.

Now Elise could feel a dull pounding deep inside her. A drum beating slowly in some great cave of ice. No, only her heart, pounding. She felt dizzy. Groped for the little telephone table, steadied herself, took a deep breath. Better. The room stopped swimming. But to move even one step felt impossible.

*Daddy can't die.*

She looked at Jared. He seemed to come in and out of focus, diffused by the tears forming in her eyes.

I left him, and now he's dead.

She was stabbing herself with the words.

No, it was really Le Palais-Royal I was running from. Dawn till midnight, he loved that place so much there wasn't anything left for me. Was that why she'd had to keep Jared all to herself? Never mentioning her wedding until afterward, knowing how it would shock Daddy and Kate. Taking pleasure in it. Jared was proof that at last she was beyond their reach.

But was she? She wanted her father now, badly.

Suddenly Elise became aware that her stepmother was still on the line, waiting. She took a breath. How long had she been standing there, in the chilly room naked? It could have been an hour. "Poor Kate," she said at last.

"There was no warning at all, darling."

*Darling* again.

"Pierre—your father—had a physical just last month."

Pierre your father. I know he's my father, damn it. Long before you came around. But the anger didn't work, didn't relieve the pounding in her heart or the pain in her head. Kate's voice went on as though she couldn't stop herself. And maybe she can't, Elise thought, feeling a pang of sympathy for her stepmother.

"He was fine last night, Elise." Kate spoke in a kind of a trance. As if by talking about Daddy's death she could somehow reverse the fact of it. "He got up early, as he always does, walked to Le Palais. The boy—you know, Jean-Paul, the apprentice,—found him on the kitchen floor. It was all so quick, darling. He couldn't have felt any pain."

She's trying to be kind—like the hangman asking if the noose is comfortable. Elise knew that she, too, must try. Whatever effort it took. "Well, Kate," she said finally, "I know how terrible this must be for you. We'll come down today if we can. I'm not sure about planes, but they do fly out of Burlington pretty often. We'll be down"—the words

7

came mechanically, like spitting out lumps of cold lead—"in the late afternoon, then, Kate."

"That's fine, darling."

No it isn't fine at all. "Good-bye, Kate." Elise held the phone for a moment longer. Then suddenly she hung up.

Jared came to her side, put his warm hands on her shivering shoulders. "Bad news?"

Elise began trembling with a shudder that seemed to start way down beneath the house, rattling every nerve in her slim body. She struggled to steady herself and then put her arms around him. Clinging. She hated women who clung. "The worst," she said, the tears streaming now. "Daddy— Daddy died this morning." She felt as if she had been carried into some dark place where she had never been before and she hung onto Jared with the grip of a drowning person.

He held her. It felt good, but not good enough. She felt like a lost child in some fairy tale. The kind where you froze to death in the forest or the witch made pudding out of you.

"Hey," he said gently, stroking her hair, "I'm sorry. Very sorry. What can I do?"

Give him back to me. Give me another chance with him.

He cupped her chin in his hand and raised her head until she was forced to look at him. "I know I kid you about him sometimes, honey," Jared said quietly, "but, well, I love you and I'm sorry."

All the things she'd never said to Daddy seemed to be pulling her away from Jared. Slowly, she moved away from his arms and began dressing. Pulled on the underwear she'd discarded so eagerly a few minutes—an eternity—before.

"We'll have to go down there. Today if we can." She forced herself to think practical thoughts. "Could you call the airport while I pack?"

He was at the phone before she finished speaking.

Elise tried to imagine her father's funeral. Who would speak? How many people? What to wear? How unbearable even to think about it—much less go through with it. She

8

thought of the publicity, the headlines Pierre Villeromain's death would make, the hundreds of phone calls. She thought of her own ancient and neglected wardrobe. At least Jared had his going-to-the-bank suit, dark gray flannel, left over from college. It would do. It would have to. Once more Elise thought about their measly bank balance. What clothes might still be in her closet at the Sixty-eighth Street house.

Do we even have enough cash to get a cab from the airport? She tried to remember what it had cost the last time. No use. She dragged her mind through the logistics. So what if I look like a poor relation at the funeral. Daddy won't know.

"You know, I don't remember what I felt when my mother died," she said, as much to herself as to Jared. "She'd been sick for such a long time, and I was only ten. Not quite ten." Almost fifteen years ago.

Jared hung up the phone. "There's a four fifteen Air New England."

"Good. We can make it."

She went into their bathroom and splashed cold water on her face. A red-eyed hag looked back at her from the mirror. At least he won't see me like this.

Their luggage, hardly used these last few years, was back in the mudroom, an unheated lean-to behind the house. Walking very slowly, Elise managed to get there.

And you thought you were free of him at last. That he couldn't hurt you anymore.

Her beat-up old suitcase was an accusation. As Elise pulled it down from the rack she remembered how she'd prized the case when Daddy had given it to her so long ago. How smooth and shiny it had been, the leather gleaming and the brass sparkling like gold. With such a treasure she could go to any palace. And here she was in a tumbledown house on the outskirts of Stowe. A house Daddy had never even seen.

She found an old cloth and dusted the suitcase.

Clothes. The thought of standing at the side of her elegant stepmother was frightening. Well, at least Jared will look fine in his gray flannel—hell, Jared would look fine in a flour sack. She lugged the heavy case back to the bedroom. For a few days, it would do for them both.

Elise stood for a moment watching Jared pack. Liking the intimacy of his clothes and hers in the same case. He packed the gray suit, some shirts and ties. Put on clean cords and a button-down shirt and a tie. Jared in a tie! Last time he wore one was to our wedding. Elise suddenly saw him as she thought Kate would see him. Quicksilver. Beautiful—maybe a shade too beautiful. And almost an adolescent. No. You're judging him again. Just what you left New York to escape. She tried to stop it, to keep that part of her mind in a separate sealed compartment. No luck. The unspoken judgments were always there, lurking. Had been, in all her time with Jared. The Pierre Villeromain in her was too strong.

She thought of the day Daddy invited her whole fourth grade class to Le Palais-Royal for tea. Served them something he called "gâteau Elise," a confection of hazelnut meringue layers frosted with chocolate butter cream. It still appeared on the menu from time to time. Even Mrs. Garfinkel, the world's hardest-to-impress teacher, had been impressed. For days afterwards Elise had been the most popular girl at Chapin. A fleeting glory: soon Laura Beekman's mother, never to be outdone, took them all to the circus.

Elise folded the last of her good silk blouses from college. She could smell the kitchen of Le Palais-Royal, the enchanting aromas. She could hear the excitement: laughter, shouts, pots clanging, sauces bubbling, the hiss of a fish fillet sizzling in clarified butter. Daddy's voice, giving orders. She could hear it just as clearly as if it were right here in their bedroom.

Those afternoons when Mummy was sick, the one time she'd had him all to herself. No Mummy or nurses or

Nanny or the restaurant itself. Fifteen years ago. She'd go to Le Palais right after school and stay until evening. Elise knew why. They didn't want her tiring Mummy. The restaurant was as different from Mummy's sickroom as a place could be. A magical place. Every pot held some miracle, and Daddy invited her to try them all. No matter if she was small and the great black range loomed over her and the saucepots and stockpots seemed bigger than the rain barrel at the farm. Daddy would lift her in one great swoop, up and up until she was squealing with fear and delight, high as the pot rack overhead; then down again, squirming, to smell, see, taste.

She remembered the time he'd taught her to make an omelette. Daddy, towering in his chef's white jacket, his blue and white checked trousers crisply pressed, a fine damask napkin knotted at his throat. She could feel the pride coming out of him like warmth from an oven as he stood her on a kitchen stool, tied a napkin around her skinny waist, handed her a wire whisk and a bowl, and said, "Well, ma petite, now comes your first lesson." As she stood there with his long arm around her it seemed to Elise that nothing bad could ever happen here. Not with Daddy to help her.

The first thing she learned in the kitchen was that nothing was as easy as it looked. Daddy could be tough—worse than Mrs. Garfinkel. First he showed her the right way to crack an egg. Just so, with the merest flick of the wrist, precisely in half, each empty half tucked one inside the other, comme ça. Then the whisking. She must hold the whisk lightly, add the cream, just a drop, now let's chop the tarragon, isn't it lovely and fresh? But hold the knife *so*, with your fingers just resting on the top of the tip, *chérie*, there! You cannot possibly cut yourself, see? And we chop with a rocking motion, that's why the blade is curved, and we never just put down the knife, my darling, we first wipe it and run it down the steel so it will be sharp for the next time, non?

11

So many, many things to learn before she even put the butter into the pan. And not just butter, but sweet butter from Normandy, and precisely the right amount, and wait until it bubbles and foams—so!—but not a second longer, or it will burn and get bitter and we can't have that, can we?

Elise felt as though she was taking a very hard examination. What she wanted most was not so much to make the omelette but to please Daddy, and it looked as though that might be impossible.

He was being patient. Studiedly patient, even smiling. But Elise could see the effort he was making. After all, everybody else here could probably make perfect omelettes in their sleep. They'd probably been born making perfect omelettes.

Now. Pour the eggs into the pan. Hiss, crackle, excitement! Just let them set a moment, now, there, move the pan quickly, jerk it toward you, see how the eggs move, all together? We shouldn't need a spatula at all.

To Elise it was thrilling as flying to the moon. She knew Daddy's restaurant was famous, that people wrote about it in *The New York Times*. And now she was actually cooking there! She watched that first omelette so intently it burned. She looked up and saw Daddy's eyes regarding her coolly, as though she were some uninvited stranger he didn't quite know what to do with. She felt a pang, a quiver, tears starting.

Then he smiled and covered her small hand with his big one, and together they flipped the burnt eggy mess into the garbage. He kissed her, and everything was all right again. "Alors, little one, I probably burned my first omelette too. It is just that when you are a Villeromain, people expect more of you."

*Especially your Daddy*, said a silent voice that lived in some dark place behind his real voice. "But look how well you have learned already, Elise," he said, making the best of it. "You crack eggs like a veteran; you are chopping nicely as well. You will do it."

12

No question of not doing it.

On her third try Elise made an omelette that caused Daddy to give her a big hug. It was properly creamy inside and not too brown outside. Her presentation on the plate was far from perfect; she'd had to use both hands to keep the pan steady when she was folding it. It looked a little lopsided. A small thing, Daddy assured her. Then he laughed in triumph, a big laugh like trumpets, kissed her again, and picked her up and swung her around until she was dizzy and flushed with a fine heady rapture. Her heart was still spinning when at last he set her down.

But why hadn't she pleased him more? Done it right the first time?

All her life Elise had had that feeling, that whatever she did, it wasn't quite enough. Not that he'd ever come right out and said so. It was just a look, a tone of voice, a Gallic shrug that said well, what more can one hope for? And now she'd never know: was that really how he had always felt?

*I could have bent a little, talked to him about myself, about him, about Kate. Even about Jared.*

Jared.

She felt his hand on her shoulder now. Warm. "Honey, we'd better move it."

She closed the suitcase while Jared wrote a sign on the back of a menu: *Chez Elise is closed for a week due to a death in the family. Back next Saturday. Elise and Jared Carter.* She smiled at the sign, at the pretentious name they'd given the restaurant as a joke. One big ratty room with the stove and refrigerator behind a counter. Chairs and tables from tag sales, enameled deep green by Jared, green and white curtains in the windows, the ancient potbellied stove giving it a touch of Vermont character. Bring your own wine or beer, wear what you like, laugh, have fun. It'd be a fern bar, Elise thought ruefully, if only we had a fern. But it worked somehow. Elise's ragouts had a small fame in Stowe, and her home-baked bread and croissants, the omelettes she'd learned from Daddy so long, long ago. She taped the sign to the window.

They were driving fast on the road to Burlington, the suitcase rattling in the back of Jared's old Chevy pickup. Elise moved close to him on the seat, feeling his warmth. For a while they said nothing. Strange random thoughts passed through her mind. Odd fragments, the shrapnel of memory. But it all came back to Daddy, to missing the chance to say good-bye. Their last phone call? She tried to remember. Weeks ago. More. Just before Daddy and Kate left for France, when Le Palais closed for August. More than a month. And she couldn't even remember what they'd said to each other.

Elise felt an unfamiliar lassitude, as though she'd come down with some tropical sleeping sickness. A feeling of hopelessness, of not wanting to make the effort her father's New York would demand from her.

Jared's hands on the steering wheel were strong and confident. She reached out and covered his right hand with her left one. He looked at her, just a glance, and smiled his magic smile, but even that wasn't enough. Elise wondered if the sun itself had heat enough to melt the chill inside her.

Then a sickening feeling came over her that had nothing to do with grief. She realized that her life in Stowe, her life with Jared and the little restaurant they called Chez Elise, were all because of Daddy, her response to him. And now, with him gone, what did it really mean?

I built my life around something that isn't there anymore. She began sobbing quietly.

Jared turned to her. "Pretty bad?"

She squeezed his hand as though they were the last two people in the world. "Pretty bad," she said softly.

The pickup truck sped onward into the blue distance.

# 2

IT WAS SEVEN fifteen when Claude got to work, earlier than usual. Already he felt tense. Today was the memorial luncheon. Today everything must be perfect, and more than perfect.

Changing into his chef's whites, he thought of the menu: the famous lobster consommé, Pierre's lobster and cheese soufflé, grilled duck breasts, puff pastry swans for dessert— swans of Claude's own invention, filled with mousse. All Pierre's closest friends would be there. The famous, the rich, celebrated food critics and restauranteurs. All wondering what would become of this place, now that Pierre was gone.

Claude walked up the worn back stairs to the kitchen, as he had done six days a week for nearly five years. His hand touched the brass knob of the kitchen door and Claude felt a pang of regret. Sharper than a knife-cut. The door creaked a little. Didn't it always? But today the familiar sound felt sinister. Threatening. From now on nothing could be quite the same here.

Claude stepped into the kitchen and felt the silence echo. Like walking into a crypt. His hand went up to the napkin knotted at his throat. He remembered Pierre wearing just such a napkin, the jaunty angle of it looking so exactly right. Claude's eyes misted.

15

Halfway across the kitchen he stopped in his tracks, as if he were about to bump into Pierre, to hear his welcoming "Bonjour, Claude!"

Claude felt like crying. But there was no time for tears. Not now. Not today, of all days. He walked to his marble pastry counter, remembering his first months here. How like a father Pierre had been. Even taking him all the way out to Forest Hills, showing him where he could afford to live, where there might be a pleasant atmosphere for the baby. Then painstakingly showing Claude how the kitchen worked, patiently answering questions, always making sure Claude had everything he needed, helping to keep Yves's temper in line, acting as a friend and mentor and inspiration too. And who, Claude wondered, will do all that now?

Claude touched the cool marble as though it were a talisman. As though he could draw its strength, its coolness, into himself. He thought of Pierre's excitement. Every day new discoveries. The kitchen, the whole place had been touched by his magic. Claude remembered those first puff pastry swans he had made, and Pierre exclaiming: "Merveilleux, Claude!" And Yves shrinking, face puckered with jealousy, as though he'd been left too long in the soup.

Claude sighed. At least it was peaceful, being alone.

And today I will make those swans. And not for the famous guests or even for his family, but for Pierre. For his memory.

Claude opened his stainless steel refrigerator, pulled out the puff pastry he'd made the day before, unwrapped it, and rolled it thin. My swans. Mine. One thing Yves can't take away from me.

It wasn't good, he knew, to think about Yves. But these last few days the man had turned into a little tin Napoléon: head chef by default. "Oh, yes, Claude," Yves had said, patronizing, "if you could make those nice little swans Pierre liked so dearly. Filled with mousse à la orange, we thought." We thought. Claude remembered biting his tongue to keep from telling Yves to go to the devil. Yves

16

making it sound as though Pierre's fondness for the pastry swans was some endearing but rather bizarre eccentricity.

"Pierre liked them best with chocolate."

"Madame especially asked for the orange." Yves's voice had been casual, laden with scorn.

Claude knew he had to block out Yves. He thought instead of Pierre, as he often did when he felt down. How fine it would be to be like Pierre. To create great dishes as Pierre had done. To one day run a restaurant that might, just possibly, be compared to Le Palais-Royal.

And now?

He dusted flour on the puff pastry. As he swung into the smooth flowing motions, moving his rolling pin on the chilled pastry, a small spark of confidence came back to him. These things I will never forget. I'll always be able to do them and do them well.

But still something seemed wrong.

Everything in the kitchen reminded him of Pierre. This very marble had been Pierre's invention, electrically refrigerated from below so that the pastry would stay cool no matter how long you worked it, even if you had to leave it for a few minutes. A great time-saver, and elegant as well. Like Pierre.

Well, at least we were together a little time. Five years might not be much out of a whole lifetime, but it was long enough to teach me what it means to be the best. He picked up his pastry knife.

"Bonjour, Claude."

Claude looked up. Seeing Jean-Paul made him smile. Good boy. Jean-Paul reminded him of his own apprentice days, not so long ago. Jean-Paul's eyes were red. Yes, he feels it too.

Claude kept his hands busy, cutting out six-inch teardrop shapes from the pastry; the bases of his swans. "How do you feel, Jean-Paul?"

"Very sad."

"And I, too," said Claude, wondering if in some way he

17

could cheer Jean-Paul up. "We were lucky to have known him at all. To have him teach us." Claude put down his knife and turned to the boy.

Jean-Paul stood silent, holding the battered old café filtre pot. Claude remembered that it had been Jean-Paul, coming in as he did every morning to make coffee in this same pot, who'd found Pierre dead. Coffee for Oncle Pierre, the boy's first chore of the day.

"Make some for me, Jean-Paul," said Claude quietly, "and we'll drink to his memory." He worked on in silence. Then he said, "He was proud of you, Jean-Paul. Of your progress. If he never said it to you, he said it to me."

Jean-Paul began blinking a little too fast. "Thank you, Claude."

The boy busied himself filling the pot with coffee. Claude thought how lonely life must be for Jean-Paul, so far away from home. If things were different with Marie-Claire, I could ask him to the apartment on a Sunday.

Claude glimpsed the others as they drifted in, Barry and Steve heading toward their huge black Vulcan ranges, then Frank the butcher, two dishwashers, and finally Yves himself.

"Bonjour," said Yves gruffly to nobody in particular as he walked directly to Pierre's little niche of an office. A battered old desk, a phone for ordering, a bulletin board with a big calendar for special events, and the priceless old looseleaf binder that held Pierre's recipes.

Claude felt something clench in his gut as Yves passed.

He'd cut out as many swan bases as the sheet of pastry would yeild. Now he scraped together all the scraps, formed them into a ball, rolled it to the same thinness, and began cutting wing shapes. He shaped the swans' bodies, folding up the front and sides so they'd rise in the oven and form an oval cup for the mousse, and put the wings on, sticking them with a dab of water. Et voilà, he had a flock of headless swans.

Working quickly, Claude made still another ball from the

scraps left by his second cutting. Rolled it out. Made necks and heads: now his swans were complete. With the point of his pastry knife he incised a few details: lines for the feathers, an indication of eyes, accenting the curve of a beak. Carefully, he lifted each swan onto a cookie sheet, then slid the cookie sheet into the refrigerator.

Concentrating, seeing nothing but the pastry birds before him, Claude at first only dimly realized that a strange noise was coming from behind him.

What in the world?

He closed the refrigerator door and looked around.

Everyone seemed busy, just as they should be.

Steve and Barry, preparing the garnishes for their duck breasts; Frank attacking a pile of duck carcasses with a flash of his razor-sharp boning knife; Jean-Paul at the central work island quietly peeling carrots for a puree.

Was it from Pierre's office? Then Claude saw Yves bent over and sobbing. Mon Dieu, he must have feelings too. Claude felt an unexpected sympathy for the man. We're all pretending this isn't happening. But it is. Claude dusted off his floury hands and went to Yves. Slumped over Pierre's desk, Yves's head was buried in his folded arms. He was sobbing convulsively.

"Can I help. Chef?" The word *chef* nearly stuck in Claude's throat.

Yves looked up, his eyes bleary. A faint aroma of brandy reached Claude's nostrils.

No. That can't be.

But there it was, no mistaking it: Yves smelled of cognac, and his voice had a slur Claude had never heard before. When he spoke it was more like gasping. "I can't do it, Claude. I just . . . can't."

Claude felt pity and revulsion competing inside him—and all at once understood. *Yves knows—has to know—how very second rate he is.*

Claude touched him gently on the shoulder. "Can't do what, Chef?"

19

Then from behind him Claude was astonished to hear a familiar voice. "Yes, Yves, exactly what is it that you cannot do?" Armand Jarnac, the maître d'hôtel, stood there looking almost as fearsome and majestic as Pierre himself.

Claude waited, feeling as though he were walking on eggs. Armand was Yves's lover. Almost anything might happen now. He watched Armand, always a model of diplomacy, struggling with . . . what? Anger, certainly. Fear? Love? Disgust?

Armand's face, typically, showed little. Only his dark eyes registered a special gleam, a quiet fire Claude had never before seen in them.

Yves's reaction was simply to look up at his friend, blink, and begin sobbing again. Armand came closer and put a hand on Yves's shoulder, much as Claude had done. Bent closer. Seemed to smell the cognac. He quickly backed away, as if from a fire, motioning for Claude to follow him into the dining room.

"Yves," Armand said in a whisper, "is overcome. It is a terrible time for this to happen, Claude, but there you have it. It's all up to us now. To you and me. I see you have the dessert well in hand. The consommé is made, just needs garnish. But the soufflés—Yves was to have made them. Can you?"

Armand tried to smile a we're-both-in-this-together smile, and Claude instantly sensed how dangerous Armand must think things had gotten. He felt his heart drop. Pierre's lobster and cheese soufflé was world famous, rich and delicate at the same time, and fiendishly difficult to make.

And Claude had never made it.

"I know you can do it, Claude," said Armand with that same terrifying smile.

"I'll try." But then Claude hesitated as all the complications of the maître d's relationship to Yves whirled through his brain. "But you must ask Yves to agree, Armand, or there's no guessing what he might do."

20

Armand nodded, and the look he gave Claude was reply enough.

They walked into the kitchen. Yves was where they'd left him. Claude only glanced at the chef and walked past him to Jean-Paul, who was just finishing his carrots. The boy looked up, his eyes filled with questions.

"We have a problem, Jean-Paul," said Claude, forcing himself to speak calmly. "I'm going to have to make the lobster soufflés, and I'd appreciate it if you can help me."

"Will I?" Jean-Paul grinned. "Just try me! The eggs are already out, you see." He pointed to a big earthenware bowl that seemed to hold hundreds of eggs. "The court bouillon is all ready, there, and we have the fine lobsters Yves ordered yesterday."

Claude felt his heart lift a little. Whatever happened, he could count on Jean-Paul. "Let's get the stock simmering to poach the lobsters," he said, looking at his watch. Half past nine. Claude saw Armand leading Yves out, one arm firmly on the chef's shoulder.

Too busy now to feel more pity, Claude addressed himself to the problem of the soufflés. He went into Pierre's office. A shiver ran down his spine as he opened the familiar recipe book, finding the notation in Pierre's barely legible scrawl. It was straightforward, deceptively simple in conception: the lobsters poached, cooled, shelled. Slice the barely cooked medallions paper thin, puree the shreds of imperfect meat into the sauce base, fold in egg whites whipped to a cloud, add some Parmesan cheese, And after that, Claude thought, it should say, *pray*.

First, he decided, he must make a trial soufflé.

Claude brought the recipe book with him to the work island, where Jean-Paul was unpacking the lobsters. Then, suddenly realizing that today he was in complete charge of everything, Claude made a quick tour of the kitchen. Did the others understand about Yves? The responsibility loomed up before Claude now, big and threatening. Could

21

he pull it off? The soup and the soufflés and the duck breasts and the vegetables—all of it?

As he moved around the room, though, Claude's confidence came back. Steve and Barry could sautée the duck breasts to pink perfection. The consommé was made, just needed garnishing.

But the soufflés? At the last minute they'll collapse and it'll be too late and I will have caused the disaster.

Claude tasted the lobster consommé, added a bouquet of tarragon, waited a moment and tasted again: exquisite! He went back to Jean-Paul and the lobsters.

Deftly, Jean-Paul was stabbing each one in the back, severing the spinal cord just where the neck met the tail. The stockpot was simmering, fragrant with white wine and bay leaves, with lemon and thyme and peppercorns. Working together, Claude and Jean-Paul slid the lobsters into the big stainless steel kettle. Stirring with a long wooden spoon, Claude watched closely as the green-black shells flowered into coral red. Then he fished them out with tongs and set them on the countertop to cool.

In the meantime Jean-Paul had gotten out sixty individual soufflé dishes and rubbed the insides with butter. Fifty-two to serve, eight reserves in case of failure. Claude went back to reread Pierre's recipe. The recipe was for six. Four egg yolks and six whites. Easy enough to multiply, but will those proportions hold true for individual servings? And what about the cooking time? Surely that must be different too? Only now did Claude notice that Pierre hadn't bothered to include a cooking time. You were supposed to know—and if you were Pierre Villeromain, you did know. Suddenly Claude had a vision of the restaurant empty, boarded up, ruined—all because the soufflés came out badly.

Jean-Paul started cracking the lobster shells. He has good hands, thought Claude, watching the blur of steel as the apprentice wielded his big chef's knife with surgical precision. Claude got another knife and joined in. In five minutes they reduced the lobsters to three piles: firm claw and tail meat ready to be sliced; shreds to be pureed into the sauce base; shells for the stockpot for next week's lobster consommé.

If there ever was to be a next week at Le Palais.

Feeling grim, Claude began making the soufflé base. Enough for all the guests and for the trial soufflés as well. And you still have the hors d'oeuvres to do and the swans to bake, and it's after ten thirty now. Claude asked Jean-Paul to separate the eggs.

He saw Armand walk casually into the kitchen. "Well Claude. How goes it?"

He's as scared as I am, thought Claude. "So far, so good."

Armand paused, considering. *"Très bien,"* he said, and turned to leave.

Claude, who never prayed, began praying now as he measured out the sauce base for his trial soufflé. He sliced one of the lobster claws paper thin and folded that into the sauce. Took down a small unlined copper bowl and picked up a wire whip and began whipping two egg whites until they mounted into a snowy foam, guessing at the amount of the egg white. Will just two of them lift up a whole soufflé? Still, two was more than Pierre's recipe called for: six whites for six people.

If only it were like the dessert soufflés I make every day. He knew the lobster meat and the cheese would slow down the rising. Claude got a rubber spatula and began folding the glossy mass of egg whites into the sauce. Gently, gently; now a little cheese. Now altogether, into the baking dish, that's it. Sprinkle a little more cheese on top. Draw the hat. With the tip of the rubber spatula he drew a circle half an inch inside the rim of the soufflé dish.

Reverently he carried the soufflé to his convection oven, set it in the middle tier, checked his watch, closed the glass-fronted door, stood back, took a deep breath, and tried to

23

think of the right words for the prayer to Saint Jude, the patron saint of lost causes.

He stared intently through the glass oven door.

But the soufflé just sat there. He knew no rising would be visible for some minutes yet. Still Claude stood transfixed. Saint Jude, help me. Just help me get through this luncheon. *Please*. He imagined St. Jude floating in heaven on a cloud airier than any soufflé. Laughing.

Then Claude remembered he hadn't done the hors d'oeuvres. While the soufflé's baking I'll roll out the cheese cigarettes, he thought.

He felt a heavy hand on his shoulder. Startled, Claude turned. Yves! Claude couldn't believe it. The man's eyes were even more red than before.

"I see you've gotten started, my boy. I thank you! But I will carry on now."

Claude started to speak, to urge Yves to go home. But how can I? He is, after all, the chef.

Yves looked barely able to stand up. "You're sure you feel well enough, Yves?" The words seemed to come out almost by themselves, and Claude regretted them immediately.

The red eyes blinked just once, ignited by anger. "Very well indeed, Montgeron. Thank you. And you may now return to your little swans." Yves lurched toward the island where the buttered soufflé dishes lay waiting.

Claude watched, almost hypnotized. His impulse was to run for Armand, but somehow he seemed rooted to the floor. Yves slipped. Claude watched as if it were all very remote, some old film on television, as Yves grabbed for the countertop and got the handle of the big saucepan instead, flipping it over onto himself. He lurched to the side, tried to recover, and then slipped again on the sauce he'd spilled. He flailed out with his other hand and sent three of the soufflé dishes crashing to the floor. Shattering. The noise filled the kitchen like gunfire.

24

It should have been screamingly funny. Any other day it would have been.

Finally Claude's body obeyed his astonished mind and he went to help, as did Jean-Paul and Barry. They got Yves on his feet, took a dish towel and wiped off the worst of the spilled sauce from his befuddled face. Only then did Claude realize that Armand had come into the kitchen again.

"Salaud!" The curse crackled more loudly than the breaking soufflé dishes. Yves blinked, looking as though he hadn't really heard. Although he knew that what was happening between the two men was a catastrophe, all Claude could think about now was the ruined soufflés.

He looked at his watch. Just past eleven. Guests would be arriving at one thirty. With a brusque gesture, Armand bade Steve and Barry help Yves down the stairs. Yes, thought Claude, and we should bolt the door after him this time.

"Très bien," Armand said, his usually silken voice stiff with anger. "And you might throw him in the shower while you're at it, boys."

Two dishwashers were already swabbing up the mess. Armand turned to Claude. "Can you do it? Is there still time?"

"I think so," said Claude as he hurried to the produce refrigerator. "If we have the eggs." Sixty would be needed. He found only two dozen.

He turned to Jean-Paul. "Quickly, run to the nearest market and get eight dozen." But what did eggs cost in a market? He gave the boy two twenties and Jean-Paul was off running. Claude got out more butter, flour, and milk and began making the sauce all over again.

He was stirring it when his oven timer buzzed. The trial soufflé! It had hardly risen at all. Disaster!

Claude simply stared at it. How? Why? The top was brown and wrinkled like the skin of a prune. He grabbed a towel and pulled it out and set it on the counter. Took a spoon, dipped in and tasted. The flavor was fine but the

25

texture was too wet. Soggy. Thank God Armand was back out front.

Claude stood there mesmerized by his failure. He imagined Madame Villeromain in tears, himself walking the streets with no job and no references, a cold wind at his back, all Marie-Claire's predictions about leaving her precious France coming true.

He checked his watch. No time to waste on worrying. Claude scraped the ruined soufflé into the garbage and immediately began making more sauce.

*Increase the amount of egg whites,* said an instinct deep inside him. *Forget Pierre's recipe. Take the chance, Claude. It can't affect the flavor much, and how else can you be sure it will rise properly?*

Steve and Barry came up from the locker room smiling. Yes, thought Claude, good. These fellows had felt the sting of Yves's temper too. But Claude felt relieved that the two young Americans hadn't seen his wretched failure with the trial soufflé.

The sauce was simmering nicely now. He turned off the flame. All was ready for the blending in of the egg yolks. But where was Jean-Paul?

Could the markets be out of eggs? What if the boy had been hit by a speeding taxi?

The door opened and Jean-Paul appeared. Claude, hiding his relief at the sight of him, whispered the bad news about the soufflé.

Jean-Paul shrugged. "A few more egg whites, then." And, with a devilish grin, "One hears of certain establishments where they resort to baking soda."

"Never." But Claude smiled.

As he stirred in the egg yolks Claude thought again about his hors d'oeuvres, unbaked, like the swans. Handing his wooden spoon to Jean-Paul, he dashed to the pastry counter. Jean-Paul could finish the sauce.

Eleven minutes later Claude's cheese cigarettes were

26

puffed and golden. He took them out of the oven and set them on the warming shelf to stay crisp.

Now another trial soufflé. And what if this one doesn't rise?

Claude's hands were flying now. Blending the sauce, tasting, pondering: it needed something. What? A touch more cayenne, maybe a bit of dry mustard. Something to pick up the flavor a little, to compensate for the extra egg whites. It was too bland.

Claude felt guilty about altering Pierre's recipe, but Pierre's recipe had failed him. And if my reputation is to be ruined, let it be all my doing.

The egg whites were waiting, warming to room temperature. Nearly time. Again, Armand was at his side, watching. Claude could see the concern in his eyes. He has more to lose than I, he thought. *Reassure him,* said an inner voice, *tell him whatever you must. But don't let him smell your fear.* "We have the eggs now, Armand," said Claude evenly. "We can still do it. Only the sauce was lost, really, and a few dishes."

But something else had been lost. Claude sensed that the incident with Yves would not soon be forgotten.

Armand moved very close. "I must tell you, Claude," he said in a voice so low it was nearly a whisper, ". . . and in confidence. Nothing's definite yet, but it may be possible for me to buy Le Palais-Royal. That's why this lunch is so important—important beyond remembering Pierre. You see, they'll all be here today. All the ones who really matter. And . . . I'm counting on you."

Claude was stunned.

Armand seemed to be waiting for a reply. "That would be a fine thing, Armand." The words sounded inadequate, but Claude could think of no others.

"Fine," said Armand, "and most difficult. If it should happen, though, I just want you to know there'll be a place for you. A special place."

27

Claude felt torn between enjoying Armand's praise and wondering if he was being manipulated. "Thank you, Armand." He managed a smile. "But now I must get on with the sauce."

"Of course. Bonne chance, Claude." Armand smiled too, and left the kitchen.

If he only knew how much I need a little luck, how I pray for it. His hands then found the wooden spoon, the butter, flour and milk. Claude's practiced reflexes took over. As his body responded to the urgency of the moment, stirring, stirring, he replayed Armand's words. Had they amounted to a kind of bribe? Something to urge me on to the limit? He stirred the sauce. If today's luncheon failed to go well, then what did any of it matter? Not Armand's dreams, not Claude's own sense of helplessness, nothing.

The sauce bubbled a little and grew silky. Behind him Claude was aware of Jean-Paul slicing lobster medallions. He felt a little better. That lad I can count on: Steve and Barry as well. It might be possible. Might just.

Claude measured some of the lobster flesh, added a little milk, and pureed it in the food processor to a silken mousse. He took the sauce off the flame and folded in the pureed lobster; then some egg yolks and cream. Then back on a low flame, stirring, stirring. Off the flame again just as the eggs began to thicken. He stuck in a forefinger and tasted. Bland!

The pallid taste of it raced through his brain. It needs more cayenne, maybe a little tarragon, a pinch of salt, he thought, fighting his panic. If it doesn't come off this time I'm done for. And since I'm adding extra egg whites I might as well risk spicing it more too. He took the sauce off the flame and set it on the counter. Eleven forty five. Time was getting tighter now. But he had to be sure he didn't rush or get clumsy. Jean-Paul sliced the last of the lobster meat.

Claude moved from post to post around the kitchen.

Steve and Barry had made their carrot puree. Claude stuck in a finger, tasted. Steve was watching him intently.

This is where Yves would explode, make a scene, chew him out in front of everyone. "Steve," he said quietly, "taste."

Steve tasted. Frowned. "I forgot the damn ginger."

Claude forced himself not to smile. Steve had taken it well. "And perhaps a little allspice?"

Steve nodded, already peeling the fresh gingerroot, chopping it fine.

The garnish for the entrée platters was ready: watercress for a touch of green and fresh raspberries to be tossed with the raspberry-vinegar sauce at the last minute. The consommé was warming over a low flame. The duck sauce was made and waiting in its white earthenware crock in the warming sink by the ranges. Claude dipped in his finger. Just right!

Back at his counter Claude measured out sauce for his second trial soufflé. Doubled the egg whites. Pinch of salt. Lobster medallions and grated cheese at the ready. Quarter past twelve! Guests at one thirty, serve at two thirty. Soufflés timed for three precisely.

He worked quickly but with care: egg whites whipped and folded into the sauce; more egg white, fold it gently; now fold the sauce into the rest of the egg whites; now the lobster medallions and the cheese. Fold, fold, not too completely, keep it light. Now! Into the waiting soufflé dish. Draw the hat. Sprinkle with cheese.

Now, please, Saint Jude, let it rise.

He carried the soufflé to the waiting oven as gingerly as if the fluted white porcelain dish had been filled with nitroglycerin. There was nothing he could do but hope.

Claude asked Jean-Paul to help him set up the trays of hors d'oeuvres. Jean-Paul began slicing the pale yellow, fine-grained bread, *pan de mie,* to make toast for the fresh foie gras. Claude kept sneaking glances at the soufflé, as though it really was explosive.

Five minutes passed. Ten.

After fifteen minutes Claude left the rest of the toast to Jean-Paul and looked at the soufflé, watching as intently as he had watched his own son struggling to take his first steps. The thought of little François stabbed at him. But no time for that now. He focused on the soufflé, willing it to rise. To be perfect. Slowly, almost imperceptibly, the delicate mixture moved up the sides of the dish. Claude had filled it to a quarter inch below the rim. Now it was just level with the rim.

He watched. Sixteen minutes. The circle he had drawn on the surface of the souffle was causing a little "hat" to form: the center rising a bit higher than the perimeter. Rise, little one!

After eighteen minutes the soufflé was nearly an inch above the rim. Higher. *Please go higher!*

But Claude knew it would rise no further. The top was golden brown now, and to leave it any longer was to risk burning it. He could see the top flecked with specks of darker brown where the cheese had melted and crisped a bit. For an instant he stood there holding his breath and hoping that against all logic it would rise a little further.

The height was not wonderful.

Finally, with the top growing darker before his eyes, he took it out. Jean-Paul was waiting, tense and expectant.

We're like two new fathers in the maternity ward, Claude thought. Another time it would be comical.

Claude could tell just by the look of the soufflé that it was a near success. Not quite high enough, but if the texture and flavor were right the height could be adjusted simply by filling the dish more.

He scooped out portions for Jean-Paul and himself. The texture was fine: light and silky on his tongue, the top crisp, the center still creamy, so that there were three distinct textures, with the half liquid center acting as a sauce for the rest. Claude breathed in the aroma and tasted again.

Yes! It seemed to be just the way Pierre had liked it. But what about Jean-Paul? The apprentice tasted, pondered, frowned a small frown.

Claude's heart sank.

"But it's fine, Claude. Perhaps a little salt?"

The relief Claude felt then was physical, euphoric. Salt, or maybe a little lemon. Minor problem, easily solved. He knew the flavor was right, the texture what he'd prayed for. I can do it, he decided, almost shocked by the realization. If I can get the timing just right, get them to rise a bit higher, I might just bring it off.

He counted in his head. This one took eighteen minutes. If I fill the rest a little fuller, that's twenty minutes at least, maybe more, because with all of them in the oven at once they'll cook more slowly. Say twenty-two minutes. Maybe twenty-four.

Claude felt sweat breaking out on his forehead. Two minutes could make all the difference. He saw soufflés falling, soufflés burnt to charcoal, soufflés exploding, not rising at all, soufflés doing everything in the world but what they were supposed to.

Quarter to one.

He squeezed two lemons and strained the juice, adding it to the sauce base. There. That'll pick it up a little. The egg whites were waiting to be whipped, a huge translucent mass.

"Jean-Paul, can you whip seventy egg whites?"

Jean-Paul grinned.

"Then we'll divide these when the time comes: it'll go faster that way."

"Mais oui."

Claude tried to remember if he'd ever tried whipping that many egg whites all at once. Formidable. But it must be done and we'll do it.

31

He got down the two biggest unlined copper bowls, bowls reserved for no other use than whipping up perfect egg whites. Then two enormous wooden-handled wire whips; they looked almost medieval. Claude wiped his forehead. Guests must be coming now.

Waiters appeared asking for hors d'oeuvres.

Claude suddenly realized that in the confusion he'd forgotten to make the little puffs filled with ham mousse. Well, and too bad. They'll have to make do with the Laurent-Perrier and the fresh foie gras and the cheese cigarettes. And he smiled. The guests would most certainly not be deprived.

Claude turned up the flame under the big pot of lobster consommé, saw that its garnish of wire-thin julienne strips of carrot and scallion was ready. When the soup goes into the dining room, the soufflés go into the oven.

He felt excitement now. And fear.

The waiters were coming back and forth, bearing empty hors d'oeuvres trays to be replenished, empty champagne bottles to be dumped. At two o'clock precisely Claude signaled Jean-Paul to begin whipping up the egg whites. He picked up the second big wire whisk, feeling like a soldier on the morning of a decisive battle. Wondering what the odds were that he'd come out of this in one piece.

Claude poured his half of the egg whites into the copper bowl, added a generous pinch of salt, and began a steady rythmic beating. Round and round went his arm, circling the bowl, engaging the mass of egg whites. Every stroke counts, he told himself as the whip moved faster and faster with a percussive whine. The egg whites swirled. Reluctantly at first, translucent and slippery. Claude cradled the big bowl in his left arm while whipping steadily with his right. His whole arm was part of the action, shoulder rotating, his wrist moving hardly at all. He knew from experience that the wrist muscles were the first to tire, that if he strained them now he might lose control later on. Big bubbles were forming in the egg whites, forming and breaking down smaller and smaller as he churned them into a rough foam like the foam of ocean waves breaking, finer and finer.

The translucence was going now. The egg whites were turning a misty gray flecked with white, more white, now almost completely white as the bubbles got smaller and ever smaller.

Claude's shoulder began aching, but he welcomed the pain. It gave him something to think of other than failing. Round and round. He kept the angle of the bowl steady despite the dull ache building in his upper arm. The beating process took on a life of its own, as though the rest of the kitchen and even the rest of the world didn't exist. His universe was reduced to the big copper bowl, his wire whip grazing the copper and the swirl of the egg whites as the foam mounted and mounted.

Pure white now but nowhere near enough air in them. He paused for breath and looked at Jean-Paul. The apprentice was keeping up, his long face intent, almost in a trance.

The egg whites mounted higher. Pure white and with a finer texture. This was the crucial stage. Too much air would make them dry, make the soufflé lumpy.

The egg whites were taking on a sheen. He could see the change, as though they were alive. His wire whip left deep tracks now, and the work was harder. Claude paused again, lifted up the whip and scrutinized the peak of egg white that clung there. Frowned, and decided to give it a few more beats.

*Two fifteen.*

After three painful minutes the egg whites were just the way Claude wanted them. He looked at Jean-Paul. Still whipping. Then Jean-Paul paused as well, lifted his whip.

"Perfect, Jean-Paul."

Claude began folding the egg whites into the sauce. Somewhere behind him he heard Armand give the order to start serving the consommé. He felt a jolt of urgency. Praying to Saint Jude, he began to fill the soufflé dishes. Almost

33

to their rims. "I'll fill, you draw the hats," he said to Jean-Paul.

Down the rows of gleaming white soufflé dishes they went, Claude scooping up the delicate mixture, easing it into the dishes and lightly smoothing over the top, while Jean-Paul drew the little circles with the tip of a smaller rubber spatula and then sprinkled the top with a fine dusting of Parmesan.

In two minutes all was ready. Claude lifted the baking sheets as Jean-Paul opened the oven doors. And how will I keep from going mad for the next twenty minutes?

"Ho!" came a cry from the ranges. He'd heard Barry's Comanche yell a thousand times before, signalling that he and Steve were about to commence their juggling act at the red-hot stoves, sautéing and broiling and finishing sauces at a pace so quick it looked almost comical. Until you tasted the results.

Claude walked closer.

Sixty duck breasts to sauté, sauce, and garnish. But, he thought, as the Americans went into action, the duck breasts can wait a little once they're done. Not like my soufflés, which can fall in a few seconds. The soufflés hadn't been in the oven five minutes, but Claude couldn't resist going back to watch them. As though by his mere presence he could somehow protect them.

Foolishness.

Still he stood there. Watching. Hoping. Praying.

The serving plates were warmed and waiting. Claude's heart skipped a beat, thinking they might remain empty forever. He and Jean-Paul stood dumb, watching their oven as though it might reveal the secret of the universe.

Seven minutes.

Claude tried to control his apprehension. Mon Dieu, it is only a soufflé. But he could imagine the gossip racing through the small world of haute cuisine from kitchen to kitchen: "That young Montgeron thought he knew it all, then single-handedly gave the kiss of death to the best restaurant in the world!"

Ten minutes.

He could see the soufflés rising now. Claude had known they must, known it logically. But what had logic to do with this terror? Suppose I filled them too full and they spill over?

No. Think of the guests. They'll be thrilled. Or horrified.

Sixteen minutes.

The soufflés had climbed nearly an inch above the rims of their dishes now. Just beginning to brown. Don't, *please*, let them brown too much!

Seventeen and a half . . . eighteen minutes. The second hand on Claude's watch seemed to crawl. The damn watch must be broken.

Twenty minutes.

Almost. Claude could hear waiters coming in with trays of empty consommé cups. Any moment now, they'd be lined up waiting.

Twenty-one minutes. The soufflés on the top rack were browning just a fraction faster than those on the bottom. But he'd planned it that way, to load from the top.

Twenty-two minutes.

The topmost soufflés looked almost ready. Still Claude hesitated. He looked at Jean-Paul. The boy stood poised, eager. Claude took a breath. "C'est le moment," he said quietly, reaching for a towel.

Jean-Paul opened the oven door and Claude, working quick as a sleight-of-hand artist, lifted out the first sheet of soufflés. They looked so fine he hardly dared to breathe.

Now the next sheet. And the next. The waiters vanished through the swinging doors, their silver trays held high.

In three minutes it was done. The last soufflé had gone into the dining room; the extras rested on the countertop, slowly deflating. Claude put a hand on Jean-Paul's shoulder.

"Thank you," he said. "We've been through the wars together, Jean-Paul."

The boy smiled. "And perhaps we've won, mon vieux."

Let's hope. Time was melting and running together in Claude's brain. Was it minutes since the soufflés had gone in, or weeks? He couldn't look at his watch. The first waiter was coming back. Claude forced himself to look at the plates on his tray. Would there be uneaten, rejected soufflés? But every dish seemed to be empty.

Maybe they only ate them to be polite, to honor Pierre.

He went back to his pastry counter. The first tray of duck breasts was going out now. Time to start filling the swans.

He and Jean-Paul were finishing the last of them when Yves walked in. The silence was immediate and chilling. Steve burned his hand on a sauté pan, cursed, and turned back to his duck breasts.

Yves looked pale as flour, but he walked. No suggestion now of the lurching, stumbling drunk of a few hours ago. Slowly, he approached Claude, a ghost, white and expressionless but somehow threatening.

Claude kept his voice level. "How are you feeling, Yves?"

A flicker of emotion crossed the chef's thin face. It might have been the beginning of a smile. "A little better, thanks, Claude. I could hardly feel worse. Or more sorry for the trouble I caused you."

The one thing Claude hadn't expected. Contrition. "We all have bad days, Chef," he said.

Again, Yves's lips flickered in the echo of a smile. "Not this bad. I see you've done it with the soufflés. Thank you, Claude. Thank you very much."

Claude made himself smile. "The first one was a disaster. Not enough height. But the final batch didn't look bad."

He tried to think of more to say—especially something that might make this man go away again. But it was Yves who spoke next, in a voice so low Claude could hardly hear it. "Tell me, Claude. Was Armand furious?"

"Well, he was upset, Chef. But he'll get over it."

"I do appreciate your help." It sounded flat, mechanical, a recording caught in a groove.

"Everyone pitched in. Jean-Paul was splendid."

Yves turned away, nodding vaguely, and went back to Pierre's office and sat down. Looking lost, a stranger who had wandered in by mistake.

Suddenly Claude realized he was very hungry. Nobody had thought about a staff lunch today and he hadn't eaten since breakfast. A waiter came back bearing a tray with a half full bottle of Cheval Blanc. Claude took it, signaled Jean-Paul, found two crystal balloon glasses, and poured. "Santé, Jean-Paul," he said.

Jean-Paul smiled. "Santé." They both sipped the legendary Bordeaux in silence. Claude felt moved as the velvety taste filled his mouth, as though this, finally, was his toast to Pierre. Then together they raided the refrigerator.

They were still eating when all of a sudden there was a stirring at the far end of the kitchen. Claude looked up, thinking, Not Yves again?

The door from the dining room opened and there stood Armand, bowing in the two Villeromain women. Claude and Jean-Paul stood up at once, as did everyone else who had been seated. Armand said, "Madame Villeromain and Mademoiselle Elise have asked me to thank you for the fine meal. The lobster soufflé was superb—truly a credit to the memory of Pierre. Our guests actually applauded."

Claude heard these words and felt better than he had all day. But they had a hollow ring as well. Would these ladies imagine Yves had done it all? No. He'd be damned if he'd let bitterness spoil his triumph. I know. Armand knows. Everyone in the kitchen knows—and especially Yves knows.

Pierre's widow spoke, quietly, but in a voice that carried. "I know how difficult it must be for you, as it is for us, to face this terrible loss. Pierre was so proud of you all, and I know he'd be especially proud today. Yves, that lobster soufflé . . ."

"Madame, may I say something?"

Kate Villeromain paused in mid sentence, caught her breath and regained her composure, smiling. "But of course, Yves."

"Madame, Mademoiselle Elise, all credit for today's luncheon must go to Claude. I was—ill, you see, feeling very bad. Claude did it all, all of it. I . . . just wanted everyone to know that."

Can it be? Claude found himself blushing as every eye in the room suddenly focused on him—especially, for some reason, disconcerted by the girl's gaze—Elise's. They all seemed to want him to say something. He felt like choking.

Before he had half a chance to think or to shape the English that was still awkward for him, the words came out of his mouth. "Thank you, Yves," he said quietly, "but it was everyone. It was Jean-Paul here, and Barry and Steve and Frank and Pepe. And, most of all, it was Pierre. He made all this possible—made us possible." Claude had to stop then, because he knew if he continued he'd end up in tears.

"Claude, that was lovely," said Kate. "We want everyone to know that for the immediate future—the forseeable future—Le Palais will remain Le Palais. After this week of mourning we'll be back in business just as if . . . as if nothing had happened. I know you can do it. You've proved that today. And I hope you will want to. Thank you all very much."

Claude heard her words but he found himself thinking about the girl, who had said nothing. Elise. Silent as a stone all through her stepmother's speech. A thin, big-eyed shadow of a girl. And married, he'd heard. Married and living far away. There was something haunted about her.

Claude sighed and turned back to his wineglass as Armand and the Villeromain women left the kitchen.

# 3

DAVE HOLLANDER JERKED upright in his bed. The apartment in the Carlyle was dark and silent. And filled with his dream. The same dream. He'd had it so many times before.

It was always exactly, maddeningly the same. High noon on Park Avenue. The deep rust red granite facade of the Hollander Industries building at the corner of Fifty-fourth Street. Dave's name, Dave's company, finely chiseled into the polished stone: HOLLANDER INDUSTRIES.

The sweat poured down his forehead. Dave lifted a hand to wipe some of it away.

In his dream Dave was struggling, both arms pinned by huge burly men, men whose faces he could never see, forcing him to watch as stonecutters chipped away at the *H* and then the *O* and the *L* and all the rest of it. Taking his name off the building. Taking it all away, all he'd worked and slaved and damn near killed himself for these thirty years. And the people on the street hurried by, not even noticing.

Dave got up, walked into the green marble bathroom and splashed water on his face. Toweled. Looked at himself in the mirror. Fifty-two years old and not an ounce heavier than when he'd played tennis for Dartmouth. Big deal. What's the good of being in shape, he asked himself, if you don't have something to be in shape for? Or someone?

39

Timmy.

Did I do it all for Timmy? Barbara would have been happy if I'd kept on canning tomatoes. Maybe I did it for myself. Dave switched off the lights and got back into bed. Sleep, damn it, you need every minute of it if you're going to function tomorrow. Today.

Three twenty A.M. Dave knew himself too well to imagine he'd get any real rest tonight. Okay then, review the numbers. Make the time count for something. He lay back, forcing himself to relax every muscle. He closed his eyes and kept them closed, his arms crossed over his chest. Feeling a little like one of those recumbent brass knights on an old British tomb.

The figures marched through his brain with a heavy, insistent beat: footsteps of a conquering army. Earnings down fourteen percent last year. And this year's first quarter was worse—off nearly seventeen and a half percent. The downtrend seemed to be easing, but the second quarter would still show red ink.

And today was the board meeting. Gerry Orloff from the Knickerbocker Trust would be there to hear Timmy's report—the report that might just turn the whole situation around.

But if the slippage continues the board might just ask for my head on a platter. Dave could almost hear them: "Sure he built it up. But that doesn't mean he can manage it in this day and age."

He thought about the old days. Days when everything worked like a perfect football play: one, two, three, score. It had gone so smoothly, so fast.

Hell, even the bank knows that, he thought. They helped finance it. Helped me buy that little canning plant in the valley. Watched me build up a whole line of soups and relishes. Loved it when I thought up the Billy Burger hamburger stands to give us a steady market for catsup and relish. Glowed with pride as Billy Burger grew from three to more than a hundred franchises in less than ten years.

Encouraged me to go public. Introduced me to DeWitt Steele.

Steele.

So he's a bean counter, so he gets off on numbers. Corporate chairmen are supposed to. He's the guy the Knickerbocker wanted for chairman, to balance me—and he does. Were they wrong? If we've reached market saturation with the burgers, is it his fault? Is it mine?

Dave turned onto his back. No point even pretending he might get back to sleep tonight. Today. He thought of his talk with DeWitt yesterday afternoon. How casually it had started. Painful for DeWitt. More so for me.

The knock on his office door. DeWitt's sleek gray head poking in. For an instant Dave had thought it must be time for their regular Wednesday squash game. Then he remembered: Steele's secretary had called to cancel the game.

"Got a minute, Dave?"

"Sure. Come in. Coffee, DeWitt?"

"No thanks, I'm supposed to be cutting down."

Banalities. DeWitt had taken the big leather chair that flanked the couch. Dave sat on the couch. "What's up?"

DeWitt was carrying a sheet of paper. A photocopy. "Have you seen the *Forbes* piece?"

"No."

"Forewarned," said DeWitt with the flicker of a smile, "is forearmed." He handed Dave the paper, watched while Dave read it and read it again.

Dave felt a jolt in his gut. One thing to know about a problem. Something else to have the whole damn world know. "Sons of bitches." It was entitled "Trouble at Hollander Industries?" It made Dave feel as though he'd eaten something rotten.

> After ten years of spectacular growth largely fueled by the Billy Burger chain, Hollander Industries has experienced a leveling off that now looks as though it may turn into a serious decline. Their first quarter

report shows revenues off 17.5% from last year, which was down 14% from the previous year. Sources close to the Hollander operation have indicated that market penetration of the Billy Burger chain has reached saturation levels. And while the chain continues to be marginally profitable, real growth for Hollander will have to come from other ventures—ventures which at this writing seem tentative at best.

The piece went on and on. "Who's behind this crap, DeWitt?" Dave kept his voice quiet. Was there a leak from inside?

"Could be anyone here—or no one. But, let's face it, they aren't far off target."

"Target is right. Just in time for the board meeting."

"That's why I dropped by, Dave."

Dave caught the change in DeWitt's voice and looked at the chairman harder. Ten years we've worked together. And well. I've always trusted him, and it seemed mutual. But now something's different. I've never seen him like this before. Is he scared?

"What's up, DeWitt?"

"I'm not about to keep anything from you, Dave. There have been a few rumblings."

"Rumblings. Somebody's got stomach trouble? You mean complaints, gripes, protests—what?"

"I don't have to tell you about the stock, Dave."

He didn't. Hollander stock had been depressed for months, trading at thirty-two and a half yesterday, down from its alltime high of forty-nine. Dave watched Hollander stock the way some people take their own blood pressure. Just about everything he had was tied up in his forty-two percent of it. "When the Street gets hold of this item," he said, manufacturing a smile, "the rumblings may turn to groans. Who, by the way, is doing the rumbling?"

"Gerry Orloff for one, as you'd expect. We're into his bank for nearly a hundred million, Dave."

"I noticed. We pay our interest. And that new meat-packing operation we financed is going to save us big money in the long run." If there is a long run. DeWitt's concern was contagious. Dave hadn't looked at the downtrend as anything more than a temporary setback until this minute.

"Well, Gerry's nervous."

"What are you trying to tell me, DeWitt?"

"You'll hate it."

"Let me decide that. I'm a big boy."

"You've heard it before, Dave. One sure way out of— our difficulties. We could start talking merger."

Dave just looked at him. How many times has DeWitt suggested we let ourselves be bought out? he wondered. How many times have I yelled for the shark repellent? Maybe it's because I think we're big enough right now. Maybe it's because I don't want anyone else's name on the door but mine. Mine and Timmy's. There were always corporate suitors sniffing around. Too hungrily. They'll get control and bleed us dry and turn us into something we were never meant to be.

Dave fought to control himself, to see DeWitt's beancounter point of view. "Look, I see you think we need a diversionary action, but that isn't it. Nix. Nada. Nyet. Over my dead body."

"It could be both of our dead bodies, Dave."

"Let 'em just try." Dave felt the adrenaline flowing.

DeWitt passed a hand over his eyes, rubbing them lightly, as though by doing this he might erase some terrible vision. "It could happen, Dave." His voice was low and there was a vibration in it that Dave had never heard before.

He's no more than ten years older than me, but somehow DeWitt seems old today. Old and tired. Dave suddenly realized that DeWitt must have been protecting him, sparing him the rumors, the rumblings, until he couldn't keep on shouldering that burden alone anymore.

He's always dealt with the board. And very well, too. Easy, maybe, when everything's going well, but for every time I see a board member DeWitt sees them ten times. Hell, it's his job to be sensitive to their feelings, to help sell our programs when it has to come to a vote by the board. It's always worked so nicely, me doing the creative part, the forward planning, new products, expansion, and DeWitt handling all those damn details I hate to bother with. But now? We're two different people with two different approaches to business. What if it comes to a showdown? How will he react? How will the board react?

"Hey, DeWitt, it isn't the end of the world. What can I do to help?"

DeWitt blinked, took a deep breath and managed to smile. "We've been through a lot together, Dave."

"And there's a lot more to come."

"I hope so. As I said, I can stall them. The timing of the *Forbes* piece is—well, unfortunate. We do have a great responsibility to our shareholders."

Dave grinned. That was Catch-22, -23, and -24. He remembered the days before they'd gone public. The memory shimmered enticingly, a distant golden age that could only be imagined. "Going public was definitely a mixed blessing, DeWitt. But hell, it made me some bucks and it sure didn't hurt you." Part of DeWitt's contract as chairman included generous stock options.

DeWitt managed to smile, but it was a thin, sad smile. "Dave," he said gently, "you're young still. You're the idea man, the builder. I'm just a manager. As you so often remind me, I'm an old bean counter. You could build another Hollander Industries. Ten more. But if something happens to me here, something that ends my career—well it means just that. The end. Ever since Louise died I guess I've lived too much for the business. It's come to *be* my life. I'm not sure I could survive a real shake-up here. That's why I'm worried."

Steele's words hit Dave with the full force of revelation.

44

He looked at DeWitt and thought, I never guessed he felt that way. The facade is so perfect: the Steele family name, the impeccable manners, the Social Register, all of it. And until this minute, if anyone had told me I'd end up feeling sorry for DeWitt Steele, I'd never have believed it.

Dave had another uneasy feeling, a feeling that came from somewhere else. A feeling that Steele was leading up to something. "You look like a man with a plan, DeWitt."

Steele smiled, a quick flicker of a smile. It came and went so fast, Dave wondered if he was seeing things. "There is something I'd like you to consider, Dave. Something I hope won't be necessary."

Here it comes. Lie down behind your camels, boys, it's going to be a rough one. Dave felt distanced from what was happening. As though he'd somehow walked onto the stage of a theater, into the middle of a drama where every actor but Dave knew his lines. "And that is . . ."

"Take the money and run. I can arrange about the stock you hold, so you won't ever have to sell in a depressed market. I can arrange all kinds of things so you and Barbara and Timmy won't have to worry about a thing." DeWitt was leaning forward now, eager, selling too hard. "Think about it, Dave! Consulting fees—whatever you need for as long as you like. No more hassles, no board meetings, no worrying about *Forbes* or the market or any of it." DeWitt paused like a sprinter who's just broken the ribbon at the finish line. Sat back again, just a little out of breath but obviously pleased with himself. Proud of having finally said these things.

He wants Timmy out too, Dave thought as he realized with a nauseating wrench how carefully Steele had thought out the details. Dave stood up, still trapped in his feeling of unreality. This isn't happening. DeWitt, whom I've known and liked for nearly ten years? DeWitt Steele, in the job I chose him for, writing my obituary while I'm still alive and kicking?

He walked to the window. Looked down on Park Avenue. At the Racquet Club, where he and DeWitt were

45

meant to be playing squash right now. Where Timmy was playing because Dave had given him the court he normally kept reserved for himself and DeWitt. As he stood there, Dave's eyes misted. He had to blink, blink hard, to drive the tears back.

"You're wrong, DeWitt," he said in a voice so low it was like a whisper.

"Wrong?"

"You seem to think I do it for the money." He felt a little more in control of himself now. He turned from the window and walked back to the couch and sat down.

"There's a farm out west of Cedar Rapids, DeWitt. A farm that has my family's blood all mixed into the dirt there. Literally. My great-grandmother was killed on that land in an Indian raid in eighteen fifty-two. She's buried there, on a little rise up beyond the windmill. Four generations of Hollanders gave their lives to that land; plowed it with mules at first, fought the Indians, went into the Union Army even though they didn't have to. They weren't a state back then. They lived and died on that land, generation after generation. I was the first one to leave, even though by my father's time the farm was more like a big business; over two thousand prime acres, huge combines that can do in a day what it once took twenty men a week to scrape together. I'll never forget the look in Dad's eyes the day I told him I wasn't coming back. He just didn't understand. I had to do something, build something, all on my own."

Dave paused, watching DeWitt's face. It was a fine, patrician face. Any Indians the old Steeles might have encountered would have been sitting on Plymouth Rock when the *Mayflower* pulled in.

DeWitt said nothing.

"Well, what I built is this," Dave said, gesturing at the big office but meaning the whole empire that was Hollander Industries. "It was my sweat, my dream—my blood just about." Dave paused again, and again DeWitt said nothing. "Well. It isn't a thing I can walk away from, DeWitt."

"I've known people who built two, three—any number of businesses."

"They weren't Dave Hollander."

"Dave, I do understand. I think I do, anyway. But I just wanted you to know—it wouldn't be fair to you if I kept my mouth shut—that it may get to be pretty rough around here. I can hold them off for a while. I'm not even guessing how long. But if we don't turn this thing around soon, and in a big, dramatic way, there's no telling what could happen. To both of us."

Dave thought. The words are right; they're just what they ought to be. Why don't I believe him? There wasn't any answer, and Dave felt too shaken up to try and dig for one right now. "Then," he said, maybe a little too fast, "let's get down to it. With the meeting tomorrow, with Tim's report, the whole new gourmet project—that ought to make 'em sit up and take notice."

"I hope so."

DeWitt left him then. Left Dave feeling sandbagged, as though somebody had crept out of a dark alley and knocked him in the gut with something cold and hard and unexpected.

And now Dave tossed in his bed, sweating, remembering all that. And DeWitt is scared enough to do it to me. He didn't set a time limit but he might just as well have. If I don't get us moving by the end of the year—by spring at the latest—the game may be up, he thought.

Six months. It seemed like an endless length of time, but Dave knew too well how fast those days could roll by. Six months to pull it back together again. To save my ass. My company. To keep my name on the damn building. My name and Timmy's.

Four o'clock now. Dave's eyes stayed resolutely shut. No point in looking like a wreck at the board meeting, even if I feel like one inside.

The night was very still. Here on the twenty-sixth floor of the Carlyle tower Dave could hear only the occasional

honking of a car's horn, now and then a distant siren. He
tried to keep his mind blank. It was an uphill struggle. All
the doubts and questions he'd felt talking to DeWitt kept
seeping into his thoughts.

I've never been afraid in my life, not really afraid, except
maybe that time Timmy fell out of the tree. Dave could
recall that moment and the jolt of terror as though it had
happened yesterday.

Eighteen years ago. Timmy a little monkey of eight, already an athlete and irrepressible. Dave, on a Sunday, in
back of their first big house in Greenwich. Calling to the
boy. Not finding him. A game, Timmy hiding. Dave calling again, louder. A rustling at the top of the old magnolia
Barbara liked so much. A giggle. A stirring. Then a scream.
Not a game at all now, but Timmy falling.

Dave felt the sweat break out just at the memory of that
helpless body falling, falling, himself running faster than
he'd ever run in his life, frantic, arms outstretched for the
catch he couldn't possibly make.

Tim fell more than fifteen feet. Fell hard. Hit with a thud
like the end of the world. *His neck's broken. He's dead.* And
Timmy just lay there, not even breathing, Dave kneeling at
his side, helpless, afraid for the moment even to touch his
son. His only son. Barbara running from the kitchen.

Timmy moved his leg a little. *Thank God, he's alive.*

Barbara rushing to the phone, the ambulance, both of
them riding in it with Tim. Tim pale as death, and Dave
cursing every jolt of the speeding vehicle. Then the emergency room. X rays. Two broken ribs and concussion, but
no permanent damage. They were so shocked, it was a
while before they could feel anything, even relief.

I was never closer to Barbara than in that ambulance.
Never have been since.

Funny, the things you remember. Dave could recall what
she was wearing; the green and ivory striped dress, her hair
pulled back with a ribbon, like some college girl. Eighteen
years ago. They'd known by then she couldn't have any

48

more babies, but even if they'd had a dozen Dave realized he couldn't feel for the others what he felt for Timmy. Then or now.

He smiled in the darkness, remembering how he'd wanted to cut down the magnolia. How Barbara laughed and asked if he intended to deforest Connecticut. "Because the minute you do he'll take to playing in traffic or rock climbing or breeding rattlesnakes. Remember, my darling, whose son he is."

Dave never forgot whose son Tim Hollander was. Not for a minute.

Finally, close to five A.M., he drifted off into something like sleep.

The board meeting was scheduled for ten. At eight forty-five Dave walked past the words that featured so prominently in his dream. Touched the *H* of the Hollander for luck almost without glancing at the cornerstone. Thought about the meeting, about Gerry Orloff, what to say to Gerry. Maybe nothing. Pleasantries. Let Gerry make the first move if he was so damn worried. Banks!

Dave's office was on the top floor, a floor he shared with DeWitt, with the boardroom, and a few other senior officers. Early as it was, Dave's secretary was already on the job. Lydia Wingfoot, what would I do without you, he thought, smiling his greeting as he passed through Lydia's office and into his own.

The coffee was made, his chromium thermos pitcher filled with it, a small basket of croissants warming on the hot tray that was built into Dave's little bar. Lydia was always after him to eat more. He poured a cup of black coffee and put half a croissant on the saucer.

Keep your strength up, Hollander, you're going to need every ounce of it.

He riffled through his mail, presorted by Lydia. No urgent messages. Idly, Dave opened an elegant brochure for a tour sponsored by the Dartmouth Alumni Association.

Three weeks cruising the Greek islands. He looked at the glossy pictures for a moment, dreaming of all the vacations he hadn't taken these last ten or more years. Of all the promises and half promises he'd made to Barbara, promises that had been broken so often they hardly talked about traveling these days.

How easy it would be to sail away from it all, to take up DeWitt's suggestion, lay back and clip the coupons and never worry about any of it, ever again.

He threw the brochure into his polished brown leather wastebasket and picked up a proposal from one of DeWitt's bean counters. Reading it, he laughed out loud. The idiot was going to save Hollander Industries by adulterating Billy Burgers by twenty-five percent with soybean analog meat extenders. Over my dead body, DeWitt, he thought. It was obvious to Dave that DeWitt must have put out the word: *think up ways to save money.* He wondered if DeWitt had ever tasted a soybean extender, or even a hamburger, for that matter.

I built Billy Burger by giving people a good product at a good price, he thought. The minute we lower the standard, we risk losing the most valuable asset we have—people's good faith.

He put the proposal aside. Time enough to talk to DeWitt after the meeting. Dave checked his calendar. *Memorial luncheon for Pierre Villeromain, 1:30, Le Palais-Royal.* Lydia's handwriting was as meticulous as the rest of her work. Dave had forgotten the lunch.

But not Pierre. He'd never forget Pierre.

Dave thought of Pierre's smile. Remembered the day Pierre asked him—rare privilege!—back into the kitchen to taste his latest variation on lobster soufflé. The smell of it, the golden puff emerging from the oven, Pierre conjuring up two dishes and two glasses on Montrachet, the proffered fork, the expectant gaze. That first taste seducing his mouth. "Bravo, Pierre!"

"You think it is . . . acceptable?"

"I think it is already a classic." No. Pierre never let me down and I won't let him down now. Nor his wife, nor the girl.

Suddenly it was quarter to ten.

Dave walked down the gray carpeted hallway to the boardroom. Smile. Be confident. You don't have a worry in the world and things like the *Forbes* article are no more than ants at the picnic. He wondered if the members of the board could smell fear the way certain animals are said to do.

The room was empty, waiting. Dave loved the Hollander boardroom, so elegantly muted in its decoration: five shades of gray set off by the rich rosewood conference table. At the far end of the table he saw the easel set up for Timmy's presentation.

He paused just inside the door and wondered what judgments might be passed on him here today, or one day soon. DeWitt came in, closely followed by Carl Sanders, the man who'd come up with the soybean concept. Dave practiced his confident smile. "Good morning."

"How are you, Dave?"

Any other day, Dave would have taken DeWitt's greeting as the offhand pleasantry it probably was. Probably. But today the question took on special meaning. What do you mean, how am I? Is the dagger already sticking in my back, DeWitt? Suddenly, against all reason, he began to enjoy the fight. He was more grateful than he should have been when Steele called the meeting to order. DeWitt had the minutes read and introduced Tim Hollander.

Even though he'd read Tim's report in draft form last week, Dave found himself leaning forward expectantly. Timmy looked fine in his dark blue suit. The room was very quiet. Bound copies of Tim's report were at every place, along with lined yellow pads and freshly sharpened pencils. Dave concentrated on making notes, hoping that the others wouldn't catch him looking too much like the proud father, but his heart was full of Timmy and he knew Tim wouldn't let him down.

Tim spoke easily, confidently, not striving for effects. He reminded everyone that in their bound reports they'd find extensive background data to be reviewed at their leisure. He defined the state of the food industry and of Hollander Industries' position in it. Tim made it very clear that Hollander wasn't the only food conglomerate showing declining revenues.

As Timmy went on, Dave looked at the eight outside board members sitting around the big table, trying to will himself into their most secret thoughts. But they were all intent on Timmy's presentation. And they were all unreadable.

"It's clear," said Tim, "that our future growth and profitability depend on new ventures. There is still potential for Billy Burger—don't forget overseas expansion, which we're just getting into—but the curve is flattening. Ten years ago our only real competition was McDonald's. Now we've got Burger King breathing down our necks, Wendy's—and that's just the burger trade. Add the Tex-Mex places, the rib joints and pizza parlors—well, you only have to take a drive through suburbia." Tim paused.

"As you know," he continued, "we've been looking hard at two possibilities: a citrus operation in Florida and a completely new—radically innovative—line of frozen gourmet foods. Not meals, nothing like a TV dinner, but ingredients: fine sauce bases, herbs, freeze-dried wild mushrooms, real buere blanc. Things like that."

Tim went on, making a concise and detailed case for not pursuing the citrus project: Florida real estate soaring in price, the weather getting more unreliable with every winter, competition too well entrenched, shipping difficulties. After ten or so minutes he summed up: "It is the conclusion of this report, and my own personal conclusion as well, that the gourmet program offers us significantly greater potential."

Dave kept his face impassive, still watching the others. Some took notes, others were flipping through the bound report. But they were all listening closely, even DeWitt. Tim added a few points in favor of the gourmet project: the revolution in home entertaining in America; the new interest in fine wines; Julia Child, James Beard, and Craig Claiborne and Pierre Franey almost as famous as movie stars. "This line, let me say again, will definitely not be gussied-up instant meals. But imagine rather a range of authentic sauce bases any good cook could be proud of: the sort of glace de viande that is the result of hours and hours of patient simmering, until an essence of beef or veal is achieved—just a few ounces from gallons of stock. But those few ounces then become the foundation of half a dozen classic sauces. And that essence can successfully be frozen. A time-saver, sure, but an honorable one. Fine restaurants do it all the time. Imagine a line of first-class frozen puff pastry dough ready to be formed into the casing for beef Wellington or dessert tarts or whatever. Freeze-dried herbs and wild mushrooms."

Even though he knew the subject and the speaker, Dave found himself caught up in Timmy's enthusiasm. Let's hope everyone else is, he thought, making notes on the yellow pad with what he hoped was the appearance of cool rationality. If there was hostility in the boardroom Dave couldn't detect it. Timmy went on, bouyed by his audience's rapt attention and by his own enthusiasm.

"The advantages are many. Start-up costs are reasonable, because we can use existing facilities with only a little modification. No new construction necessary. We estimate that the whole project through test market can be brought in for under five million. Depending on packaging and advertising, it could be as low as four. If the test market is successful we can go national within a year. We'll be first. And I assure you, we'll be the best."

Tim stopped speaking and asked for questions.

"Does the line have a name yet?" Eric Bartholet.

Timmy smiled easily. "We're testing several. Nothing's final at the moment."

53

DeWitt spoke up. "I want to compliment you on your presentation, Tim. I for one am in complete agreement. Hollander Industries needs to get moving again, and this project can do it. May I call a vote?" Tim folded his flip chart and made as if to leave. Not being a board member, he didn't have a vote. "Do stay, Tim," said DeWitt, smiling, "and see the results."

Dave's heart swelled. The boy had done a fine job, whatever the outcome of the vote. He'd congratulate Tim later, in private. It was always a struggle to restrain himself in public, not to play the proud father. He turned his thoughts back to the vote, dreading a rejection more than he cared to admit. DeWitt asked for a show of hands.

"Those in favor?"

The first hand raised was Jocelyn Turner's. Dave smiled and raised his own hand, followed by Bob Fraser, Carl Sanders, Bartholet, and Ponte. Only Orloff and de Vos abstained. Let 'em, Dave thought with a flush of relief. Damn bean counters.

"Seven to two in favor then, motion carried. Thank you." DeWitt looked pleased, a different man from the pale worried person Dave had talked to only yesterday.

One hurdle passed, but only the first of many.

Steele thanked everyone and wound up the meeting. There was a scraping of chairs, a rustling of papers, a murmur of voices. Some of the board members made a point of congratulating Timmy. Dave watched this with pride, deliberately staying in the background.

So where are those rumblings DeWitt was talking about? Not here. Not now, he thought. But Dave knew DeWitt too well to think he'd been imagining things yesterday. They seem pleased right now, but they're watching. Watching me, Steele, Timmy—the whole shooting match.

Finally all but the two of them were gone. DeWitt came up to Dave. "So far, so good."

"Thanks for your support, DeWitt."

"Dave, it's my ass, too."

Dave made a quick run to Timmy's office on the floor below, down the fire stairs he always used, too impatient to wait for the elevator. Tim stood up when his father walked in.

"Beautiful, Timmy. Just beautiful."

Tim blushed. "They seemed to like it."

"They ate it like caviar. Now we've got to get moving, fast and furious."

Dave looked at his watch. Time to leave for the luncheon. Suddenly he felt hungry. Not just for food but for action, as though he were in training for tennis again. He rode down in an empty elevator, thinking about the board, DeWitt, Timmy. And Pierre.

The afternoon sparkled. He decided to walk the ten blocks up Park Avenue. On such a vibrant day it seemed all the more shocking that Pierre was gone. He remembered the first time he'd gone to Le Palais-Royal. More than fifteen years ago now, with Barbara. He thought of how she'd looked then. Radiant. Never complaining about the long weeks he spent in California trying to will some new life into that decrepit old tomato canning plant. Then, finally, he'd shaped it up to a point where he could be in New York most of the time.

Dave walked up the avenue reliving that night. Just how often, he asked himself, in any lifetime, do you get an evening that's perfect, truly one hundred percent glorious? As that night had been. As Pierre had helped make it.

Was I ever that young, that much of a stranger at places like Le Palais-Royal? He could remember dialing for a reservation—a week in advance—and wondering if they'd take him in, if there was some secret password into that legendary kingdom. If you had to have a famous name or a title. Their dinner had to be at Le Palais, no question about it. Dinner at Le Palais-Royal, a suite at the Plaza. Timmy off with Barbara's sister for the weekend. It had to be perfect. To make up for all those days and all those nights away.

There was a table. The voice on the other end of the line

was French, to be sure, but friendly as well. Armand. Dave hadn't known his name. He remembered drawing out five hundred dollars in cash, not knowing if a place as regal as Le Palais took credit cards. Then to Tiffany's. There he selected a bracelet for Barbara, a gold bangle set with crisscrossing bands of small diamonds and sapphires.

Dave crossed Fifty-seventh Street. A cab swerved past him, horn blaring. He stopped abruptly, blinking. Damn near walked right into it. But despite the shock of his near accident, the past drew Dave back. Back to the year he'd been twenty-seven, when Billy Burger had just opened its hundredth franchise and the sky had no limits. *Newsweek* had named him to its list of young industrialists to watch.

All he'd really wanted that night was to recapture a piece of magic: the feeling he and Barbara used to have when they first met. A feeling of being all alone no matter where they were. So crazy deep in love that nothing else mattered.

How lovely she'd looked that night. Blue silk. No one who saw her walk into Le Palais-Royal would have imagined that Barbara Hollander spent her days chauffering kids to the Little League and the orthodontist, that the English border of her flower garden was a triumph of pure sweat and determination over a tiny budget and no help from anyone. That night she'd been a shimmering vision of romance, and from the tilt of her chin to the glow of her smile Barbara had existed only for Dave.

And Dave had felt like a king.

How gracious Armand had been, smiling as though the Hollanders came to Le Palais-Royal every night of their lives. Armand showed them to a corner table for two. It delighted him all the more to discover the famous restaurant for the first time through Barbara's eyes. They started with champagne, quenelles de brochet Nantua for an hors d'oeuvre, then filet de boeuf Villeromain and a Bordeaux to go with it. For dessert, a Grand Marnier soufflé that Dave could taste in his memory to this day. He could taste the whole evening, in fact.

With coffee he gave her the dark blue leather box from Tiffany's. Barbara slipped the bangle on and just managed not to cry. Pierre sent them a Grand Marnier. The whole evening glittered. Later they walked back to the Plaza hand in hand and made love like teenagers all night long.

Fifteen years!

The old days. Dave kept walking, in no special hurry, and tried to remember the first time he'd met Pierre. After the success of his anniversary dinner he'd made a point of lunching there as often as he could. At least twice a month, sometimes more often. He thought, I met Pierre when we were setting up a private dinner to celebrate going public. Supper for two dozen people in the back dining room. Consultations with le maître himself.

Suddenly Dave could see Pierre more clearly than the traffic cop on the next corner. Pierre, tall and imposing and wearing his toque blanche for the occasion, solemnly inviting Dave to have a glass of wine as they discussed the menu. "I leave it to you, Mr. Villeromain," Dave had said, "and price is no object."

The smile that spread across Pierre's rather solemn face had nothing to do with money. "Thank you," he said quite formally, "for your confidence. You shall not be disappointed."

People still talked about that dinner. The miracle of lightness that was the crayfish mousse that began it. The unexpected delicacy of the tiny quail grilled hunter style. The richness of the hot wild boar terrine. The subtlety of the stuffed breast of veal. And—Dave's only suggestion—the soufflé Grand Marnier that followed. After dessert Dave invited Pierre to join the group for a cognac, which Pierre did to a standing ovation. From that moment on Dave tried to have a word with Pierre every time he visited the place—more and more often as the years went by.

The avenue seemed dense with memories. Dave was crossing Sixty-second Street, still remembering Pierre. Two busy men, Pierre almost without a private life as far as Dave could tell. Until he married the painter, Kate, who kept very much in the background. Pierre beamed when he mentioned her. Bad shock for her, Dave thought. They'd only been together five, maybe six years. What'll she do now?

Dave remembered the day Pierre created oysters Hollander for him. Seeing the words lettered on the menu in that wonderful copperplate script. At first he thought it was a mistake: *Huîtres Hollander.* A variation on the more famous oysters Rockefeller: poached Belon oysters on a bed of watercress puree, lightly glazed with cheese. Forget how fine it tasted. In that moment I suddenly felt, yes, by God, I've made it, and made it on my own. Even when the red granite skyscraper went up and his name was carved on its cornerstone, Dave hadn't felt quite such a jolt of recognition. Hell, I paid for the building, but to be so honored by Pierre was something beyond price. He glowed at the memory of that moment.

Dave still had that menu framed in his bar at home.

Sixty-fourth Street. Dave turned left. I wonder if Pierre realized what he meant to me? How many times I tried to apply his standards to my business? I do it to this day, and I guess I always will. Pierre's standard was at once the simplest and the hardest to achieve: only the best of the best would do. Compromises were unacceptable. Period.

Dave paused now on the sidewalk in front of the restaurant. He did not want to go through that familiar door. Facing the building itself, the proud old white limestone house with its wrought-iron and glass front doors, the brass handles gleaming, Dave felt the sadness all over again. Deeper now. This might be the last time I come here. After today there might not be a Palais-Royal.

He took a deep breath, not letting himself think about that possibility just yet, and walked up the steps.

There was Armand, pale but himself, at his usual station behind the old lectern. Sleek as an underweight seal in his black dinner jacket, poised like a dancer, every dark hair in place. Armand's face was serious, though. There was no trace of the famous smile. To Dave, Armand had always seemed a smiling enigma, almost inhumanly perfect. A beautifully polished mirror giving no hint of what might be behind the gleaming surface.

"Armand," said Dave, taking his hand, "I'm terribly sorry."

"Yes, Mr. Hollander," said Armand. "So sudden."

Dave passed on to where Kate Villeromain was standing at the head of a three-person reception line, next to a thin, pale, dark-eyed girl and a strikingly good-looking young man. The daughter, Dave thought, and her husband. He kissed Kate Villeromain lightly on the cheek. She's holding up well, poor thing, he decided, murmuring gentle words of sympathy. A fine-looking woman. Younger than Pierre by at least ten years. Kate had a delicate pink and white complexion, and her face seemed rounded everywhere. No hard edges. But a strong face all the same, a face with character. He recalled Pierre's obvious devotion to his second wife. "She makes me human, David," he'd said once, "she makes me understand there is more to the world than my oven door."

Kate smiled and thanked him for coming and introduced Elise. "It's a terrible loss, Elise," Dave said. "New York won't be the same without him." She seems distracted—as she has every right to be, he thought.

"Thank you, Mr. Hollander," she said in a voice only slightly louder than a whisper. "I think I miss him more every day."

Dave shook hands with Elise's young husband and passed into the front dining room where several people were standing about drinking champagne. He accepted a glass and looked around for someone to talk to. This place. This incredible legend of a restaurant. Whatever would become of it now?

Dave looked at Kate. She'd never shown much interest in Le Palais. Pierre joked about it: "It's why I love her, David.

59

Another sort of woman would be underfoot all the time—what do you say? Fixing it up a little?'' No. Kate won't wan: the place. Armand? Maybe. He's a part of it, surely. Maybe h already owns a piece. The daughter? Unlikely. Other guest came in that Dave knew. Only Harry Pierrepont made sub dued small talk. Then they were escorted into the back dinin; room, seated, and served the famous lobster consommé. Dav sipped the consommé. Thinking.

The concept formed itself in his brain with the sam spontaneous rightness of a bubble creating itself in a glass o champagne. Like many big ideas it was an obvious one. I had been here all the time, really. Right here on East Sixty-fourth Street. Right in this room.

It has everything, and more than everything: the name, the credibility, the cachet. An image for the new line o foods. The glittering legend of the best restaurant in the world! Dave was oblivious of the small talk around him. A waiter came and removed the consommé; replaced it with a glorious lobster soufflé. Dave ate, barely tasting the exquisite food.

This is the big idea, the concept that'll pull us out of our slump. It was hovering right in the room, lofted on the ethereal fumes of lobster and cognac. A mirage, but not really a mirage at all. A very practical idea, in fact.

Dave smiled into the Laurent-Perrier that had been served with dessert. The simplicity of his idea was startling. It was all right here. The world-famous name, the reputation, the legend. An incredible standard to meet, but Dave knew they'd do it. Maybe they could even use some of Pierre's own recipes. The lobster consommé would freeze—no vegetables to go mushy.

Délices du Palais-Royal.

Dave could see the packages, advertisements in *Gourmet* and *Architectural Digest* and *The New Yorker*. I'll talk to the advertising people this afternoon. And Timmy, and the lawyers. The place has to be for sale!

I'll buy Le Palais-Royal!

# 4

KATE STOOD AT the closet door and finally forced herself to open it. Pierre's clothes, patiently waiting for him. The packing boxes were waiting too, lying open on the floor. Like little cardboard coffins, she thought, helpless now, feeling half paralyzed with sorrow. Get on with it, she told herself sternly. This is only making it worse.

She took down a dark blue pinstripe, immaculate like all his things. Kate stood holding the walnut hanger, frozen all over again as she realized that the last person to touch the suit had been Pierre. He got it for our wedding. That beautiful day came flooding back, and she felt her eyes mist over. Kate sat down on the edge of the bed, holding the suit, just barely aware that her hands were clutching the soft fabric as though it were a lifeline, a last way to hold on to him.

I could hire someone: I don't really have to do this myself.

But Kate knew she did have to clean out the closets and the drawers. How else could she ever finish saying goodbye? Kate made herself go through the pockets, taking out the spotless handkerchief and folding the suit neatly, and put it into the first box. And then the next suit, and the one after that, working quickly now. Blocking out the memories. All the suits and shoes from the closet, the belts and neckties, so many of them ties she'd chosen. How Pierre hated to shop.

Finally the closet was empty and Kate used the momentum she'd worked up to go on to Pierre's bureau drawers, to the shirts and the sweaters, the socks and the underwear. Kate had considered offering Pierre's things to Jared, but the boy was all prickly with pride. He might take it the wrong way and think she was patronizing him somehow. Not to mention Jared's being a little shorter than Pierre and very much thinner. Good as they are, it'd cost a fortune to alter the suits properly, she told herself as she put the cover on the last box.

The pickup from the thrift shop would be here in half an hour. Kate lifted two of the boxes and carried them down to the front hall, then came back for the rest. It felt good to do something physical, however slight. With the boxes neatly stacked by the door, Kate walked into the living room and inspected it with a suddenly appraising eye. Almost as though she'd never seen it before. The prospect of meeting Pierre's lawyer had done that—and a lot more. Kate looked at lamps, tables, carpets and paintings.

Would Elise want that? Those? Would I?

She hated the kind of person who felt it necessary to put price tags on things: a two-hundred-thousand-dollar house, a thousand-dollar dress. People who had cash registers for souls. And now here I am doing it myself. Again she thought of Jared, and of Elise. Kate's thoughts had an unaccustomed edge on them now, an edge that made her uncomfortable. Almost ashamed. He can buy his own clothes now, he's married to an heiress.

But quick as the thought formed she reproached herself. How very complicated it was, the relationship between her and Elise, between Elise and Pierre. She'll never know, and I surely won't tell her, how deeply she hurt her father. Running off like that. Sneaking into marriage. How Pierre had worried about her. And that first snapshot she'd sent. "He looks," Pierre had said sadly, "like a film star." But she's never asked for a penny, I have to give her that.

Would there be so much money after all? Pierre, French to his toes, had hardly ever talked about money. We lived so comfortably, she thought. Time and again he hinted I wasn't to worry. But I never thought to ask him even one specific question. About insurance, for instance. I must have wanted to be taken care of. Like some helpless woman in a book.

But Simon would know. And thank God for Simon. "Simon knows all my business affairs, chérie," Pierre had said, right in this room, maybe only a month or so ago. "If anything should ever happen to me, just call Simon Doughty."

Could Pierre have known? She shuddered at the idea. Well, Kate thought grimly, this afternoon will tell.

Kate stood in the living room she had so cheerfully redecorated and for a moment felt like a stranger in her own house. Is it mine? Could he have left it to Elise? Who else did he have besides those cousins in France?

Elise and Jared. Well, it would be only natural if they were up in the guest room asking questions of their own: who gets what? And how much is it, anyway?

She remembered the half drunk cup of tea she'd left and went back up to her bedroom. Kate stood for a long time, holding the cold tea, looking out the window but not really seeing anything. Reliving yesterday. They'd driven up to the farm. Pierre had wanted his ashes buried on the hill behind the apple orchard. "And no marker, my dear," he'd said in the one brief talk they'd had about funerals. "It must be simple. Natural. Plant a tree if you like, but nothing cold or carved in stone."

Again the chilling thought came to her: He knew. All Pierre ever did was by intuition, and no matter what the doctor says about his last physical, he sensed it. Tried the only way he knew to prepare me. If only he'd done more.

63

Such an enormous *if*.

They'd planted the tree, just the three of them, Jared wielding the spade, making it look easy. Such a small box to hold a great man, Kate had thought, grasping it tightly, a plain utilitarian shoebox-size casket of unpolished steel. She remembered the gaudy urns the undertaker had shown her so proudly. *At least I spared him that.* A fine seedling copper beech, his favorite tree, marked the place where Pierre's ashes would rest forever. He was right, she thought, taking pride in the wonder of his perfect taste. *It is more fitting. More like him. More alive, even in death.*

Kate didn't know how long she'd been standing at the window, in a trance. *If only I could stay like this forever, never moving, never having to make another decision,* she thought. *I don't want to go to Simon, not this afternoon— or ever.*

She felt all the grief come back again, filling her chest the way water must fill the lungs of a drowning woman: inevitably.

*Snap out of it, Kate!* But still she stood at the window looking inward and back. Knowing she shouldn't. Helpless. Tasting the salt of her own tears.

She closed her eyes and tried to imagine what her life would hold now. The house she'd buy. Something much smaller, less formal. A carriage house in the Village? She could almost see it: pale yellow with white trim, its big carriage door turned into an arched window, light streaming in through pale muslin curtains. Everything simple. And upstairs a studio, a big north skylight slanting up, and her easel, all set up and waiting.

*If I can afford it.*

God. All the decisions she'd soon have to make. *How indulged I was, with Pierre. How protected from real life. Amazing. All the bills going to the restaurant.* She turned from the window at last and looked around the bedroom. Such a pretty room.

But no. It holds too many memories. I'll be better, far better, when I'm out of here.

But would she be? Kate heard a knock on her bedroom door.

"Come in."

Elise came in with a tray. Smiling. Fresh tea and sandwiches—crusts trimmed off, the way Kate loved them—and one perfect peach, improbable as it was for October.

"How are you feeling, Kate?"

Kate managed a smile. "Elise, how sweet of you. I was just up here moping. Feeling sorry for myself, I guess."

Elise set the tray down and sat on the edge of Kate's bed. "Hey," she said gently, "we all feel terrible. I've had this . . . this feeling of guilt somehow. As though I'd murdered Daddy. I was rotten to him, Kate. There never were big scenes or screaming arguments or anything. But I always felt, from the time I was a little girl, that he was shutting me out—in favor of Le Palais. So then I showed him I could do some shutting out too. . . . I hate myself for it."

Kate was astonished and secretly pleased that the girl could be so perceptive. "We can't always help ourselves, darling. We get drawn into these situations. And he was a bit obsessed by the restaurant."

Elise stood up. "What really gets me is, now I can never tell him how sorry I am."

Instinctively, Kate put her arms around the girl. "He loved you very much, Elise. Never doubt that. Your father wasn't always an easy man to talk to. Sometimes the portcullis would come down and stay down, and there were things he just didn't discuss. Ever. At least, not with me."

"Like his business?"

"That's very French, I guess."

Elise smiled a quick, self-deprecatory smile. "You might not believe how ignorant I was before I married Jared. About money, business, how to balance a checkbook—name it."

"I dread this afternoon, Elise."

Kate felt closer to her stepdaughter now than she ever had. She longed to think of ways to keep this new intimacy alive. She is all I've got left of him, Kate thought. We ought to stick together.

"You, too?" Elise walked the length of the bedroom, turned, and came back to Kate's desk where she'd set down the lunch. "We're lucky, I guess, that there's Simon. I sure wouldn't know where to begin, not about anything legal." She paused, grinning, and said, "Well, I'd better fix something for Jared."

"Thanks for the tray, darling."

"Enjoy. You haven't been eating enough, Kate."

Elise left, and the warmth of her visit seemed to remain in the room. It pleased Kate and surprised her at the same time. She looked at the tray and realized she was hungry. Ate half a sandwich. Took a sip of hot tea. Then she looked at the peach, at first with a painterly eye because it was a splendid thing; the palest yellow blushing into a deep, almost burgundy red, dusted with the lightest of fuzz. Pure Impressionism. Kate's hand itched for a paintbrush. Yes, and I'll do still lifes too. But she ate the peach instead of painting it.

What do I wear?

She overcame the feeling that it didn't matter. That nothing mattered. Chose a beige suit with navy and cream braid trim in the manner of Chanel. Lay the jacket on the bed and thought, once more, of Pierre. Of that bed. How he'd made love. The magic of it. His hands both gentle and knowing, his eagerness, his almost boyish joy in it. In me. Yes, he was an artist in all things, she thought, and smiled at the memory. And what we had can never be taken away from me, no matter what happens at Simon's office this afternoon.

But the dread was still alive in her. And a terrible foreboding. Nonsense, she told herself. Still the apprehension persisted like some unwelcome odor.

She put on the skirt, a cream silk blouse, the jacket. Examined herself in the mirror. Brushed her hair, put on a touch of coral lipstick. A walking ruin, she thought, setting down the golden tube.

Kate carried the tray downstairs. How nicely Elise had done it. Thoughtful of her, too. The thinly sliced chicken for one sandwich, cress and cucumber for the other. And her confidences about Pierre. Touching—pathetic, really.

She's lost almost as much as I have. Or has she? And who am I, to try measuring such a thing? She put the dishes and teacups in the dishwasher, wiped off the tray, and sat down in the library to wait for Elise and Jared.

An hour later they emerged from their taxi before the stern granite facade of the Wall Street building that housed Simon Doughty's law firm.

Kate remembered meeting Doughty several times, but she'd never been to his office. She knew, rather vaguely, that he was a partner in an old firm, that he'd handled Pierre's affairs for years and that the men had been friends as well. But I don't really know Simon, she realized. Would that matter now? The elevator door looked like the entrance to a bank vault; it was that thick, that heavily encrusted with polished steel and gilded bronze. She, Elise, and Jared were beyond small talk now, and to Kate that seemed a mercy.

Simon himself came out to greet them, grave but smiling. He is the very picture, Kate thought, of a Hollywood actor cast as a fancy lawyer. All starch and pinstripes, club tie, the gold wire-rimmed glasses, the fringe of white hair. And he holds the secret of all our fortunes. Simon led them down deeply carpeted hallways to his own spacious office. It fits him as well as his suit, she decided; all that polished walnut and shiny brass, the Persian carpet, the leather chairs greener than money.

"A sad, sad time for all of us," he began when they were seated. "It was brave of you to go through with the memorial luncheon. People were touched. Very touched. And here we are. . . . The news may be a bit unsettling to you, Kate and Elise," Simon continued. "But it really oughtn't to be as bad as it seems."

Kate felt a stab of pure unexpected terror. Pierre had debts we don't know about, a secret life. Gambling, maybe. She found Elise looking at her, but the questions in both their eyes stayed unspoken. Right now, what could be said?

"Pierre," Simon went on, "was of the old school, as I hardly need to mention. And he felt, rightly or wrongly, that financial matters were a man's concern. That his womenfolk shouldn't have to worry about a thing."

And he was right, Kate thought grimly, I shouldn't. But what in the world was Simon leading up to?

Simon's dry New England voice cut through the layers of silence. "I won't go into all the details now unless you insist, because there really are a great many of them, and they're complicated. That is the nature of wills, especially thoughtful ones." He paused again, and the silence seemed to grow more dense.

"Pierre died a wealthy man," Simon explained. "Like many wealthy men, the bulk of his estate lies in assets that are not immediately liquifiable. That is, real estate: the restaurant—which Pierre owned outright—plus its very good name, which must be worth a great deal; the house on Sixty-eighth Street, which has a mortgage but not a very large one, as these things go nowadays; and, of course, the farm. Aside from a lump sum for his cousins in France and a few charitable bequests, he has left his entire estate equally to you, Kate, and to Elise. Fifty-fifty. That is, you each own half of the restaurant, the house, and the farm. And the contents thereof and whatever cash and securities remain."

Kate took a deep breath. There seemed to be more air in the office now. How enormously relieved she felt that at least it wasn't some sort of terrible financial disaster.

But Simon wasn't quite finished. "I must tell you that I tried to talk him out of the fifty-fifty part of this arrangement. Tried to persuade him it could backfire, that it should have been forty-nine to fifty-one, just to prevent any friction." His quiet voice cut into Kate like a buzz-saw. "Well, he wouldn't hear of it. Insisted on equal shares." Another pause, and the pause seemed to say what the lawyer might not want to put into words: they might be in treacherous country now.

How very like Pierre, Kate thought, cutting up his estate as though it were some magnificent pastry. Imagining it would be that simple. Elise and I could end up as mortal enemies if she feels one way about a thing and I, another. But I won't let that happen. I'll do everything in the world to make sure it goes well between us. Whatever she feels.

Kate looked at Elise. Unreadable. The tension in the quiet office was like a living thing. Finally Simon spoke again.

"The first thing you'll have to face is the taxes. Inheritance taxes. The law may change, but as things are today, they'll fall due in a year, with penalties and interest charges for any delay. I'll have to get two independent appraisals each of the estate, the restaurant, the town house, and the farm. But the bottom line is, individually or together you ladies will have to raise a very substantial amount of cash within the year."

Kate felt dizzy. She had come to her marriage with Pierre with very little money of her own, the small fruits of six years of widowhood and the sparse income of her painting. Even now, Kate knew, her private checking account had only a few thousand dollars in it. Pierre, so completely French, had taken care of every expense and given her only a modest household allowance.

"These estimates will take time," Simon continued, "and I realize your plans may be unsettled. I'd assumed you'll want to sell Le Palais—"

"Do we have to decide that right now?" Elise broke in quickly. Her voice had a catch in it, something strangely harsh, almost metallic. It reminded Kate of a mousetrap snapping shut.

"Of course not, my dear. You don't have to decide anything right now. I just wanted you to know where you stand, so you can look at the alternatives and make the best decisions. But one thing you must consider: the restaurant's value will never be higher. The name is legendary. Should Le Palais-Royal fall into less capable hands, one wonders what might happen to that reputation. Of course, that wouldn't affect the value of the real estate, but . . ."

His "but" hung in space.

Finally Kate forced herself to speak. "For myself, I'll want to sell the Sixty-eighth Street house in any event—it's just too big for me now. I rattle around in it, and that's not good for anyone." Again, Elise was unreadable. All she did was nod, a little bob of her head, as though someone had mentioned that it might rain tomorrow.

Simon smiled. "Well, I think I've probably given you more than enough to consider," he said gently. "And please understand that I take a more than professional interest in the Villeromain family. Pierre was a dear, dear friend, and there isn't anything you might ask of me that I wouldn't try very hard to do."

Bring him back to me, thought Kate in a wave of panic. Make everything the way it was.


"I'm in shock," said Elise in the cab. "I mean, all this is just too much. How can we sell the farm when Daddy's buried there? And the tax people hovering like vampires. And the idea of selling Le Palais . . . it's awful."

Kate reached over and took Elise's hand. "I know, darling, it's ghastly. I was thinking just that, when he went on about the value falling and all. But it seems we haven't much choice."

There was bitterness in Elise's voice: "Simon made it sound as though we could end up penniless if we're not careful."

Suddenly Jared laughed. To Kate's ears it was not a merry sound. "A few days ago, honey," he said, "you were telling me we might not make this month's mortgage payment.

Now you've got, maybe, millions. Don't complain, okay? At least, not where I can hear you."

Elise leaned over and kissed him on the neck. "Touché," Elise said. "It's really ludicrous, Kate. Last week we were fighting over pennies, practically."

Again, Jared laughed. "And now we're fighting over millions. I love it."

"Not fighting. Fretting."

The cab pulled up in front of the Sixty-eighth Street house. Kate felt exhausted. She paid the driver, and for a moment they all stood on the sidewalk looking up at the house where Elise had grown up. Where Kate had found such happiness. She felt an urgent need to do something—anything—to bring them out of this strange edgy mood. "Why don't we go in and have some tea. We'll all feel better."

They sat around the kitchen table. Elise spoke first. "It doesn't have to be the way Simon said. It isn't written in stone that Le Palais has to go downhill. Listen. Coming up in the cab I began thinking. Why don't we keep it going? I mean, ourselves? The three of us?" She paused, looking from Kate to Jared. "I mean, why should we let some creepy tax people take away what Daddy worked all his life to build up? He'd have hated that and, well, so would I."

Run Le Palais? Kate was stunned. Why the three of us would be no more fit to do that than to perform heart transplants. The girl's crazy.

Kate felt as though the floor had given way under her. "Darling," she said at last, "that's a very large order. Even for your father, Le Palais wasn't easy. I know you and Jared have a little restaurant in Vermont, but Le Palais-Royal . . ."

Elise looked at her stepmother and something very like anger flared up in her eyes, but Jared spoke before she could lash out. "Honey, that's plain crazy."

Good for you, Jared, Kate thought, tremendously relieved that he'd said what she was biting her tongue not to say.

He went on, clearly angry but controlling his temper. "I mean, you might have asked me first, okay? What about us? What about Stowe? We're just going to bag all that?"

Elise was sitting next to him at the table. She reached out and took his hand. Treating him like a child, Kate decided. Not wise.

"Jared, I just had the idea five minutes ago. Of course we'll talk about it. Maybe it is crazy, and impossible. But when fate drops an opportunity like this on us, hell, we have to at least consider it. That place is Daddy's real legacy—much more than money. And I don't like to see it treated as though it were some meaningless stock certificate."

Kate felt the room closing in on her, felt as though she might suffocate. The air in the sunny kitchen seemed thick. What Elise was proposing had to be impossible. And she'd be fulfilling Simon's prophecy, risking the restaurant's reputation. Ruining everything.

There was a long pause; finally Jared filled it. "If I move anywhere, it'll be to Aspen. Honey, if you really have to run a fancy-schmantzy restaurant, sell out here and buy one there."

"It isn't a question of just any restaurant, Jared. It's Le Palais-Royal. It's the best restaurant in the world. But even if it weren't . . . well, it was my father's. You can't know— nobody else could—how he loved it, how proud of it he was. I spent a lot of time being jealous of that place. But now . . ." Her words trailed off. Elise had a terrible feeling that nothing, ever, could make them understand.

Kate felt herself making a great effort. I've got to make her see I'm not the enemy. "Elise, you may be right," she said. "It is an enormous thing you're suggesting. Not just a spot of work, but a lifetime of total dedication. If you really think you can do it, well, I'll help. But all I ask is that you think it over—carefully. Are you really qualified?

Elise laughed, a sharp and defiant sound. "Of course not.

But that doesn't mean I can't learn. I'm not proposing I leap instantly into Daddy's toque blanche, Kate. I doubt I'd cook at all, just learn the ropes and help run the place. Cover for Armand when he's busy—which is all the time. Just be there."

"And Jared?"

"Yeah," said Jared—too quickly, Kate thought—"what about old Jared? You casting me as a waiter, maybe? Head dishwasher?"

"You could do lots of things. The business part. Buying."

"Honey, you don't realize one very basic thing. I hate this city. Any city."

Elise looked at him, loving him and hating him in the same moment. Then she felt a recklessness come over her. "You think I like Stowe, Jared? But for you, I'd have gone crazy with boredom years ago."

Something changed in his face. The anger had made him flush; now he went pale. "Yes," he said quietly, "I guess I did think you liked it."

Kate felt the tension building. Soon there'd be an explosion. "Why don't you give it a try?" she said, with a cheer she was far from feeling. "Give yourselves a little time and see how things work out. It's the only way to find out if it'll work for you."

"Thanks, Kate." Elise smiled warmly now. "It's good to get a little moral support. By the way, is that apartment free? The one on the top floor of Le Palais?"

Kate had to think. Yes. It was empty. Pierre had fixed it up years ago to put up chefs who'd just come over from France, until they found a real place to live. "Jean-Paul is in that room on the second floor but, yes, the apartment is free."

"I suggest we move in, Jared." Elise smiled like a little girl looking forward to Christmas. "Then you can see what it's really like, being involved with a place like Le Palais. I mean, if it doesn't work out, well, it doesn't. You'll have a

73

chance to see New York and we'll be out of Kate's hair as well. It'll be fun."

Kate found herself feeling sorry for Elise. She was putting her marriage—her whole life—in jeopardy. Jared's resentment was a visible, palpable thing, and Elise couldn't—or wouldn't—see it.

"I mean," Elise went on, a little breathlessly, "no one in Stowe will exactly be heartbroken if we keep Chez Elise closed for a few more weeks."

"Maybe not. You really want this, don't you?" Jared was talking as much to himself as to Elise.

"Very much. And you will too, when you see how it is."

"I will?"

"Well," said Kate, suddenly brisk, trying to match Elise's enthusiasm, "why don't we go over to the restaurant and take a look at the apartment. I hardly remember it."

As they put away the tea things, Kate forced herself to move, to speak, to support Elise. It wasn't easy. She thought of the fragile rapport that had sprung up between them only this morning: the lunch tray, Elise opening up for the first time. I've got to preserve that, build on it. She's all I have left of him.

But as they walked down Madison Avenue toward Sixty-fourth Street, Kate knew they were heading for trouble.

# 5

As HIS TAXI sped down the FDR Drive toward the towers of lower Manhattan, Armand thought, Next year I'll be fifty. And while he had never shared the American obsession with youth, the birthday would be a turning point. What shall I have achieved? Will it be a glorious day or a sad one? Will I be alone, or with Yves—or with someone else? Will I celebrate at Le Palais-Royal or . . . where? But he could not see himself anywhere else.

The taxi hit a pothole and the sudden jolt triggered a memory: his first meeting with Pierre. Could it be nearly twenty-five years? Pierre just starting up the first Palais-Royal, the little place on Fifty-fifth Street. Pierre in the bustle of carpenters and plumbers and painters, interviewing. How intimidated I was, a kid waiter of not quite twenty-five. What did I know? But Pierre was kind and gentle, the way a good king in a fairy tale is kind.

"If you're willing to work, Armand, we can go far together."

And I did. And he did make me feel like a part of it, that first day and every day since. And I gave him everything, hours beyond counting: the late nights and the early mornings, the sweat and the smiling, the smoothing-over when some bitch got the wrong table and made a scene.

The taxi pulled off the FDR Drive and began to thread its

way through the narrow streets of the financial district. He felt a stranger here: Wall Street! Symbolic fountain of wealth, the churning catalyst of all commerce. He looked up at these soaring towers and envisioned the money that had built them. Sums beyond counting. The cab stopped in front of the Pierrepont Building, austere in gray granite, taller than its neighbors. All of Armand's apprehensions came down on him now. Pierrepont must have billions. My dream costs so little: pennies, really, as things go down here.

Armand had made up and discarded speech after speech. What he counted on was the obvious affection that Harry Pierrepont had for the restaurant, his easy rapport with the staff, his often stated respect for Pierre. I have taken good care of him all these years. Now is his chance to take care of me, thought Armand.

But would it be that simple?

Somewhere inside Armand was buried a deep French mistrust of the very rich. He hoped that Pierrepont would want Le Palais as a plaything, content to own it and play the gracious host, letting the restaurant's cachet enhance his own status. Armand stood on the sidewalk like any bumpkin tourist, staring up at the tower as though at any moment it might come crashing down on him. He looked at his watch. Fifteen minutes to spare.

The rich are often stingy, counting every penny as though it were the last. But Harry Pierrepont isn't stingy. He thought of the generous tips, the checks at Christmas, the way Pierrepont ordered, his fondness for great vintages and his apparent disregard of the great prices that went with such wines. No. Harry Pierrepont wasn't stingy.

But is he really in control of his business? Armand had only the vaguest concept of what a man like Pierrepont actually did at the office. He is the sole male heir of the Pierrepont fortune, There is a sister who lives in Texas, a few distant cousins, but really it all comes down to Harry. Suddenly Armand felt like a beggar. Going to the rich man hat in hand, beseeching favors. But he'll get good value for his money. Le Palais makes money now, and when I take over it will make even more. He'll have all the prestige and the fun of it, while I do the work. From his point of view it ought to be a bargain.

Still, Armand could not shake off the feeling that he was coming to Pierrepont as a beggar, and the pain of it ran through him like an electric current.

Yesterday I felt as though I'd known Harry Pierrepont all my life, but I haven't really. In all these years I've never seen him outside of the restaurant. We've never had a long talk, never been alone for more than a minute or two. He probably thinks of me as some sort of upper-level servant. Or worse. Maybe all his smiles and good cheer and tipping are just a way to get a better table.

He took a deep breath and walked into the building.

The lobby looked like some great cathedral, with floors of marble inlaid with marble, more marble on the walls, and all of it polished to a mirror finish, columns soaring, cool steel enriched with warm gilt bronze, hidden lights and an awesome hush. People moved in the vastness, but the lobby seemed to swallow up every sound. Then he was alone in the gilded, bronzed, paneled, curlicued elevator as it glided silently up and up. Armand felt as though he'd left his stomach in the taxi.

On the fifty-third floor he stepped out of the elevator into a silence even more impressive than the quiet of the lobby. Armand had to remind himself that this was a place of business. He felt more of a stranger than ever, as though his papers might be questioned at any moment. The floors were old parquet, softened here and there by antique Persian carpets. Everywhere there was space, richness, silence. A perfectly groomed woman with steel gray hair and a gracious manner asked him his name and invited him to sit down.

But Armand remained standing. Feeling like an understudy suddenly called upon to fill in for the star, and eager to do it but terrified at the same time.

What would Pierre do?

But Pierre would never have been in this situation. Never. Not even in the beginning. I am Le Palais now, he told himself by way of a pep talk. For an instant he felt better. There was truth in it. When Mr. Pierrepont sees me it must be as though the restaurant itself had walked into his office, and with an irresistible offer at that. And he began forming and reforming the phrases that would untie the purse strings.

In a minute or two a young man appeared, introduced himself, and asked Armand to follow him. They walked down a wide central corridor that seemed to cut right through the tower, turned left, and then left again. To Armand the walk seemed like miles.

Harry Pierrepont was alone in his large corner office. He sat behind an old mahogany partner's desk whose sole ornament was an elegant scale model of the Pierrepont America's Cup winner, the twelve-meter sloop *Blue Moon*. Even Armand, in no way a sportsman, had heard about the *Blue Moon*. Mr. Pierrepont looked exactly as he always looked: like a very cheerful marzipan pig, pink and scrubbed to the shining point and just slightly rumpled in the way that only the very rich can afford to look rumpled. Pierrepont saw Armand and beamed. Stood up and walked around the big desk.

"Armand!" he said, a slight astonishment in his voice, as though the visit were completely unexpected and altogether delightful. "How good of you to come!"

Graciousness radiated from him like perfume from a hothouse gardenia. It's only a reflex, Armand told himself, resisting feeling flattered. In people like Mr. Pierrepont such manners are bred from birth. Pleasant, better than the opposite, but all the charm in the world won't buy me a ride on the subway, much less Le Palais-Royal. Still, Armand smiled his warmest smile. In any game that involved charm he was a world-class contender and proud of it.

"I'm glad you could see me, Mr. Pierrepont."

"Can I get you some coffee? Tea?"

"Coffee, please, Mr. Pierrepont." Pierrepont touched an invisible button and spoke softly into an invisible receiver.

Armand examined the model sloop. It was made with the same care a master jeweler might use: each cleat fully rendered, all the rigging workable. Probably, thought Armand, it has tiny toilets that actually flush. Once again his mistrust of the rich came over him. There was something faintly obscene about a grown man having such a fabulously costly toy. "She's lovely," he said, meaning it.

"The one true love of my life, if you can believe Mrs. Pierrepont," Harry said with a rueful smile, "and like all great loves, an expensive one. She won't even be competitive in the next Cup race, Armand; beautiful as she is, she's outmoded. Damn Aussies! Still, I have no regrets."

"Many men," said Armand, one philosopher to another, "live all their lives and never know such an emotion."

"Pity."

The young man who had escorted Armand from the reception desk now came into the office with a large silver tray that held a blue and white antique Chinese coffee service. Harry poured and handed Armand a cup.

"If I didn't say so at the time, Armand, you did a wonderful job with the luncheon for Pierre. Just splendid."

"Thank you." Armand hesitated for a moment, searching for the right words, words that would show Pierrepont he was a businessman as well as a restauranteur. "Really, that's why I'm here." There was a pause that seemed to last centuries. "I want to buy the restaurant, Mr. Pierrepont," Armand continued, "and to do that I'll need financial backing. I thought of you first because I believe you love Le Palais-Royal almost as much as I do."

For a moment Pierrepont said nothing at all. Armand wondered if his host was setting some kind of trap for him but kept on talking all the same. "I think it will be possible to keep Le Palais intact. To maintain Pierre's standards. We have Yves, Pierre's sous-chef. We have Claude Montgeron on desserts and, well, you know Claude. And we have me." Armand tasted the coffee. Excellent. "It is too soon for an actual price to have been determined, Mr. Pierrepont. Obviously, the Villeromain ladies are still in mourning, and so I have mentioned nothing of my plan to them. But no doubt the place will be sold, and the idea of it falling into the hands of people who might not care as much as I do—well, frankly, it apalls me."

"And so it should." Pierrepont smiled, his round blue eyes positively twinkling. "Just what sort of arrangement are you proposing?"

"A generous one. If you will underwrite a loan to buy the restaurant, I will give you a one-third share—and of course repay the loan at whatever interest rate prevails."

Again Pierrepont smiled, more elfin than ever. "For fifty-one percent I might just be interested, Armand."

Armand felt the jolt. I should have expected it. Underneath his marzipan face this man's a horse trader. It's just a game for him, and if he can score a few points off my need for the place, all the better. He might be bartering for soybean futures or slum real estate for all he cares. And he has the advantage of me, because he knows I do care, and deeply.

But Armand hadn't mastered the delicate diplomacy of Le Palais-Royal for nothing all these years. With the appearance of absolute composure, he smiled. "You drive quite a sharp bargain," he said easily, as though his entire future weren't riding on the deal. "But fifty-one percent is out of the question, Mr. Pierrepont. I must have control, you see. With Pierre gone, nobody in the world knows the place as I do."

There was a brief pause and Armand took care not to fill it.

"Agreed."

Armand could feel a chill come over the room.

"You know, Armand, we're all gamblers downtown. It's in the air. A point here, a point there, it adds up." He paused and sipped his coffee. "I am interested. And I respect you too much to play games with you. You did well to come to me first. When Pierre went . . . Well, let me be frank: I thought it might be all over with Le Palais. It would give me great pleasure to be a part of its continued success."

Armand could hardly believe what he was hearing. So I was right to stand up to him. And it might work after all. Might.

Pierrepont sat back. Held the palms of his hands together in the attitude of a man praying. "You say you can do it. And I'm positive you can do the front of the restaurant to perfection, as you always have done. But the actual food? It'll take a miracle."

"You were at the luncheon, Mr. Pierrepont."

"Yes, yes, of course. And it was excellent. But we were all—well, in a daze, really, Armand. Can you keep it up day in and day out, up to Pierre's standard?"

"I am sure I can—we can. Yves will be with us, and Montgeron. And the rest." But Armand suddenly had an image of Yves, dead drunk on the day of the memorial luncheon, and a great shiver of doubt ran through him. "I have every confidence, Mr. Pierrepont," he said simply. "It can be done, and we are the people to do it."

"Well, Armand, as you've said yourself, it will be some time before we get right down to it. To the details of buying or not buying Le Palais-Royal. I want you to know I am more than sympathetic to your desires. Believe me, I am. And don't worry too much about percentages or things like that. When the time comes—if it comes—we'll resolve the little details."

Little details. From somewhere at the bottom of his anger Armand conjured up a smile.

"The way estates are settled these days, Armand, it'll be months before the dust clears." Pierrepont paused and adjusted the angle of the model yacht just a fraction of an inch. "Which is really a good thing, because we'll all have a chance to see how the day to day operation goes on. By the way, when is the Tastevin banquet, Armand?"

It was more than disconcerting. Can he possibly know

I'm meeting with the Villeromain women later today to discuss the banquet? he wondered. But when Armand spoke his voice was calm.

"The last Sunday in November—the twenty-eighth, I believe."

Pierrepont smiled. Armand had learned to look very carefully now at that well-known smile. "I'll make you a proposition, Armand. If everything goes well on a day to day basis up till then—nearly two months, that'll be—and if you and your people can bring off the Tastevin banquet the way it deserves to be brought off, then I'm with you in buying Le Palais-Royal. I'll be at the banquet, naturally, and Justin Bosch will cover it for *The Times*, in fact, everyone will be there. Everyone, that is, who really counts in this town. The people who can make or break a restaurant's reputation. And you know they'll be doing a lot more than just tasting wine, Armand. They will be judging every bite they eat and every nuance of the service. Watching for any small sign of slippage."

He paused. A small pink flicker of tongue darted out of Pierrepont's mouth and moistened his equally pink lips. Armand could feel him relishing the moment. "So astonish us, Armand. Delight us. And we'll go on with this little chat after that. Now, I ask you: is that a fair challenge?"

"Eminently, Mr. Pierrepont. You will not be disappointed, I assure you." Armand smiled his smoothest smile.

Armand walked from his home to the Villeromain's. Stretching the time. Planning his approach. Feeling a bit like a hunter stalking game. Maybe I can slip in my offer to buy Le Palais. They'd be fools not to consider that I might want to. Strange sensation, just strolling down the avenue on a weekday afternoon. He looked at the other pedestrians and wondered who they were, where they might be going. None of them seemed to be in a hurry, most of them well dressed. People, he thought with a sense of wonderment, who have no need to earn a living. Or who earn it in ways that didn't demand regular hours in some conventional office. Horse traders?

He paused, looking idly in the window of a gallery that specialized in oriental antiquities. A complicated and snarling dragon, carved of wood, leered at him from behind the glass. Beast in its cage. Somehow the dragon, carved hundreds of years ago in a posture of frozen anger, reminded him of Yves. Of what Yves had become lately. The tantrums must be meant to tell me something, but what?

Armand stayed for many minutes at the gallery window, not really seeing the dragon anymore. He drifted back in time to the days when Yves had first appeared at Le Palais-Royal. Fifteen years ago now, and Yves just in his twenties, fresh from the hotel school in Lausanne, shy and eager and very good in the kitchen. Was it just an impulse that led me to put him up that first night? Or did I guess even then how it might be?

Armand didn't know the answer to that one. Time had blurred the memory, but even now, fifteen years later, he could remember the warmth. The sharing. Yves had come for a few days and never left.

When did it change? There hadn't been one single incident. A few inevitable squabbles but nothing you'd call a fight. Just—diminishing affection. It seemed to have something to do with Claude.

Ever since Claude had appeared in Le Palais-Royal, Yves had been edgier, more given to sudden outbursts of temperament. It was never that way with any of the other cooks. Yves sensed that Pierre had a special fondness for Claude—and why should he not? Claude's skill was so obvious, his manner so modest that everyone liked him at once. All but Yves. Yves sulked, held it in, exploded. Acting the spoiled child again. While Pierre ruled the kitchen Yves kept some sort of lid on his behavior. But ever since Pierre's death—uncontrollable. And again Armand thought of the incident at the memorial luncheon.

He remembered Kate's speech after that luncheon, about how everything would continue as it had been. He had no doubt that Kate was a woman of her word. But was she really in control? How had Pierre divided up his estate?

Armand walked down Madison Avenue, past the Carlyle. He turned the corner at Sixty-eighth Street, wondering if he'd be able to make Kate see the urgency of going ahead with the Tastevin banquet without seeming desperate. Kate had always appeared to be a reasonable woman. A bit distant. She kept herself at a remove from the restaurant. There was a mystery about her because of that. Not that she was anything like mysterious in her manner. Au contraire—the soul of frankness.

Or so she has always seemed.

Again he thought of the restaurant. Somewhere Armand remembered hearing that in the old days the manufacturers of Rolls-Royce automobiles used to seal the engine so that no unskilled hands could ever touch the mechanical wonders within. And we were like that, Pierre and I. In our own special world, with our own private standards of perfection.

Unbearable to think that now it might all be over.

He arrived at the Villeromain house and stood for a moment on the sidewalk. Pierre's house. Pierre's restaurant. Pierre's legend. Pierre's wife and daughter. It would always come down to this. I may own the bricks and mortar but it will always be his. They say you can't take it with you, but he did.

Slowly, he climbed the stairs. Kate opened the door herself. "Armand," she said, offering her hand. "It was nice of you to come. We're just having tea, even if it is a bit early."

She led him into the library, Pierre's favorite room. Elise and Jared waited. They smiled—too quickly?—nodded. A tension was in the air, and Armand couldn't tell what it was or who was causing it. But this situation is tense, will become more tense, he thought, forcing himself to take the long view. They're upset, maybe in shock, and worried about their futures just the way I am. But no. Not quite in the same way.

The Villeromains will have money. They have this house and the restaurant and each other. While I—what do I have?

Tea was poured, small pleasantries exchanged. But it is not to drink tea or to make small talk that I am here, and they must know this. Still Armand hesitated to speak. It was almost as though by speaking he might break some spell, some enchantment that had—so far—kept him safe in this strange and perilous quest. He asked himself what Pierre would do in such a circumstance, but no easy answers came to him. Pierre would do something brilliant. Something bold and unexpected, possibly, or subtle and fantastically clever.

It seemed intimidating even to conjure up an image of what Pierre might do and so Armand forced himself to act on his own. "Well," he said as soon as there was a tactful opening, "Le Palais resumes on Monday."

Silence.

They know this—or they don't care.

He continued, speaking gently to hide his growing apprehension: "I've taken a small advertisement in the *Times* to announce that. The message runs tomorrow, and I will be there all day accepting reservations. But what we really must talk about now is the banquet. The Tastevin banquet." Armand saw the boy frown, Elise's beautiful husband. He'd obviously never heard the word before. But there'd be no need to explain the Confrérie des Chevaliers du Tastevin to Kate or to Elise. The winetasting club was world famous, both for its exclusivity, its influence, and the magnificence of its entertainments. The membership included the crème de la crème of the gourmet world: vintners from Europe and California, restauranteurs, wealthy amateurs. The Tastevin's very existence was devoted to preserving and elevating the highest standards of viniculture and dining. Pierre had been one of its leading lights for years. Armand remembered the famous portrait, painted by Kate and commissioned by the Tastevin. Their first meeting.

Funny how everything seemed tied to the Confrérie. The

past and the future. Maybe she has some sentiment for the Tastevin. That's it! She must have.

Armand looked at Kate and addressed his words to her. She is, after all, the head of the house now. Or should be. "I feel odd, this afternoon. It's the first time I've discussed a thing like this with anyone but Pierre. Ordinarily, we schedule special events as a matter of course. It amounts to nothing more than rearranging some tables, perhaps, maybe closing off the back dining room and designing a special menu. But the Tastevin requires much more. A certain investment on our part. Naturally, I need your permission before we proceed."

"Investment?" There was something in Kate's voice that made them all look at her with concern. She said the word almost as though Armand had made some indecent proposition to her.

Now what does she mean by this? Is there less money than I guessed? Maybe they're desperate to sell. So much the better! He smiled a gentle and reassuring smile. "Not a very large one, Madame Villeromain, but there will be a question of ordering special vintages we may not have in stock, and much more elaborate floral decorations. A special theme, perhaps. All will be paid for, of course, but there is the commitment up front. The whole purpose of the banquet is to astonish—for les Chevaliers to experience only the rarest of vintages and exotic foods. Pierre accepted months ago, but we hadn't—he hadn't gotten down to actually planning it. I think it's important that we proceed with the banquet. It will signal to the world that Le Palais-Royal is still Le Palais-Royal."

"I see," said Kate quietly. "This is a time for careful planning, Armand. Pierre never really discussed the business aspects of the restaurant. I know it's a great success, although the profits aren't as splendid as an outsider might imagine. Now, with Pierre's death, Elise and I are faced with some very heavy inheritance taxes. It would be ridiculous to pretend we're penniless, but for the time being, at least, we do have to watch our budget very carefully."

Kate paused. It seemed as though she'd been speaking for hours. How, she asked herself, can I make anyone understand what I don't really understand myself? All these complications about money. From what Simon said, I'm rich. Why do I feel so poor, so back-to-the-wall?

Armand looked at her expectantly. "Of course, Armand, we must do whatever you feel is best for Le Palais," she said.

He nodded soberly. "The sum I speak of is not enormous, just out of the ordinary. No more than ten or so thousand dollars should cover everything nicely, depending on what is in the cellar, and what we buy. And all will be recouped eventually—at a profit. I think—I hope—there is no question of not going forward with the banquet. It will honor Pierre's memory. But beyond that, it is the best way we can tell the world that Le Palais-Royal is in business to stay."

Elise spoke up, her first words so far, other than the noncommittal greeting. "I think there's no question about that, Armand. To back off now would make us look as though we'd already given up."

Armand sensed something in Elise's tone. An edge, a special tension. Steel in her voice. Thin, flexible, and very sharp. It surprised him. Maybe she wasn't such a little country mouse after all.

"I am honored by your encouragement, mademoiselle."

Elise laughed, small explosions of laughter with no merriment in it. Hysteria, he thought. She is struggling even harder than I am to keep some measure of self-control.

"I guess this is as good a time as any to tell you, Armand," she said with a forcefulness that astonished him. "I've been thinking a lot about Le Palais. And what I'm thinking is that I'd like to be a part of it now. To join you and Yves and the rest. To help run it if I can. To try and keep it going the way Daddy would have wanted—the way I'm sure you want to do it. Naturally I'll need you and Yves. And everyone, really. Everything the same . . ."

Armand felt himself choking, as though a bone had caught in his throat. As though no air was getting to his lungs. Numb with astonishment, he could say nothing. Luckily, Elise went on.

"I think that's what Daddy would have wanted. Anyway, what we're going to do—if it's all right with you—is to move in to the apartment on the top floor of Le Palais-Royal and just sort of learn the business."

Just sort of learn the business? Who is this girl?

Armand found his voice, the words came out gently. "Of course," he said, managing a smile, "we will be delighted to have you, mademoiselle. And to help you in any way we can." His manner was calm, confident. Underneath it Armand was shattered. Groping for anything he might now rescue from the ruins of his hopes. If she's there, on the premises, a sort of hostage, then that'll buy me some time. I can keep the place going while I arrange to buy it, he thought. Maybe she'll be helpful. If not . . . We'll deal with that when it happens. The important thing was to make the best of it. Buy time.

"You think it's foolish of me, Armand?" Elise's voice was soft as ever, but there was a challenge in it all the same. Armand had a feeling that the question was aimed not only at him but at Kate and the husband as well. Her question so completely captured his own feelings that for a moment Armand was entirely disarmed.

As she means me to be. There was more to Elise than he'd thought.

"I think it is very brave of you," he said softly. "I think that your father would be pleased if he could see you now. Yes. It will be a fine thing to have a Villeromain in the restaurant again. A continuity." Armand paused. "I—all of us—will be very pleased to have you there," he finished.

As Armand spoke these words he wondered if they rang false. If she'd believe him. It was the only way to respond, whatever he truly felt. Besides, all he could think about now was getting through the next few minutes without making a complete fool of himself.

Elise jumped up and kissed him. "That's the nicest thing

anyone's said to me since . . . since all this began." She looked from the astonished Armand to the others. On her face was an odd mixture of defiance and pathos.

In that moment Armand felt sorry for her. He could sense her danger; her husband and her stepmother must have reservations about this sudden decision. That it was an impulse he had no doubt. But they won't stop a Villeromain, he thought, finding to his surprise a kind of reluctant admiration for the girl.

He watched Elise as she went back to her seat next to her husband. What can her life with him be like, if she's so willing to change it? There was silence, and Armand had no words to end it. With a sickening jolt he could see Jared in black tie, meltingly handsome, standing behind the oak lectern in the foyer of Le Palais-Royal.

I'll kill him first.

The pang remained, sharp as a knife-wound. They could do it, and what might I do to stop them? They own Le Palais. I'm nothing but a hired employee, no matter if I've given almost half my life, the best part surely, to making Le Palais what it is. If this little girl decides to turn my restaurant into a discotheque starting tomorrow, she can do it. He could feel the trap closing. The uncertainty that he'd felt, ever since Pierre's death, was multiplied now. The small sense of hope Armand had gotten from this morning's interview with Mr. Pierrepont evaporated as though it had never happened.

I must get out of here, right now, before I do something I'll regret.

"Well," he said, smiling one of the most costly smiles of his life. "I really must be going. There's a lot to do at the restaurant." He rose and shook hands all around.

Kate saw him to the door. "I hope I didn't alarm you, Armand," she said. "About the money, I mean. Of course we'll go ahead with the banquet, whatever it takes. Let's make it—spectacular!"

Well at least I've achieved that much, he thought.

# 6

ELISE STOOD AT the curb watching Jared load the taxi, quick and strong and graceful. Lifting her heavy suitcase as though it was weightless. He can do anything, she thought, if he'd just put his mind to it. If only he'll give me a chance at Le Palais. But Elise could feel the force and weight of her husband's pride, the burning need to resist all favors. The obsession with living his life just the way he felt like living it, making up the rules along the way.

There wasn't much to load, just the one suitcase they'd brought from Vermont plus two cartons of things Kate had pressed them to take along: sheets and towels, a few books, an alarm clock, and a funny old threadbare stuffed toy from Elise's former bedroom—a dog named Charlie, playmate of her lonely childhood. "I'll be cleaning out anyway, darling," Kate had said, smiling, never guessing that Elise still cringed inwardly at the word "darling."

Kisses, waves, and they were away. Elise imagined Jared standing beside Armand at the front of the restaurant, dazzling the customers with his merest smile. Maybe replacing Armand one day, if the Frenchman were to leave, unlikely as that might be. Elise looked out unseeing as Madison Avenue moved past the taxi window, praying she'd find something for Jared to do in the restaurant.

They brought their cartons and the suitcase into the service alley that ran along the east side of the building. Elise turned her key in the service door. My key, she thought, feeling the power in it. My key to my restaurant! It stuck a little. She had to wiggle it. Finally, exasperated, she stepped aside and asked Jared to try. He had it open in a second. "You were pushing too hard, honey," he said, holding it open while she carried in the first of the cartons.

Sunlight streamed into the apartment, which stretched from the front of the house to the back on the top floor: sitting room in front, bedroom in the middle, the bathroom with its old-fashioned claw-footed tub, then a tiny kitchen. Needs a good cleaning, Elise decided, and went down to borrow a vacuum from the restaurant.

An hour later the apartment had been thoroughly vacuumed and dusted and Elise was hanging the curtains Kate had given them, a pretty floral chintz. The curtains suddenly made the place seem like home. "There!" she said, stepping back to admire the effect.

Jared was across the room, unpacking books. "Nice," he said, standing and coming close to her. "Very nice."

Something in his voice made Elise sense he was working at it. Jared and flowered chintz aren't really the first combination you'd think of, she decided, reaching for the second pair of curtains. Still, it was nice of Kate. Generous. Inheritance or not, I've got to watch the pennies. She glanced over her shoulder at Jared. He had gone to unpack the suitcase now, putting things in the bureau. Three dress shirts. Three may be all he owns, she thought, and decided they'd both need new clothes. Well, that would be justifiable. And it might make him feel better about the whole thing. Moving here. It might make him feel a little more comfortable, more at ease. Elise knew in some dark instinctive corner of her heart that unless Jared somehow felt better about this new life, and soon, there'd be no telling what he might do.

She got down from the chair she'd been standing on and once again admired her efforts. Well, it was a beginning. For one blessed restful moment she just stood there enjoying the way Kate's curtains looked with the sunlight dancing through them, not thinking about Jared or Armand or the whole strange and maybe hopeless world of Le Palais-Royal. A world that even now, inaudible and unseen, was humming and churning right underneath this apartment.

She felt Jared's arms as they twined around her from behind. When his arms were around her Elise always felt safe again, safe and warm. He knows that, he has to know that, and he's doing it to comfort me. He's trying! Just thinking that made her feel better.

"No bookcase," he said, "but I could build one."

"You could build anything." And suddenly he was the old Jared again, Jared the king of the mountain, Jared in charge. She looked at the books, stacked neatly in a corner. Some poetry left over from college, five old cookbooks of her father's. "Would you? That'd be great." She turned in his arms and thought, Maybe, just maybe, please God make it be more than maybe.

"Know what I was thinking?"

"What?"

How about going on a shopping spree? Let Le Palais-Royal buy us a few things. We both need stuff if we aren't going to disgrace the restaurant. Dresses for me—*dresses,* Jared! Suits for you. Shoes. The works!"

He looked at her as though she'd just arrived from outer space. "Only last week you made it pretty damn clear the mortgage's due and we've got two hundred and something in the bank. Shopping? You're kidding."

Here comes his pride again. Everybody duck. Elise paused for a moment, choosing the words that would bring her safely through the minefield. "Jared Carter, do you mean to say that if you came into a little money you wouldn't buy me a present?" She cocked her head, grinned, reached up and touched his cheek.

He smiled. That smile.

"I see what you mean. I guess. But you know I feel pretty weird about all this . . ."

"This what, Jared?"

He shrugged. "It's all pretty damn fancy, honey. Not only your father's restaurant, but the house, the people. God. The people at that luncheon. I felt like—well, like they were talking down to me. Treating me like some little kid."

"We are kids to most of them. I mean, they're Daddy's friends. Kate's the youngest of them and she's fifty, at least."

"I didn't mean about age."

Elise tried another smile. It didn't fit right. It felt like some faded dress from a childhood closet, nice enough once but too tight for her now. Awkward-making. "Some of them scare me, too."

"I didn't say they scared me." The edge was forming in his voice now, sharp and cold as ice at the rim of a winter pond. "It's not being scared, honey. It's being uncomfortable. Hell, those people don't care any more for me—for us—than they care who shines their limos. I feel invisible around them."

"I promise you are far from invisible."

"You don't think André wants you here?"

"Armand."

"Armand. Just about turned green yesterday when you told him we're moving in."

"He was surprised. But Armand's a part of Le Palais-Royal too, just like Yves. We made that clear—at least, I hope we did." Elise felt another army of doubts marching on her.

"Why not just take the money and run? Think what we could do with it in Stowe."

Stowe. It always comes back to Stowe. As though the sun rises and sets only upon Stowe goddamn Vermont. Elise felt the anger simmering up in her. All the things she'd never said to him these last five years. She walked to the window, absentmindedly touching Kate's chintz. Took a breath. "When you wanted to buy that wreck of a house, who went along with you? You think that was my idea of a honeymoon? Who shivered those first three winters and sweated in the kitchen and said nothing if you decided to

93

split and go skiing all day? I just want a little of it back now, Jared. It's not really asking a whole hell of a lot, is it?" For an instant Elise had a vision of herself as Jared must see her. Flushed with the emotion. Shrillness threatening. Or tears.

"I never knew you hated it that much."

There was a kind of awe in his voice and Elise knew that she had reached him at last. That she had penetrated the golden armor and touched whoever it was that lived inside.

And she would have given anything in the world to take back her words.

Jared walked to her. Panther's stride. Then his arms were around her again. He kissed her and she kissed him back and she felt the electricity of it and the shared need. And it came to her then, a thought whose simplicity was startling. Astonishing, because she had never thought of him in quite this way. He needs me, too, the lovemaking is a way for him to prove something. To himself? To me? But then she was so caught up in the glow of it that she clung to him as though they were both drowning and only love could save them.

They stayed like that for a time beyond measuring. Finally she found words.

"I didn't hate it, Jared. You know that. And God knows I didn't plan this. All I ask—"

"Is that I change my entire life. And you think that's not much? That you wave some kind of solid gold wand and zap! I turn into a New York smoothie? Making small talk with turkey-throated old ladies dripping with emeralds?"

His resentment or fear or whatever it was seemed to have a life and a power all its own and she cringed from it, sure in her heart that she must deal with it too. Defuse it. Turn it into something positive. "Won't you give it a chance, Jared?" she asked. "Just a few months?"

He tightened his grip on her convulsively. A reflex. He'd never been violent with her—unless you could call his lovemaking a kind of sweet violence. But Elise knew the strength that lay coiled in his muscles and for an instant— just an instant—she felt afraid.

He kissed her forehead and said, "Let's go shopping."

Elise felt a sense of relief so quick and startling it was almost painful. Quicksilver Jared. She laughed, a little too loudly, and raced across the room for her purse, her coat. Before he could change his mind. In a few minutes they were out on Sixty-fourth Street hailing another taxi. "Madison and Forty-fourth, please," she said.

"What's that?"

"J. Press. If we're going on a spree, it's got to be the best. Daddy always had his suits made there, but they've got very nice stuff off the rack too."

"God forbid I should darken the door of Le Palais-Royal in a suit off the rack." She looked at him quickly, apprehensively, but he was smiling.

The afternoon went by in a whirl, and soon Jared was caught up in the fun of it, the giddy rush of spending after so many years of counting every last penny. At J. Press they picked out three dark suits—two grays and a navy blue—a tweed jacket and a blue blazer, two pairs of flannel trousers, some tan whipcord trousers. She dragged him across the street to Brooks Brothers for shirts, to Paul Stuart for ties, and finally to Church's for three pairs of dress shoes.

He laughed. "You weren't kidding about a spree, were you, honey? That's more clothes than I've ever owned—a lifetime supply."

"We strike," she said happily, "while the iron is hot. When the IRS catches up with us we may be threadbare again."

The tailored clothes would be finished in two weeks. The rest of their loot they carried in shopping bags, but Elise still managed to hold onto Jared's arm as they walked up Madison Avenue to Fifty-seventh Street. She couldn't help noticing the looks Jared gathered from the women passing by. They wonder if he's some movie star, and he could be, she thought, basking in Jared's own private heat wave, warmed by the reflected glory of simply being at his side. In Stowe it was different, although equally electric. In Stowe she was used to the impression he made.

"My turn," she said as they walked into Bonwit Teller. She found a dress that had a pleasing combination of style and simplicity and richness: a sheath of fine silk with an unadorned boat neckline and three-quarter-length sleeves. Ladylike she thought, but not old lady–like. Too impatient to look further, she ordered the dress in three colors: navy, burgundy red, and a soft celadon gray-green that was very like the color that dominated the inside of le Palais-Royal.

They were like children on an unexpected holiday, giggling together, filled with happy secrets. He's doing it for me, she thought proudly as Jared endured the fittings at Press, the speculative looks of women in the streets, in the shops. The dresses Elise had chosen fit perfectly, not even the hemlines had to be altered.

She charged them on her American Express card and felt a twinge of panic. It was a Villeromain family card and for years she'd kept herself from using it except in the worst emergencies. But the card kept coming year after year, and now, finally, she felt that maybe she deserved it. But suppose they've cut it off? Suppose they think we're thieves? But the card had worked in all the other stores and it worked now. They picked up the dresses and went on to the shoe department.

Elise looked at the rows of bright pumps in daring styles, bearing incredible prices—incredible for one who for years had bought nothing fancier than L.L. Bean boots. It was a candy store of shoes. She looked at Jared and thought she sensed a certain restlessness growing. She knew he hated shopping. Quickly, Elise chose three pairs of low-heeled pumps in styles as simple as her new dresses and in complementary colors: navy and wine and the deepest emerald green. "I feel like Cinderella," she said as they walked out onto Fifty-seventh Street again.

"With no pumpkins in sight," he said. The gallantry touched her.

But she wasn't so sure about those pumpkins.

"One more stop," she said. He groaned. "For you, Mr.

Carter." She led him into the discotheque glitter of Bloomingdale's and bought him a dozen pairs of conservative black socks to wear with his new finery. And another dozen definitely unconservative brightly colored Jockey bikini briefs to wear underneath. Jared smiled.

The sun was setting when they got back to Le Palais. Again they walked down the alley to the service door. Elise managed the lock easily this time and it seemed like a small but fortunate omen. They could hear the noises from the kitchen as they climbed the service stairs, up past Jean-Paul's little room on the second floor and then up again to their place on the third. Tomorrow, she told herself, it all begins tomorrow, and that's soon enough.

Elise looked around her. The curtains definitely helped. But she found herself wondering, Will this be my home? Will it really happen? Jared came close.

"It may be a dumb thing to say on top of a famous restaurant, but your husband is starving."

"Me too. Of course we could raid the icebox. Or just go down and dine like the paying customers. But somehow I wouldn't feel right doing that—yet."

He smiled. "I've got about twelve bucks in my pocket."

"But I've got the trusty green card."

They wandered hand in hand down Madison and soon found a friendly-looking bistro. It was a little early for the supper crowd but the bar was doing good business. A bored young man led them to a table at the back. Menus appeared. They asked for a carafe of red wine. The waiter brought bread and butter and poured their wineglasses half full.

She lifted her glass to Jared. "To our first shopping spree. That wasn't so painful, was it? You're going to be something in those suits."

"And you in your dresses. Thanks, Cinderella. I kept remembering you running around all the supermarkets in Stowe, comparing the prices of toilet paper."

Elise smiled. "This was a temporary madness. But necessary. Hell, we deserve it."

97

"Deserve? If you say so." He tasted the wine, then took a big sip. "Know how I really felt?"

Elise felt herself hesitating. Dreading what he might say. She too sipped the wine, buying a few seconds of time. Jug wine. Gallo Hearty, she knew it well. At three fifty a glass this place probably made a fifteen hundred percent profit. Restaurant thoughts. "Tell me," she said very quietly.

"I felt kept. Like some rich lady was buying me. Buying, as they say, my favors."

Keep it light. She smiled. "You've got pretty good favors, young man. Might test drive 'em myself one of these days. Or nights." He smiled too, but now that the words were out they hung in the air between them, invisible but menacing.

"You know it isn't like that," she said, unable to leave it. "We never thought about money, not really, not until now." Elise laughed, a short laugh touched with bitterness. "There wasn't really very much to think about back in Vermont, Jared, was there?" The waiter appeared, saw that they hadn't glanced at the menu and vanished. Elise felt all the fun of the afternoon melting. Worse, she felt there was nothing in the world to do about it. "'Kept,'" she said evenly, "is different."

Elise felt another presence at her elbow. She looked up, annoyed. A balding middle-aged man stood there. Three-piece suit. Piano key smile. Big tortoiseshell eyeglasses. He smiled twice in quick succession, as though practicing. "Forgive me, dear lady, dear gentleman," he said, "but I saw you come in and I had to speak. My name is Marshall. Marshall." He paused, awaiting their astonishment. There was none. "I see you're strangers."

"Very strange," said Jared in a voice Elise knew too well. His time bomb voice. She felt sorry for Marshall Marshall.

"Have you ever done any modeling, young man?"

"In clay. In kindergarten."

"Well you ought to. I represent Pinnacle." Again he

paused. We ought to know Pinnacle, Elise told herself. We are hopeless bumpkins.

"What's Pinnacle?" Jared was trying for control, but not very hard.

"Hottest model agency in town. And you, sir, ought to sign on with us. You'll be making fifteen hundred a day in no time. Truth." Marshall Marshall pulled out a slim black leather wallet with gold corners that looked as though they were really gold. Out came a crisp white card. "Call me anytime," he said, "and we'll arrange for some test shots, a head sheet, the works."

"Thanks," said Jared, reaching for the card.

"May I ask your name?"

"Jared Carter. And this is my wife, Elise." Jared emphasized the word *wife*.

The man smiled. "I'll expect to hear from you, then, Jared. My, my. We won't even have to change your name." He bowed and did a neat little spin and vanished into the gloom by the bar.

"Don't hold your breath, faggot," said Jared quietly.

"Jared. He was only trying to be nice."

"His next move is to ask me up to see his etchings or something. Couldn't you tell?"

"No. How could I?"

"Hell. It doesn't matter. Just makes me a little mad, is all. Coming up to us like that."

"He might be legitimate. You could model, you know."

He looked at her, reaching for the menus at the same time. "That'll be the day. Shall we look at these?"

Elise felt reprieved as she studied the menu with more attention than it deserved. She ordered a quiche first and roast chicken following. Jared asked for a steak.

The waiter went off with their orders. Jared ate a piece of bread, took some more wine, looked at Elise as though he had discovered some bewildering new aspect of her. "Women never come on to you? I mean like that creep?"

"No. I don't think so." Elise thought, and thought again. "Well, maybe once. But it wasn't . . . overt."

"You're lucky."

Her quiche came and Elise was pleased that it wasn't nearly as creamy as the ones she served in Stowe. "It's okay," she said, "but only okay."

He took a sip of the red wine, set down his glass, and leaned closer. "Honey," he said, "what now? I mean, what are we really supposed to be doing in your father's restaurant? If you don't mind my asking."

She set down her fork. "You know I haven't planned anything. We've got to feel our way. Not upset the status quo. Get to know the place, the people. We'll study it. There'll be a lot to do. For both of us."

"I'd like to believe you."

The edge was back in his voice again. Elise realized with dawning apprehension that the same edge or something like it had been creeping in and out of his voice ever since they'd left Vermont. "You sound like I've got a gun at your head."

He smiled at that. "It's just that the idea of changing our whole life seems very weird to me."

She took a breath, an athlete going into the final heat of competition. "Ninety percent of whatever we have is us. Inside us. It isn't geography, this place or that. I'm still me. You're still you."

"But you aren't, honey. You're different. I know it's hard for you to see, that it's been a tough experience for you, your dad dying and all. But it isn't as simple as you seem to think."

"You just hate New York, or think you do, and you haven't really seen it yet. New York can be terrific, Jared." Elise could hear the note of pleading in her voice and it disgusted her. Their entrées came. For a moment Elise let the food distract her. The roast chicken looked beautiful but it was dry and overcooked inside. She could tell from the way Jared was attacking his steak that it should have been more tender. Restaurants!

100

They ate in silence for a few minutes, hunger compensating for the mediocre food. Jared's silence had its own dark meaning for her. Finally he spoke, gently. "Whatever you do with Le Palais-Royal, it'll always be your father's. I don't mean to knock it. It's a big achievement, and I would like to be part of it—of something fine anyway. But I can't make myself what I'm not, Elise. Why can't we build something together? Something that's truly our own?

She looked at him across the table. Fighting the feeling that he was miles and miles away. You can't be what you're not, but what are you, really?

"Daddy's funeral," she said at last, "did something really scary to me. Beyond the sadness, I mean."

"What was that, honey?" Sympathetic. Reaching.

"It made me wonder . . . where I will be when I'm Kate's age. When I'm fifty." She let that sink in for a moment, fighting the temptation to ask him if he'd ever seen anything sadder than a fifty-year-old ski bum. Right now I can look at him and imagine he'll be young forever. But he won't be. Neither of us will be.

"Fifty, for God's sake? Half a lifetime away."

She squeezed his hand. Feeling that if she let go even for a second he might disappear forever. "I have to make you see this isn't some kind of a whim. It's a thing I have to do."

"Right. Let's not talk about it anymore, okay?"

"Deal." But Elise knew she'd achieved nothing. She wondered: Is there a magic key to his understanding? Something I've missed, that I haven't done right? The pain she felt now was all the sharper because their afternoon had seemed so fine. Almost carefree. She signaled for the check and signed it, and they left. Marshall Marshall was nowhere to be seen.

It was dark now. They walked east on Sixty-fourth Street. As they neared the restaurant a gray limousine glided to a halt. Its driver, immaculate in a dove gray uniform that matched the car precisely, held the door as a silver-haired man squired a dramatically beautiful woman out of the car and up the stairs. Her diamonds flashed cool brilliance in the lamplight. Her laughter caressed the night air.

"Back to reality at last," said Jared as they slipped into the service alley.

A diamond is every bit as real as a lump of coal, Jared, she thought, but kept the thought locked up inside her.

Elise stood outside the kitchen door. A chill came over her that had nothing to do with the chill of early morning in October. It was scary, laying everything on the line. Maybe I'll make a mess of it, maybe they will all resent me. Maybe Jared's right and we ought to be trying something less ambitious. But Elise knew in her heart that this was a thing she must do. That if she didn't try she'd regret it the rest of her life.

She opened the fateful door.

Jean-Paul was standing at one of the ranges making café filtre, singing softly to himself in French. Thank God it's only him, she thought, looking affectionately at his stringbean back. Jean-Paul was almost family, a special favorite of Daddy's. "Bonjour, Jean-Paul!"

He turned, grinning a grin that transformed his rather serious racehorse face into something very friendly. "Bonjour, Mademoiselle Elise." He offered her coffee and she accepted eagerly. Delicious. So far so good, she thought, putting aside her fears of Yves's reaction to her invasion of his kitchen—Yves and all the others.

She watched Jean-Paul as the apprentice made his rounds, setting up for the day's culinary operations. Lifting the big stainless steel stockpots from the refrigerator and skimming off the fat that had hardened on the surface overnight. Setting the stockpots on top of the big Vulcan ranges to resume their slow and careful simmering: one pot for beef stock, another for chicken, and a third for fish fumet. Elise offered to help, impressed by the boy's quick efficiency. Very politely, he declined. I wonder if I could even lift one of those stockpots, she asked herself, realizing how very little she knew about running a kitchen on this scale.

Elise was startled by the vast difference between her childhood memories of this kitchen and what really happened here. I remember being the kitchen pet, Pierre's girl, and all the fun of tasting different things every day and learning to make omelettes and to roll out dough. But I never saw any of the real work, never felt the strain and sweat of it, or the tension. She felt that tension now, even before the workday had really begun.

Jean-Paul rendered the fat he had skimmed from the stockpots. Nothing would be wasted here, Elise knew: the chicken fat would enrich pâtés and the beef fat would be sold to the soapmaker whose van made rounds every week. There were mounds of vegetables to be prepared: peeled, shaped, blanched, maybe pureed. Sauces to make, meat to be butchered, fish to filet. Jean-Paul's job was to make the initial preparations so that the more senior chefs would waste no time when they arrived; a complicated routine the boy obviously knew well and took pride in.

Elise sipped her coffee and watched him. Two young American men came in together now, laughing and joking. Barry and Steve. Recent graduates of the Culinary Institute, they manned the sauté and broiler operations at mealtime, working as a team. They began working as a team from the beginning, checking the posted menu and preparing their garnishes, making sure the appropriate sauces were made and warming in their white earthenware crocks in the specially built sink set into the service counter that flanked the ranges. In this sink water was kept perpetually circulating at a temperature just below the simmering point so that the sauces would be piping hot but in no danger of curdling.

An older man came in twenty minutes later. Frank was Le Palais-Royal's butcher, in charge of preparing all the day's meat and fish for cooking. Elise watched them all. Awed. Knives flashed. Hands flew. The chefs were like

103

friendly robots, precise, economical of movement, operating swiftly but at the highest level of expertise.

Claude Montgeron came in, solemn-faced, and shook her hand. "Welcome, mademoiselle," he said, and smiled shyly.

"I'm honored to be here," she said, remembering him vaguely from her visit to the kitchen after Daddy's memorial luncheon. The pastry chef. Why is he unhappy? He had, she thought, a very nice face. Nobody will ever mistake him for a movie star but there's a lot of strength there. And, better—kindness. But Claude seemed embarassed by her presence so Elise turned away and went to watch Jeff bone a capon. Major surgery. Even in this first hour and a half she was becoming aware of the enormity of all she had to learn. Thank God I didn't imagine I could waltz in here and take over the kitchen.

It was about nine thirty when Yves came in. "Bonjour!" he said jauntily, walking toward his office. Daddy's office, Elise thought with a sudden jolt. Yves saw her then and stopped; turned and came to her. "Mademoiselle Elise, it is a pleasure to have you with us."

"Thank you, Chef." Is he a little too effusive, she wondered, or am I being paranoid? He must be wondering— they all must be—what is she up to, exactly? And with a blast of astonishment Elise realized she didn't really know the answer herself.

"Now," he said, polite as any courtier, "what can we do for you?"

"If there's anything I can do to help—that will let me learn?"

"Can you flute mushrooms?"

"I can try."

He led her to the central work island that dominated the big room, a big slab of butcher block with a pot rack above and drawers and cabinets below. A large basket of perfect white mushrooms had already been set out there. Yves picked up a small vegetable knife in his right hand and a mushroom cap in his left. Popped out the stem. "These we save, maybe for a soup," he said. Then, moving so fast his hands were almost a blur, Yves produced a perfectly fluted mushroom cap in seconds. Symmetrical grooves all around it, radiating out from the center of the cap like spokes from a wheel. "It may take practice," he said gently, "but you have time. I don't suppose you've brought your own knives?"

"No."

Yves frowned, a cloud passing. "A custom, no more. Most chefs prefer it. Bring them every day or keep them in their lockers."

"Where are my father's knives, Chef? I'm sure he'd like me to use them." There was a pause. The possibility of a confrontation. Does he think he's inherited Daddy's knives as well as his job? Yves smiled, but only with his mouth.

"But of course! Here." He led her back to Pierre's little office. Opened a drawer in the shabby desk. Elise saw that it had been fitted with a rack holding five knives. She saw Daddy's chef's knife, fourteen inches of carbon steel and a well-worn wooden handle. Elise picked it up. Just holding the perfectly balanced knife made her feel better, as though Daddy were with her right now. She picked up a vegetable knife and went back to the pile of mushrooms. Which now looked insurmountable. "We'll need one hundred, Mademoiselle Elise," Yves said briskly. "Then we'll go on to something—more challenging."

She nodded, fighting the feeling that Yves was mocking her. Elise picked up the first mushroom, flicked out its stem, and tried to hold the knife as she remembered Yves doing. Slowly, holding the knife steady, she revolved the mushroom cap. The damn thing split in half. Flustered, hoping no one had seen, she reached for another mushroom. Slowly. Gently. She made one successful cut and then another. Eight more and the thing was done. She set it down beside the one Yves had done as an example.

Disaster. Hers looked deformed, out of balance, entirely lopsided.

How can I be so clumsy? Her cheeks were burning. I'm probably red as a beet, and I deserve to be. Concentrating fiercely, she reached for another mushroom. She was still reaching when she felt a hand on her own. Startled, she looked up.

Claude. "If I may, mademoiselle," he said, "there is a bit of a trick to it. Perhaps Yves was not clear about the angle of the blade."

Perhaps Yves wanted me to fail, she thought, grateful for the lesson, that Claude was interested enough to care. Gently then, Claude began the cut. Immediately she saw what she'd been doing wrong. The blade had to be at something like a forty-five degree angle to the cut. She'd been holding it vertically, as though she were slicing an onion. He finished. A perfectly fluted mushroom. Even better than the one Yves had done. "Thank you, Claude."

He smiled and his face changed. Grew younger. Suddenly Elise realized that the pastry chef must be only a few years older than she was. Surely not yet thirty. Amazing. "Anytime, mademoiselle," he said shyly. He managed to meet her eyes, and smiled again. "And should you wish to learn *pâtisserie*, I am here."

Her relief was a warm and physical thing. Like coming indoors to a well-built fire on a snowy night. "I'll do that, Claude," she said, reaching for another mushroom.

It took six tries before Elise carved a respectable-looking mushroom. After that the chore went faster. Practice and practice until you can do it in the dark, she told herself. It was nearly twelve when she finished the last of the mushrooms. She felt tired and exhilarated at the same time.

"Will you be joining us for luncheon, Mademoiselle Elise?" Jean-Paul stood at her elbow. She hadn't thought about lunch. And I haven't been thinking about Jared, either, she realized with a surge of guilt. Well. Jared was a grown man, and he knew that if he wanted to join her down here he'd be very welcome. But the logic of this was no consolation. She fought the urge to run upstairs to him.

But what will I say? I'll see him when I go up to change for my session with Armand. That'll be soon enough.

She smiled at Jean-Paul. "You bet I will!"

"It is my turn, you see. Each of us takes turns to prepare the staff meals. So you may regret."

"Not likely, if what my father said about you is true— and I'm sure it was. He thought very highly of you, Jean-Paul."

The boy blushed and looked down at the floor as though the soft black rubber grid that cushioned the tiles might hold the secret of eternal gratitude. "Thank you. I hope to be worthy of Oncle Pierre's praises."

And so do I, Jean-Paul, she thought as the boy turned and fled in a mixture of elation and embarassment. Even though Daddy never really did praise me.

And that is unfair, unfair, Elise. You know damn well you backed off, isolated yourself in school, kept that distance away from this restaurant, his life, Kate. No question of praise, or blame just distance. The desolation of that closeness now lost forever swept over Elise violently. The impact almost sent her reeling. She gripped the edge of the work island so hard her knuckles showed white. Then it passed. She took a deep breath and walked over to Claude's pastry counter to watch him make fruit tarts.

A few minutes later Jean-Paul called them all to luncheon by banging loudly on a big copper pot with a wooden spoon.

Elise hung back, unsure of herself again. I'm not really on the team yet. Will they ever accept me? "You are shy, mademoiselle. But you will surely starve if you have good manners at mealtime. You see, we are quite rough and rumble here." Claude again.

She smiled. "Rough and rumble?"

"As in football."

"Ah. Rough and tumble."

Claude nodded happily. "Yes. Exactly. As I said." He followed her to Jean-Paul's impromptu buffet as she helped

herself to a bit of everything. It looked wonderful: a big po*
of chicken sauteed with tarragon, a bowl of jade-green
string beans in butter and nutmeg, rice, bread, a salad. Red
wine or Perrier. They pulled up milk cartons and used them
as benches. Yves joined them, smiling, joking.

"Delicious, Jean-Paul," said Elise after tasting the suc-
culent chicken.

But her mind was not in the kitchen. She thought of
Jared—and Armand, whom she wanted to join very soon at
the front of the restaurant. I have to learn it all, every bit of
it, every last detail, from where the garbage goes out to
how the customers come in. The day hadn't gone badly
thus far, but it was only a beginning. How will I look,
standing beside Armand? Will people laugh? She ate as
quickly as she dared, just this side of rudeness. Dessert was
a walnut torte left over from last night's dinner service.
Gossamer layers of nutted meringue spread with walnut
butter cream and garnished with chocolate curls and walnuts. "Claude, it's magnificent."

"Your father's invention, Mademoiselle Elise. All I did
was make it."

"All God did was make trees and rivers, Claude. I think
your torte is that miraculous." There was laughter at this
and Claude blushed and suddenly for the first time that day
Elise relaxed a little. Felt that maybe, after all her doubts,
that there was a chance of her being accepted here.

She excused herself and took her plate to the big dishwashing machine and stacked it as she had seen Steve do.
Back up the service stairs. Elise's heart was pounding as
she rushed up the two flights, but not from exertion. She
dreaded another scene with Jared. Yet she knew another
scene was bound to happen. They hadn't really resolved
anything last night, only defined the problem a little. She
opened the door. "Jared?"

Silence.

He's gone out for a sandwich. Why didn't he come down

and have lunch with us? I should have come up and made him.

Elise felt sticky after her morning in the kitchen. Quickly, wasting not a second, she showered, dried her hair, and changed into the pale green dress she'd bought yesterday, half expecting Jared to walk in at any moment. Thinking of something one of her nannies used to say: "Silence was the stern reply."

Where had that come from? Some old poem probably.

But silence had been a part of Jared's attraction from the beginning. It seemed that everyone at Harvard had been so facile and eloquent that their words took the place of real emotions. No danger of that with Jared. *He's running, or he's with Kate for some reason, or figuring out how to make me a bookcase.*

She examined her face critically and applied new makeup. *Damn Jared! It was tough enough without having to worry about him as well.*

Elise brushed her hair and swept it back into the simplest of twists at the back of her head, hoping the guests would take it for understated French chic. Well, it would have to do for now. Later, there'd be time to discover how to truly live up to the elegance of Le Palais. To find out who did Kate's hair, who kept her stepmother's coiffure looking so impeccably right from morning till night. But that would come later.

The face in the mirror was almost the face of a stranger; some half remembered acquaintance, a person met at a party long ago. Not a dab of perfume, not a glint of jewelry. *I look plain as mud, silk dress or no silk dress.* Suddenly it all seemed more hopeless than ever. But Elise made herself turn from the mirror and walk out of the apartment. *Maybe he'll be on the stairs. Bringing me flowers.* She thought of Jared last summer, climbing high into the mountains and coming back with great bunches of wildflowers.

Would he ever do that again?

109

Would he have a mountain to climb again? And woul
the flowers be for her? Elise walked into the front of th
restaurant feeling that a part of her was missing. The sigh
of Armand manning his lectern was disconcerting. He wa
so very good at it. I'll never be the diplomat he is, knowin
everyone's name. It's taken him years and years of practice
He is smoothness itself. It must be built in.

There was nothing forced in Armand's smile. If the quee
of England had walked into Le Palais-Royal instead of Elis
Villeromain, she could hardly have expected a warmer re
ception. "Ah, Mademoiselle Elise!" Armand's handsom
brown eyes fairly glowed. "What a help it will be to hav
you here."

She decided to believe he meant it.

"Anything I can do, I'll be glad to, Armand." His atten
tion was distracted then as a patron came in. Elise stood a
his side as Armand checked the man's name against his re
servations list. A name, it seemed, that Armand did not al
ready know. Armand bowed slightly and escorted the ma
to his table. The first customer of the day. Le Palais spar
kled. White tablecloths and napkins, white freesias in cryst
bud vases, Baccarat goblets for wine and water and the spe
cial Palais-Royal plates, plates designed for the restauran
and made in Japan of fine procelain in the palest celado
green to complement the slightly deeper green silk moir
that covered the restaurant's walls. The silver was Jame
Robinson's handmade reproduction of the classic Georgia
rat-tail pattern. Pierre Villeromain would have nothing less
Even if it does mean that the waiters have to watch the sil
ver like hawks. Elise looked at the front dining room an
felt a surge of pride. Magnificent. And Daddy was righ
real silver does make a difference, and if a few butter knive
turn up missing, it's just another operating expense, lik
heat and electricity.

Expenses.

Another fear, another worry. I don't know the day to da
expenditures here, and it's a safe bet that Kate doesn't ei

ther. Elise looked at the gleaming silver again. What must it be worth? The freshest of fresh flowers. All the linen was Irish damask, and Elise realized she had no idea how long it could be expected to last.

I've taken it all for granted, all my life. I thought elves came in and did it in the moonlight.

She remembered Daddy on the subject of flowers: "You may be able to afford just one flower, Elise, but it must be the best flower in the shop, the freshest and the most fragrant. And one of such quality is enough—better, perhaps, than vulgar masses past their peak and poorly chosen." She smiled, remembering. Once they'd walked into the Plaza together—Elise must have been nine or ten, she couldn't quite recall—and there stood an enormous bronze urn spilling over with flowers. Pierre had leaned down and whispered "Gangster funeral!" in her ear. To this day every time Elise saw a huge pretentious flower arrangement she thought about Daddy and the gangster funeral.

Armand came back from seating the first customer. They waited, but no one came in. Elise could see that Armand's reservations book was full. Maybe they've canceled. Maybe it's all over, right now, even before I start in. Maybe people are staying away in droves now that the word's out. Now that the great chef of Le Palais-Royal is gone forever.

Armand took his place at the lectern, a rock of assurance, sleek as a seal in his bespoke dinner jacket, studying the reservations book as if it were the Bible. He looked at her and smiled conspiratorially. Elise could have kissed him. They were in this together and Armand had managed, without flowery speeches, to let her know that he understood the situation. Like a whipped enemy, some of Elise's fears and doubts began slinking away now. The morning had gone rather well, really. She felt she'd made some progress, discovering the way things worked in the kitchen. Claude was obviously a treasure, and everyone else seemed to be doing nicely. And if Yves was to be a problem, well, she'd have to find a way to deal with him.

In the silence that followed the seating of the first customer, Elise left Armand's side and walked across the foyer to look more closely at Kate's portrait of Daddy. There he stood, forever stirring his pot. PIERRE VILLEROMAIN, PROPRIETOR, said a small brass plaque at the bottom of the frame, along with a message announcing the painting as a gift from les Chevaliers du Tastevin.

The banquet. There was another thing to worry about. All of us. We'll have to begin planning in earnest now.

She went back to stand by Armand. Robert the barman stood behind the little zinc-topped bar Daddy had found in the Paris flea market. It had room for just four bar stools and for a few people to stand. Against the far wall was one little table for two. In desperate cases people could be served meals there, but Daddy had never liked the idea. Daddy, she remembered with a rueful smile, would much prefer someone waited, starving graciously, rather than dine on Palais-Royal cuisine in an ambience that was less than the best that Le Palais-Royal could offer. It must be perfect, from the size of a table to the crispness of the little almond cookies that were offered with the coffee.

As she stood there about to face her first customers Elise felt like an attendant at some ancient and splendid ceremony, a gilded ritual extending far back in time. She felt small and completely insignificant. What had she done to contribute to all this magnificence? It was as though she were a traveler with false papers, sneaking across dangerous borders, holding her breath for fear of being stopped. Unmasked.

She prayed the fear didn't show.

In something like a trance she heard Armand's confident voice: "Mrs. Vanderwicken, it is good to see you."

Elise looked up and managed a smile. Minnie Vanderwicken was a gray-haired matron in steel-rimmed glasses. Her tweed suit and sensible shoes were built for the ages. Only the famous Vanderwicken pearls—each big as a hazelnut, two strands of them, which fell to her waist—

gave a clue that this was the dowager of one of the oldest families in America. She smiled fleetingly at Armand and examined Elise with undisguised curiosity. Elise felt like a bug under a magnifying glass.

"And are you Pierre's girl, young lady?" Her voice had the unmistakable cutting edge of authority.

"Yes, I'm Elise Villeromain."

Minnie Vanderwicken's face changed. She smiled a motherly smile and took Elise's hand in both of hers. "You poor thing," she said. "I've been thinking of you. Couldn't make it to the luncheon, but we did think of you—and, of course, your dear father."

"That's very kind of you, Mrs. Vanderwicken. Thank you."

"Fiddlesticks! We all owe the Villeromains an enormous debt of gratitude. Before Le Palais—well, New York was a wasteland, my dear. A wasteland!" The taller woman who had come in with Minnie Vanderwicken said nothing. Armand escorted them to a table in the front dining room while Elise stayed by the lectern trying to regain some composure.

If every little conversation is going to fluster you, maybe Jared's right, she told herself. Maybe you ought to be back at Stowe where everything's less intimidating.

Behind the bar Robert was polishing already sparkling glasses. Elise couldn't get over her feeling of being on trial, of being watched. Of performing on a wire, and without a net.

The next arrival was Dorothy Dutton and a party of five. Not being a reader of gossip columns, Elise was grateful that she'd met the lady at the memorial luncheon. "Good to see you, Mrs. Dutton," she said, smiling, as Armand rejoined her just in time to lead the party off to their table.

Elise took a deep breath. At least she'd remembered the woman's name! Armand was back again, sooner this time. The door opened and more people arrived. They would be full after all. Elise felt the rythmn picking up. There wasn't

113

time to think now, or to be afraid. She had to concentrate on greeting people, on smiling, on checking their names with the book if Armand was taking someone to a table. It was a mystery to Elise how Armand chose where to seat people. During a brief lull in the stream of arrivals she asked him.

"You know, of course, about the file?" Elise looked at him questioningly, feeling more and more like an interloper from Mars.

"File?"

He smiled benevolently. "I see that you do not. Well, no matter. The file was your father's invention, and a clever one. A simple index of file cards, arranged with tabs alphabetically." Armand looked about him with a conspirator's guile and saw that there was no one close enough to hear. "Later I will show you. There are some who would give much to read this file. As people become known to us, they achieve a place in the file. It mostly deals with their preferences: do they prefer the front room or the back? A favorite wine? We check to be sure it is on hand when they reserve. Special foods? Anything like this. But then, over the years, the file grew more complex." He paused, leaned closer, almost whispering now. "It began to deal with relationships as well. Who should not be seated in the same room with whom. Personal matters. A marriage going sour, wives who might arrive when the husband is already here with another lady—that sort of thing. Very delicate, in some cases. Tact is essential."

"I'm sure it is." Elise was astonished. Another complication to learn. Another technique to master.

"So, automatically now, when someone reserves, I check the file. It takes only a few seconds, and the results are well worth it." He turned toward the main dining room. Elise turned as well. "As for seating strangers, naturally I give them their preference if that is possible. Do you see the lady in red?"

It was impossible not to see her. A dramatic beauty, dark-haired and aristocratic-looking, and somehow mysterious.

114

Armand smiled. "I have never seen her before, but she is a lady who needs to be noticed. So I seated her party there, in the center of the first dining room. Only because the lady is decorative. Now, should another such lady appear, I will separate them as much as I can, so that the sphere of the one will not intrude upon the sphere of the other. I think of such ladies, and certain men as well, mind you, as rare ornaments, to be set where they can be most effectively seen. They like it, and so do many others. Mrs. Vanderwicken doesn't wear those pearls because they keep her warm."

Elise looked at him and nodded. I don't ever want him as my enemy, she thought. Armand knows too much and thinks too subtly.

She could tell he was enjoying his new role, the role of instructor. "And do you see those two men? The one with the red face and the other with the white hair?" Elise had noticed them coming in. The red-faced man looked positively combustible. She had found herself hoping he'd have his inevitable seizure after lunch, not on these premises. Armand interrupted her thoughts. "The red-faced one is trying very hard to sell the white-haired man something the white-haired man doesn't especially want to buy. So I put them in a quiet corner of the banquette."

A couple had come in while Armand was talking. Elise tried to guess who they were, where they'd be seated. They didn't look like typical Palais-Royal people. The man was tall and spare, almost gaunt, really, and while his suit was decently tailored dark gray flannel, there was an air of just-out-of-mothballs about it. He looked like a man who didn't often wear city clothes. The woman, obviously his wife, from the gentle way she deferred to him, wore a navy blue silk suit of the indeterminate cut favored by the Queen Mother. Elise thought of another navy silk suit—the one she had fished out of her closet to wear to Daddy's memorial luncheon. It's her special-occasion outfit, Elise guessed with a quick, exciting flash of intuition. She was sure she must be right. They were perhaps in their late fifties, scrubbed and bright-eyed.

115

"A table for two for Collins," said the man. He had a pleasant unhurried voice with no particular accent. Elise had a sense that the Collinses were not from New York. Armand consulted his book. At first he seemed unable to find the notation. The woman looked anxiously at her husband. "I made the reservation last week," he said, "all the way from Lakeville." Impulsively, the woman turned to Elise. "It's our anniversary, you see," she said eagerly, suddenly a girl again. "Every anniversary Will and I come to town and see a show and have lunch at Le Palais-Royal. We save up for it."

Elise was smiling trying to think of something appropriate to say when Armand found the notation. "Of course, here it is," he said, positively beaming. "This way, madame, if you please."

"Enjoy your lunch," said Elise quickly, feeling about ten years old and distinctly inadequate.

Armand returned. "I should have recognized them," he said. "The lady is right. They do come every year."

"Would it be out of the question for me to send them a bottle of wine on the house?" Elise asked as the thought came to her. The Collinses were touching, saving up all year for a meal at Le Palais! She hadn't known people did things like that. For an instant Armand frowned, but the frown soon melted and turned itself into a smile. "You are indeed your father's daughter, Mademoiselle Elise. Pierre would have given away the house if I let him. But yes. An excellent gesture, I think. They won't forget it, and they will tell all their friends."

"Champagne, then, seeing it's their anniversary." She selected a bottle of nonvintage Laurent-Perrier Brut, one of Daddy's favorites. Then Elise wrote a message on the thick, pale celadon green notepaper the restaurant kept for guests: *To Mr. and Mrs. Collins, with best wishes on their anniversary*. She paused for a moment, wondering how to sign it. Then, boldly, *Elise Villeromain*. She gave the note and her order to Olivier, the wine steward, and pointed out the recipients. With increasing pleasure Elise watched as the elegant black back of Olivier disappeared into the wine cellar to execute the first official action she had taken in her new role at Le Palais-Royal. And Armand approved! For the first time today, she felt like a real part of the place. Not just a fly on the wall. And there had been something special in Armand's eyes when he'd said "You are indeed your father's daughter."

If only it's true. If only I have even a fraction of what Daddy brought to this place.

She turned to Armand. He was on the phone explaining that, alas, Le Palais was all booked for both Friday and Saturday. We aren't finished yet, then. People are coming back. They will give us a chance. She glanced at her watch. Nearly two thirty already. Time to go back and change. Elise felt she'd seen enough of the front operation for one day. Maybe, depending on Jared, she'd come down for a while tonight. She told Armand where she was going and walked back through the two dining rooms toward the kitchen. Elise took care to walk slowly, observing, smiling, nodding. By every sign she could understand the staff was performing flawlessly. Nowhere could she see a customer waiting in vain for service, or any other sign of discord. It was almost frightening, the smoothness and perfection of the service. A hundred different operations meshing with silken efficiency. It was the result of training, practice and constant vigilance. But, more than skill, it came from caring, from an eagerness to excel.

The sight of Le Palais functioning so well made her proud, and with the pride came a new determination. I can do it, she told herself, and I will.

The back dining room was slightly smaller than the front one. As she passed through it Elise noticed Mr. and Mrs. Collins looking a bit ruffled as Olivier appeared with a silver ice bucket containing Elise's gift. Mr. Collins started to protest, softly, and Olivier handed him the note. He read it, blinked, handed it to his wife; then he spotted Elise. She smiled. He gestured that she come to his table. "You are very kind, Miss Villeromain," he said rather formally. "Will you join us in a glass?"

"I'd love to," she said, wondering if this was breaking form. And if it is, to hell with the form, she thought as Olivier materialized with another champagne glass. He opened the bottle. Just the faintest hiss greeted them as he deftly slid out the cork. Olivier poured for Mr. Collins and waited deferentially as he tasted the wine. "Delightful!" Something young in his voice now. Olivier filled all three glasses and Elise raised hers.

"Happy anniversary, Mr. and Mrs. Collins. We're flattered that you chose us for your celebration." They all sipped the elegant wine. "No question about it," said Mr. Collins. "If we couldn't dine at Le Palais-Royal, we'd stay home."

"Will teaches French, you see," his wife said as though that explained everything, "so it's very important to him. That it be the best."

Elise laughed. "It's important to us, too, Mr. Collins." She said good-bye and walked back to the kitchen. What a pleasure, hearing the Collinses' loyalty to the restaurant. But mixed up with the warm feeling of accomplishment Elise sensed a dread, a foreboding.

Where will I be this time next year? Where will Le Palais be? Will those people have to find someplace else to celebrate in?

She climbed the service stairs to the apartment. The door was unlocked. She could hear Jared moving around. Called his name and got no answer. Walked down the hall to their bedroom.

Her heart plummeted.

He was packing.

The suitcase—her old suitcase—was on the bed. Jared stood there, folding things, methodically filling the case. Half filling it, really. But for the new shoes and shirts and underwear, none of the new things she'd bought him yesterday were ready yet. He never was one for long explanations, she thought, fighting nausea.

118

"Can we talk about it, Jared?"

Her words just hung there, frozen in the quiet air. He closed he lid; looked at her for the first time since she'd come in. ared's eyes had a flat clouded look more disturbing than inger, as though he were already somewhere else. As though ie couldn't quite see her, or this room, or the restaurant. His voice was equally remote. "We came down for a funeral," he said, "and we left our lives—yours and mine—back in Vermont. And I"m going back to pick up the pieces while there's till a chance." He paused, seemed to take a deep breath. "And 'd like you to come with me, if you will."

Elise wondered if words could reach him now. If it made iny difference. "Can't you give me just a little while? A few weeks? Why right now?" Even as she spoke Elise hated herelf for begging him.

"Free ride. Bobby Parker's in town and he's driving back n half an hour. There's room, if you want to come."

"Vermont will still be there in a few weeks, Jared. Give ne a chance."

He was still looking at her, his eyes clouded with that incustomary faraway glaze. "I spent part of the morning up iere, honey," he said softly, "going stir-crazy. I felt like I was inderwater, drowning, everything closing in on me. I guess you can't understand that. You swim so well in these waters."

*I don't*, she wanted to shout at him, *I'm more frightened han you can imagine, and I need you, Jared. I need your presence, your love.* But all that came out of her mouth was a sudden ;asp. She felt as though she was choking on her thoughts, ind everything became confused, a churning of loss and reentment, of needing him terribly and hating herself for it.

"Just like that," she said at last. A statement.

"You're right, you know, honey. A few days don't mater. Better sooner, because you can bet anything I'd be ;oing some day."

"We've been here only one day, Jared."

He closed the case. The finality of those old brass catches licking shut echoed in her heart like the slamming of some enormous vault. "Honey, I've got to do what feels right To me. Now."

"And it doesn't matter what I feel?" She might have been talking to smoke.

"If I were here for a million years, I wouldn't fit in," he said as though he hadn't heard her.

Black defeat flooded Elise's heart. What more could she say? Or do? Jared went to the closet and put on his old tweed jacket. At least you could wait till your new suits are altered, she thought, clutching at straws. But Jared hadn't really wanted the clothes, or the restaurant.

And maybe he doesn't really want me, either.

Elise knew she couldn't stop him, any more than she could go with him. She watched him finish his packing, trying to distance herself from it now, trying to pretend it was just some old movie she didn't really care about. But the instant she tried to tell herself, If he loved me he'd stay, a taunting, laughing voice answered, If you loved him, you'd go.

Elise felt the tears welling up. Blinked. Felt the very breath going out of her. Drowning.

"Like I said, there's room in Bobby's car, honey." There was a kindness in Jared's voice.

She could only shake her head, a sad little gesture, but less hurtful to him than the words she was choking back. Don't make it worse, Elise. Don't make him burn his bridges and don't burn yours. She clutched the bedpost with a frightening tenacity, feeling that if she didn't have it to cling to she'd fall right off the face of the earth.

He turned and walked past her. Burningly handsome. She closed her eyes, but the pain stayed with her. The door closed. Elise lowered herself to the bed. The tears came slowly. Then rage at the brutal unfairness of it all. She rose from the bed and walked as far as the door and couldn't force herself through it. I won't go chasing after him, no matter what. Maybe someday he'll understand, we'll work it out, maybe I'll even go up there to him. But not now. Not when he's hurt me this badly. Not when I feel like this.

* * *

Elise lost track of time. Finally, in a daze of grief, she got up and looked at her watch. An hour had passed. She got herself out of the green dress. The dress itself seemed to mock her. Elise remembered yesterday afternoon—a million years ago—how she'd felt buying all the fine new things. Especially the things for him. She managed to hang up the dress, then went into the bathroom and changed into jeans and an old turtleneck. Washed her face mechanically.

When she could bring herself to look in the mirror Elise began crying again. Forced herself to rinse her burning face again. Pressed a cold towel to her eyes. And once again the impulse came over her to follow him. I can be on a plane, get to Burlington in an hour, be back at Chez Elise waiting for him. Cooking for him.

There was a knock on the apartment door.

"Yes?"

"It is Jean-Paul, Mademoiselle Elise. We wondered, is there anything we can do for you?"

She hesitated. Had they seen Jared leaving? Finally, with an effort of will that threatened to consume her altogether, she spoke. "Thanks, Jean-Paul. I'll be down in a minute."

Elise was watching herself in the mirror with a strange detachment now, almost as though she was an observer at some theatrical performance. The girl in the mirror dabbed at her eyes, slowly refreshed the few touches of makeup, straightened a vagrant strand of hair.

Elise saw herself in that moment, but she saw Daddy as well. He seemed to be a very real presence here in the apartment. Not angry, not sad, just a presence. Someone to be reckoned with. Help me, Daddy, she pleaded in the resonant silence. Because if you don't, who will?

She forced herself to walk down the stairs to the kitchen.

# 7

CLAUDE STOOD AT his chilled marble pastry counter, slowly turning the pages of a picture book about the Statue of Liberty. There she was, from every angle, including shots taken from an airplane. How fine it would be, one day, to take little François on the boat ride to the statue! But that happy thought was soon replaced by a greater urgency, the challenge of recreating the statue in sugar as the center-piece of a dessert tray at tonight's banquet for the president of France.

He turned to a frontal view of the statue and reached for the thick, flexible copper wire that would become the arma-ture supporting his statue's frosting body. The crown would be tricky, and the angle of the arm must be just so. He began working quickly, fired up by the challenge. Lost in his conception of the sugar statue.

As he worked, deep in concentration, Claude could feel an uncomfortable prickling sensation at the back of his neck. He glanced up to find Yves staring at him from across the room.

Waiting for me to fail. Wishing me bad luck. But what did I ever do to him that he feels this way? I work hard, saved his ass the day of the memorial luncheon. He even went out of his way to let the Villeromains know what I did. But still, Yves holds a lot of bad feeling for me. Maybe

122

he's just an unhappy man. Maybe I am doing something I don't realize that annoys him.

It was a mystery and a sad one. Once again, Claude felt a stab of regret that Pierre was gone. Whatever Yves's problems might be, he'd always contained them when Pierre was on the scene.

The armature grew, a tangle of wires that might seem formless to anyone else. Claude's hands were quick and sure and he found pleasure in the physical act of creating the statue, even though it was destined never to be eaten but only admired. That the president of France might be pleased by the statue was every bit as important as the freshness and texture of the fruit sorbets that would surround it on a great silver tray.

He looked at the photograph, planning the exact mixture of frosting that would duplicate the look of weathered copper. His fingers worked nimbly, almost as if they had a life of their own. The armature was finished now, and he was building up the base of frosting, a special quick-drying formula he had perfected in the kitchens of La Tour d'Argent. Shaping the lady's skirts now, duplicating every curve and fold of the original.

Claude felt a presence at his side. A friendly presence. He looked up and smiled.

Elise.

For an instant he watched her as she watched him working. Claude felt a glow deep inside him. How fine she is, how slender. A girl who must be capable of great passion. Claude felt an undercurrent, a tension between them, unspoken but very real. For one crazy instant lasting no longer than a heartbeat, he thought, Yes, maybe we could get together—but no. Impossible. She, Elise Villeromain, the owner of all this, a lovely girl, of course, but she could never be more to me than an employer. Patronne. Claude was afraid to speak. Afraid that she'd guess, and maybe take offense at his presumption. Or, worse, laugh.

"It's going to be beautiful, Claude," she said.

"Well, let us hope. Not really a thing I believe in, confections that don't get eaten, but it is in the grand tradition . . ."

She laughed. "And he is the president of France. I was thrilled when Armand said the ambassador had chosen us."

She wants me to be pleased, to be happy here. His hands kept on moving, building, shaping, refining the statue. And thank God for the work, that I have something to distract me. "It is good for the restaurant."

She hesitated a moment before replying. "And the restaurant needs all the good it can get right now, Claude."

"But we are full every day, no?"

"Yes. For the moment. But Americans love nothing more than a new superstar—or to see an old star fall."

"Even a restaurant?"

"Or a president or an automobile or an epic film. Other people's failures make some people happy."

"Human nature," he said, watching Yves out of the corner of his eyes. "La comédie humaine."

"You seem so calm, Claude," she said suddenly. "You've probably cooked for so many presidents and kings it doesn't mean much anymore."

She is being a little girl, a bit of a tease. Or am I imagining all this? He shrugged. "One exiled king, at La Tour d'Argent. A disagreeable man. So afraid of assasins he had guards in the kitchen, brought his own eggs, his own flour, all that."

Elise laughed. "Can I get you some coffee, Claude?"

He nodded and she went off to make some fresh. Then, so quickly that it could hardly have been by chance, Yves was there. Squinting at the statue. It is his right, he is the chef de cuisine now, Claude reminded himself. But it took only one look at the nasty smile that was forming on Yves's lips to understand this was not some casual tour of inspection.

"Her poitrine is too big, Claude. We want Liberty, not Mae West."

124

And what does a homosexual like you know about tits, Yves? Claude asked himself, resisting the temptation to strike out with the pointed spatula he was using to shape the frosting. Instead Claude picked up the book. "Regard," he said evenly. "And let us have our joke after the president's dinner, shall we, Chef?" Claude kept his voice low. No point in making a big scene. But there was a threat in it, a subtext that must be unmistakable to Yves: *Don't push me too far, Chef, or I'll be gone.*

Yves just looked at the photographs. Irrefutable.

Rub it in a little, thought Claude, suddenly reckless in his anger. "Alain Sailhac called yesterday, Yves. Asked me if I had changed my plans since Pierre's death."

Yves glowered and Claude immediately regretted his outburst. Should have saved Alain for the final showdown. Sailhac was the executive chef at Le Cirque, one of very few restaurants in New York ever mentioned in the same breath as Le Palais-Royal. Claude watched Yves's face darken, as though a bruise was spreading from within. Not pretty.

Claude's hands were busy again, now adding frosting to the statue. And as he worked a grim thought came to him: Maybe this is what Yves really wants—to drive me away.

The simplicity of it was startling.

Yves stayed just where he had been, inches away. The pause lasted only seconds by the clock but to Claude it seemed to stretch out for minutes. Finally Yves spoke. "You would be so disloyal? I am shocked, Claude." His indignation sounded operatic and Claude didn't believe a word of it.

"All I did was answer the phone. I made him no promises, Yves. But you must understand; my loyalty was to Pierre."

"How about to Pierre's daughter?"

Claude looked up and saw Elise. She moved so lightly he hadn't heard her come back with his coffee. How much had she heard? Now he really regretted speaking out. But he smiled.

"Of course, mademoiselle. And to Pierre's daughter. It was nothing, in any case."

Elise's eyes seemed to grow wider, darker. And once again, despite his anger and embarassment, Claude felt the pull of longing for her. "I hope so, Claude. Have some filtre."

Claude smiled again. Back to routine matters, please. He took the coffee and sipped it gratefully. "Magnifique!"

Yves seemed to have grown roots. Speechless, he remained where he had been. If his face grows any darker he may explode right here, thought Claude. Finally the chef de cuisine managed a weak little smile and went bustling back to his office.

Only then did Elise say what was on her mind. "He really annoys you sometimes, doesn't he, Claude?" Her voice was so low that Claude knew her words were meant for him alone. "I only heard the end of that," she went on, "but I sure hope you aren't thinking of leaving us."

"Oh, no, Mademoiselle Elise. Not . . . not for the immediate future, at least. But you are right. Sometimes he has a way of making me angry." And I could run this kitchen blindfolded, and do a better job than he does, and have a much happier crew.

Claude paused, thinking. Thinking how hard this must be for Elise, so new, just finding her way in the restaurant.

He sipped his coffee. Hot and strong. "Sometimes," he said quietly, as much to himself as to her, "I think of myself in a small country inn, a dining room seating no more than thirty—luxurious, of course, but also informal. A place, perhaps, where presidents would not dine so often as they do here." Elise had her own small cup of café filtre. She said nothing but listened intently. He continued. "But then I think, such a place would be amusing, and I could make it a fine place. But it would not be Le Palais-Royal. And I think also that I am not yet thirty, that there is more to be done here—or somewhere." He paused wondering what kind of an impression his words had made. My English is not fluent yet. She probably thinks I am too full of myself.

"Do you think Le Palais has a future, Claude?"

Something in the way she said this made him choose his words as though they were precious stones to be set in some legendary crown: carefully, one by one. Precisely. "I think it surely can have a brilliant future, Mademoiselle Elise. As it has had a brilliant past." But if that future includes Yves, it will not include me. Not for very long. He thought it, but gave the thought no voice. Elise looked terribly vulnerable just now, standing close by his side and looking up at him with the wide expectant eyes of a very young child waiting to be reassured that Christmas would, indeed, soon be coming. Then she smiled, and her face changed completely. Became joyous.

"I pray you're right, Claude. I pray a lot. It won't be easy."

"Nothing worth having is easy, mademoiselle," he said, his fingers busy again with the sugar frosting.

She left him and walked across the kitchen to help Jean-Paul, who was shaping carrots into ovals the size of olives. Claude watched her every step of the way, basking in the way she moved, lightly—no hip-wiggling for this girl. And again he felt a quickening of need for her.

There is the sort of girl I should have married.

He remembered the scene in the park, just last week. So ordinary on the face of it, two young parents and their toddler son. Himself and Marie-Claire and little François.

As usual his wife hadn't wanted to leave their flat. "The park is unsanitary, one never knows whom the child might touch there. Or what diseases he might catch." Claude had looked at her then. Really looked. No wonder she'd gotten so fat. Marie-Claire hardly left the apartment except to shop. Going the three blocks to the playground was a vast journey for her. It involved bundling up the child like a little Eskimo, even though it was still October and not really cold at all. It involved cautions and dire predictions and Marie-Claire swathing herself in the red wool coat she'd bought last spring that was already bulging at the seams, stressed by the weight she'd put on over the summer. She's only thirty-one, he thought, just four years older than I, but she looks and moves like a woman of sixty.

Claude might have been better able to tolerate her fatness if only she were jolly. But the spirit in Marie-Claire that had first drawn him to her was gone now, changed and congealed. It had turned from something sparkling and merry into something sour, the way good wine, badly stored, can turn to vinegar.

He'd watched her dispassionately as she struggled into the red coat and thought. The pastry chef's wife. Like the title of some satirical Daumier cartoon. A cruel cartoon. The little boy came running in and took a great leap and Claude caught the child and swung him around and up, up nearly to the ceiling. The boy whooped his pleasure, eyes sparkling, pink cheeks glowing. Marie-Claire stood by the door with an expression of grim resignation: the martyr.

"If we must go let's get on with it, Claude," she said. This was delivered like a proclamation from some not very friendly branch of the government. "You'll only get him overexcited, and then he'll cry, and then he'll come down with something, some dreadful germ from the filthy park, and who'll have to deal with all that? Surely not his father, the great pastry chef."

Claude said nothing. He had heard the song before. He set François down and took the boy's hand, opening the front door of their apartment.

There was sunshine in the park, sunshine and bright autumn leaves and laughter. For a moment it seemed cruel to Claude. Simple pleasures were here all around him, and yet somehow Marie-Claire contrived that he should have none of them. Well, almost none. Today is a pleasure. Every minute I spend with my child is a pleasure. If it weren't for the boy it would be so easy to leave her, and she knows that and uses it.

One day, Claude knew, there would be nothing left for him to give her. He dreaded to think what might happen then. But in the meantime Claude was determined to spend every moment he could with his son. To warm himself and renew his love with the joy the boy gave off like sunshine.

In the park François wanted to swing. Marie-Claire sat on a bench, away from the other mothers who had come here with their children. She has made no friends here. Come to think of it, she made no friends in Paris, either.

Claude had often suggested that she try, but English seemed beyond her, and she withdrew into herself and her complaints about the apartment, the neighbors, America, Claude. He looked at her through the swing. A lump, sullen in her red coat, drawing pleasure out of the fine day as a sponge soaks up water.

The boy shrieked with laughter: "Papa!" He was just learning to talk, and Claude feared for his English because Marie-Claire spoke only French to him. Claude took the other tack and spoke English whenever he could, which Marie-Claire counted as a betrayal, a personal insult.

They played at the swing for a time and then Claude lifted François to the ground. Went back to Marie-Claire. "Shall we get him an ice?"

She sniffed. "Unsanitary!"

"Come with us then," said Claude cheerfully, "and you can call the ambulance when François and I are writhing in agony in the gutter." She will not poison the boy's fun, he promised himself grimly, not while I breathe.

Claude tried to remember the last time he had heard his wife laugh. There was a kind of disdainful snort she gave from time to time, an expression of amused disgust, but to call that laughter would be to insult humor.

He bought his son an orange ice in a little paper cup.

"You're making a mess! He'll have no manners at all."

Claude could feel his enjoyment draining away as though

she'd pulled the plug on his happiness. He forced himself to laugh. "Manners? I certainly hope not!"

François was experimenting, seeing how much of the ice he could heap on the small plastic spoon that came with it. Claude knelt close to him, carefully guiding the spoon to the child's eager face. "Gently, gently, little one," he said. "It is all for you, not for the ants on the sidewalk." The boy laughed.

Marie-Claire stood aside, hands on hips. Planning the next attack, he thought. Yes. It had come to that. A kind of combat.

They walked on.

The sun was beginning to set when they got back to the imitation Tudor apartment complex where they had lived since their arrival in New York four years ago. The apartment was agreeable, solidly built in the 1930s, five small rooms. It was drenched in shadow now. Marie-Claire was stingy with electricity, buying bulbs of such feeble wattage that the apartment had a kind of underwater gloom. It reminded Claude of a film in which the director was trying a bit too hard to recapture the sepia tones of some old photograph. Now, as Claude bent to help his little son take off the parka, scarf, and thickly knitted cap his mother had imposed on him, the dim light in the apartment seemed symbolic of his whole life: shadowed where it might have been bright, closed in where it should be open. A prison, and very close to unbearable. But how can I leave her, and risk hardly ever seeing my son again? The pain of even thinking such a thing stabbed him.

He made a light supper. Later, after the baby had fallen asleep in his arms, Claude carried the boy to his nursery and tucked him in bed, bending to kiss him good night. He felt the unbearable sweetness of that soft little cheek, knew the trust in the closed, dreaming eyes. Still sleeping, little François smiled. Claude thought his heart might break then and there.

He closed the nursery door and went out into the hallway. The television blared from their bedroom. She must lie in bed and watch the mindless square of glass all day. The more mindless since she was so adamant about refusing to learn the language.

It was only ten o'clock, but Claude felt tired. The exhaustion went all the way to his soul. He undressed, showered, climbed into bed.

"It isn't working, is it, Claude? Your fine venture across the ocean?" Her words struck him with the force of a flung brick. "You know I want to go back, that I've never been happy here, here in this miserable provincial dump."

He closed his eyes tighter, then opened them wide. There was no hiding from it. Maybe he was even grateful, in a way, that she'd brought it out in the open at last. "What is it you want me to do, Marie-Claire? Throw away the best pastry chef's job in America and run back to Chateaubourg so you can hang around your father's gas station like you used to? Is that your idea of a fine life?"

She was brushing her hair. The sparkle had gone out of that, too. "You took me away from everything I loved," she said, the tragic heroine now, a princess captured by brigands, imprisoned in a high tower. "And gave me—nothing!"

"You are right in one thing, Marie-Claire. I did for sure make a mistake. I thought you loved me. That our love would fly across the ocean and land with us. That when the baby came he would magnify that love. I was wrong and I'm sorry."

She sniffed. "What have you done to make me happy?"

"More than you seem able to admit. When we married all you wanted was to leave Chateaubourg. Fine. So did I." He sat up in the bed, watching as she continued brushing her hair with slow, lazy strokes. There was a burning in Claude's belly, pure outrage. He took a breath and managed to control his voice. "In Paris—you remember Paris?—you did nothing but complain: the place was too small, the stairs too steep, my hours too long."

"Truth, every word of it."

"But you made no effort, damn it! You expected everything to come to you on a silver tray, and why? In paymen for what? You never tried, Marie-Claire, in Paris. And you make no effort here. Not to work, not to make friends, no even to be a good mother. You sit here in darkness like a toad in winter, nursing your grievances. Of course you are unhappy. I'm coming to think you may have been born unhappy." Saying the bitter words brought Claude no relief Still, it was better to get it out in the open, instead of bottling everything up the way he had been.

Marie-Claire put down the hairbrush, sighed operatically and got into her nightgown, flesh rolling on flesh, pale and soft. *Once I thought she was irresistible.* Claude nearly smiled, but the irony was too painful now. *At nineteen might have killed to see her naked, to touch those breasts* He tried, struggling, to conjure up the joy that had beer between them then. And there had been joy. Passion, even But now it was all blurred, like an old watercolor left out in the rain.

Claude stood at his pastry counter finishing the sugar Statue of Liberty. Taking a quiet pride in this small perfecti ble skill. His confrontation with Marie-Claire had beer three days ago, and since then he'd hardly seen her. Some times he imagined it had only been a dream. But it hadn' been. She had been quiet, very quiet these last few days. Speaking in monosyllables, saying only what was necessary. Asleep when he got up at five thirty, often in bed when he got home.

At least one good thing had come of it: Claude felt a little easier, a little less troubled about Marie-Claire.

He looked across the kitchen and found, as he often did these days, that Elise was looking his way. He smiled. Wha was it about her? Her face so fine and mobile, quick to smile, yet in unguarded moments so apt to look sad. She watches me as much as I watch her, he thought, and cherished it.

And they were allies in the kitchen. Claude had sensed that from the beginning. Elise was well aware of Yves's hostility. Where will it end? he wondered as his hands stirred the sugar glaze he had just colored to simulate Liberty's weathered copper patina. He picked up the soft brush, almost like an artist's brush, and began, slowly and carefully, to paint on the statue's finishing touches.

Then Claude began imagining how it might be in some perfect world where he could be alone with the girl who was working at the other side of the kitchen. They were walking hand in hand through a green countryside. There was a cool breeze. Birds sang. And although it was a place Claude had never been before he seemed to know the way. Down this path, across that field, up yonder hill. And finally they were at the top of the world, just the two of them, and they could see for miles and there were no other people to see them. He turned to her and drew her close.

Claude blinked, not wanting to let go of the magic.

He sensed her at his side and wondered if he were still daydreaming. Or if he had finally gone crazy. But there she stood, right there in the kitchen, and the only music was the clang of copper pots and the rush of water in the sink. Elise.

Get control of yourself, fool. You're acting like a schoolboy. This is most unprofessional.

Still he could feel the electricity of her. The warmth. Without her saying a word there was already communication between them. A special closeness. No. I am dreaming. Or going mad. But if this was madness Claude thought it might not be such a bad thing.

"She's beautiful, Claude, whatever Yves said."

"Thank you, mademoiselle. He was joking. I hope." The words seemed to catch in Claude's throat. He could feel, the way an animal might sense danger, Yves's speculative glance from across the room. My being so much with Elise

133

doesn't help Yves's temper. If she befriends me as her fathe[r] did, how can I help it? And why should I want to?

There was a pause while Claude struggled to think o[f] something more to say. Anything. But she spoke first.

"Claude," she said smiling, "I don't mean to pry, bu[t] you are a mystery to me. Tell me about your family, how you came here. All that."

Suddenly he was terrified. As though she could see righ[t] into the furthest corner of his heart. *How could I tell he[r] what I've been thinking?*

His hands continued to work on the statue. Nearly don[e] now. "It is not a very interesting story, mademoiselle," h[e] said slowly, fighting for control, selecting each word[.] "I . . . was born in a small town in Brittany—Cha[-] teaubourg—son of a baker. I helped Papa, of course, foun[d] I liked it, he thought I had some skill. An apprenticeshi[p] was arranged through a friend of a friend, as these things ar[e] done in France. Lasserre, at sixteen! That was a thrill, I ca[n] tell you. Two years there, then La Tour d'Argent. Thir[d] assistant pastry chef. By then I was almost nineteen an[d] about to be married, to a girl from my village. That hap[-] pened." Claude paused, thinking how to describe the disas[-] ter of his marriage.

He could not.

He made himself smile. "Then, soon after we were mar[-] ried, your father came over. He heard of me somehow. W[e] talked. He was very persuasive. It seemed magical[,] mademoiselle, an entire new life, so many opportunities[.] And here I am."

She had been watching him closely during all of this[.] Claude felt instinctively that his every word somehow hel[d] for her a special weight. That she was interested, deeply an[d] truly. That it was something more than noblesse oblige, th[e] owner chatting it up with the hired help.

"And here you are," she said, smiling a little smile tha[t] made his heart leap. "And thank God."

134

When she smiles, something fine happens to her face. Lights go on inside her.

It was contagious. Claude smiled back.

"Thank your father, mademoiselle."

She laughed. "I'm afraid I sometimes confuse them. My father and God. Claude, could we drop the 'mademoiselle' please? I think Armand and Yves do it to tease me. To make me feel like a little girl again." She lowered her voice until it was no more than a whisper. "And maybe as a little bit of a put-down, if you know what I mean."

Claude understood very well but said nothing.

"At any rate," she went on, making a small and rueful move, "I am an old married lady, so mademoiselle isn't quite it."

"Not old, Elise." Claude almost strangled on it. Just saying her name like that, without the framework of distance and respect that "mademoiselle" or "madame" might impose. It sent shivers of intimacy right through him.

Don't be stupid, he told himself sternly. She is only being the gracious lady, cultivating you because you might be useful. She'd be equally kind to the dishwasher.

Claude felt so young right now. Unsure of himself, of her, of anything. If he followed his instincts he might offend her. If he didn't he might lose the chance forever.

But there is something between us. Something special. I can't be imagining it all.

Then she was gone. The moment passed.

The statue was done now, perfect, glazed, her arm raised to hold the sugar flame. Liberty. *Elise.* Stop it, Claude, you're behaving like a schoolboy.

Claude went to the chef's office—he still thought of it as Pierre's office—and picked up the worn loose-leaf notebook that held Pierre's recipes. The dessert section filled half of it. Here were notes, recipes copied out of the antique cookery books Pierre collected, the occasional magazine or newspaper article, recipes sent in by friends or patrons of Le Palais-

135

Royal, odd little notations that were no more than concepts to be worked out in the future.

Claude had often turned to this book for inspiration, and the book never failed him. He flipped page after page almost idly, waiting for some piece of Pierre's culinary magic to ignite his fancy. He was engrossed in the meringue section when her name seemed to leap off the page at him.

*Gâteau Elise.*

It was a meringue torte in the Viennese manner, layers of hazelnut meringue frosted with mocha butter cream, topped with whipped cream and chopped toasted hazelnuts. And beside the recipe a note: "Birthday, October sixteenth." Next Tuesday!

Claude smiled and decided he would make the gâteau for Elise as a birthday surprise. Secretly. I must remember to order the noisettes, to have them toasted and peeled and waiting.

Tuesday was only five days away, and just thinking about it made Claude feel better. How fine to have something to look forward to again.

"Well, Claude," said a voice so close it startled him, "It's good to see you studying the Bible."

Yves. Mocking.

They all called the recipe book Pierre's Bible. But hearing the joke on Yves's tongue made the humor curdle. Yves was standing outside the little cubicle—his office now—in an attitude of exaggerated patience. Waiting for the trespasser to clear out.

Claude stood up immediately, putting the book back on its shelf and walking out of the office. Conscious of Yves's glance. Of the malice in it. Claude forced himself to think of something to do. A dessert to create. Keep yourself busy, he told himself. Give yourself no chance to think, to brood over things that can never be.

There were beautiful raspberries. I'll make a raspberry bavaroise and serve it with fresh raspberry puree. He went to the produce refrigerator and took out a big basket of rasp-

136

berries and brought it back to his counter. Looked up and saw Elise again.

Looking at him.

Impulsively, he tossed a raspberry to her.

With instinctive grace she caught it. Smiled. Slowly brought it to her lips, her eyes never leaving Claude's eyes. Crushed it with her tongue. Slowly. Smiled again and swallowed.

As Elise savored the haunting mixture of sweetness and tartness, she thought, He really is something, our Claude. But how can someone so young and talented and good-looking be so sad? Maybe he's just shy. But married and with a baby. Not for you, Elise.

She turned away then, ashamed to be thinking the kind of thoughts she had been thinking about Claude.

And Jared gone only a few days. He might come back any time at all. What kind of woman are you? she asked herself. But Elise knew the answer: Lonely. Scared of where I'm going, of how the restaurant's going to do, of the way Kate might or might not help me. Scared of damn near everything. Well thank God for Claude. For having at least one friend in this place.

Claude stood at his counter watching her intently, wondering if the slow and sensuous way Elise had eaten the berry was some sort of sign. Something more than just an attractive girl enjoying an out of season framboise.

# 8

KATE WANTED TO meet Dave Hollander without Elise. But how can I? she asked herself. And what will Elise think if she ever finds out? The very idea of going behind her step-daughter's back was repugnant to Kate; so was the idea of more conflict with Elise, and these days Elise was so terribly caught up with her plans for the restaurant—it seemed to Kate almost like an obsession—that she was hardly capable of being rational. Well, she'll think I'm the wicked step-mother either way, Kate realized, letting herself out the front door and locking it. But I have to meet Dave, and I have to let Elise know about it. Not on the phone, though. On the phone it's too easy for her to make excuses, to say she's too busy.

Having made the decision Kate felt better. She under-stood Elise's feelings and she was sympathetic—up to a point. Her sympathy stopped when Elise's dream threat-ened to destroy the value of the Villeromain inheritance for both of them.

It was ten thirty in the morning. Much too early for even the earliest luncheon guests at Le Palais-Royal. Kate let her-self in the front door of the restaurant. She'd never felt at ease going in at the service door, not that it wasn't immac-ulately clean back there, but rather because she'd never felt at home in that kitchen. Even Pierre stopped inviting me there after a while.

Armand had his back to her, checking the levels of the bottles on the shelf behind the little bar. He turned at the sound of Kate's footsteps. "Bonjour, madame! It is good to see you."

"Hello, Armand. I just dropped in to have a word with Elise. Is she here?"

"Yes, madame. In the kitchen."

Kate always felt a quiver when she passed her portrait of Pierre. It's true what people say: it does almost seem alive. She looked up at it now, briefly, then forced herself to look away. What would he think? she wondered. Would Pierre feel betrayed because I'm not interested in running Le Palais?

No.

What would really break his heart would be to see his restaurant in decline, to see us all just making do, lowering his standards. Somewhere she'd have to find the courage to handle this situation in a way that would honor Pierre's memory. With renewed determination Kate pushed through the padded waiter's doors into the kitchen.

As always, Pierre's kitchen overwhelmed her; today more than ever. The noise; the clanging, chopping, stirring. The laughing and shouting. The joking in French, English, and Spanish. The orchestrated chaos, the comings and goings, men carrying huge steaming pots, crates of vegetables, sides of meat, and huge silvery fish. At a glance it might have been a battlefield.

Well, she thought, and that's why the chef is literally the chief, the general, the supreme commander, whose orders and leadership must be obeyed without question. It seemed a terrible sort of setting for a girl so fine and sensitive as Elise.

Yves was by the dishwashing station, screaming in broken Spanish at a terrified boy who stood blinking back tears, wringing a dish towel behind his back, twisting it so tightly it looked like a rope. Yes, and I'll wager he wouldn't mind throttling Yves with it, too. Kate remembered Pierre's anecdotes about Yves's temper. *What he is,* Kate thought with revulsion, *is a bully.*

She went to him. "Good morning, Yves," she said with her brightest smile. "Isn't it a lovely day?"

His reaction amused her. Instantly he stopped screaming, turned, blinking, and bowed his dark head for an instant like some small boy surprised in mischief. The mask of anger transformed itself into a mask of good cheer. Yes. A bully.

"Madame Villeromain! Welcome! What brings you to honor us today?"

Kate smiled a frosty little smile. By this time everybody in the kitchen had become aware of her presence. A silence had fallen, and the tension was almost palpable. "Oh, nothing really, Chef. Just wanted a word with Elise."

"Would you like some coffee, madame? A pastry?"

"No, thank you, Yves."

Elise came up to her. Kate kissed her stepdaughter on the cheek. She thought Elise was looking pale, overtired. She could be quite lovely, if she'd just make a little effort.

"Kate! How are you?"

The question in Elise's voice remained unspoken: *And what are you doing here?* It was the first time since Elise and Jared had moved to the restaurant that Kate had dropped in.

"I'm bearing up, darling. How are you? How's Jared?"

Suddenly Elise realized that she hadn't told Kate about his leaving—not Kate and not anyone else. Well, there's no one to talk to, except possibly Claude. No. Not even Claude. Elise tried to smile. "Shall we sit down in the dining room? Would you like some coffee or tea?"

"No thanks, dear, I've got to make this a quick visit."

They went into the empty back dining room and sat down.

"I just didn't feel like telling anyone, Kate," Elise said as soon as they were alone, "but Jared split. Went back to Stowe the day after we moved in here."

"Elise, I'm terribly sorry. Is there anything . . . no, I don't guess there would be. Anything I can do."

"Nor I. I just never realized—it's such a tiny little world up there in Stowe—how terribly uncomfortable he'd be anywhere else. I guess he just needs to think about it some. And so do I."

"All you asked was that he give it a try."

"It seemed fair to me, but then, I'm not Jared." Elise stirred the air with her hands, a small and hopeless gesture. "Well, Kate," she said, "that's my problem. What's yours?"

Kate smiled serenely. I will not become upset just because Elise's manners seem gruff to me. She's a different generation; she grew up in a different country. "Ours, dear," Kate said gently. "The problem is both yours and mine, I'm afraid."

"Daddy's will?"

"The estate. I find it confusing—frightening, really. All those taxes, all the details. I guess neither of us is used to things like that."

"I'm definitely not."

"I just want you to know everything that's going on, Elise. It's so important we trust each other, come what may."

Elise just looked at her, and the look held both alarm and suspicion. "You're very mysterious, Kate. What's up?"

"Someone's coming to tea this afternoon. I'm pretty sure he wants to make an offer for the restaurant. I want you to hear it from his lips instead of secondhand from me. Or from Simon."

"Wow. That's a little heavy. Why didn't you tell him flat out we're not interested?"

"Because it's important to hear his valuation of the place—and of its reputation. It won't be the only offer, if we can believe Simon Doughty. We owe it to ourselves to at least consider them."

"We do?" This seemed to be a completely new idea to Elise. Kate watched her as she wrestled with it.

"Darling, whatever happens, we have to know what the alternatives are. The offer is going to be a large one, I know that. So large it may seem irresistible."

"Not to me, it won't. Who's coming?"

The defiance in her voice was building. Kate knew she must tread very gently now. "Do you remember David Hollander?"

"Vaguely. Friend of Daddy's?"

"Yes. And something of a tycoon besides. Hollander Industries."

"Billy Burger." The contempt in her voice was unmistakable.

"What's Billy Burger?"

Elise laughed, but it was not a merry laugh. "Part of the ruination of America's taste buds. A chain, a very big and successful chain, of gaudy fast-food hamburger restaurants. Haven't you seen their advertising? Billy Burger is about seven feet tall, a sort of a clown, and he sings and dances and lures little kids into those garish plastic places where they overdose on thin little patties of dubious beef and greasy french fries. Just this side of poison."

Kate smiled. "I'm so provincial, living in New York. Never been to one. In any event, Mr. Hollander seems to be interested in Le Palais. In possibly buying it. And he wants to see us."

Elise leaned back in her chair, looking to Kate more and more like an overwrought child. She's too young to have all of this thrust on her.

"Well, Kate, it comes down to this, doesn't it? Are you with me or against me?"

Kate looked at her. "I don't know. I love you, Elise, and—"

"You do?"

Kate forced herself to remain calm, to understand that quick challenges were the style of young people everywhere today. But the effort suddenly seemed almost too much for her. Like lifting some enormously heavy weight.

"I try to, Elise."

"I do know that, Kate. And I don't always make it very easy for you, do I?" Elise reached across the table and touched Kate's hand gently. "It's just that, well, I guess I expect you and everybody else to feel the way I do about this place. However crazy that might seem."

"Darling it may not be crazy. If it's possible to help you without ruining all of us forever, I'll help. That's a promise. But we have to hear these people. We can't play ostrich, no matter how comforting it might seem at the moment."

Elise sighed. "You're right, dear Kate. As usual. What time is the chopped meat prince showing up?"

"Four thirty."

"I'll be there."

"Thank you."

Elise stood up, set the chair neatly in place, smiled. "I'll try. I really will try."

Kate stood up too, came to her stepdaughter and kissed her cheek. "That's all either of us can do, isn't it?"

She walked toward the front of the restaurant.

Elise stood there watching Kate's retreating back, thinking. Then she looked about the magnificent dining room. Thought about the years of love, the fabulous taste, the plain hard work it had taken for her father to build Le Palais-Royal. It seemed hopeless to try it alone.

Jared didn't want it. Kate doesn't . . . why am I trying? It's like climbing Everest barefoot without a guide.

If only Jared had stayed, how different it might be. If he'd backed her up in this. Elise had stopped counting the times she'd found herself at the phone about to call him. But always something held her back. She thought of Kate, and for one brief moment Elise felt sorry for her stepmother.

She is trying to be fair, as she sees fairness, but no one who isn't me can possibly understand how deeply I care. How hard I'll fight.

143

For several minutes, Elise stood just where Kate had left her. It was all coming at her so fast. If only, she wished, fighting back a feeling of absolute panic, if only I had someone to be on my side in all this.

But there was no one.

The magnificent dining room was quiet and empty. And hers.


Letting herself into the house, Kate thought of David Hollander. She went straight to the kitchen to see what she might serve at tea later on. Smiling suddenly, remembering her astonishment at his call. How gently he'd eased into his subject: "I know it's too soon, Kate, but I've asked my people to get independent appraisals, to do all the groundwork, so that when you do feel ready . . ."

"Mr. Hollander, I'm ready now. And I appreciate your interest. We're really not sure, Elise and I, that we will sell. I have no interest in running the restaurant, but Elise does."

There was a pause.

"I see. I'll just have to be persuasive then."

There was something in his voice that Kate responded to immediately. A quiet confidence, an easy warmth. I've never thought twice about the man, but he's obviously special. And very interested in Le Palais. Kate knew she'd met Hollander once or twice before the memorial luncheon, but she couldn't recall where or when. She conjured up his face, as strong and as kind as his voice, wondering what it must be like to be that rich, that famous. To have your name on one of the big corporations.

And in that moment Kate felt the loss of Pierre with a special vividness. How wonderful it had been, that feeling of security that went so far beyond material comfort; the confidence, that sure knowledge he'd be there in any crisis, strong and loving and decisive.

Only Pierre wasn't here now.

"Thursday at four thirty?" she'd asked, opening up who knew what Pandora's box.

At four thirty-two the doorbell rang.

There stood Dave Hollander looking lean and dynamic in a tan gabardine suit, a blue button-down shirt, and a navy tie striped with precisely the right shade of green. Kate smiled her greeting, her pleasure partly due to her painterly appreciation of colors well put together—but there was something else. Something at once warm and disturbing.

It was with a sudden shock that she realized she was responding to him as a woman.

"Thanks, for letting me come," he said, breaking the silence. "I know it's been a terrible time for you."

Kate struggled to collect herself. "We're trying to cope, Mr. Hollander. With mixed success, I'm afraid. But do come in. Elise ought to be here soon."

Tea was ready in the library.

"Do you take sugar, Mr. Hollander?"

He smiled. "Black, please. Can I persuade you to call me Dave?"

"Of course. And call me Kate. We're hardly strangers, are we?" It was only then that she realized he'd been calling her Kate from the first. Americans. It wasn't presumption, but only their easy style.

He laughed. Not too much and not too little, a fine resonant laugh. "I may become a pest. That's how eager I am to buy the restaurant."

The doorbell rang, and Kate rose to let Elise in. Odd she doesn't use her key, Kate thought. Is she making some kind of a statement? Not very subtly telling me she doesn't think of this house as her home? Or am I just overthinking everything?

"Hi, Kate. Am I late?"

"Just on time, dear. He got here only a minute ago."

They walked back to the library. Dave rose; smiled and offered his hand. Elise took it after a second's hesitation. Whatever might happen now, Kate felt a tremendous sense of relief that Elise had bothered to come. That she wouldn't

145

be left alone one minute longer with this disconcertingly attractive man.

"Hello, Mr. Hollander."

"How are you, Elise?"

"Terribly busy, since you ask. Trying to learn the restaurant business—on the level of Le Palais-Royal."

He smiled again, and Kate realized it would take a lot more than Elise's barely controlled brusqueness to put Dave off his game. She actually began to enjoy herself a little.

"That's the best level there is."

"I think so."

Kate poured Elise a cup of tea. There were small sandwiches: cucumber, smoked salmon with dill butter, and cream cheese with watercress.

"Well," said Dave, plunging right in, "I guess Kate has told you about my interest in the restaurant." He watched their reactions. Primed by her stepmother, he was focusing on Elise. But somehow Dave's attention kept wandering back to Kate.

"Yes," said Elise with a chill in her voice. "She has."

"I don't know how to tell you what Le Palais-Royal means to me. Knowing Pierre—it was more than just a friendship. He really changed the way I look at many things, not just a menu. Pierre stood for quality. . . ." Dave paused, realizing then with an almost visceral shudder what it was about Kate: *quality*. She radiated it, the real stuff, effortlessly. He made himself go on. "He stood for the best of everything. I've never known anyone with higher standards."

"No," said Kate softly, "nor have I."

He looked at her and smiled, remembering something Pierre had once said about her: "She saved me, you know, David. Saved me from becoming a completely obsessed old man. Opened new doors and windows in my life. Made me see how much there is—can be—outside the walls of my restaurant."

"When Pierre died," Dave went on, "I couldn't believe it.

146

He was so vitally alive. I couldn't imagine a world without him. And when I came to your memorial luncheon—came without a thought in my head of doing anything but honoring his memory—well, all of a sudden I was struck with it. With the possibility of my acquiring Le Palais-Royal. Keeping it going the way it deserves to be kept going."

Elise looked at him carefully and thought, Very convincing. Maybe he even is sincere. Maybe he really does believe that's why he wants the place—and maybe pigs can fly. She felt an answer was expected of her, and she wanted to lash out at Hollander. But she looked at Kate and remembered how her stepmother had taken the trouble to come to the restaurant, to make her see that they needn't be at odds about this.

"I'm really in a fix, Mr. Hollander," she said, taking it slowly, choosing her words with care. "Because that's just what I want to do. And I realize I may not be able to. We're—I hope you don't mind a few family secrets—we're going to have to come up with some pretty big estate tax payments before long, and there isn't much cash. What it comes down to is, we don't know yet where we'll be financially a year from now. But if I possibly can keep control of the restaurant without selling, I—well, I've just got to try."

He looked at her with a kind and unwavering gaze. "Pierre would be very proud of you, Elise."

Elise felt herself blushing. Why does he have to be so damned nice? Why can't he be a sneering villain with a waxed mustache and a lisp? She felt she was being manipulated, and by an expert. And some of the anger she had been repressing came back to her in a rush. But still she didn't reply.

"You see, I can help you do just what you want to. I wasn't actually planning to get behind the stove, you know. Just to make sure Le Palais has the resources it needs to keep going. I'd hoped—naturally, I haven't mentioned this to anyone yet—but my plan was to keep the staff intact—right down to the last dishwasher. Armand, of course, and Yves

147

and Montgeron. Everyone. And if you're a part of it now, that's fine by me. I'll give you a contract for any length of time, ironclad."

"I wasn't planning on being anyone's employee, Mr. Hollander." Elise said this with a finality that made *employee* sound like some dread disease.

"If you accept my offer, Elise, you'll never have to be anyone's employee, ever again."

There was a hush in the room. Brass tacks time.

"I've had it looked into," Dave went on. "The real value of the house, the restaurant's reputation, all that. Not of course down to the last bottle in the cellar, but in general terms. And the general terms are, I'm prepared to offer you ladies four million dollars for Le Palais-Royal."

Kate heard this awesome news in a kind of trance. Four million, she thought, shaken. That means the taxes will be at least two—on the restaurant alone! We'll be beggared unless we sell.

"Four million?" Elise repeated the words as though she were learning a new language. "Incredible."

Dave flushed slightly, and Kate liked him all the more for not being a hundred percent in control. "You think that isn't enough?"

Elise laughed. A laugh with a cutting edge to it. "Just thinking about that much money makes me dizzy. A few months ago I was worried about paying the phone bill."

"I think you can stop worrying." He smiled, in control again.

"If we sell."

"If you sell. Especially if you sell to me. You will get other offers, naturally, if you haven't already."

"Not a one," said Elise.

"The important thing is to sell to someone who's going to respect Le Palais."

"That's just my problem," said Elise too quickly. "I have visions of Billy Burger singing and dancing his way through my father's restaurant. It's a long, long way from

148

cheap hamburgers to the cuisine at Le Palais-Royal, Mr. Hollander."

Dave smiled, overcoming his immediate urge to lash back at her. "About as far as you could hope to get, and that's why the idea intrigues me. But one doesn't really contradict the other. General Motors can make the Corvette as well as their little economy cars. They both serve a purpose."

"The enrichment of Hollander Industries?"

Dave laughed. He was beginning to enjoy the game. "The enrichment of Elise Villeromain, if you'll accept it."

Kate had watched this struggle as though it were a championship tennis match, fascinated by what it revealed about Elise. And about Dave. But now Elise was getting out of hand.

"Elise takes Le Palais very personally, Dave. I think that's understandable."

"Of course it is. And as I said, Elise, we'll write the contract any way you like. So you can have any title you want: manager, patronne, whatever."

Elise set down her teacup. "What I want, Mr. Hollander, can't come out of any contract. Not the kind you're talking about. I want to be the Villeromain of Le Palais-Royal. Not some kind of puppet, not a figurehead, but truly in charge. For better or worse."

"But you would be."

"Nominally, maybe. But can you really sit here and tell me there wouldn't come a time when we disagreed, no matter why, and then what would my fine title be worth? About as much as yesterday's soufflé!"

Kate watched, feeling helpless, as the girl cut deeper and deeper. Part of Kate admired Elise's spirit. Agreed with her sentiments too, for all that. But another part saw this reckless child plunging heedlessly into who knew what.

"Naturally, for that much money, we do expect control. It's only fair." Dave's reply was gentle, as though he were explaining things to a very small child.

Elise smiled. "I'm sure by your lights it is fair. And that

what I'm trying to do may strike you as crazy." She paused, took a breath as though gathering her strength for the next attack. But when she spoke her voice was low. Reasonable. In its way as persuasive as Dave's. "But all the wise opinions in the world aren't going to stop me from trying. And when it comes right down to it, I also have another concern about selling."

Dave leaned forward a little. He sensed they were really getting down to it now, that the next few minutes would make it or break it.

"Tell me about it," he said quietly.

Kate had no idea what might be fermenting in Elise's mind.

"If I—we—were to sell, and please understand this is really hypothetical, because I won't unless I'm backed to the wall, I'd want a very strong guarantee that the buyer wouldn't exploit Le Palais-Royal in any way, or cheapen its image. Maybe I'm getting paranoid, Mr. Hollander, but I have these visions of little plastic replicas of Le Palais-Royal defacing the highways of America, the way your hamburger places do."

"The name of the restaurant is worth a lot in its own right," Dave said. "At Hollander Industries, we're experimenting with a new line of gourmet foods—the highest quality, sauce bases and concentrates, freeze-dried wild mushrooms, things like that. There's a possibility we might want to bring out the line under the name of Le Palais-Royal."

There was a silence that seemed to spread in the room with the dark insistence of spilled ink. Elise smiled a cool and triumphant smile. Her worst fears about Hollander had just been confirmed. She looked at Kate.

"Just happens to be a possibility? Really, Mr. Hollander. Neither Kate nor I are businesswomen, but we're not morons, either."

Dave felt his fuse igniting and fought back. If I show the anger I could wreck everything—if I haven't already.

"These things happen in a business like mine, Elise. That's how we got to be in the *Fortune* Five Hundred. You make fun of Billy Burger. Have you ever eaten one?"

"No."

"I wish you would before you condemn us. Those operations serve excellent food. Nothing's artificial, nothing's frozen, the beef is top grade and it's ground fresh every day in every shop, and they're flame broiled to order, not microwaved or fried the way some of the others do it. It's all fresh and well prepared and people respond to that."

"No doubt. Kate, what do you think about all this?"

Kate frowned. Why must she put me on the spot like this? She looked at Dave and saw the expectancy in his eyes. "I think we shouldn't jump the gun, darling. We really don't know what Dave's proposing. Would it be such a crime to have the restaurant's name on something that was of the finest quality? I think we'd have to find out more about it all, taste the products, and then decide. He isn't suggesting bubble gum."

Elise closed her eyes for a moment, almost as if she were praying. Maybe she is, thought Kate and a pang of sympathy ran through her. There seemed to be so little she could do to help Elise.

"The idea of dragging Daddy's name through supermarkets. Doesn't that shock you, Kate?"

"If it were done badly it would upset me, yes. But shock me? No. As I've said."

Elise stood up. She looked first at Kate and then at Dave, and her sense of having been betrayed was vibrant in the quiet room.

"I guess maybe I'm overreacting, Mr. Hollander. But I can only tell you what I feel, and what I feel is disgusted." She turned and ran from the room.

Kate sat dumbfounded for a moment—a moment too long. They heard the front door slam. Kate got up and started to go after Elise, then stopped. "I'm sorry, Dave. She ought to have better manners. Elise has been going through a pretty rough time. She took it very hard, losing Pierre, and then—other complications. I guess you caught her off base."

Dave picked up a smoked salmon sandwich and ate it slowly. Sipped his tea. Smiled. "Are you ready to believe I admire her for standing by her convictions, Kate?" he asked. "She's tough. So was Pierre. And I do sympathize with her. Naturally, her point of view isn't my own. And I gather you're somewhere in between?"

"Somewhere. Precisely where, I probably can't say." Kate sighed. "It's such a muddle!"

"Yes. It is that." But Dave felt a sense of relief all the same. Elise had left and taken her anger with her. And Kate Villeromain looked even more beautiful when she was upset a little. "Well," he said after a pause. "Kate, I appreciate your help in this—even though we didn't make a whole lot of progress, I know where I stand now. And that could be half the battle."

Kate smiled, a fleeting ripple of a smile. "I see you're determined, Dave. There's no predicting how Elise will react if you pursue this."

"I guess I'll just have to take my chances. But I've taken up enough of your time, Kate. I'd better be getting back to the office. I hope I can call you, maybe for lunch?"

"I'd like that." Kate paused, surprised at her response. Yes, she thought. I would like it. Very flattering, Mr. Hollander. And if I ought to be ashamed of myself for feeling like this, too bad.

"I'll call you tomorrow, then."

"Please do. And don't worry too much about Elise. She'll grow up one day."

"I hope it's one day soon." He paused, rising.

Kate got up too. "I just hope," she said softly, "that Le Palais doesn't go to pot in the meantime."

"It won't. Not while you have Armand and the rest."

"Dave, I'm sorry our meeting didn't work out better for you."

They were at the front door. He extended his hand and she took it. He grinned. "It'll take a lot more than what happened here to scare me away, Kate. The restaurant could fall into much worse hands than mine."

"I'm sure it could."

"Thanks. You've been great about this."

And he was gone.

Kate stood in the doorway watching him as he strode down Sixty-eighth Street toward Park Avenue. Tall and strong and athletic; confident strides. A warmth suffused her, thrilling and frightening.

# 9

KATE LOOKED AT the telephone as though it might explode if she touched it. Why, she asked herself, am I so nervous about making a simple phone call to Dave Hollander?

She knew one answer to that: if she pursued Dave's offer to buy Le Palais-Royal, she'd be risking the loss of whatever fragile relationship she still had with Elise. But that wasn't all of it. There was something about Dave. Something that stirred in Kate feelings so unexpected they terrified her.

She sat in her desk chair and tried to force these feelings out of her mind. Impossible. Irrational. And disgraceful. Maybe, she thought, grief has unhinged my mind, as they used to say in the old days. And she looked around the bright, comfortably furnished room, longing for Pierre with an intensity that did nothing to comfort her, or to drive the confusion from her brain.

The only way I can possibly deal with Dave is to treat this as a businesslike situation. He made an offer that must be considered, both by Elise and by me, if we are to salvage anything from Pierre's estate. Since Elise didn't seem capable of being rational on the subject of the restaurant, Kate knew she would need to assume the role of impartial evaluator for both of them. However unattractive it might seem.

She took a deep breath and picked up the business card

he'd given her: HOLLANDER INDUSTRIES, 351 *Park Avenue, New York, N.Y. 10017.* David G. Hollander, President."
What, she wondered, does the G stand for?

Kate picked up the receiver and dialed. Even the tiny clicks and humming sounds of the phone connecting seemed ominous somehow, as though they were a code to which she hadn't the slightest beginning of a clue.

Kate had expected an army of secretaries.

Dave answered. She was shocked.

"Dave Hollander speaking."

The simplicity of it astonished her. There he was. Dave. Accessible, not only to her but to anyone in the world who cared to dial his number. Her first thought was that it cheapened him somehow. But then she reconsidered. No. It was just efficiency and self-confidence. Dave wouldn't need the props with which some other executives shored up their frail esteem.

"Hello?" he said, an undercurrent of impatience vibrating on the line.

"Dave? It's Kate Villeromain." She felt as though she had climbed a very high mountain without oxygen. Scary but wonderful.

"Kate. I'm glad you called."

The warmth in his voice encouraged her, led her on, a map through the minefield. "I wanted to apologize for the other day," Kate heard herself saying. "For Elise."

"Thanks, Kate, but I really do understand Elise. She wants that place desperately, and I guess she's young enough, she can't help letting it show." He paused, then laughed softly, a low ripple of sound. "I know how she feels, Kate, because I feel the same way. As you know."

He has an instinct for saying just the right thing, but how do I know if it's real? Dave's frankness was disarming—perhaps it was meant to be. A chill crept up Kate's spine. For a moment she hesitated.

"Dave, I want to invite you for luncheon. How about

155

Friday?" He'll be busy Friday. President of Hollander Industries. And it's only the day after tomorrow.

Dave laughed again, the same low easygoing sound. But Kate thought there was a difference in it, a subtle change.

"This is going to sound stupid, Kate, but I was sitting here trying to get up the nerve to call you for lunch."

She smiled. He hadn't forgotten.

"Let me look," Dave continued. ". . . Sure. Friday's fine."

"Le Palais-Royal at twelve thirty?"

"I look forward to it."

"That's fine, Dave. I'll see you there."

"Good-bye."

"Good-bye, Dave." She hung up the phone with a sense of having slain dragons. Of having taken the situation in hand for the first time, really, since Pierre's death.

Or did the situation take me? She looked at herself in the dressing table mirror and liked what she saw.

The day after tomorrow.

At Le Palais-Royal.

When she reached for the phone again there was no hesitation. Armand answered on the first ring, and with a measured glee Kate decided there were some advantages to being an owner after all. How many people in the world can call Le Palais on two days notice and be sure of getting a good table? she asked herself. And she was defying Elise and she knew it, and the sensation was unnervingly pleasant.

But am I also betraying Pierre?

The reservation was made. Kate wondered how she was going to get through tomorrow and the next morning.

There was mail to answer, a few notes of sympathy that still needed her attention, the inventory to complete, real estate people to contact—plenty to do. But for the moment Kate just sat at her dressing table thinking of Friday. Of Dave. Of what Elise's reaction might be when she saw them together.

Shall I warn her, soften the blow a little? It was all so delicate, elusive, like trying to hold smoke in your hand. Elise is going to be difficult, and I'd better get used to it, Kate decided. She always has been difficult, and not only for me. Caused Pierre a lot of pain, and she'll do the same to me, too, if I let her.

If.

Dave put down the receiver and leaned back in his chair, grinning. Feeling like he'd just won the lottery. At least one part of his life was going right.

For a moment it seemed she was in the room with him. He could see her clearly: the tilt of her chin, the widely spaced eyes with their soft amber gleam, that magnificent skin. The kind of complexion cosmetic makers dream about. And her voice. The British accent had softened now, after years in the States. But musical.

Kate.

Dave was in awe of her. Torn between his affection for Pierre's memory and this new feeling. Whatever it was. But maybe it was crazy even to daydream about Kate Villeromain. Things like this don't happen in real life. Not to guys like me. Good old pragmatic Dave Hollander. Anyway, what would a woman like Kate see in me, the man who defaced America with his hamburger joints?

Dave sat alone in his corner office and wondered what Kate would say if she knew what was going on in his head. In his heart. *Kate.* Silently, he said her name again and again. Like a schoolboy.

Not the time to get silly.

He made a conscious effort to put her out of his mind. Picked up the stack of papers Lydia had left for his attention.

The image of Kate wouldn't go away.

Dave stood up, as if by moving he could escape her. Paced the length of the room and back again. Looked out a window, down at the Racquet Club. What I need is a good hard game of squash. Walked to his desk and dialed Tim's extension. But his son was out of the building, meeting with the advertising agency about packaging. Dave put down the phone, feeling a little better. At least one Hollander was keeping his head.

Still Kate seemed to fill the office.

Dave replayed Monday's visit: the beautiful old house, the elegant tea, Kate, the bad scene with Elise. Poor kid, she doesn't know what she's letting herself in for. It's that crazy determination so many kids get: damn all and full speed ahead. Not knowing or caring how miserable she was making Kate's life. Kate, who shouldn't have a worry in the world. How he wished he could wave some kind of a magic wand for Kate. Do more than just offer money.

Why is it so terribly important that she likes me? Unanswerable. When Dave thought of her there seemed to be a new edge on all his perceptions. The air seemed a little keener, the sun a little brighter, the balancing act of his business a little more risky.

Dave tried to sort out his feelings about his own wife, Barbara. It had been so fine once, full of love and caring and the joy of Timmy.

And when you hear that tired old phrase, "They drifted apart," it always sounds stupid, he thought. But that's what happened. My fault as much as hers. These last ten or so years. Barbara refusing to spend time in the city, me not able to be with her in the country. It faded so gradually neither of us realized what was happening. Like color bleeding out of some old photograph, seeping away bit by tiny bit until all the brightness turns pale and suddenly you have to squint a little to recapture the way it was.

How long since they'd had a real talk, a passionate, tearing argument? Or a passionate night in bed.

*Kate*.

How Pierre had glowed when he spoke of her. Dave searched his memory now. Remembered Pierre's face, always so mobile and alert, changing. A special softness would come over him when he mentioned her.

And I never gave it a second thought. Could there be room for me in her life now?

The very thought was dangerous.

Friday. Kate woke with a start and the room seemed filled with portents. Sitting at breakfast, she closed her eyes and tried to conjure up his face in every detail, his walk, the way he moved without effort. Painter's tricks. He must play a lot of sports. And what could he see in me, whose idea of a workout is walking to Bendel's? She sipped the fragrant tea and laughed at her foolishness. Still and all, you're not in bad shape, Kate. You've kept your figure. When you're fixed up a little you're not about to scare anyone.

But suddenly, like a very young girl on her first date, Kate found herself thinking about what she'd wear to lunch.

I wonder what his favorite color is? Suppose I wear blue and he hates it, the way Pierre hated orange? She ate half a slice of toast and put the rest aside, mindful of where she'd be eating lunch. Poured a fresh cup of tea and brought it upstairs to take a look at her wardrobe. Well, she thought, holding up a dress and then rejecting it, anyone in the world would take a little extra care about what they wear to Le Palais-Royal, Dave or no Dave. She knew she must choose carefully. Nothing too festive, but not deep mourning, either. Pierre would never want that.

Kate held up dress after dress in front of her to see the reflection in her closet door mirror. As though the mirror itself might hold some clue to her future. Finally she chose a suit of silk tweed in a dark burgundy color, rather severe, cut in the Chanel manner, lightened a little by a silk blouse of the palest shell pink with a soft bow at the throat. Her only jewelry was her grandmother's brooch of angel-skin coral, a fine Georgian piece that was nothing more than an oval of the pale pink stone set in a thin ribbon of gold, the ribbon itself inset with the smallest possible seed pearls and twining on top into a charming stylized bowknot.

As she pinned the brooch to the silk jacket Kate struggled to organize her thoughts. Be businesslike, she told herself, today's lunch is a question of millions and millions. How very right Simon Doughty had been about the will. Kate could imagine Pierre going all bullheaded, insisting. His sense of fairness wrestling with Doughty's logic.

How could he have known? Pierre, so very shrewd about most things, an utter child about others. Fifty-fifty. Maddening. Just as Doughty had said, the whole thing had backfired. It was a trap, as tight and confining as steel.

Or was it?

Fifty-fifty.

When the idea came to her it was almost shocking. She sat down, took a deep breath and considered.

Fifty-fifty. *If I own half, why can't I sell half?* Feeling almost dizzy, Kate went to the phone and called Simon Doughty.

There was a pause after she finished speaking, and it went on long enough for Kate to wonder if he'd understood her. Maybe I'm blabbering like an idiot.

"Yes, Kate," he finally said, "surely you could do that. Perfectly legal. Solomon's solution, if you recall, cutting the baby in half." She could feel his disapproval, Doughty's sense of correctness offended, perhaps, by her suggestion. "Of course, if the other party is in violent disagreement, it might engender a lawsuit. Elise could try and get an injunction to stop you."

Now it was Kate's turn to pause. Yes, and she might just be contrary enough to do that, and we'd both be tied up in the courts for years and nothing would be accomplished. "Well, Simon, thank you. It was just a thought. I'll be in touch if anything further develops."

"Good day, Kate."

*Good day.* The man was right out of the nineteenth century. But sound as granite.

Kate took one final look in the mirror, decided that with a little luck she'd pass muster, and left the house. A lovely day. She walked down Sixty-eighth Street and thought, I am having luncheon at the best restaurant in the world with one of the most attractive men in New York.

Five minutes later, Armand escorted her to the corner banquette in the second dining room.

From where Kate sat she could see the length of the room. She felt her heart leap. Armand escorted Dave into the room, and she watched him with pleasure as he walked toward her.

He smiled. "Hi, Kate."

She put out her hand, pleased to see it wasn't trembling.

"It's good to see you again," he said, sitting down.

"What would you like to drink, Dave?" She wondered if the struggle showed in her voice, her effort to keep this light and easy.

A waiter had materialized silently, the way waiters did at Le Palais, never hovering or pushy but simply there quick as thought, almost before you realized you needed one. To Kate it had always seemed miraculous but she knew from Pierre that this smoothness was the result of Armand's long and rigorous training.

"White Lillet and soda with a slice of lime."

Thank God we're in a restaurant, she thought, and there'll be waiters and menus and the wine list to distract me. And so many people I won't dare make a fool of myself. Or will I?

Dave's drink came. He lifted his glass to her. "Thanks for asking me, Kate. You, and Le Palais too—that's really a treat."

Kate only smiled, raised her sherry glass and took a small sip. She was watching his hands, the strong square fingers, lightly suntanned from—what? Sailing? Tennis? Something, she was sure, that would take skill and grace and daring.

"Dave, I want to apologize for Elise. She gets so emo-

161

tional about anything connected with Le Palais. I guess it's understandable, but it isn't always fun."

He put his glass down. "Don't be too hard on her, Kate. Kids can all be monsters from time to time. Even my own boy, Timmy, who's just about perfect in my eyes, went through a rebellious period in college. Dropped out for a year to do good works among the Indians—excuse me, the Native Americans. At the time I was furious. I saw it as throwing away a terrific education. But it was a thing Tim had to do and I know I'd feel awful if I'd done anything to stop him." He smiled. "Not that I could have, in any case."

"What's he doing now, Dave?" So there is a son. Where's the boy's mother? Kate watched Dave, taking pleasure at his obvious pride in the boy. So many parents are at war with their children, she thought. Please let it not happen to Elise and me.

"He's with me at Hollander. Nepotism running rampant. But Tim's doing well, very well. Working on this new gourmet project."

"And not, I'll wager, making the sort of scene we had the other day."

"Well, Elise cares. That's good. What I have to do is convince her I care too—that we all do."

Kate lifted her glass. "To your new venture."

"To Le Palais-Royal," he said solemnly, "and may their fates be intertwined."

May our fates be intertwined, Kate thought and then stopped the thought in its tracks. What must he think of me? Her mind raced. The smooth old sherry burned on her tongue.

"Pierre," said Dave, startling her, "would be proud to see you looking so beautiful, Kate."

A flush was building, and she remembered with a shudder that it was less than a month since Pierre's death. "Thanks, Dave. I've been feeling anything but. In many ways I guess I'm still in shock. He was so thoroughly alive, such a force, that I keep expecting him to walk into any room I'm in."

"But that's natural, and very nice, when people have been as happy as you two were."

Her voice was very low when she was able to speak. "Yes. We did have something very special. But—heavens! This is a gloomy subject for the table."

"He'd be proud of you, Kate, that's all I meant."

The waiter brought menus, blessed diversion. Dave was much too attractive, and his remarks about Pierre were cutting too deep.

"What do you feel like, Dave?"

He laughed a mellow laugh. A laugh like bronze, muted but resonant and fine. "This is one place, maybe the only one in the world, where you can't possibly go wrong." He paused, skimmed the menu again, and said, "It would be tempting fate not to have the oysters Hollander first. Then, I think, the Dover sole, grilled."

Kate had forgotten oysters Hollander. He's really a part of the place already, she thought, and wondered if Elise knew. "It must be quite a feeling to be on a menu—especially this one."

"I never get over it. Of course, I'm not on every day of the year."

"I think I'll have the asparagus first, then the quenelles de brochet. I can never resist those here." Kate gave the order, then asked for the wine list.

It was a mistake to come here with him. It's too full of Pierre. Had to be. I should have known that. She thought of the portrait out in the foyer, watching them. Well, I did it, and I'll see it through.

"Have you ever tasted consommé Katharine?" Kate made sure her voice was light, her tone casual. Sooner or later we'll stop the small talk, and then where will I be?

"I will the next time it's on the menu. What is it?"

"A winter soup—pheasant consommé garnished with

163

wild mushrooms. He thought there was something English about it."

The wine waiter came up and handed Kate a book bound in dark green leather. Should I ask Dave to order? No. That might seem coy. She scanned the pages. Pierre had once told her the total number of bottles—in the thousands.

"The Meursault Goutte d'Or, I think, Robert. Is nineteen seventy-seven a decent year?"

"Excellent, Madame Villeromain."

"We'll have it then. How does that sound, Dave?"

"Like drops of gold. It's one of my favorites."

Robert vanished and Kate picked up her sherry glass, more to have something to do than to actually drink it. She noticed that Dave, too, had barely touched his Lillet. Well, he has to go back to the office and do whatever tycoons do in the afternoon.

Kate was thinking of what to say next when she sensed a presence at her side. She looked up, wondering if it was possible even in Le Palais-Royal for the wine to have come so quickly.

There stood Elise.

Even though Kate had expected her, the physical fact of Elise's being here was startling. The girl looked severe and quite pale in a dress of navy silk. Kate could feel the sudden chill, see the tensing in her stepdaughter's throat. That tension was contagious: Kate felt it herself. Only Dave seemed undisturbed, genuinely pleased to see Elise.

"Hello, Kate," Elise said quietly. "Mr. Hollander."

It sounded more like a dismissal than a greeting.

Kate managed to smile. "How are you, Elise?" she asked, bound and determined that no cracks would appear in the facade of her goodwill toward the girl. Especially not here. Already Kate saw that heads were beginning to turn in their direction. She made herself smile.

Elise looked as though she was about to face a firing squad. "I'm all right, thanks, Kate. But I want to apologize to you—and to you, Mr. Hollander—for flying off the handle the other day." A small self-deprecating ripple of a smile flickered across her lips quick as a snake's tongue. "I still haven't changed my mind, but there's no point in getting all emotional about it, is there?"

Dave answered before Kate could think what to say. "It's a good thing for Le Palais that you do care, Elise," he said gently. "Your father would be proud of you."

A touch of color appeared in Elise's cheeks. "I hope so. Listen, I've got to go help Armand. It's nice to see you. Enjoy your lunch."

And she was gone.

Kate felt a sense of relief, as though she had just been reprieved at the very foot of the gallows. Her fear of some terrible incident vanished. "Thanks, Dave. Kindness is probably the one thing she didn't expect from you."

He smiled. "I wouldn't want to make it too easy for her."

Kate found herself almost startled by the subtlety of him. By his instinctive understanding of the girl. Well, of course. You don't get your name on a big corporation by being stupid. And in that moment Kate knew that if Dave were in charge of the restaurant there'd be nothing to worry about, regardless of what Elise might think. The room was full now, but there was nobody close enough to hear. Kate decided to take the plunge.

What does it matter if he refuses? If he's shocked by my presumption? It is a solution, not the best one maybe, but logical. And Simon says it's perfectly legal.

It was the chilly little visit from Elise that decided Kate. She'd put an end to that kind of stress forever. But now that she was on the brink of telling Dave of her idea, Kate felt a sense of foreboding. A feeling that she was poised to take an irrevocable step, to make a move that might forever alienate her from Elise. She closed her eyes for just a moment. I will not, she told herself firmly, be manipulated by a headstrong girl half my age, even if she is Pierre's daughter.

Kate opened her eyes and smiled at Dave. "Dave, you

remember what I said about the will? About it's being entirely on a fifty-fifty basis?"

"Of course. Why?"

"It may sound crazy, but how would you like to buy my half of this place?" Having come right out with it, Kate sat back and waited for the explosion. Or the laughter, or the scorn.

Dave took a long careful sip of his drink.

The waiter arrived with their hor d'oeuvres. The silence lasted only a minute or so but to Kate it felt longer than eternity.

Finally Dave spoke. "Kate, that's brilliant. Why didn't it occur to me?"

"It just came to me this morning, Dave, and I called our lawyer—Pierre's lawyer—and he says it's quite legal. Naturally, I'd hoped such a thing wouldn't be necessary, but it seems it may be."

Dave took another sip of his drink. "Damn," he said, quietly and reflectively. "That is something to think about."

Kate, remembering suddenly that she was his hostess, quickly took a bite of the jade green asparagus.

Dave went on, his enthusiasm building. "Sure it's legal. It's the way to get you out of the line of fire, to let me and the company do the maneuvering, and help you financially at the same time. Very good, Kate."

"Thanks. Can I give you some asparagus? It's wonderful."

He smiled. "Only if you take one of my namesakes here in exchange."

"I'd love one." She passed him her butter plate and on it Dave put one of the lightly glazed Belon oysters and some of the watercress puree they rested on.

Too good to be true, Kate thought, as she forked the oyster and lifted it to her mouth. There has to be a hitch, a conflict. Maybe it isn't really legal after all. "Well, Dave," she said. "Oysters Hollander are very worthy of the new owner of Le Palais-Royal."

It was his turn to flush with pleasure and embarrassment. But the minute Kate said the words she regretted them, wondering if any waiter, if any of the other diners might possibly have heard her. Even worse, what would Dave think of such an indiscretion? But all Dave did was smile.

Kate took another stalk of asparagus, lifting it by the end in the European manner, dipping its head in the golden sauce of lemon and orange, butter and egg yolk. How well it's going, she thought, and how very careful I must be to make sure it keeps on going well.

The atmosphere in the dining room was seductive. A murmur of contented voices, the occasional soft chime of a crystal wineglass, from time to time a tantalizing aroma. Only a very few people might suspect how fragile it was, all this perfection and ease. Kate knew, and the knowledge frightened her. How lovely it would be not to have to think about Le Palais-Royal at all, she decided, just let Dave do what he so very badly wants to do.

His voice brought her back to the reality of the moment. "Well, let's not count our truffles before they hatch," he said, "but, subject of course to my legal people checking it out, you have my word on it. I accept."

"On principle. Oh, Dave, I'm nothing like a businesswoman. We haven't really talked price except in the most general way, and I'm not going to spoil this lovely lunch by haggling."

Dave looked at her, charmed by the words, impressed by her poise. "I'll bet you couldn't haggle if you tried."

"Come with me to Orchard Street some day and you'll see haggling."

"I may just do that." Dave ate the last of his oysters. "I'd mentioned four million, Kate, and it was rough. You'll get other offers, you're bound to, and I'm sure the estate will do its own appraisal. You owe it to yourself to consider all of them."

"I appreciate your advice, Dave. But maybe you flatter us. I haven't heard about any other offers."

167

"You will. Bet on it. I have an advantage, Kate: I can move very quickly. Other people, to raise that kind of money, might take longer. There's always something going on behind the scenes."

She looked at him and wondered what might be going on behind the impressive front of Dave Hollander. Keep to business, Kate. You're safe as long as you stick to business.

The wine waiter arrived with the Meursault. Silently he poured half an inch in her wineglass and she tasted it. Nodded her approval. The waiter then filled her glass one third of the way and did the same to Dave's. Once more she lifted her glass to him. "Good luck with it, Dave."

"And to you, Kate."

The wine was followed swiftly by their entrees. And there was another, blessed pause while they each tasted. "If I do say so myself, Dave, you must have a quenelle."

He reached deftly with a spoon on the bottom and a fork inverted on top, using the silverware like chopsticks to scoop up one of the delicate ovals of pike mousse and some of its pale pink sauce. Deposited the treasure on his plate and tasted.

"Magnificent, Kate. Would you like some sole? it's fabulous."

"Ought to be. It was swimming off Calais this time yesterday."

"Only at Le Palais."

Kate sipped her wine. "No, other places do it now. Pierre was the first to fly in European fish—quite an astonishing thing at the time—but it's what happens in the kitchen that makes the difference."

"And there definitely is a difference."

Kate felt herself growing less cautious. It wasn't the wine—she'd barely tasted it. It was Dave. Something about him that made her want more. "Dave, tell me something. When you reached for my quenelle you did it—well, as gracefully as a waiter."

He laughed. "But I *was* a waiter. In college. Weird as it

sounds, that's what got me started in the food business. It was mostly a beer and hamburger place, but the owner knew what he was doing. Best hamburgers I ever ate. Elise'll never believe this, but when I finally set up Billy Burger I tracked him down, old Roger Pickens of Hanover, New Hampshire. He was retired then, but he still knew all there is to know about hamburgers. Came on as a consultant. Real terror behind the scenes, a maniac for freshness, for quality. Roger could smell rancid grease at thirty-five thousand feet, or if someone was trying to pass off grade Z frozen beef as the fresh prime chuck he insisted on."

"Just like Pierre."

"Exactly like Pierre. They would have gotten on, Pierre and old Roger."

"It seems funny, Dave. Here we are in the best restaurant in the world, talking about hamburgers."

He smiled. "It's a subject dear to my philistine heart, Kate. It was hamburgers that made me able to afford this place. You'll never hear me say a bad word about them."

"We'll leave that to Elise."

There was an honesty to the man that Kate decided must run bone deep. How many other men would be so open about such humble beginnings? She listened to his words, watched him enjoying the meal. And felt herself sliding deliciously into an emotional state.

Intoxicating. Maybe dangerous.

"I hope, one day, that you'll be able to tell your story to Elise."

He lifted his wineglass and took a slow, contemplative taste. "I'm working on it, Kate. Never doubt that."

Kate ate the last of her quenelles, broke off a piece of her otherwise untouched baguette, put it on the plate and maneuvered it with her fork to soak up the last of the exquisite sauce Nantua that had enrobed the fish dumplings. "In a way," she said softly, almost to herself, "it will be sad not to own it anymore. I'll miss it, Dave, even though I've never had the slightest desire to run Le Palais."

"But you'll still come here I hope? I'll see to it that Madame Villeromain is never presented with a bill."

She smiled. Gallantry became him just the way every other generous gesture seemed to do. "It isn't that, Dave. After all, you may make me quite rich. But even though I do love good food, this isn't my sort of place. Deep down, I'm really not this grand."

"But it just might be possible to get accustomed?"

She watched the smile forming on his lips. And she laughed a gentle laugh. "Need you ask? But, left to my own devices— and I surely will be—I might not make the effort."

Dave heard this and couldn't stop himself. To hell with caution, he thought, either she feels something for me or it's all a pipe dream, and I might as well find out. Now. He reached across the table and laid his hand on hers. Squeezed a little. "I could help you make that effort, Kate."

Kate withdrew her hand as though she'd been burned— and it did burn, his touch. The gentle pressure that was so strong in its message. So frightening.

She looked up to find his eyes fixed on hers. Pleading. She forced herself to act casual, as though they were discussing nothing more urgent than the weather. Kate turned her head slightly, half smiling, and looked around the dining room. Fighting for breath and hiding it. Feeling trapped, threatened, utterly panic-stricken. The dining room of Le Palais-Royal was just as it had been a few heartbeats ago. A million light years ago.

The pause lengthened.

It's too soon, she told herself. You don't know this man, or what he's really like, or what he really wants. You could make a mistake that might wreck your life, that would forever cheapen your memory of Pierre.

Something in her changed at the thought. As though a door had slammed shut, a door that might have led to unimaginable treasures of loving. Or to shame, disgrace.

I can't afford it, she told herself sternly. I'm too fragile as it is, what with losing Pierre, taking on Elise, the money problems. All of it. The sudden resolve seemed to strengthen her. She smiled at Dave.

"Dave, you're very kind. It's hard to describe quite what a state I'm in. So much has been happening to me lately, most of it pretty . . . pretty heavy, as Elise might put it." She paused for a moment, searching for words that might explain the inexplicable. "Please never think I don't appreciate your concern, your kindness. Not to mention your interest in the restaurant. What I need, I'm afraid, is a little time."

He looked at her, thinking, You've blown it, Hollander. Coming on too strong, too soon. What kind of a clumsy asshole is she going to think you are, damn it? After this, will she even want to do business with you, let alone anything more personal? It seemed to Dave in that moment that two of his most cherished dreams lay in ruins on the table like so much shattered crystal. I may not get the restaurant now. Or Kate.

A waiter materialized out of nowhere. "Some dessert, Madame Villeromain?"

"Not for me," she said softly. "Dave?"

"I wish I could, Kate, but I'd probably better be getting back to the grindstone soon."

Banalities exchanged between near strangers, Dave thought. And near strangers is probably all we'll ever be to each other now, thanks to Bigfoot-in-Bigmouth.

"Coffee?"

"Sure," he said. "Filtre, please."

"Two filtres," Kate said to the waiter, smiling graciously. Feeling like a condemned prisoner who'd been reprieved at the very last minute. "So," she went on, forcing herself to be far more casual than she felt, "you don't think it's altogether out of the question? This selling of half?"

"I hope and pray it's in the question, Kate. There isn't anything I want more."

Liar, said a voice inside him.

# 10

ARMAND SAT ALONE in the living room of his house on Seventy-eighth Street, thinking of Yves. Yves was out somewhere, and this was another sign, a symptom of everything that was going wrong between them. Even a few months ago, there would have been a note, a phone call. Something.

Armand stretched, relaxed, picked up a magazine and restlessly put it down. He looked around the room and thought of the good times they'd had, all the Sunday shopping expeditions to find furniture, carpets, decorative touches for the place. The room was pleasing, everything familiar and well loved; the apartment had become a refuge for both of them, a gentle contrast to the high-powered world of the restaurant. A refuge too, from other people, other temptations.

More than ten years we've been together, that's pretty good. Longer than most marriages. The place is the same, my clothes are the same; the soft old corduroys, the cashmere pullover he gave me a few years ago, the old Italian loafers that fit like skin. But nothing is really the same, and there's no point in pretending it is.

The sadness Armand felt was a physical thing, a feeling close to nausea. I planned so well—we planned. What dreams we had! But it's all changed now, and Pierre's death is only part of it.

He sighed a long and heavy sigh. Sometimes it was so bad, this feeling, that he had trouble breathing. In Le Palais it was better. In Le Palais there were a thousand other things to think about, all the details that, together, added up to the perfection that had become something like a religion with Armand. He sat absolutely still for several minutes, his mind as blank as he could force it to be. Blankness was far preferable to the dark thoughts that kept trying to crowd in.

Armand heard another metallic sound, sat forward, straining to hear. Yves's key in the front door. A moment of panic; then a quick resolution. At least here was something to deal with. Someone real.

Yves walked into the room to find his lover calmly reading *Manhattan Magazine*.

"Bonjour, Yves," said Armand gently, the irony of a morning greeting at nearly midnight so light that it might well pass unnoticed. And the unasked question too: Where have you been?

"Bonjour," said Yves, walking directly to the bar and pouring himself a generous cognac.

Every bone and muscle in Yves's body ached, throbbed, vibrated with pain. He had walked nearly the length of Manhattan and back again, seen a movie whose name he couldn't remember, grabbed a snack in a Soho café, washed it down with two glasses of unspeakable California Burgundy, walked some more, up the far West side of Greenwich Village, walked unseeing through the crowds, past the boutiques and gay bars and laughter.

On one nameless empty street there had been a quiet bar, light coming through its windowed doorway, and just outside, lounging against the wall, a young man. A beautiful young man, his profile fixed by the golden light from within, black leather jacket, T-shirt taut over sculpted muscles, tight jeans, leather boots. His face was blank, the fallen-angel mouth defined by a faintly mocking sneer. Light glinted off a hundred steel nailheads that decorated the jacket. As Yves came closer the young man shifted his stance, lazily, a slight but provocative flexing of his slender hips.

Yves forced himself to look straight ahead. To walk on by. But as he walked away a sound of soft laughter came curling after him, maybe from the boy or maybe from the bar. Yves shuddered. The boy seemed like a dark messenger from the future. A reminder of what Yves might be forced to seek if there were no Armand in his life. And in that moment the thought of being separated from Armand became unbearable. The decision Yves had been wrestling with all the long, long evening was resolved in an instant and by pure chance. The young hustler had done it, driven it home and made it entirely clear. Yves knew that he needed Armand more than ever now. Needed his strength, his confidence, his love.

He took one drink of the cognac standing up, rolled it around the roof of his mouth, enjoying the aroma and the warmth of it. Then he sat down. Knowing in his heart that he must stay, that there could be no thought of leaving. Knowing, too, that there was one thing he must say to Armand.

"Armand, we must talk."

Armand looked up, smiled, put down the magazine. "But of course."

"Claude must go."

For a moment Armand said nothing. Then he smiled, encouragingly. I will not become angry. It's better, far better, to have it out in the open. Yves is at least trying to be reasonable. I must be reasonable too, and more than reasonable.

Armand was touched by what he saw on his lover's face. By the rage and the sadness, the hesitancy and the final resolution to say what must be said. "I understand, mon vieux, that you don't get on. But you must try for a little longer,

Yves. You know how crucial it is just now. We must give every appearance of stability. Of being a team. Of continuing Le Palais-Royal at the highest level. Like him or not, cher Yves, Claude is necessary."

Yves looked at Armand, taking great care in forming his reply. Armand saw this and thought, Good, let him take care. Let him understand what it means to weigh every word. Let him begin to learn.

Yves spoke quietly. "There are other pastry chefs."

"Of course there are. Good ones too. But, dear Yves, you're missing the point. If so much as a dishwasher leaves us now, the word will get out. People will say it's a trend, that Yves and Armand can't hold onto people, that the rats are leaving the sinking ship. You know how gossipy it is in this business. Sometimes I think even the garbage cans have ears."

Yves took another drink.

Armand watched attentively, wondering where he'd been and what else he might have been drinking. But Yves looked sober enough. Drawn, tired, too pale, no doubt about that. But drunk? Armand thought not.

"What you don't see, Armand, is that Claude is a troublemaker. For all his soft manners, for all his quiet voice, he is a sneak. Claude is poisoning the air at Le Palais, cleverly playing up to the girl—to Elise—convincing her that it is he, not me, who should be the new chef de cuisine!"

"And you, dear Yves, are playing right into his hands by letting all this upset you so." Armand stood up, went to Yves's chair and tousled his hair playfully, an old gesture. "Yves, Yves," he said softly. "You know I've spoken to Mr. Pierrepont. You know what he said—that if we can bring off the Tastevin banquet he'll back us in buying Le Palais. Do you realize how close that is? It's less than a month. Can't you bear with me that long? Just be a little patient. Once we actually own the place, everything will be different. I promise."

Armand's hand rested on his lover's head. He reached

down with the other hand now and began slowly massaging the muscles at the base of Yves's neck. For a moment there was silence. Armand could feel Yves relaxing under his touch.

"Yves," he said quietly, almost a whisper, "do you know what I want, more than anything in the world?"

"What is it?"

Armand leaned over and kissed him on the forehead. "I want you, cher Yves. I want you."

Yves set down the glass. Got up and put his arms around Armand. Hugged him tightly for a long moment.

"You do?" There was wonderment in his voice.

"Only you. Come to bed now, mon petit," Armand said with a new urgency in his voice. "It has been a long time."

Arm in arm they walked upstairs. Quickly undressed. For Armand there was a little sadness mixed in with the love-making. But at least we're together, he seems better now. Happier than before. If the fire of his anger can be replaced with this, then we've really achieved something.

Yves moaned with pleasure.

For the moment, at least, Le Palais-Royal was safe.

# 11

ELISE TURNED OVER onto her side, clamped her eyes shut, and tried to concentrate on blankness. *Damn* Jared! Would this be another sleepless night? I think of him more now than I ever did when he was beside me. And maybe that's the truth of it. Maybe that's why he left.

Her memory of him was a quicksilver thing. It kept seeping into places where she didn't want it, turning up at the most inconvenient times, all bright and shiny. Jared burned in her brain, in her heart. And while she tried to tell herself it was finished, tried to act as though she had no regrets, acting was just what it came to. Bad acting at that.

Three weeks and he hasn't so much as called.

She turned onto her back, opened her eyes, and stared at the shadows on the ceiling. A streetlight filtering through branches. Her mind wandered among the shadows; Elise saw patterns, a pointing finger here, a dagger there, somewhere else a line that was almost precisely like the silhouette of the mountain you could see from the kitchen window in Stowe.

Will I ever see it again?

The empty room seemed to be closing in on her.

This is my fault more than Jared's.

She was very aware of her breathing: in and out, in and out.

What if I'd just come down for Daddy's funeral and gone right back again? Jared and I would be together right now. Planning what to do with the inheritance. There'd be no sticky questions about selling or not selling Le Palais. Kate would be happier, God knows. And I wouldn't even have to think about the hamburger king. She closed her eyes. Got to get some rest or I really will fall apart.

But there was Jared again. Elise sensed him so completely that for a moment she was sure he was here, in this room, in this bed. She reached out for him. Felt the cool emptiness of the sheets on the other side. Drew her hand back sharply.

I'm not being fair to him. Sure, he's never called—but did I call him? Between my pride and his we've got quite a little war going on.

Elise knew it was more than just pride. Daddy was tied up in it too, and her own need to be as good as he'd been. Or at least to feel worthy of him. How could Jared be expected to understand?

If I can't have Jared and the restaurant too, what do I do? A voice inside her said: You'll never know unless you talk to him.

Jared wasn't the only imaginary presence in the room; Elise could sense her father too. Every day and in every part of Le Palais-Royal, he was there somewhere. In the wine cellar and the kitchen. In the dining rooms and, inevitably, inescapably, shockingly alive, in Kate's portrait. She felt that he was watching her, witholding his judgment, waiting. And she'd be betraying him if she gave up on Le Palais.

Jared came back to her once more and she felt angry. He wants me for some kind of meek little indentured servant, bowing to his every whim, right out of some Victorian novel. Do it his way or not at all.

Again she turned over in the bed.

But I need him. She remembered, shivering, the first time he touched her. Like being blessed by a king. Well, Jared is royalty in Stowe. Jared, king of the ski bums. And I ate it up. Basked in it, that I was the one he chose.

And she remembered how it had been, Jared waiting tables in their little place, her behind the counter cooking. Watching him move around the room, smiling, making jokes, pouring wine, flirting a little, taking orders. Trailed by the eyes of every female over the age of five. Giving off more heat than their old cast iron stove.

I've got to call him—or I may never sleep again.

She got out of bed. Went to the bathroom, scrubbed her face with a cloth, dressed in her kitchen clothes and debated having a cup of coffee before she called him. No. No delays. No excuses. No fooling around.

She walked decisively into the bedroom and picked up the phone without giving herself a chance to think twice. Dialed the familiar number. Elise felt a wave of doubt as the various hummings and clickings found their way from East Sixty-fourth to their tumbledown house on the edge of Stowe. There were two phones up there: one in the kitchen of Chez Elise and one in their bedroom. She looked at her watch. Not quite seven. Well, he's usually up pretty early, she thought.

The phone rang in Stowe. Kept ringing. Now Elise remembered that other call: Kate's call about Daddy. How they'd let it ring because they were doing something more important.

He's out of town. Closed the place down and put it on the market. Can he do that without my permission? The phone rang and rang. Five times now. Six.

He's dead, and nobody told me.

"Chez Margot, good morning," said a groggy but definitely female voice. Then, when only silence came from the other end: "Hello? Hello? Shit, Jared, it's some kind of a wrong number or something."

Elise slowly put down the receiver. Blackness closed over her. She was alone in a cold and empty place. At first she felt a kind of numbness. She sat down on the edge of the bed. No more hoping he'll come back to me. That he'll give it one more try. To be part of my life again. Part of me.

179

Elise shivered, hugged herself for warmth, stood up and went to the closet. The blackness moved with her, and the chill. She pulled on a raincoat and grabbed her keys and left the apartment. It seemed impossible to breathe in Le Palais-Royal. She went down the stairs and let herself out the service entrance, praying she wouldn't bump into any early arrivals. No one. Standing in the dark alley she breathed deep, deep breaths.

Of course he'd find another woman. I should have known that. Jared hasn't been ten minutes without a woman since he was fifteen.

*Chez Margot!*

Elise walked blindly out of the alley, turned left, and headed toward Fifth Avenue. The morning was cool. There was a light mist. She crossed Fifth Avenue and walked into the park. The mist made everything flat, gray and dreamlike, but Elise didn't see the beauty of it. She passed a man walking a dog and hardly saw them. Two joggers passed her.

Chez Margot.

The park is probably filled with muggers, she thought, absolutely indifferent to the idea. How can they hurt me when I don't have anything left to lose?

She followed a winding path, had no idea where it led, cared less. Here in the middle of the park the mist seemed thicker, more dreamlike. She had no sense of time nor of how far she'd walked. The path climbed a little hill and on the top of it there was a bench. Sitting on the bench was an old lady all in black, feeding pigeons and talking to them in a low, confidential voice.

Elise walked on. That's how I'll end up, alone and half crazy, my best friend some dumb bird.

Jean-Paul was in the kitchen when Elise walked in ten minutes later. He smiled, said "Bonjour!" and seemed not to notice that she was late. The offhand kindness of his greeting warmed her a little. There are good people here,

180

people who want it to work, she thought. She managed a smile and accepted his offer of a cup of coffee. Put twice the usual amount of sugar in it.

Elise sat on a stool and looked around the big immaculate room, trying to extract whatever warmth and reassurance there might be in the orderly rows of copper pots and sauté pans, in the gleaming knives and the big black Vulcan ranges that seemed to crouch behind the serving counter like machines of combat. Not by chance, she thought, do the old French kitchen terms have a military ring to them: *chef, brigade, batterie de cuisine.* And it will be a battle, and I'm in it for keeps. She felt a little better now, focusing her hurt, her anger.

The coffee was very hot, almost scalding. Just the way Elise liked it. And the heat of it and its potency jolted her a little. Good. A reminder that life went on.

Carrying the coffee cup, she walked through the double service doors into the dining rooms. They were just as empty as the kitchen, but the sense of anticipation was different out here. This was not an arsenal before battle but the empty stage before a gala performance. She paused for a moment. She could almost hear the well-bred laughter, the murmur of cultivated voices, the chime of fine crystal, the resonance of wealth and power.

Elise walked into the foyer, sipping coffee, and looked up at her father's portrait. The portrait looked back at her, and beyond her.

I won't let you down now, Daddy. Even if I did run away before. Even if I did break your heart a little. Or a lot.

She felt better after that. Turned and walked back to the kitchen. A new sense of resolve filled her heart. It didn't take the hurt away, but it was a contrast, something to hold onto.

She was in the kitchen pouring another cup of coffee when Claude walked in. Elise took one look at him and set the coffee down. For an instant she was afraid to speak. Something terrible had happened. He walked slowly, as if in a trance, feeling his way as though each step might land him in quicksand. On his face was an expression of bewilderment. Elise's heart took a small leap of sympathy. From somewhere the phrase *he never knew what hit him* floated into her head. Claude looked like that now. Good, kind, wonderful Claude.

Elise realized that, for the first time she was seeing him in street clothes. He'd always come into the kitchen dressed immaculately in his chef's whites. Now he wore faded jeans and a turtleneck and running shoes. He looks about eighteen, and totally lost. She went to him, put her hands on his shoulders. "Claude. What's wrong?"

He looked at her, startled, and Elise realized that he was so much in shock—or whatever it was—that he hadn't really seen her. His efforts to recover were terrible to see.

"Oh," he said. "Elise." Looked around the kitchen. Jean-Paul was peeling vegetables at the work island. Claude lowered his voice. "Can we be alone for a moment?"

She led him into the rear dining room. Sat him down at a table. "Claude, you look like you've seen a ghost. Can I help?"

He tried a little smile; Elise thought it was the saddest smile she had ever seen. Closer now, only a few feet away, she could see how red his eyes were. Must be from crying.

"Did someone die?"

"Worse."

He passed his hand across his eyes as if that gesture could erase the memory of whatever it was.

"Last night, very late—well, no later than usual—I got home. And there was nothing. Only a little of the furniture. The better pieces all gone. No baby François—my son. No wife. She has stolen him, Elise, cleaned out our bank account, sold off the television and the rugs. That would be bad enough. But she has also stolen my baby. My son." The word *son* came out like a sob.

Elise came closer to him and touched his shoulder. He

182

was trembling, struggling to contain his sorrow. "Claude, that's terrible."

"I must go after her, you see. Get the boy at least. I don't think I could face another day without him."

"Drink this."

She handed him her coffee cup. He took it and tasted a little, then put it down.

"I must go after them," he repeated, as much to himself as to Elise.

It came to her on a shrill wave of alarm: He's come in to quit. For an instant Elise was numbed by the shock of it. Not *Claude.* Not Claude, of everyone in the kitchen. Claude, who had been so especially kind to her, Claude, whose genius was so conspicuous it set Yves on edge with jealousy. She realized all at once how much she depended on him—how much Le Palais depended on him too.

She felt torn like some martyr in a medieval painting. Pulled apart by her sympathy for Claude on the one hand and by her growing concern for Le Palais-Royal on the other. With the Tastevin banquet coming up like judgment day.

She knew too well what a tiny, gossip-ridden world it was, this world of New York haute cuisine. How quickly the word would go out—"Le Palais is slipping, they've lost Montgeron already. Who'll be next?"

Her first thought was how to keep him. No matter what it cost. What would Daddy do in a fix like this? She paused, let him recover himself a little.

"Claude—do you have any idea where she's gone?"

"Oh yes. There is only one possibility. She will go home, to her fat pig of a mother. It is my hometown also. Chateaubourg. A small town in Britanny."

"Claude . . . before you do anything you might regret, you must think. Make plans. Don't just rush off like a madman. If I remember anything about French law, they're

183

pretty strict about keeping mothers with their children, no matter whose fault it really is."

For a moment he couldn't look at her. "You are right. They are very strict about that."

"Is there any chance you can persuade her to come back?"

He picked the coffee cup up but put it down again, slowly, precisely, as if it were a test to see how little noise he could make. Elise could see him struggling for control—knew the feeling too well. "The truth is, Elise, I don't want her back."

He looked away from her, and she was almost relieved. Elise wasn't sure how long she could stand the sorrow in Claude's brown eyes. He's never said anything about her. Maybe he couldn't really admit it to himself, either—any more than I could face up to the fact of Jared's leaving. She must really be a bitch, that Marie-Claire. To walk out on a man like Claude!

"I'm sorry to hear that, Claude. She'll divorce you?"

He sighed. "Perhaps. Blackmailing me with the baby. Things . . . haven't been good between us for a long time. Maybe from the beginning. I was nineteen when we married. Too young."

Elise ransacked her brain for a way to comfort him. For words that might help keep him here. "It happens," she said, helplessly, thinking about Jared. Would there ever have been a right age for Jared and me?

"I'll go to France, get a job. At least I'll see the little one."

"If she lets you."

He looked at her, startled.

Elise continued. "Claude, don't do anything in a panic. Right now you're very upset. Naturally. But to go chasing after her—that's probably what she hopes you'll do. You still have family in Chateaubourg?"

"My father. My sister too. But my sister would kill Marie-Claire as soon as look at her."

"Talk to your father then. Have him see her. Find out what she wants. She's probably every bit as upset and angry as you are. And definitely have your father talk to a lawyer. Find out what your rights are. It may not be necessary for you to go, Claude. From a selfish point of view I hope you can work out something that keeps you here. If you haven't been told lately it's my fault, but you're a very valuable part of Le Palais-Royal. We—I need you here."

Even as the words left her lips Elise knew they might backfire. She watched him react.

Claude stood very tall, stretched like a taut wire. Clenching his fists. "Monstre!" he said, a low hissing sound, making it into a curse. "How can you think of the kitchen when my life blood has been stolen from me?" Then he turned and ran from the room.

Claude turned the key of his apartment in Forest Hills, half expecting to hear the sound of his little boy's laughter, the interminable drone of Marie-Claire's soap operas on the television. He took a deep breath and forced himself to open the door.

Emptiness awaited him, the same emptiness that had ambushed him the night before. The same echoing spaces, the same disorder left by the movers or whoever it was that had taken away the furniture. It wasn't a big apartment, but now it seemed endless. The echo of remembered laughter had a resonance in Claude's ears that made him wince with pain. His life seemed as empty as these sad rooms, and all he could think about was getting little François back again.

But Elise was right: it might be impossible.

I was terrible to her, unforgivably rude. But it seemed all she could think about was keeping me at Le Palais. I'll write her a note apologizing before I go. She just doesn't understand—how could she?—what the child means to me. The one real bright spot in my whole life these days.

In the restaurant his anger had been beyond controlling. But the long subway ride out here had forced Claude to think, to cool down a little. Whatever her motives, there was some logic to what Elise had said. I can't simply go to

Chateaubourg and steal the boy. And what would I do with him if I did? Marie-Claire would have the gendarmerie on my trail in five minutes, and Interpol and the FBI as well. And what kind of a home can I make for the child anyway, working the hours I do, whether it's here or in France?

Claude's sense of hopelessness grew darker and deeper. To get the sort of job I need, I'd have to be in Paris. And even in Paris—even if La Tour d'Argent would take me back—that's a four-hour drive and I'd only have Sundays off. Assuming Marie-Claire would let me near him.

The apartment seemed filled with questions to which Claude had no answers. He sat down on one of the few chairs that hadn't been taken away. At least the bitch hadn't ripped out the phone. He stared at the telephone for a moment, then dragged his chair to the spot where it rested on the floor. Lifted it to his lap and dialed the overseas operator.

The connection was almost instantaneous and very clear. The very clarity of his father's voice made Claude's heart leap. It seemed as though he could smell the applewood fire in the ancient black iron woodstove the old man refused to part with, or taste the good Breton cider that Papa would surely be enjoying with his supper; it was nearly suppertime in Chateaubourg.

"Papa? How are you, Papa?"

"Claude! Claude! The frost has eaten my raspberries, but you don't want to know about that. How are you, and the baby, and Marie-Claire?"

The hesitation before the old man spoke her name had a message for Claude. Papa had been too reticent to say it, but Claude knew the old man had never liked Marie-Claire.

"Well, Papa, that is why I'm calling. She has left me. Left with the baby. I assume she'll go to her mother."

"Conasse!"

"Papa, please."

"She is a cunt, and a cunt's cunt, and everybody knew it

186

but you, poor boy. Well, Claude, I apologize to my grandson and to his father. But to that bitch, never."

Claude smiled. He felt exactly the same way.

"I was going to hop on the next plane, Papa, but—"

"Don't spend a sou chasing after that one."

"But Papa—"

"Claude. I love you. It is not necessary to say that but I say it. And I will love the little one. Before . . . before you married your wife I did not speak. You seemed so happy, so eager, so ready to take on the world that I held my tongue. And now I bite my tongue for not having spoken up. The bitch was always clever, too clever by half, leading you on. And she's been clever now. In France, even today, a woman can be Messalina herself, and in the town square at high noon, and still the judges will give her the custody of the child. Even divorce is a long and complicated thing, although possible. For a country whose churches are filled only with tourists, we still cling to the trailing skirts of Rome in many ways, Claude."

"Yes," said Claude. "I know."

"Claude—this is important. Do you like it where you are? In New York? In that restaurant?"

There was a pause. "Yes," said Claude. "I do like it. Very much."

"Then it is settled. Stay. Stay until I find out exactly what the bitch is up to. Stay until I talk to my friend St. Remy the lawyer. Stay until we have a plan, Claude, until we know for sure what will work. I do know this—whatever the attitude of the courts, she has run out on you. You are an abandoned husband." And the old man laughed.

"It is not funny, Papa."

"No. It is not funny. But perhaps certain things can be salvaged. Having left you, she has no claim to your support. But, being Marie-Claire, she'll try to pry out of you every last franc. Give her nothing if she asks. Make your support conditional when you do give it, conditional upon

187

having a certain amount of time with the boy. All of August, for instance."

Suddenly it seemed to Claude that an enormous burden had been lifted from his shoulders, a burden that had threatened to crush him altogether. What Papa said made every kind of sense. It struck Claude vehemently that Papa's advice wasn't much different from what Elise had said earlier on, at Le Palais-Royal. *Except then I was crazy with pain, and now I'm better.*

"You think that might be possible, Papa?"

"I know it is possible, idiot. Everything is possible, with a bit of planning, with the help of good friends. Which I have in Chateaubourg, never forget. Which Marie-Claire and her wretched cheating cochon of a father have not."

The very force of Papa's anger was reassuring to Claude. *How he hates her! How blind I was not to see what everyone else saw.*

"Thank you, Papa. You're splendid. You will call me when the boy turns up?"

"Does a duck quack? They may be here already, if she left yesterday afternoon. Count on me, Claude."

"I will. And thank you, Papa."

Again, the old man's laugh. "I do feel for you, cher Claude. But I can hardly tell you what pleasure it will give me to have my bit of revenge on the one who has made you so unhappy."

"We must be very careful that she doesn't find some way to take it out on the baby." There was the briefest of pauses. Claude could hear his father taking a deep breath.

"She wouldn't dare. This is a very small town, Claude, as you may have noticed. I'd hear. Go back to your kitchen, my boy. I'll handle Marie-Claire."

"I love you, Papa."

"Go make pastries, dunce."

When Claude hung up he was smiling. *August, all of August, with François! I'll be with him more in a month than in a year of keeping chef's hours.*

He didn't stop to have lunch, but let himself out of the depressing apartment and ran for the subway.

Elise forced herself to get up from the bed. Washed her face, put on a little makeup and walked down to the kitchen. Feeling as though she was going to her own execution.

When Yves came in she told him about Claude, simplifying it, saying he had a crisis at home, that he might be in later or might not. Yves merely sniffed, as though such erratic behavior was to be expected from the likes of Claude. Together they went to see what was in the dessert refrigerator.

Claude, as usual, was far ahead of himself. There were four fruit sorbets, a mousse of chocolate and another of lemon, seven batches of puff pastry ready to be rolled out to make the bases for fruit tarts or other confections, praline in a big glass jar, a sheet of chocolate ready to be shaved into decorative curls, and two elaborate gâteaus.

"Well, Yves, all we really need to do is make some cookies and stand ready if someone orders a dessert soufflé."

"Yes," said Yves thoughtfully; "and I can easily do that."

Elise had half expected Yves to gloat, or to make some scathing remark about Claude. But he was remarkably even-tempered this morning. He nodded and left her with the air of one who has much more important things to do than trifling with desserts.

Elise went back to the dessert refrigerator and looked at the beautiful things Claude had made. We're all right for the moment, for luncheon and maybe even for supper. But what in the world will we do if he's gone to France? She went back into Yves's little office—Daddy's office—and dialed Claude's home number. Nothing.

Elise put down the phone and went to Claude's pastry counter to try making a crème anglaise à la orange to be served with the mousse au chocolat. She was in the midst of separating a dozen eggs for the sauce when Claude walked in immaculate in his chef's whites, and on his face there was something very like a smile. It faded when he saw her at the pastry counter, becoming something much more complicted. A mixture of sadness and hope.

"Elise," he said quietly, "can you forgive me? I was very upset this morning."

Elise felt a current that was almost electric in its urgency. Partly sheer relief that he was back, partly something else: a warmth and a rapport she hadn't felt for any man since Jared walked out. "Claude, there's nothing to apologize for. We've been missing you all morning and I'm delighted you're back."

"I did what you suggested, Elise," he said, coming very close and speaking quietly. She realized Claude was eager not to have the entire kitchen know of his problems. "I called my father in Chateaubourg. And he'll take care of everything—at least, for the time being."

And the time being is all that matters, thought Elise, because if the next few weeks don't go right, then the time being may be all we have. She smiled.

"Claude, that's wonderful! I'm so pleased. Sometimes it's better to let everything simmer down a little."

"Especially the pastry chef?"

His smile was full and warm now, back in focus. Elise was so relieved to have him back that it was a moment before she noticed the change in him. But there was a change. Claude has always been so subdued, acted older than he is. But now, whatever had happened with his phone call to France, it was as though something had been ignited in him. Something happy. Something hopeful.

Elise looked at him analytically and wished—prayed— that whatever it was might happen to her.

"I was just about to start making a crème anglaise for your mousse. Maybe you'd like to take over?"

"My pleasure."

She handed him an egg, feeling a small quiver of pleasure as their hands met. He's very attractive when he smiles—

suddenly, for the first time, Elise found herself thinking about him as a man, a young and virile man who had just been walked out on. Well I sure can relate to that, she thought ruefully. We have that in common.

As the supper hour approached Elise changed and took her place at Armand's side. Armand was Armand, but tonight he seemed a little keyed up.

Elise learned why when Harry Pierrepont arrived, fifteen minutes early for his seven o'clock reservation. Greetings all round. But then Pierrepont leaned close to Armand and spoke so softly it was almost secretive.

"Armand, could we have a word in private someplace?"

Armand smiled blandly. "Of course. Elise, may I leave you for a few minutes?"

"Sure. I'll man the fort."

Armand led Pierrepont to the farthest corner of the bar, made him the champagne kir, Pierrepont liked so dearly, then stood next to Pierrepont while Pierrepont talked. Something about their very posture looked conspiratorial to Elise, rather like those scheming lawyers in Daumier's cartoons, bending with the supple elegance of serpents, hatching plots.

Well, he's an old and favored customer, not to mention one of the richest men in the world, so of course Armand kowtows to him. I would too, probably.

But there was something in the air at the far end of the little bar. What would I give to hear every word? Elise wondered. But there was no chance of that. If I were Armand I'd want Le Palais. If I were Armand I'd probably turn to the richest person I know for backing. And that person is Pierrepont, and here he is.

Elise felt a sense of dread. A sense that here was another threat coming at her, not altogether unexpected maybe, but a threat all the same. A threat very possibly backed up by the fabulous Pierrepont fortune.

Or maybe I'm flipping out. Maybe they're talking about

some new vintage, or God knows what else. Daddy used to say that sometimes clients gave him tips on the market. Maybe it's that.

But Elise knew in her bones it was more. The two men at the end of the bar were up to something. Something conspiratorial.

Something they don't want me to know. Elise shuddered. She looked up and saw her father's portrait.

They're up to something and it has to be about Le Palais-Royal. I'd bet my life on it.

Claude pulled a batch of puff pastry dough from his refrigerator. "Go make pastries, dunce," Papa had said. He smiled. Papa and his old crony the lawyer St. Remy would make short work of Marie-Claire. As he rolled out the cool dough Claude thought of the two of them, scheming by the old iron stove, a bottle of calvados between them. François isn't alone, with Papa nearby. He'll give the boy more attention than I ever could. He'll fill in—Marie-Claire's so lazy she'll be glad to have his help.

The pastry got thinner. Claude envisioned his father meeting François after school, taking him for long walks through the forest, teaching him how to fish, just as he had taught Claude. And for a moment Claude felt a pang of regret that he'd be missing all that. But then the pain was softened by his knowledge that at least the boy would have someone special to love him. Someone fine and wise and good-humored. Someone watching closely. Someone not Marie-Claire.

Somehow, thinking about Marie-Claire made Claude think of Elise. And thinking about Elise stirred a memory. A memory of a dessert named for her.

He left the pastry and went to Pierre's office to look in the recipe book. There it was, and the date of her birthday. Tomorrow! Lucky she's out front, that gives me at least an hour. Quickly he finished shaping his tart bases and set them to bake. Checked to see that he had all of the ingredients, the hazelnuts and all the rest.

Her birthday. She must be—how old? Younger than me. Mid twenties. Hard to tell, she's so slender, so quick. Sometimes she looks like a little girl, and a lost little girl at that. Other times, like this afternoon when I came back, it all changes. Something catches fire inside her and she glows, and then Elise is definitely not a little girl at all.

He smiled and began toasting hazelnuts.

Elise's birthday.

Claude worked like a demon, a highly secretive demon, making the mocha butter cream, the chocolate butter cream, chopping the toasted nuts, whipping up egg whites for the meringue layers. And all the time he thought of her, of her concern this morning, her sympathy, her desire to keep him here at Le Palais. *We*—I need you here.

Claude smiled.

While the meringue layers were baking he had a word with Yves, and to his surprise Yves smiled too, agreed they must create a little surprise. Claude spoke to Steve and Barry as well. The afternoon took on a new momentum. It had a life of its own, a special happy velocity. As Claude put the gâteau together and frosted it lovingly, writing her name in chocolate glaze on top, he knew that Elise had put the magic in his day.

Even when she isn't here I think of her. Even when it seems like madness. Impossible I could ever touch a girl—a woman like that.

He warmed to the thought of her. Felt a tingling that seemed to ripple all through him. A pulsing in his groin that made him vividly aware: the need was quick and urgent.

I want her, he realized with a kind of happy astonishment. Impossible as it is, I do. *Stay away*, said a cautionary voice inside him. *Stay away, she's not for you.*

The voice of caution had no heart, no eyes, no balls.

He examined the finished gâteau.

193

Gâteau Elise. That's taking on something, he thought, trying to duplicate her father's creation. Suppose it's sacred to her? Suppose she thinks it's presumptuous of me? This could be the end of everything—what little there has been between us.

But it was done, it looked fine, and Claude covered it with foil to hide it from her in case she chanced to look in his refrigerator. He closed the door and thought of Elise.

Elise's birthday dawned sunny. She woke after a dreamless sleep, dressed quickly, and went down for coffee. It was only when she looked at the menu Yves posted every day that she realized it was her birthday.

My twenty-fifth birthday and I'm all alone, just like someone in a tacky old song. The sense of abandonment that she'd felt yesterday morning when Claude left came back now, redoubled. The kitchen was empty, but Elise knew she'd feel isolated in the middle of a mob.

Every man I get close to walks out on me. *Chez Margot!*

Jean-Paul came in, grinning like a puppy with secrets. His cheer was contagious. Immediately she stopped moping. They began chatting about the day's specials, about the news from France that Jean-Paul had a baby sister. Well, she thought as she sipped her coffee, Jared never remembered birthdays anyway. And she recalled how hurt she'd been the first time that happened, how she sulked the whole day until he had to ask her what was wrong, and he held her and then disappeared and came back an hour later with an armful of late wildflowers for her because that day they had no money at all. Elise was able to smile at that now. He never remembered his own birthday, either. Let's be fair.

Jean-Paul chatted on, and it dawned on Elise that she was already thinking of Jared in the past tense, as if he were someone long dead and dimly remembered. The sense of relief she felt was astonishing. Like being told she'd just won the lottery.

The morning took on its usual shape; people drifted in on their own private schedules and before long the whole place was humming. Elise knew it by heart now and she enjoyed every minute. And if her contributions were small ones they still counted for something. Now Yves asked her to flute a hundred mushrooms and she merely nodded, secretly pleased that he took it for granted she'd sculpt them to an acceptable Palais-Royal standard. She remembered her first attempts; it seemed ages ago, but it was only a few weeks.

She fluted her mushrooms, trimmed some baby carrots, and transformed fifty perfect lemons into one hundred perfect lemon crowns. The staff lunch was informal as ever and, as usual, she ate quickly, then ran upstairs to shower and change to go out front.

Armand greeted her with his usual silken "Bonjour, mademoiselle."

"Bonjour, Armand," she replied with her best imitation of lightness. You Quisling, she thought, then dismissed the thought as unbecoming. It's perfectly natural for him to want the place, and it's natural for him to get his backing lined up before he approaches us. Really, Armand's been decent to me. Kind, even. But the uneasy feeling wouldn't go away. Elise smiled and greeted people just as Armand did, but all the while she wondered what was going on behind his practiced smile, behind the glass-smooth facade. What's the worst he can do but up the bidding? If it comes right down to it, I'd much rather see Le Palais go to Armand than to Kate's miserable hamburger king.

At half past four that afternoon a florist's deliveryman arrived bearing a huge gardenia plant. The fragrance threatened to overwhelm the kitchen. Elise carried it upstairs before reading the card. As she opened the little white envelope a tiny glimmer of hope crept across her heart: Maybe it's from Jared. Maybe he really does care after all.

Happy birthday dear Elise,

Your real present is waiting at Sixty-eighth Street. Why don't you take the night off soon and we'll celebrate?

Love, Kate.

Beautiful plant. Lovely gesture. Why is my heart on some cosmic elevator ride, down and down and down? Stupid to even dream Jared would send something like this. Jared probably wouldn't know a gardenia if one dropped on his beautiful head.

It was Claude's turn to make the staff supper and less than an hour after the gardenia appeared they sat down to it. A superb hot terrine of chicken and veal and wild mushrooms, all aromatic with thyme and a hint of garlic. With it a white wine and mushroom sauce, rice, bright green broccoli flowerets sauteed with shallots, bread, and a salad.

Praying her attention wasn't too obvious, she watched him carefully. Decided he was pulling himself together nicely. Quiet, but Claude was almost always quiet. His fine dark head and compact body were such a contrast to Jared's bronze-god looks that for an instant Claude seemed almost a stranger.

She found a place at the far end of the table, as far as it was possible to get from where Claude was serving his terrine. I hope he doesn't think I'm avoiding him. But no. Everyone in the kitchen knows my routine by now. They expect me to eat and run, to go out front with Armand.

Elise cleaned her plate and told Claude how fine it had been and went upstairs to change.

Armand, as usual, was studying his reservations book. And smiling to himself. He saw her and held the smile. "I watch, fearfully, for any falling off, mademoiselle, but so far there is none. We're booked up nearly a month in advance."

"Glad to hear it. But it's really the Tastevin banquet we have to worry about, isn't it?"

The smile faded. For the first time she could remember, Elise sensed that Armand was struggling to control himself. He stayed frozen in time, expressionless, like a film that had been stopped cold. She knew he must be well aware of the banquet; after all it had been Armand who was so persuasive that they must honor their commitment to do it. Something's up, there's something to do with that banquet that bothers him, and he's not telling me about it.

He recovered himself quickly. "But of course. That's when we'll be judged by all the people who count. That's the night we must truly astonish them."

People began arriving then and there was no more chance to speak. Dorothy Dutton came in wearing the famous ruby necklace that had belonged to the maharaja of Jaipur, kissed Elise on the cheek, and was shown to her table by Armand.

Within an hour Le Palais was full, and Elise had the familiar sense of excitement at just being a part of it. Armand rejoined her and now they took turns, strolling through the dining rooms at about twenty-minute intervals to see that all was as it should be. They were together at the lectern when a very beautiful young woman stormed past them, not in tears but in a fit of anger that looked incendiary even at a distance.

Elise was alarmed. "Should I go after her, Armand?"

"Non, mademoiselle, it might only make matters worse, and you would not be thanked for it. Sometimes we are witness to very private moments—happy ones often enough, now and then sad. Le Palais is a place for denouements, Mademoiselle Elise. People propose marriage here, end relationships here, using the setting as a sort of bribe, I've often thought—a guarantee that good manners will be maintained whatever the provocation."

"You must have seen a lot in your time."

He frowned. "The book that must never be written. There was a fine moment a few years ago when a very famous political figure was in the back room with his mistress

197

and his wife appeared, unannounced, asking for a table. Fire in her eyes."

"What did you do?"

Armand smiled and Elise realized all over again why he was the best-loved maître d'hôtel in New York.

"Le Palais-Royal, mademoiselle, is fortunate in being equipped with a rear entrance. The distinguished gentleman and his lady were hastened out through the kitchen, down the service stairs and into the alley. Madame Politician was shown in not five minutes later to find only a freshly set table, the seats still warm from guilty passions."

Elise laughed. "You're a hero, Armand."

"I try, mademoiselle. We must spare our guests any discomfort, from whatever source, if that is possible."

The evening seemed to take forever, but Elise was determined she'd see it through until the last Poire had been sipped and the last Havana snuffed out.

I will not quit early and sulk.

Finally the last guests left in a soft cloud of satisfaction. Elise smiled and wished them good night, barely supressing a yawn.

Armand stayed for a moment at his lectern, then made his routine tour of the front of the house, checking the locks on the doors and turning off lights. At last he followed her back through the dining rooms to the kitchen.

Deferentially, he stood aside as she pushed her way through the quilted green leather-covered doors with their round windows. She stepped into the familiar kitchen and blinked.

Pitch dark.

She was alarmed. The fuse must have blown, or the wiring shorted out, and where would they find an electrician at this time of night? Then suddenly there was applause and whistles and laughter. Matches were lit and candles began to glow and two dozen inharmonious voices broke into "Happy Birthday." From the back of the kitchen there erupted the merry pop and hiss of champagne bottles being opened and poured.

Elise hoped Armand, standing right behind her, wouldn't see the tears that were filling her eyes. She blinked fast, praying for control.

The song ended and the lights came up. There on the work island, centered upon an immaculate white cloth and surrounded by pale pink tea roses, was a magnificent cake.

Good God, it's the one Daddy made for me! Gâteau Elise.

Just the sight of it nearly had her in tears again. Only Claude could have done it. Without having to be told, she knew this. He must have come upon one of Daddy's old recipes.

There was one slender candle on the cake. She made a wish and blew it out. More applause. An old superstition, she thought, but I've always believed it. So did Daddy. Why didn't I wish for the success of the restaurant?

Her wish had come to her out of nowhere: that Claude should be happy.

Someone handed her a glass of champagne. There was a general merriment, a clinking of glasses.

"To Mademoiselle Elise!" said Armand, raising his glass.

"To the restaurant—to Le Palais-Royal, and everyone in it," she replied, looking at Claude as she spoke.

Claude was already looking at her—they all were. Elise had a sense of occasion learned from a master, from Pierre Villeromain himself. She remembered vividly how Daddy used to follow through on ceremonious occasions. She went from person to person all around the room, touching glasses and saying something special, something personal to each one, from little Hector the dishwasher to Yves himself.

Finally she came to Claude. Typically, he was in the background, quietly chatting with Jean-Paul.

"Claude—how can I thank you? And how did you learn about the gâteau?"

199

His smile was a shy one, a little boy's smile. "In Pierre's notes—with the date also."

"He made it the first time for my eighth birthday. Invited all my class at school to Le Palais for tea. We felt so grown-up."

"Gâteau Elise," he said softly. "It has a fine sound."

"It has a fine taste too. Daddy couldn't have—"

"Forgive me, but he could. Still, I am pleased if you like it, Elise."

People were beginning to drift away now. It was past one. The glasses were emptied, the remains of the gâteau wrapped in plastic and returned to the refrigerator, plates and forks consigned to the dishwasher. Elise stayed until the last of them had said good night. She poured herself a tall glass of water and stood half leaning against the work island, thinking about all that had happened these last few days. The good and the bad of it.

Twenty-five years old. One quarter of a century. And what have I got to show for it? One broken marriage, one crazy attempt to run this place, a lot of lost sleep, and a tax debt that would sink a battleship.

And for what?

She took another sip of water.

"No one," said a voice from behind her, "should be unhappy on her birthday."

She turned. Startled, even though the voice was a familiar one. There stood Claude—Claude transformed. In his street clothes again and looking vulnerable as any teenager. Jeans and a turtleneck again, like yesterday. But very different from the sorrowful Claude of yesterday. He carried a small box wrapped in shiny foil.

"For you, Elise," he said shyly as he handed it to her. "I could not—in front of the others."

Whatever it is, it's precious, she thought, holding out her hand. She remembered her silliness yesterday when she handed him one egg. How shy she'd felt then, as though the egg itself had some special meaning. Now this.

The shadowed kitchen seemed cool all of a sudden, and Claude, the only warmth in it. The only warmth anywhere.

"Claude, really! After making the gâteau—and I'll bet you organized the whole thing." She began to unwrap the package. The foil was kitchen foil and the object inside was nestled in several layers of baker's parchment.

"I had—not the time to find proper gift paper," he said anxiously.

Inside the parchment was a small antique crystal bud vase, a thick cylinder about six inches tall, deeply engraved with scrolls and swags of tiny flowers.

"Oh, Claude, how lovely! It must be very old."

The smile flickered on his lips.

"It belonged to my mother." He paused. "And also to her mother, I think."

"But Claude, it's much too precious . . . You're very kind, but I couldn't."

He looked at her, and in his eyes she saw an expression of wariness. A forest animal surprised. A deer. She could sense how much he wanted—needed—her to have the vase. How important it must be to him, beyond any value the vase itself might have. He's such a mixture of boy and man.

"I would be honored for you to have it, Elise."

A smile began to form on his lips as he saw that she would accept his offering.

Elise took it, looked at it closely, turned it so the carving caught the light. She knew in that instant that something more than a fine piece of old glass had passed between them. Still on the work island was the vase of pink tea roses from the party. Elise took one and found a knife to trim its stem; poured water from her own glass into the little vase and put the rose in it. Set it down and stepped back a little to scrutinize the result.

"There. It's perfect."

Then she went to Claude and kissed him. She felt he might be too shy to come to her.

But now he wasn't shy at all.

It started as an almost sisterly kiss, just the lightest touch of her lips on his. She felt herself lingering in the kiss. Nice place to be. Felt his arms embracing her. Tightening. Felt the warmth of his body and the thrust of his tongue.

Felt herself responding, her hands moving on his neck. And his hands, caressing her.

Finally she broke from the kiss with a sense of wonderful discovery; looking up at him. She smiled. Claude's arms remained around her and he showed no sign at all of wanting them anywhere else.

"Come," she said softly, and took his hand, holding the vase in her other hand. And she led him up the stairs.

Inside the apartment she turned on the little lamp on her bedside table and set the vase down beside it. Claude was at her side. Silent. He took her into his arms again and this time there was no hesitation at all. He said her name, and it seemed to Elise she had never heard the word before. It came to her as a gift.

"Elise." His statement of wonder.

And he kissed her.

*"Elise."*

He came to her like a starved man. Quickly, as if by some unspoken mutual signal, they undressed. And once more he took her into his arms and said her name. The little bedside lamp cast a soft amber glow. Elise felt his body and hers, smoothness and fire. She had already responded to the man. Now she responded to his need for her, eagerly and generously, and soon she found that his need was hers, one and inseparable.

They couldn't get enough of each other. Minutes passed. Hours. Finally they lay panting, entwined side by side, and Elise could feel the warmth of him all the length of her body. A fine warmth it was, strong and gentle at the same time.

Claude brushed his fingers across her lips, lightly as a butterfly's wing. "Happy birthday," he whispered, not knowing if she was awake.

"The happiest I ever had, thanks to you," she said, kissing his lips, his throat, traveling the length of him, kissing.

Dawn found them together, Elise sleeping in his arms with a serene half smile on her face. She woke and looked up at him, and her smile widened.

"You're sleeping with an older woman, Claude. This is my twenty-sixth year."

He kissed her and it began all over again.

They made love and didn't notice when a ray of sunlight slid through the shutters and found the old crystal vase, which caught the sunbeam and held it and refracted it into a thousand crystal rainbows. Later, as they dressed, she looked at Claude with an expression somewhere between pleading and reverence.

"Don't ever leave me," she said.

# 12

DAVE OPENED THE door of the top secret test kitchen. He loved the place, crazy as that might seem to a stranger, had helped design it. Deep in the heart of the building, it was deliberately windowless for security reasons, spacious and perfectly vented, gleaming with stainless steel and white tile.

If today's tasting goes as well as yesterday's, we're nearly there. A big nearly, maybe, but progress all the same. The world's first real frozen hollandaise! Dave walked briskly through the main kitchen, nodding and smiling at the technicians who worked there, testing and tasting on-line products that Hollander Industries was already marketing.

Beyond the big kitchen was a smaller one. Not much bigger than the kitchen in a large house, it was equipped with everything a master chef could wish for. Dave knew that well, because he'd gone over the lists of implements and accessories himself, working with Gérard Rideau, the chef he'd hired just for this project. And there was Rideau, stirring something in a copper saucepan. A good choice if I do say so myself, Dave thought, watching him work. Not Pierre, but that would be asking for miracles.

"How's it going, Gérard?"

Rideau looked up and smiled.

"Come, Mr. Hollander, and taste for yourself."

Dave could feel the quiet pride in Gérard's voice. On the butcher block counter was a big electric warming tray. On the tray were three small copper saucepans. Dave already knew what was in them. Gérard had been experimenting with variations on the classic sauce hollandaise for over a month now. One saucepan would hold the basic hollandaise, another the orange-flavored sauce maltaise, and the third a variation spiked with dill that Gérard thought would go well with fish.

A freshly baked loaf of French bread lay near the warmer to cleanse the mouth of anyone who tasted all three sauces in succession. But Dave bypassed the bread and simply did what he'd seen many a chef do: he stuck in his forefinger and licked it off. The hollandaise was just the right temperature. Hot but not too hot. He felt the freshness of the lemon flowering on his tongue, felt the smoothness of the sauce's texture caressing him. This is one very sexy little sauce, damn it. I may not be the world's biggest gourmet, but I'll match this against anyone's hollandaise. Even Pierre's.

Dave turned to Gérard, bowed in a good imitation of a French diplomat's bow and said, simply, "Congratulations, Gérard."

Gérard beamed.

"Now," he said, "comes the bad news."

If he'd kicked Dave in the gut it couldn't have been more of a shock. What could be bad? He managed a grin. "You had it sent in from Le Palais-Royal?"

"Not that bad, Mr. Hollander. But I think the dill sauce doesn't really work the way it ought to. I think we should suggest—as another variation—that they add their own fresh dill. Not too much to ask, do you agree?"

"Sure I agree," Dave said. The relief he felt was so great it frightened him. I'm really on the edge with this one, he realized, knowing it too well and not knowing what in the world to do about it. "People love to do things like that. Gives them more of a sense of having made it themselves."

The kitchen door opened and Timmy walked in.

Dave looked at his son and gave him a friendly nod, consciously trying to control the pleasure he felt in Tim's presence here, now, just at the moment of their first breakthrough.

"Am I late?"

"Just on time. And wait'll you taste it." Dave watched while Timmy tasted all three. He took a little piece of bread after each, turned to Gérard at last and said, "Fantastic! I think you've got it. Maybe the dill sauce is a little bland, but the others are great. Really great."

"Our sentiments precisely, Tim," said Dave, pleased that the boy was developing a palate. At his age I didn't know things like hollandaise existed. "We're going to forget the dill. Suggest they add it fresh, just before serving."

"Dad, have you let DeWitt taste these?"

"Not yet. But I'd sure like to get his blessing." Yes, and I'd like to get DeWitt back on my team again, like in the old days. I'd like to find a way to make him stop dancing all around this project and get his full weight behind it, instead of the bobbing and feinting he's doing these days. Dave couldn't shake the feeling that his old friend was psyching himself up to sell Dave down the river, if it came to a showdown. All the same, he reached for the phone.

Ten minutes later Steele came into the kitchen. "Well," he said, rubbing his hands together in a parody of anticipation, "You guys look like the cats that ate the canaries."

"We've made a breakthrough, DeWitt. And I wanted you to be the first to taste it."

Steele walked up to the warmer, broke off a piece of bread, and dipped it into the hollandaise. Gérard cringed but said nothing. Steele tasted, chewing contemplatively.

How much of my future is in that guy's mouth right now? Dave knew that the chairman couldn't stop the project now, but he did have the power to influence the board negatively, to prevent the gourmet line from going national.

"Well I'm just a country boy," said DeWitt at last, the same DeWitt whose schools included Choate, Princeton, and Harvard Business School, "But it tastes pretty damn fine to me. I wonder, though. Are we bullshitting ourselves? I mean, Dave, will it really play in Peoria? Maybe we should scrap the whole thing and get into tacos. Tex-Mex is big right now."

Dave fought the anger and didn't quite win. "And so were Hula-Hoops big, DeWitt. This stuff is eternal. This line has about four hundred years of history going for it. It isn't some trendy fad."

DeWitt laughed a humorless little laugh. "Just joking Dave, only a small witticism. I think the sauce is fine. But these are lab conditions. Gérard, with all due respect, isn't Mrs. Peoria. How will it taste to her?"

Dave smiled for real now. An idea was forming and he knew it was a good one. "Funny you should ask, DeWitt. I've been planning—plotting is what it really amounts to—a small dinner at my place, to try and convince the Villeromain girl we're on the up and up. I've already got her stepmother's agreement—orally, anyhow—to sell her half interest in Le Palais-Royal. But the daughter's sticking. She thinks we're going to turn the place into some kind of an upscale Billy Burger."

Steele laughed. "Are you?"

"No, DeWitt, a massage parlor. What do you think, for God's sake? It gives us instant credibility. A priceless name. At four million it's a bargain. I don't know how much we'd have to spend in advertising to equal the value of the name alone."

"If you say so. Tim, how many Billys could we open for four mil?"

"Sixteen to twenty, depending on the price of the lot."

"Eighteen, let's call it. And after the first year each one of them might bring in, conservatively, a net profit of about fifty thousand?"

"With luck, fifty," said Timmy. "Some of them are only bringing twenty or so these days. Some less."

As well you know, thought Dave.

"DeWitt, we've been over all this," Dave said quietly. "Nobody's ever going to be a bigger fan of Billy Burger than his old dad here. But we can't have all our eggs in that particular basket. Billy's fine, but Billy's the past. If we're going to have a real future we've damn well got to diversify. But you know that."

"I know it. The board knows it. I just wish I felt about it the way you guys do."

"Maybe my dinner will convince you, and Elise Villeromain as well." Dave said. "I hadn't fixed a date, but let's do that. How about next Sunday? Has to be a Sunday, because the restaurant's closed then. My place at the Carlyle, drinks at eight?"

Steel whipped out a slim gold-edged agenda. Flicked pages, made a note with a thin gold pencil. "Looks fine by me, David."

"Great. I'll confirm the others and get back to you. Can you make it, Gérard?"

"Oh, yes. Definitely, and with pleasure."

"Let me get on the horn then, and see if the others are willing." Dave left the test kitchen with a sense of uneasiness, a feeling that maybe DeWitt Steele wasn't quite leveling with him. Well, who said it was going to be easy?

Only in the privacy of his office did Dave let himself think of Kate, of how badly he'd screwed up with her— Dave Hollander, to whom so many things in life had come easily, inevitably. Well, he thought, the game definitely isn't over. Not for me and not for her. He dialed her number, wondering if she'd have anything more to do with him after that lunch. Not that it had been a real disaster. But they'd been on pretty thin ice for a while there, and both of them knew it.

He hadn't seen Kate since, or dared to contact her. Let it cool down a bit, play it easy. Now just the sound of her voice answering the phone made him feel about sixteen again. Sixteen and decidedly horny. Forcing himself into some semblance of control, Dave outlined his plan, the reason for the party, the importance of having both Kate and Elise there.

To his astonishment and relief, she agreed.

"Dave, that's a fine idea. I wish I could guarantee Elise, but that child is unguaranteeable. Since our lunch, I've had two more incidents with her. She isn't a bad girl, mind you, just . . . just very fragile right now."

"I can understand that. I mean, think what she's been through. It can't be easy, trying to take on Le Palais-Royal."

"That's just what I fear, Dave. That it may be impossible. That she may get hurt."

"Kate, let me talk to her. God knows what I'll say, but if persuasion will do it, I'll be persuasive. Sunday at eight, my apartment in the Carlyle. Black tie."

"It sounds wonderful Dave. Frankly, I'm fascinated to try your new inventions."

"I hope you'll find them fascinating after you've tasted them. Not a word about that to Elise, though. I want to surprise her."

"Good luck, then, Dave. I look forward to Sunday."

Dave hung up and replayed the conversation in his head. Perfectly fine, absolutely cordial, even maybe a little more than that. Or am I imagining things? Reading in meanings that aren't there? Well, at least Kate had agreed to come. It would have been the easiest thing in the world for her to make some excuse—or to simply refuse, period.

He reached for the phone again, to call Elise, but stopped. Better in person. Twenty minutes later he was climbing the front steps of Le Palais-Royal. Would she be there? He rang the little ivory-colored bell.

Elise herself opened the door.

"Hi, Mr. Hollander. Can I help you?"

Could she? Elise's voice was level, businesslike. Dave smiled, feeling the effort. Hoping it didn't show.

209

"Elise, I came to invite you to dinner, you and a friend. My place, twenty-sixth floor of the Carlyle, eight o'clock next Sunday. Your stepmother will be there, and just a few other people."

"I—I really don't go out much these days, Mr. Hollander. We're terribly busy right now, and—"

"I know that. And I do understand. And you can be sure I have an ulterior motive. I want to convince you, the only way I know how, that I'm really not the monster you imagine me to be. I promise not to serve hamburgers."

To Dave's astonishment, Elise smiled; a big, happy, and apparently completely genuine smile.

"Mr. Hollander, guess what? I'd love to come. I've been horrible to you, really horrible to Kate, and if this is a chance to make peace, then I'd really like to do it. May I bring Claude Montgeron?"

"Elise, you could bring Vlad the Impaler. This makes me very happy. I don't know Claude, but I hear sensational things about him. Please do bring him."

Elise smiled again and Dave thought how very charming she could be when the tension went out of that almost too slender face. When the big dark eyes took on a touch of merriment. Something he hadn't expected in Elise Villeromain, a young lady of surprises. Well, let there be a few more pleasant ones.

"I'll see you around eight, then," he said.

"Eight it is. And . . . thank you."

"My pleasure," Dave said, automatically. Wondering if by some miracle it would be.

Dave turned, walked down the stairs, and headed to the Carlyle.

All of a sudden he felt very tired.

The first person Dave spoke to the next morning was Gérard Rideau.

"Expense is no object, Gérard. If you want to serve Petrus, go right ahead. Or any other damn thing, just so long as it shows off our creations. What I want to do is to impress the Villeromain girl. And she's bringing Montgeron, one of their top chefs, and he may be the most critical of all."

Gérard only smiled.

"A challenge. Très bon!"

Dave smiled too. It can happen. It must.

"I will have some menu proposals for you this afternoon, Mr. Hollander," said Rideau as they parted.

Dave went back to his office and thought about Kate, wondering if there was something more he could do, something—anything—that would make up for his stupid rashness during their luncheon.

Take it slow, ease into it, don't frighten her off. He smiled to himself. Sounded like a formula for taming some wild animal. Kate was anything but wild. There was a fineness to her, a quality of gentle confidence that seemed to Dave almost royal. Just being near Kate Villeromain threw him into a state of preadolescent confusion. A bull in a china shop was balletic by comparison.

But maybe it was an illusion, all wrapped up somehow in his desire to own Le Palais-Royal. Dave knew he couldn't force it, couldn't make it happen if it wasn't meant to happen. And for a man as used as Dave was to having what he wanted when he wanted it, this was maddening. Kate filled his thoughts and filled his heart in a way he had never imagined a woman could do again. Kate's mere existence had forced Dave to come to grips with the empty shell of his own marriage.

He knew that, whatever might come of his interest in Kate, it was cruel and even dishonorable not to face the fact that there was nothing left between him and Barbara except their shared love of Timmy. And if his life had depended on it, Dave couldn't have said how or when, or even why his love for Barbara had turned into the dry husk it was. There had been so much, once. So much closeness, such an intuitive rapport, a passion that seemed like forever.

He sighed, and wondered if anything remotely like that would touch his heart again.

That afternoon Gérard presented Dave with a variety of possible dinner menus and a new, sensational, wild mushroom sauce.

Dave tasted the sauce. Rich, glossy brown, and studded with chanterelles, the wild forest mushrooms of France, it would glorify a steak, turn an ordinary roast chicken into something immortal.

"Bravo, Gérard. How long has it been frozen?"

"Nearly a week."

"Let's definitely have this on Sunday."

"Très bien. I propose starting with poached trout or baby salmon, with our hollandaise. Then a simple flattened, grilled veal chop, a fine vehicle for this mushroom sauce. Vegetables. A salad. Then a dessert made with our frozen puff pastry." He paused. "A pear tart, I think."

Dave smiled, imagining it. "I like that a lot, Gérard. Is there any way you could work in the sauce béchamel? In the long run, that'll be one of our best-sellers. At least, it ought to be."

Gérard pondered.

"With the veal chop, something green. Vividly green. A puree of broccoli or possibly watercress. We could use some of the béchamel for that—very subtly, of course, just for cohesion. But still, it would be there."

"Do it. How about wines?"

"To begin with, for the fish, a Traminer. Hugel would be my choice, just a bit spicy, excellent wine. With the veal, a Bordeaux, perhaps Cheval Blanc, but I'll have to go shopping. Champagne with dessert and as an aperitif as well. I will make little cocktail hors d'oeuvres, something based on that puff pastry."

"That sounds splendid, Gerard. Pierre's favorite champagne was Laurent-Perrier Grand Siècle. It might be tactful to have that."

"Tactful and a superb choice. I'll go shopping this afternoon, and get back to you. And we'll do a trial of the whole dinner before Sunday."

Dave smiled and left the test kitchen thinking that even if some unforseeable disaster prevented him from buying Le Palais-Royal, the new gourmet line could still be a success. But it would be so much easier, so much more elegant, if the restaurant's legendary ambience were a part of it.

Every time he thought of the restaurant, which was often, Dave thought of Kate; how she haunted his dreams, how his need for her seemed to grow, even though he knew nothing might ever come of it. Kate!

Back in his office, Dave began sketching seating arrangements. In all of them, he was at one end of his oval dining table, and Kate at the other. The illusion of a relationship, a mockery of his hope? He put aside the paper and called the Carlyle to arrange for flowers, for a waiter to help with cocktails on Sunday and to serve at table.

Would Sunday ever come?

Dave felt the urgency of it like a physical ache. It must go right. He must convince Elise that Le Palais-Royal would be in good hands if she sold to him.

It'll be perfect. Has to be.

Sunday was four days away. Could he get through those four days without going out of his mind? All his life, Dave had taken pleasure in organizing the details that made his ideas come alive. It might be a big tomato canning plant in the San Fernando valley, or the architect's proposals for every last square inch of the Billy Burger restaurants.

He threw himself into the planning of his dinner party with the determination of a general planning a major invasion of some very hostile land. He had to restrain himself from becoming an irritant to Gérard. Dave knew that his chef was one of the most accomplished to be found anywhere: hadn't he searched for months before finding Gérard?

Then there was DeWitt. Friend or foe? Dave had worked

213

with the man for years. Now he realized how little he knew him. DeWitt had been widowed—how long? A few years, surely. Hadn't mentioned bringing a guest. Dave picked up the phone and asked him.

"No, David. I'll come alone. Wouldn't miss it for anything."

"I look forward to seeing you, DeWitt."

Dave put down the receiver, trying to measure the distance that had sprung up between him and Steele these last few weeks. When had it started? Why hadn't he noticed? Would DeWitt sell him out to the board, just to save his own aristocratic neck? No easy answers to that. Or to anything.

Sunday came at him by inches. Gérard's trial run at luncheon on Friday went off flawlessly. Dave loved every magnificent bite of it, then found himself worrying whether it hadn't somehow been too perfect. Maybe, he thought, we're using up our good luck. Even knowing the foolishness of his doubts didn't stop them from coming.

On Friday night he had the dream again, the nightmare of being forced to watch as his name was cut off the cornerstone of the Hollander Industries building. Woke up sweating, as he always did when the dream came, sweating and taut as a bowstring and cursing his own stupidity.

He lay in the dark room trying to force himself to relax; deep breaths, concentration, fighting the damn frustration. At six fifteen Dave got up, pulled on a sweat suit and running shoes, and headed for the park. Eight times around the lake and he began to feel human again. Tired, but definitely human.

Home, shower, plan the day. Cramming it full. Two movies Timmy had told him not to miss, a much needed visit to his tailor, the new Impressionist show at the Met, lunch from a hot dog vendor by the park, a walking tour through SoHo looking at galleries filled with artwork he didn't understand. Down to the South Street Seaport, feeling weirdly like a tourist. Caught a glimpse of the Brooklyn Bridge, decided to walk over it, something he'd never done.

Dave stood near the tower of the bridge, on the Brooklyn side, feeling a good kind of tired, rubbernecking up at the soaring Gothic pointed arches, looking out over the glittering, near empty harbor, past Liberty to the Verrazano Bridge, the sea, infinity.

He walked down the stairs at the end of the bridge. Remembered the new restaurant someone had told him about; found his way past the old arch-windowed warehouses to One Main, had a beer, checked out the view. Spectacular. Taxi home. Legs burning a little. When had he last taken a whole day, all on his own, not doing a single deal, using every last ounce of willpower to force himself not to think about Hollander Industries or DeWitt Steele or tomorrow's dinner party? Or Kate.

As the taxi drove back over the Brooklyn Bridge and up the FDR Drive, Dave found himself wondering where she was right now. Doing what, and with whom? Useless even to speculate, which didn't stop Dave from speculating.

Sunday. Coffee and the *Times*. The table was set for tonight, flowers perfectly arranged, all done by the almost supernaturally competent staff of the Carlyle.

Gérard arrived in mid afternoon with three bulging shopping bags. The sauces and puff pastry had been in Dave's freezer since Friday. Half an hour after Gérard's arrival the kitchen was organized to the chef's taste, sauces thawing gently in warm water, veal chops flattened and ready for the grill, the trout cleaned and waiting for their brief, last minute poaching.

Dave showered, dressed, fumbling, as always, with his black silk bow tie. At seven thirty the doorbell rang and Dave was pleased to see Edward, his favorite of all the Carlyle waiters: tall, black, and unflappable. Edward spoke with the velvet lilt of Barbados. All was in order. Dave paced the big living room, wishing he believed in prayer.

215

From the kitchen came a faint but tantalizing aroma. Hors d'oeuvres baking. The Laurent-Perrier was chilling in a silver ice bucket, glasses set out in glittering formations, a few dishes of toasted pecans. Dave looked at his spectacular view.

After what seemed like hours, the doorbell rang again. Kate stood there, looking magnificent. Dave wanted more than anything to take her in his arms and kiss her thoroughly. Instead, he smiled and extended his hand, which she took graciously.

"You look wonderful, Kate." As he spoke the words, Dave wondered if they were excessive. Hell, no more than the truth. She walked into the big living room, admired the room, the view. Feeling like a schoolboy, Dave showed her the layout: the dining room, the two bathrooms. He stopped short of the bedrooms.

As he twisted the wire off the cork of the champagne, Kate said, almost to herself, "I am truly amazed that Elise agreed to come. Maybe she's growing up after all."

Dave looked at her. Beautiful when pensive, irresistible when smiling. Damn!

"She was actually pleasant, Kate, when I asked her. I went in person. I was afraid she'd hang up on me if I phoned."

That made her laugh, and Dave felt a small surge of hope. But before Dave had a chance to build on that, the doorbell rang again. Edward got it, ushered in Timmy and one of the best-looking girls Dave had ever seen, tall and olive-skinned with lustrous dark hair and brown eyes you could drown in. She might have been a Medici princess.

"Flavia," said Tim, "meet my father. Dad, this is Flavia Montebrunello."

There were smiles and handshakes. Kate joined them and Dave poured more wine. Their talk was easy, the girl confident and charming. She was studying art restoration at the Metropolitan Museum.

It was beginning to seem like a real party. Dave knew—

should never have doubted—that Kate would hold up her end of the social duties, come what might. It was Elise who frightened him now, and the chef she was bringing. And the enigma known as DeWitt Steele.

Almost in the instant that Dave thought of DeWitt, he appeared. In his bespoke dinner clothes DeWitt looked both elegant and, to Dave's eyes, just slightly sinister. But his manners were as finely cut as the cloth on his back, and DeWitt fit in perfectly, chatting amiably with Kate and Flavia, complimenting Dave on the wine, accepting the delicious little puff pastry tarts filled with melted chevre and walnuts as Edward passed them on an octagonal silver tray. Dave knew it was useless to keep thinking of DeWitt as the enemy. But the events of the last few weeks had demonstrated too clearly that the man was not climbing out on any limbs to be a friend.

Dave watched as Steele ate, with obvious pleasure, one of the little pastry tarts. Could he suspect that the puff pastry was straight from Délices du Palais-Royal? Dave glanced at the old French clock on the mantel. Nearly eight thirty. Would Elise be capable of simply not coming?

Kate seemed to sense his mood.

"Dave, don't worry if Elise is a little late. She often is. I think it's a reaction against her father's militant punctuality."

A few minutes later Elise and Claude arrived, Elise in a street-length dress of navy silk and Claude in a dark blue suit. Dave instantly regretted making the invitation black tie. What did it matter, really? The food would be as good if they were all in blue jeans.

Dave was almost shocked by the social effort Elise made. She kissed her stepmother charmingly, shook hands all round, accepted a glass of Laurent-Perrier, and seemed to be the very picture of diplomacy.

Dave smelled a rat.

But maybe not. Maybe she had turned over some new leaf. Certainly, Elise was most attentive to young

Montgeron—which made Dave wonder where her handsome husband might be.

Edward came in with a replenished tray of cheese tarts. Dave felt his breath stop as he watched Elise eat one. She smiled. "Claude, you have to taste these," she said, taking another and popping it into his mouth: "Maybe we can steal the idea for Le Palais."

Score one for Billy Burger, Dave thought. Still, this was only the beginning. Anything and everything could still go wrong.

Dave felt a hundred subtle tensions. Maybe imaginary. Maybe not. He looked around the living room. There was Kate, apparently engrossed in conversation with DeWitt Steele. She could melt rocks with her charm if she wanted to, he thought, hoping and praying she'd want to. Timmy and Flavia were chatting happily with Claude and Elise. Everything that could go right seemed to be going right.

Why, then, this terrible sinking feeling in his gut? Dave went to join them.

They were just finishing the second round of champagne when Edward came in to announce dinner.

The dining table was oval, napped in pale salmon, lit by tall ivory candles in crystal holders and ornamented by a low arrangement of rubrum lillies and white phlox. Dave had checked the table at least six times this afternoon. Every time, it had been perfect. Now, feeling like a traitor to Gérard, he checked it again. Perfect again.

They sat down and Edward came in to pour the Traminer. The seating arrangement looked better in real life than it had on paper: Kate at the opposite head of the oval, flanked by Steele and Montgeron, Elise on Dave's right—guest of honor or mortal enemy?—and Flavia on his left. And Timmy—there was no avoiding the imbalance—between Claude and Elise.

For one crazy moment Dave had a vision of Tim getting together with Elise. Fat chance. But they were amiable with each other.

In came Edward with the trout. Gérard had glazed the fish lightly with hollandaise, then dusted the sauce with parsley minced so finely it was like a green powder. Edward passed more sauce in a sauceboat and Dave was pleased to see that everyone took some.

He tasted the sauce, trying to act like a host at a dinner party, not like a man whose entire future might depend on the reaction of Elise Villeromain to the damn hollandaise. The lemony smoothness filled Dave's tongue. It tasted exquisite to him. But what would Elise taste? Or Claude? Or DeWitt?

He turned to Elise.

"I'm really glad you could come, Elise."

"My pleasure, and Claude's. You know how it is in the restaurant business: we never have a moment to behave like normal people. This is fun, Mr. Hollander."

"Can I persuade you to call me Dave?"

She smiled, just a glimmering. "You can persuade me to do just about anything, Dave—anything but sell you my restaurant." Her tone was friendly but there was no mistaking the steel underneath it.

"How's it going, your apprenticeship?"

"It's murder. I've got so much to learn. But thank God for Claude, and Armand."

The fish plates were taken away and Dave noticed that they were clean. A small indication, maybe, but a good one. Score two for Billy Burger.

Edward poured a taste of the Bordeaux for Dave's approval. Château Haut-Brion 1967. Magnificent. Smooth as old satin and with an enticing hint of violets in the bouquet. For an instant Dave wondered if any entrée, however good, could live up to the legendary wine.

In came the veal chops, looking exquisite. Each plate held one flattened chop, the marks of the grill making perfect black treillage patterns on the pale meat, the wild mushroom sauce glistening and Gerard's puree of watercress making an intensely green contrast, set off by a small portion of fluffy wild rice, a sprig of fresh watercress garnishing the puree, and a lemon half cut into a crown. Just the way they do 'em at Le Palais-Royal, Dave noticed.

Dave had feared disaster, but as the meal spun out in course after magnificent course he slowly came to believe that nothing like that was going to happen, that his guests were actually enjoying themselves, each other—and especially the food. He looked at Kate, gracing the other end of his table, and wondered if it was too much to hope that, one day, she could take that place forever.

The entrée plates were whisked away. Edward poured more Laurent-Perrier, then brought in individual pear tarts encased in puff pastry so light it seemed ready to float off the plate.

Now.

Dave tapped his wineglass with a spoon. He stood and lifted his glass. Edward, on cue, led in Gérard, splendid in his chef's whites, a little shy.

"I'd like to toast our chef, Gérard Rideau," Dave said, "the author of our experiment here tonight. It was wonderful, Gérard. Thank you." All the men stood, Raising their glasses. Applause. Gérard merely smiled, bowed, said thank you, and left the room.

Elise turned to him.

"Dave, it certainly was delicious. But what's the experiment?"

He smiled.

"Do you remember, a few weeks ago, when I mentioned that Hollander Industries is developing a line of frozen gourmet foods?"

"Vividly. I made such a fool of myself."

"Not a bit. I probably came on too strong. Anyway, we've been eating the prototypes. The puff pastry was frozen. The hollandaise, frozen."

Dave paused, looked up. Without intending to, he'd captured the attention of the entire table. No one was talking.

Claude, in particular, was watching him with fascination. Dave smiled and went on.

"The mushroom sauce was frozen, and so was the béchamel that went into the watercress puree."

Elise laughed. "I'll be damned. Well, Dave, you sure fooled me."

Then DeWitt spoke up, a glint of mischief in his eyes. "Now, folks," he said, "let's not be polite. We really want your true opinions. There is a lot riding on this project and we have some of the finest palates in New York right in this room. Claude, would you serve that puff pastry at Le Palais-Royal?"

Dave felt like strangling DeWitt with his bare hands.

There was a pause that seemed to last months.

Claude smiled. "Absolutement. In fact, I frequently do."

Another silence, even more resounding.

"I don't understand, Claude." DeWitt's voice had taken on an edge, like some prosecuting attorney questioning an obvious perjuror. "You couldn't serve this pastry. It doesn't exist yet—on the market, that is."

But Claude was impervious to goading.

"Well, no, not as you say literally. I use my own puff pastry, frozen. If there is some left over, it freezes perfectly. No difference. Gérard's was beautifully made. I would serve it proudly, Mr. Steele."

Dave felt like dancing on the table.

Steele's eyebrows were doing a peculiar little dance of their own invention, up and down in either surprise or indignation. Maybe both. But Claude hadn't finished.

"As for the sauces," he went on, "I am truly astonished. Never had I heard of freezing hollandaise—yet it was excellent. And the champignon—the mushroom sauce—it was very fine as well. Béchamel, of course, we all freeze. I think, Mr. Hollander, that you are on to something. Something delicious."

Dave could have hugged the man.

"Thank you, Claude. I couldn't ask for higher praise—except, perhaps, from Pierre himself."

Coffee was served in the living room. Edward poured, then offered after-dinner drinks. Only DeWitt asked for a cognac. The talk was easy. Gérard's wonderful food had mellowed everybody, the superb wines had relaxed them, and the surprise had delighted them.

It should have been a triumph.

But Dave felt hollow inside. He sensed he'd never feel quite complete again unless Kate were truly a part of his life. Yet he knew he couldn't approach her. Not yet. How long it might be, before she felt sufficiently at ease with him, with her grief for Pierre, Dave had no idea. What he did know was that he wouldn't give up on her until she forced him to.

DeWitt was the first to leave. "School day tomorrow," he said cheerily, shaking hands all round, thanking Dave profusely. A little too profusely? "Very cleverly done, Dave."

Was there something hidden there, Dave wondered? Some subtle put-down? To hell with DeWitt.

Elise and Claude left a few moments later, taking Kate with them. "We enjoyed it very much, Dave," Elise said as she shook hands in the foyer. "Thank you for asking us."

"And I thank you, Mr. Hollander," said Claude.

"Thanks, Dave," was Kate's good-bye as she stepped into the elevator.

But no thanks? Don't call me—I'll call you? Dave turned and went back into his apartment to Timmy and Flavia, who were getting their coats.

"Dad, you got him, right between the eyes."

Dave managed a laugh. "Let's hope so. Thanks for coming, Tim, and for bringing this lovely lady."

Then they were gone. Dave felt entirely alone even though Gérard and Edward were still there, cleaning up. He went to his bedroom and wrote two checks and sealed them in envelopes: a generous tip for Edward and a thousand-dollar bonus for Gérard. He thanked each of them separately and discreetly presented the envelopes.

Gérard left, soon followed by Edward.

Dave wandered back into the big living room. It seemed so very empty without her.

There was still a half full bottle of Laurent-Perrier in the ice bucket. Dave poured himself a glass and walked to the tall French windows, stepping out onto the little balcony. The chill night air braced him.

He lifted his glass—to what?

To the confounding of DeWitt Steele? The persuasion of Elise? But she hadn't really been persuaded, only polite.

To Le Palais-Royal, then. At least he had half of it—or soon would.

Manhattan spread out before him, its billions of lights framed darkly by the East and Hudson rivers. Dave's balcony faced south. His view took in the towers of midtown, the more distant, taller pinnacles of the financial district, and beyond, past the bridges strung with lights to the sea.

Everything tonight had gone the way he'd dreamed it might. By any measure a great success. Why, then, didn't he feel better?

Dave knew the answer. He knew he would never feel quite complete again unless Kate was at his side to share things with him.

# 13

ARMAND HANDED ELISE the paper. She forced herself to make a show of studying what was written there. Trying to mask her anger. *God, they both know how much I want to be a part of Le Palais. They know how hard I work. That it's already cost me Jared. And they couldn't even let me in on planning the Tastevin menu!*

The list of wines and courses swam in front of her eyes. It might just as well have been posted over a McDonald's counter. Or Billy Burger. Elise couldn't make sense of the menu. She heard Armand's soothing words. *He treats me like a child. Well, buddy, I am definitely not a child and maybe it's time you and Yves found that out.*

"Yves and I discussed it last night, Mademoiselle Elise," Armand said blandly, "but since Reverend Romney will be coming in this afternoon, naturally we want you to be there when we present our suggestions to him."

"Naturally," said Elise softly, taking a small measure of pride in her control, that she'd managed to keep herself from telling him off. "And Claude as well, surely."

*Can Armand have any sense at all of what he's doing to me by acting this way? Could he think he's being clever?*

There was the slightest hesitation before Armand answered. "If you wish, certainly."

Elise folded the menu and slipped it into the pocket of her jeans. "What time is he coming, Armand?"

"Three."

"I look forward to meeting him."

Elise watched as a smile formed on Armand's lips. The anger was burning inside her. She turned and walked back to the kitchen, controlling every step, forcing herself not to run, not to kick over a chair, not to start breaking things. Maybe I'm being unfair to Armand. He's practically given his life to this place. Maybe he's entitled to resent me. To think I'm just some silly kid playing at the restaurant business.

She went back into the kitchen and quietly asked Claude to join her upstairs, taking care to make it look casual. Conscious all the time that Yves was around somewhere.

In the apartment she sat on the bed. Pulled out the menu, seeing it clearly for the first time. Handed it to Claude.

"Armand just presented me with this. It's Yves's ideas for the Tastevin menu."

Claude sat down next to her. Put an arm around her. Immediately Elise felt a little better; more confident. Together they studied the menu.

*Haricots aux Foie Gras, Truffle Vinaigrette*
*Montrachet*

*Mousse de Truite Chaud, Sauce Béarnaise*
*Mersault Les Perrières*
*Le Sorbet de Tomate*
*Veau Orloff*
*Château Margaux 1900*
*Filet de Boeuf Villeromain*
*Le Richebourg*
*Les Légumes*
*Le Fromages*
*Riz à la Impératrice, Sauce Framboise*
*Château d'Yquem*

225

Claude laughed. "Surely he is not serious?"

Elise felt the relief building inside her. Thank God Claude agrees. I wasn't imagining all that. Every cliché in the recipe book. That isn't dining, it's gluttony.

"I'm afraid they're both serious, Claude. It's a bit much, isn't it?"

"We shall have to call the ambulances, Elise, if anyone actually eats all this. Beans and foie gras—that fad was over five years ago. And veal orloff: it will smother that famous Margaux."

"What would you suggest?"

She watched him thinking, reviewing ideas in his head, rejecting, creating, all in seconds. Yes, she thought you can do anything, and do it beautifully.

He smiled, loving the challenge. "To begin with, much less. Cut the damn menu practically in half. Nobody today wants all those courses, or all that richness. The tomato sorbet is an affectation—a cliché of the nouvelle cuisine, like the bean salad. In summer, perhaps, in the country, as a first course it might work. Here, never. So. Out with the beans. Out with the sorbet. The mousse of trout? Maybe. But not with a béarnaise—too rich before a meal that is all richness. The veal Orloff—much too rich. Your father's beef is not a bad idea. Simply roasted, with a Madeira sauce. The rice pudding is a joke. So heavy, with all that candied fruit—ugh!"

Elise smiled. His disgust was a physical thing. She could feel the little boy in Claude; the quick rippling emotions, the joy in creation. The rebellion against anything below his standard. How very lucky I am, and Le Palais too, to have him.

"I want you at that meeting this afternoon, Claude. When Armand invited me—I think it was an afterthought, really—I insisted on that. Put my foot down. I keep forgetting, I do own the place." For the time being anyway.

"It might not hurt to gently remind them of that," he

said, stroking her neck with a tender warmth. A shudder of pure pleasure went right through her. Not easy to keep my mind on business, here on this bed with this sexy man. But business it would have to be, for now anyway. The whole fate of Le Palais-Royal might depend on this banquet.

"Or not so gently," she answered. But we'll have to come up with a counterproposal. And not spring it on Armand, mind you. We do need him on our side. You write it up and I'll sell it to him—or try to."

"Très bon!" Claude smiled, getting into it. "I propose then something more interesting and less rich to begin with: perhaps those wonderful tiny oysters from the West coast."

"Olympia oysters?"

"Exactly. And very simply sauced, just a glaze of some sort—sauce aurore maybe—and presented in little barquettes of puff paste, for style. Elegant but light. And different, which the trout mousse is not. No sorbet. No Orloff. Perhaps a terrine of duck or pheasant, they're in season now, you have them on your farm. Then the Boeuf Villeromain as Yves suggests—but not with the famous Margaux. The Margaux is the reason for the banquet. It, not the food, is the real centerpiece of the meal and it must be presented that way. With no competition. Because when the nineteen hundred vintage Margaux comes on people are going to forget what they're eating. They'd be mad not to."

Claude paused as if for breath, kissing her neck. Elise squeezed him.

"So," he went on, still very close, close enough so she felt his breath, felt his body pressing against hers. Felt the warmth and the love of him. "I propose that we serve with the beef something complementary but lesser—and almost any Bordeaux in the world will be lesser—and then have the Reverend Romney's wine all by itself at the end, with just bread and cheese. Which nobody will eat, but there ought to be something. Then the dessert—and that must be ethereal. Perhaps . . . yes! Raspberry soufflé with raspberry

227

puree as a sauce. Refreshing and deluxe at the same time. Cookies, I suppose. And the coffee and etcetera."

Elise was writing it all down as fast as she could. Feeling the joy in him, feeling the beginning of something good in herself—a new sense of confidence. *That other menu is a mess. Daddy would be spinning in his grave if we dared serve anything like that.*

She finished scribbling, made a fair copy, and showed it to Claude. He smiled and nodded his agreement.

She kissed him, and for one brief warm moment it seemed as though they might not get back to the restaurant at all that day.

"You smell good," she said softly. "You smell of flour."

He broke away, laughing. "And my puff pastry calls, Elise. Chère Elise. What would the owner think if she caught me necking with the kitchen help when I ought to be working?"

She kissed him again.

"She'd be furious."

They walked downstairs together. Doubt seemed to lurk in the shadows now. *Am I kidding myself? Can Claude and I really pull it off ourselves?*

The kitchen looked exactly the way it had looked fifteen minutes ago, but everything had changed. Elise could feel the change in herself and it frightened her. *I didn't ask for a showdown, but if it comes to that I've damn well got to be ready for it. And ready to face the consequences. Otherwise I'd better pack it in right now.*

She walked through the kitchen and out to the front of the restaurant. To face Armand.

"Armand," she said, keeping her voice even; "I've looked at your menu—showed it to Claude as well." *Did his eyebrow elevate just a little?* Elise waited, breathless. But Armand said nothing. "We feel it's too heavy. Too rich. And we have a few suggestions I'd like to propose to Reverend Romney."

She handed him the paper. Armand read it carefully. Elise felt the weight of every second. Felt as though great chasms were opening up in the floor in front of her. Icy, bottomless crevasses

Armand smiled. Elise's fear turned to wonderment.

"It is," he said, "a fine menu, mademoiselle. Flawless. And . . . I do see what you mean about the other. But we have Yves to contend with, do we not?" Do we not. The last few weeks I've done damn little but contend with that one.

"I guess we do, Armand."

"Leave it to me. Has Yves seen this?"

"No."

Armand looked at his watch.

"We have just ten minutes. In the interest of diplomacy, mademoiselle, may I suggest we propose both menus? The first, after all, is a catalogue of classics—it might just appeal to the reverend. We can recommend your menu as . . . well, healthier. And let him decide."

"That may be dangerous. Suppose he chooses the heavy one? What I'm thinking, Armand, is that the original menu might just get us laughed at. In the press. And Le Palais can't afford that."

"I'll speak to Yves."

Elise left it at that and raced upstairs again to change into something that wouldn't alarm the Very Reverend T. Q. Romney.

As she dressed Elise tried to remember what little she knew about Romney. He had money, that was for sure. Somewhere in the background was Romney Mills, whose sheets half of middle America slept in every night. The highest of High Episcopal, pastor of a fancy congregation on upper Park Avenue. Famous in wine tasting circles.

But really I don't know beans about the man. He's taking a big chance, trusting us now that Daddy's gone. I've got to make sure he doesn't lose by the gamble. That I don't either. All that and Yves as well. Going to be a fun meeting, this one.

At three precisely Elise walked into the dining room,

where Armand and Yves were waiting. The two menus lay side by side on a round table that had been cleared for the occasion. Yves sat staring at them. Saying nothing. Soon after Elise sat down, Claude joined them. And at three minutes after three Reverend Romney appeared, pink and puffing a little, murmuring apologies.

The Most Reverend T. Q. Romney was a pink and white conglomeration of cheerful twinkles. His real calling, Elise decided isn't religion at all. His gods are Cheval Blanc and Margaux, his saints the Baron de Rothschild and Dom Perignon. His fervor was contagious.

"It is not by chance, my dear Miss Villeromain, that at Saint Swithin's we celebrate Mass with an unpretentious but nevertheless quite acceptable Beaujolais-Villages."

I bet you do, she thought, mistrusting the charm. And I'll bet all your twinkles can turn into daggers if things don't go exactly the way you want them to. Reverend Romney was obviously making an effort to please her, but he radiated an aura of privilege, of having been pampered all his life long. Like so many of the clients of Le Palais-Royal, this was a man who'd grown accustomed from birth to having the best of the best, and having it the way he wanted and precisely when he wanted it.

There was a little small talk. Romney accepted Armand's offer of coffee. A waiter appeared with the coffee and a platter of Claude's cookies.

"Well, Reverend," said Armand at last, "we look forward to the challenge—the challenge of making this Tastevin banquet unforgettable—as your nineteen hundred Margaux will surely be. We've actually designed two menus."

Armand paused then, just for a moment. Elise was watching Romeny's every reaction, trying to read the man beneath the jolly facade. But she had a sense of Yves sitting on her left, silent. Glowering. What had Armand said to him? Where would it lead?

"This," said Armand smoothly, handing Yves's menu to

Romney, "is in the great nineteenth-century tradition. A banquet out of Carême or Brillat-Savarin."

Romney studied it carefully, his pink lips pursed a little, and the smallest hint of a furrow formed in his shiny forehead. Slowly he set down the paper. Elise watched him with an almost eerie fascination. As though he held the key to her whole future in his small, perfectly manicured hands.

"Yes, Armand, it certainly is right out of the history books. And the other?"

Armand passed it.

"Much more contemporary, Reverend. Lighter and not so complicated but, naturally, elegant all the same. And with a difference where your Margaux is concerned. This menu presents it quite alone, but for the cheese. Glorifies the wine, as it were."

Elise felt a surge of affection for Armand now, a feeling she'd never had for him before. He's really trying, as best he can, to sell our menu!

Yves' face held the same sullen expression it had when the meeting began. Claude was very quiet. The silence was dense with expectation.

Romney smiled. "Lovely," he said, "quite absolutely smashing, Armand—everyone. And how thoughtful for you to develop two plans. The classic one is fine in its own way as well, mind you. But my doctor would shriek in protest. Veal orloff—no, never!" He laughed a merry little laugh, and to Elise it felt as though she'd been reprieved from the gallows.

"And the framboise soufflé!" Romney went on, actually licking his lips in anticipation. "Always one of my favorites at your father's table, my dear. So. It's settled then? We'll go with the simpler menu?"

"Absolutely, Reverend." Elise found her voice now. "We'll do you proud, I'm sure."

"Yes," he said, and Elise felt a faint suggestion of doubt in his voice. "I am sure you will, my dear."

Armand spoke then, perhaps a little too quickly. "We'll begin looking into the wines, then, Reverend Romney. Some, of course, we'll have on hand. Others we may have to purchase. But we'll check the prices with you before we commit."

"Not to worry," said Romney, merriment dancing in his round blue eyes, "all I want is the best, as the poet said."

Armand smiled. "Then you've come to the right place, sir."

Quickly then, they ran through Claude's menu one more time, pausing only for some delicious speculation on certain vintages, which Chateau and what flowers. Then Romney took his leave.

Through it all Yves's silence had loomed dark as an approaching thunderstorm. Elise had watched that, praying the storm wouldn't break—at least, not while Romney was with them. Only when the Reverend had closed the front door behind him did Yves speak. His voice seemed thick, clotted with anger. He looked at Elise. At Claude.

"You plot against me. Why?"

Elise took a breath. Nothing had prepared her for the bluntness of his attack. "Yves, please. We're in this together, all of us. If I'd had a chance to see your menu, we could have talked about it. But you didn't give me that chance, did you? Naturally, I asked Claude's advice. All any of us want is for the Tastevin banquet to be a big success."

"Some of us want that, mademoiselle," he said. There was an unstated but obvious threat in his voice. Yves got up from the table, turned on his heel and stalked out of the dining room. If the padded swinging doors could be slammed, Yves would have slammed them.

Elise stood too, gathering her energy to go after him. But Claude's hand came to rest on her arm, and he shook his head. She turned to Armand. "He has a temper, Armand. Yves doesn't seem to realize it's his enemy, that temper. That it hurts him more than the people he aims it at."

"He is upset, mademoiselle. Yves tends to be, shall we

say, emotional. But it will pass. It always does with Yves. Claude, thank you. Your menu is an improvement. As the Reverend Romney saw at once."

"Thank you, Armand," said Elise, "for being so helpful about that."

Claude went back to the kitchen, but Elise stayed a moment longer, wanting to say more to Armand, more about Yves, about the whole situation at Le Palais-Royal. Wanting to, but not quite daring to. I've had one victory today, maybe that's as much as I can hope for. She sipped her coffee, set the cup down. If I sack that grumpy little troublemaker, will Armand go with him, out of protest? A dangerous thought. Elise could imagine the kitchen without Yves. But the front of the restaurant without Armand? Unthinkable.

"He seems," she said thoughtfully, half to herself, "to take everything very personally."

Armand spoke with his usual assurance. "Don't worry, mademoiselle. I will take care of Yves."

But as the words left his lips Elise found herself wondering if they were true. What is their relationship, really? They're two grown men, lovers or not—even though Yves hardly acts like a grown-up some of the time.

"I hope so, Armand," she said, and left the dining room.

Elise got back to the apartment to change and found the phone ringing. Immediately, alarmingly, she thought of Jared.

"Hello?"

"Elise, it's Kate. Sorry to interrupt, but could you possibly come over for a few minutes? There's something we've got to talk about—and not on the phone."

What now, for God's sake? Elise hesitated. "Sure, Kate," she said after a little pause. Keeping her voice noncommittal. "As long as it won't take too long. You know how it is over here."

"Half an hour, tops," said Kate cheerfully. "We'll have tea."

Kate put down the phone to find that she was trembling. *It has to come sometime. I've got to tell her what I intend to do. For her sake. For mine. And to be fair to David.*

The decision didn't make Kate feel better. *This*, she thought, *will tear it. It'll be the final break between Elise and me. Please God I may be wrong, and she'll understand. But if she doesn't, at least we'll know just where we are.*

It all came back to Dave Hollander. So many things did, these days. *Keep it businesslike*, Kate reminded herself. She remembered his voice, the gentle way he'd handled a potential awkwardness: "Do it any way that seems best for you, Kate. But I would like to announce this to my board as soon as possible."

"I've been cowardly, Dave," she'd replied, feeling so close to him, he might have been in the room instead of on the other end of a phone line. "I've got to tell Elise soon. Let's make it today. I can't have her hearing this from anyone else. Supposing the papers got hold of it."

"It will make news. Do you want me there?"

"I'd like that, Dave, but this is a thing I've got to do myself. She won't be pleased, but I doubt she'll actually murder me."

"You'll be fine. Let me know how it goes."

"I will."

And Kate had put down the receiver, already replaying the conversation in her mind. Perfectly correct, utterly straightforward. But why was there always this extra tension between herself and Dave Hollander? Kate knew the answer yet refused to admit it.

She picked up the phone again and called Le Palais-Royal. And as she waited for the connection, Kate thought of all the years of trying to get closer to her stepdaughter. The gifts and letters she'd sent to Vermont and rarely been thanked for. The shopping trips when Elise was in town, Elise's grim acceptance of Kate's thoughtfulness as though it were some kind of ordeal. And the heartbreaking moment when Elise had married Jared without even telling her father. Even then Kate hadn't given up on the girl. But maybe, she thought, it's time to draw the line.

Kate busied herself preparing tea. Thinking about her talks with Simon Doughty. Dear Simon. Crossing every *T* and dotting every *I*. He'd spelled it all out, made the situation clear even to Kate, confusing as it was: her share of the estate taxes must be at least a million. And that, with what would be left, she'd be able to have a comfortable, completely independent life.

That had been frightening. It made Kate realize that ever since she was eighteen, she'd been taken care of, or taking care of someone else. To face the world alone, with endless choices and no immediate responsibilities was almost more than she could take in.

Making an effort, she recalled her dream of a place where she could start painting again. Some little carriage house in the Village. A real studio at last, and time, time even to travel a bit without worrying about every penny. Time to sort out her life instead of always living for others. Was that too terribly selfish?

She had no appetite for lunch, but set the tea things ready, cut some of the small, crustless open-faced tea sandwiches she liked. The thin Limoges tea set Pierre had found on one of their August excursions to France. This will go to Elise, Kate thought as she set out the graceful ivory-colored teapot so delicately painted with small sprigs of wildflowers.

Elise seemed to be everywhere in the silent house.

Kate made more sandwiches than either of them could possibly eat and warmed the teapot. Studying her large collection of different teas, she realized she didn't know which was Elise's favorite. If she had a favorite. So, feeling a bit daring, Kate chose her own favorite: a smoky Lapsang souchong. She was just pouring boiling water onto the tea in the warmed pot when the doorbell rang. Like the knell of doom.

When they were settled in the library and Kate had poured out the tea, she took a deep breath and got right to the point. "You know, Elise, from the beginning I've not wanted to be involved with Le Palais. And of course you know about the estate taxes, how we're going to have to come up with no less than two million within a year."

Elise just stared at her stepmother. The silence thundered.

Kate plunged on. "David Hollander has been very generous in his offers to buy the restaurant. I do understand how you feel, Elise—never think I don't. But it's all gotten to be too much for me, being caught in the middle like this. Damned if I do, damned if I don't. Well. To make a long story short, there is a way out. I've decided to sell my half interest in the restaurant to Hollander Industries."

Having said it at last, Kate had an eerie, distanced feeling, as though she had just stepped off a very high cliff and hadn't quite begun to fall yet. She looked at Elise and felt sorry for the girl, knowing how deeply she cared for the restaurant and how traumatic the last few weeks had been for her.

"Oh, Kate." Elise looked at her stepmother as though Kate had suddenly grown fangs and claws.

"Can't you understand even a little, Elise? If we weren't faced with all those taxes, it might be different. I respect what you're trying to do with Le Palais—truly I do—but I don't want to be a part of it. You're making the restaurant your life, and that's fine. But now I've got to get on with my own life."

"Take the money and run? And you expect me to pat you on the back and say how swell I think you're being?" Elise set down her teacup with a click that had an air of finality to it. "Kate, make no mistake. I think you're selling out in more ways than one. You're spitting on everything Daddy cared about—on his whole life's work. How can you only think of the damn money? Can't we work out some other kind of arrangement?"

Kate held her tongue for a moment, fighting for control.

"Elise, if you'd only listen. If you'd just take off the blinders for a few minutes, you might understand what this is all about. If you'd at least try to understand that yours isn't the only point of view here. I didn't make that will. I didn't want any of this—especially not any of this dissention. I've looked at it from every angle. I even asked Simon if there was a way for you to buy me out. There isn't. No bank will loan money—not that kind of money—on something so speculative as a restaurant."

It was doubly painful for Kate now, to see Elise cringing from the reality of the situation. Kate made her voice gentle. Tried to forget her irritation.

"Elise, Elise. You aren't losing the restaurant by this. You're just getting a different partner in it."

"The hamburger king."

"Dave doesn't want to change Le Palais. Far from it. He wants the restaurant for what it is—for what it has been."

"Has been? If anything, we'll make it better!"

Kate could see the fire in Elise now, and a part of her admired it. "I hope so, darling. And Dave will help if he can. He has all the backing, all the money you'll ever need."

"Junk food money. That man will drag Daddy's name through the gutter, mark my words."

"Was the food we ate at Dave's dinner party junk food? Give the man credit, Elise. He's smart and he can do a lot for Le Palais."

"Smart enough to get around you, Kate. Smart enough to get his greasy hands on the restaurant Daddy just about gave his life to build."

"Elise, think about it a little. You're upset now, and I guess I've given you reason to be. Really, I am sorry. But the situation is tearing me apart and—"

"That makes two of us, then, doesn't it? Three, if you count Daddy's memory."

"Your father liked and admired Dave Hollander."

"If you say so. Kate, let me go to the banks. Somebody must be willing to lend me the money to buy you out."

"Elise, you have to think. And hard. Even if you were to find a lender, all you'd be doing would be saddling yourself with an enormous debt—and the taxes coming due in any event."

Elise sat back in her chair. Slumped, almost. Her face looked pale, and Kate could see how very tired the girl was. Tired and wrought up.

"Why do you hate Dave so?"

It was a moment before Elise replied. When she spoke Kate could see the tears brimming at the corners of her eyes. "Oh, Kate. You know it isn't him personally. Dave's all right, I guess. It's what he represents. The commercialism of it."

"He's already told me he'll make any arrangement you like. You can be part of Le Palais forever, even if you do sell out."

"Selling out is just what it seems like. Kate, look. I've had quite a day so far. This hasn't made it easier. I do understand how you feel. And maybe I'm not such a moron as I may seem about the money. Can we put all this on hold for a while? Right now I've got to get back to Le Palais. We're just starting to crank up for the Tastevin banquet—remember that? Every food critic and gourmet in town will be watching us like vultures."

"You'll be fine, Elise. I'm sure of that."

Elise smiled a thin and scornful smile. "Are you? Good. I wish I were. Kate, let me tell you how I feel. I feel betrayed. If there were some legal way to stop you, I'd do it. As for Hollander, I guess I'll have to make some sort of peace with the man. Hating every minute of it. I will talk to him, but not today." She stood up, and Kate rose too.

"Elise, let me talk to him, have him call you. At least I can help with that."

Elise smiled a funny trembling smile that seemed to be balanced between tears and hysteria. "I guess I ought to thank you for that."

"Don't thank me, dear. But try to understand."

"I will try, Kate. But trying doesn't make it happen." She turned and walked out of the room.

Three days passed. Elise hadn't heard from Kate and hadn't called her. Or Hollander. *There'll be time enough for all that later on,* she decided, looking at the menu that was posted for the banquet. Cleanly written out in Yves's familiar hand. No bloodstains on it that the eye could see. The design was ready for the printer too. The menu would be more than just a menu; it would be a keepsake, something the members of the Tastevin would cherish. An elegant little folder on thick cream-colored paper, on its front cover a reproduction of a Picasso pen drawing, a merry satyr dangling a bunch of grapes to tempt a voluptuous nymph. And beneath the drawing the Tastevin name and motto: "Confrérie des Chevaliers du Tastevin, Dimanche le 15 Novembre 1984, Jamais en Vain, in Vino Veritas, Toujours en Vin."

Inside, the actual menu as it had evolved since their fateful meeting with Reverend Romney. The wines had all been chosen now, their price and quality and vintage assured. Elise knew the menu by heart, but she reread it all the same, as if it were a roadmap to her entire future.

*Les hors d'oeuvres*
*Champagne Laurent-Perrier Cuvée Grand Siecle*
*Barquettes des Huîtres Olympia, Sauce Aurore*
*Meursault Les Perrières 1961*
*Meursault Les Perrières 1961*
*Terrine de Canard en Croute, Sauce Poivre Verte*
*Château Margaux 1959*
*Filet de Boeuf Villeromain*
*Les Légumes*
*Les Fromages*
*Château Margaux 1900*
*Soufflé Framboise, Sauce Framboise*
*Château d'Yquem Sur Saluces 1955*
*Café Filtre*
*Eau de Vie Framboise/Cognac Martel Napoléon/*
*Eau de Vie Poire Williams*

The menu was posted where the special-events menus were always posted, by the calendar just outside the chef's office. Daddy's office—now Yves's.

Elise went to Claude's pastry counter. Watched as he experimented with shapes for the puff pastry boats that would hold the tiny oysters at the banquet. He pulled a baking sheet from the oven. On it were six barquettes, all different. Claude set them on the counter and regarded them with a critical eye.

The first was shaped like an Indian's canoe. "Because the oysters are so completely American," he said. The second boat was hardly a boat at all, just an oval shaped into points at both ends. Claude looked at it, squinted, frowned and put it aside. The third boat on the tray was fanciful, a galleon complete with castellated poop deck and jaunty bowsprit. The fourth was shaped like a stylized scallop shell and the fifth was another sort of shell, an oyster's shell, deliberately rough-hewn. The sixth shape was made in the image of a Breton fisherman's dory, broad of beam and sturdy, with an elegant upsweep to its bow.

"The galleon," said Claude with a touch of regret, "really doesn't leave enough room for the oysters. And there is too much pastry in it—too filling so early on." Sadly, he pushed it aside next to his other reject.

Suddenly Yves appeared, looming out of nowhere.

Elise restrained a shudder of revulsion. She felt a prickling down her spine, a warning. Jungle reactions. For a moment the three of them stood there in silence. Across the big room Elise could also see Armand, who must have come on some errand of his own.

Yves didn't see Armand. His attention was riveted on the six pastry boats. "If this is our navy, mon vieux," he said, "we have lost the war." The sneer in Yves's voice hung in the air like vapor from some fetid swamp.

Elise looked at the pastry boats, at Yves, and at Armand, who had stopped whatever he'd come in for and was watching the little tableau from ten feet away. Suddenly something in her changed, as though an invisible switch had been thrown. The man was incorrigible. "Tell me about it, Chef," she said with the utmost politeness. "Don't you approve?"

A purple flush engulfed Yves's cheeks. When he spoke it was in a voice choked by some inner rage. "This . . . this is the work of an amateur. Nothing like the standards of your father, mademoiselle."

"You know as well as I, Chef, that Claude was personally chosen by my father. And from La Tour d'Argent at that. These barquettes are just experiments. We've already rejected two of them. The others? Well, it's hard to decide. They each have a lot of interest. I'm sure Claude will appreciate your criticism, as long as it is constructive criticism, Yves." She lingered on the word *constructive*.

Yves's lips quivered. He was obviously under the influence of emotions beyond his control.

"Cochonne!"

*Bitch-pig*. The word slipped out in a hissing undertone like something ugly slithering out from underneath a rock. Elise felt her head jerk back a fraction as if to avoid a physical blow.

She stared at Yves, barely able to comprehend that he'd risk such an insult to her, right here in her father's kitchen. For a few seconds the shock itself had a kind of numbing effect. But that quickly turned into plain cold outrage. The man was sick, the proverbial one rotten apple who could easily spoil the lot.

Elise had forgotten Armand. She almost forgot Claude, until she felt the warmth of Claude's hand on her arm. Comforting. Restraining.

Too late.

"Et ta soeur!" she said without thinking, plunging right down into the gutter language with Yves. *And your sister!* As the words left her lips she regretted them, but it was too late.

She was doubly angry at having let herself be dragged down to his level. But it was no longer a hot kind of anger. It was cool and surgical now, sharp as a carbon steel chef's knife. Elise looked up and saw Armand close by, silently watching.

"I'm sorry, Armand," she said, directing her words over Yves's head, "but this has gotten out of hand. Yves, you're fired. You can leave right now and pick up your things later. I'll arrange with Armand about your pay. But you've thrown your last tantrum in my kitchen."

Yves just stood there, blinking. She wondered if he'd truly heard her. Armand said nothing.

Finally, after an ominous pause, the maître d' spoke. "You have gone too far, Yves. Much too far."

What did it cost Armand to say that? Elise wondered. His face was impassive, but the words carried their own cargo of feeling, and the feeling was pure pain.

"As you wish, Mademoiselle Villeromain. It is, of course, your kitchen." Yves managed to put a nasty emphasis on the *your* but Elise was beyond caring about innuendoes. He turned and walked out of the kitchen, and through the service door at the back.

Slowly Elise took a deep breath. Looked at Claude. Claude was regarding her with an expression that managed to hold both awe and love.

But Elise had one more thing to do.

"Claude," she said in a voice so low it was all but a whisper, "if you'll accept the job, you are now the gros bonnet—the chef de cuisine of Le Palais-Royal."

She looked to Armand, half expecting this to be the final blow for him; that he'd run after his lover and leave the restaurant forever. But if this was a blow Armand gave no sign. His head nodded once as if in agreement. Elise didn't press the issue.

"It is a great honor, mademoiselle," Claude said gravely. "Thank you."

"Thank you, Claude. Nobody deserves it more."

She walked with Armand up to the front of the restaurant. Stood by the bar, silence all around them. Wondering what she could say that would make him understand.

"Armand, I'm sorry. I didn't want to do that and I sure didn't enjoy it. But he's been, well, disturbed ever since my father died. God knows, it's been tough for all of us. I've tried and tried with him. So has Claude, believe me. I think he needs help, really I do."

Armand reached out and touched her arm. The simple gesture was almost shocking to Elise; usually he was so reserved. The touch was a gentle one, and there was something in it like a plea.

"Mademoiselle Elise, it is my fault as well. I promised you this would not happen. That I would control Yves's temper. I failed. And this is the result. Please, don't blame yourself."

"Thank you, Armand. If there's anything at all I—we can do, you'll let me know?"

"Of course. And he should seek help—you are right about that. But what we must all think about now is the banquet."

She managed a smile. "Of course. The banquet."

She walked back into the kitchen.

Claude was making new pastry boats. Elise stood by the work counter in a state of shock, just a little dazed, slowly comprehending what she'd just done. Astonished by her own boldness. *If I hadn't been really furious, I never could have pulled it off.*

Barry came up to her, grinning. "Bravo, Elise!" he said in a whisper. "The wicked witch is dead."

Elise could only smile at that, and the smile seemed to kindle warmth all through her. Just the way she felt herself. Something dark and ugly had been exorcised from the kitchen.

Now they could get back to work again.

That evening Armand caught himself doing what he had once fired a waiter for: looking at his watch. Usually at Le Palais-Royal the meal service was a fluent, orchestrated thing, with each table on a schedule of its own, each with dozens of details to be supervised and Armand in charge of it all. Time flew. Tonight it crawled, and with every dragging second he wondered where Yves was, what Yves must be feeling. And what could be done about it now.

I didn't want it to happen this way, he thought, smiling graciously at the third richest woman in New York. I tried and tried, just as Elise says she tried. And I believe her—why would she not? Poor Yves. If he'd only listen, if he'd only exercise just a little control. It was this same childlike quality in the man that had always appealed to Armand.

So unlike me. Too unlike, perhaps.

Now Armand had to force himself not to look at his wristwatch. Another bit of self-control on top of all the rest. He wondered if it might break him finally, if he might not just crack right here in Le Palais-Royal. How would it be to throw it all away in one huge gesture, to begin screaming and wailing and breaking things?

To act like Yves.

Armand walked through the dining room, nodding to a table here, tasting a vintage La Tâche there, and checking, forever checking on every last little detail.

But really Armand was somewhere else.

He was reliving a beautiful night twelve years ago when a young chef named Yves, just in from France and with no apartment as yet, had come to spend the night in Armand's guest room.

How fine he was then. Full of fun. Full of hope. It had been a Monday night, the restaurant closed, Yves arriving from the cheap hotel with his one big suitcase. The suitcase too new, Armand remembered that particularly. All shiny, untraveled and somehow eager. Like Yves. Armand had made a little supper. Showed Yves the guest room, small but perfectly comfortable and just down the hall from his own bedroom. And they'd had a glass of wine—Beaujolais it was, nothing intimidating—and they ate the little supper and drank more wine.

I saw him to his room, got out towels, and then, in the doorway, he turned to me. Reached out with his hand and just brushed my cheek. As though he couldn't quite believe

I was real. He knew. Must have known, must have sensed. I took him in my arms, it was as though he'd been away a long, long time, and had come home at last.

Armand blinked, fast. Blinked back tears of loving and regret.

This will not do. He smiled at Elise, who stood at the old lectern. Does she sense what I feel? What hell it is?

Armand knew that it might have been possible to make an arrangement with Elise. That the whole situation might have gone on much as it had been with her father.

But for Yves's damn fool temper. He thought of Harry Pierrepont, of his half promise. Of the banquet.

First and above all we must get through the banquet.

Hard enough to do that with Yves on hand. But without him? it seemed too much to think about just now. Guests were leaving. Armand knew he was operating on some kind of automatic pilot and he silently thanked all the saints that his reflexes worked so well. That no cracks appeared in the facade.

Finally, all the good nights were said, the lights switched off, Elise and Claude gone upstairs, Jean-Paul lingering to make sure the kitchen was entirely buttoned up for the night.

Elise and Claude.

That was an open secret now. As I suppose Yves and I are an open secret, speculated on. Maybe laughed at.

Armand walked out into the chilly air of one forty-five in the morning. Walked west on Sixty-fourth and up Madison, past the darkened boutiques. Past another man in evening clothes, who leaned drunkenly against a mailbox waving for a nonexistent taxi. Fourteen blocks to Seventy-eighth Street; he'd timed the walk often, a minute per block at the outside. Now the minutes dragged the way the afternoon and evening in the restaurant had dragged. Armand walked briskly as ever, but his legs felt like lead. He saw his future sinking. Maybe I want the time to go more slowly, maybe

I'm just not up to facing Yves. Not tonight. Not on top of everything else.

But Armand knew it must be, that there was no avoiding whatever awaited him at home. He felt as though some dark river was sweeping him along. A hideous feeling, all out of control. His grand plans for Le Palais seemed to vanish in the cold and darkness. Armand shuddered, only partly from the cold. But his feet kept on moving and Seventy-eighth Street came closer and closer.

His own front steps loomed up at him, formidable as Everest. Armand turned his key in the lock, dreading what he might find behind the door. Yves raging drunk? Yves dissolved in remorse? Recriminations? Does he expect me to have defended the indefensible?

Perhaps.

The house was silent; the only light came from the far end of the hallway. From their bedroom.

Armand walked toward it, thinking about condemned men walking the last mile. He paused before the half open door. Reflexively his hand reached up and felt the angle of his immaculately centered black silk bow tie.

He opened the door.

Yves was packing. Slowly, deliberately, and with every indication of being quite sober. It took Armand a moment to realize that this was that same suitcase Yves had brought here so long ago.

Armand paused, groping for the right words.

Yves kept on packing and did not look up.

"What is this, mon petit renard?" My little fox. Well, he was that once, quick and young and clever. Saying the old pet name nearly made Armand choke with regret.

"I'll finish here, Armand, and pick up some things from my locker at Le Palais, and then I'll go."

"What do you mean, go? Who said anything about going?"

"Elise, for one." For the first time Yves raised his head and looked Armand right in the eye. His expression held a resignation that was heartbreaking to see. Once again Armand thought of condemned men. Yves paused a little before he continued.

"Yes, Elise. Bitch-in-heat Elise. But aside from all that merde, it was over with us anyway. Has been for quite a while, hasn't it, Armand? Better a clean break. Better not to drag it out, don't you think?"

The words came at Armand with the force of a thunderbolt.

Yes, poor dear Yves, that is precisely what I think, and what a fool I've been not to realize you must have known, too, that you felt what I felt. Feel what I don't feel.

Armand was startled, deeply saddened. Suddenly he didn't want Yves to go. Not like this.

"Yves, Yves. Where will you go, this time of night?"

"To a hotel. There are many."

"But there are questions of money. Elise will make some sort of settlement—"

"And there are mails. And telephones. I'll let you know where I am, Armand." He closed the suitcase and to Armand it sounded like the shutting of the gate of eternity.

Yves smiled a brief regretful smile. "Once I loved you, Armand. Once you were all the world to me. I would like to remember that—at least, some of it—happily."

"And I too."

"In the end you were too much for me, Armand. Too strong, too sure of yourself. I got lost. Confused. Trapped, because I'd been stupid enough to imagine everything would stay the same always. The way it used to be. With Pierre to guide me in the restaurant, you up front. With the two of us here. This bed."

He paused as though to go on might be too much.

"We had good times." As Armand said the words he knew they were true, and all the sadder for the truth in them.

"Mais oui," said Yves quietly, lifting the suitcase from the bed. "I have more to pack, mon vieux, but it can wait until I have some permanent place to live." He smiled, just a flicker of a smile. "Don't blame yourself, Armand. I know I did it to myself. Couldn't help myself. Called her what she is—a pig."

"It would have been so easy to have said nothing."

Again, the flickering smile. "Would it? For you, perhaps, dear perfect, always-in-control Armand. But you don't have to slave in that kitchen all day, feeling them nibbling away at you, at your position. Seeing the looks that pass between them—between her and Montgeron. They imagine I didn't notice! That I'm made of stone. Disgusting."

"He is a very good chef, old friend."

Suddenly Armand realized how utterly tired he was. Wanted this scene—all scenes—to be over. And for all his regret at the loss of what had been between them, what he wanted most in that moment was for Yves to leave. To leave him in peace. And in control.

Yves wasn't quite finished yet. Armand felt in his heart the churning of several emotions. But his basic impulse underlying all, was to somehow cushion the blow to his lover. He knew he must force himself to persuade Yves to stay—if only for a day or two. But before he could speak Yves answered.

"Montgeron is too good by half, and well he knows it, the hypocrite. So modest, our Claude. So quiet, quiet as a mouse, just waiting, waiting, biding his time until, sure enough there she is, Elise, going after him, taking him into her bed and her bed still warm from the other one. The beautiful one."

"What business is it of ours who she sleeps with?"

"Can't you see? That one uses his prick as a weapon—anything to gain power in Le Palais-Royal."

"Do you really think that?"

"I know it, and so would you if you spent more time in the kitchen."

"I think, petit renard, that I've spent all too much time there. Especially today." Yves cringed at the sound of the

248

old pet name. Armand came closer to him. Put a hand on his shoulder. "Yves—don't go like this. Not so late at night. Stay. We can talk in the morning."

Yves turned and walked to the closet and pulled out a windbreaker. Put it on. Zipped it up. "I must go to Le Palais now. To be sure it is empty. Can't face even the dishwasher after what happened today. If it pleases you, I'll sleep in the guest room tonight. Tomorrow, I'll find a place to stay, and a job. For the gros bonnet of Le Palais-Royal there will be many jobs."

Armand smiled. One small consolation, at least. "Yes, of course there will be. You can name your price."

Something glittered in his lover's eyes then and Armand prayed it was a beginning for Yves, that this wouldn't wreck him altogether.

"Don't wait up, Armand. I must say good-bye to the restaurant."

Armand thought how it would be for him if the situation were reversed. If he'd been forced out instead of Yves. And it could happen yet, he thought.

Yves walked toward the door. Armand followed, trying to think of some other reassurance. Another way to tell him things were going to work out. But no words came.

Yves opened the door and turned to him.

"Take care, little fox," said Armand.

Again, the flicker of a smile played across Yves's lips. "We'll talk tomorrow then." He went down the steps, turned again. "Sleep well, Armand."

The words came to Armand like a blow: He thinks of me as a traitor, a Judas. As having gone over to the other side. Armand stood there in the open door, still wearing his superbly cut dinner jacket and black bow tie, and watched Yves disappear into the night. For a moment the urge to run after him was very strong. Then Armand sighed. Exhaustion came down on him all at once.

Yves walked to Park Avenue and found a taxi right away. Left it at the corner of Sixty-fourth Street.

As he let himself into the service entrance of the restaurant he felt a mild surprise. *She hasn't changed the locks yet, bitch.*

The brandy he'd drunk earlier was wearing off now. Still, Yves walked carefully. *They would be upstairs, the bitch and the usurper Montgeron, the apprentice Jean-Paul.*

*Won't do to have them hear me. Won't do at all.*

Yves' logic was clear, invincible. He made his way to the staff locker room, knew every inch of the hallway, the lockers, the showers and the bathroom beyond. Found his locker and quietly opened it.

Nothing much to take, really. He peered into the locker. A shaving kit, an extra pair of shoes, one umbrella, and an old tattered raincoat. A faint beam of light slanted down into the locker room from the service alley outside. It was light enough for Yves. He sighed.

*Twelve years, and this is all I've got to show for it.*

Slowly, Yves groped his way along the dark corridor, up the stairs and into the kitchen. Thought of the cognac he'd drunk all afternoon, how it hadn't done a thing for him, only made him a little slower, a little more sad.

*Armand must be slipping. Didn't notice a thing.*

The sight of the empty kitchen gleaming softly in reflected moonlight made Yves feel like a ghost come back to haunt the place. The silence, the faint blue-gray light, the muted glimmering of polished copper and stainless steel all contributed to the eerie effect. *It's as though everything that happened to me here happened a long, long time ago. I'll drink to that!*

Yves walked through the kitchen feeling invisible. Walked through the two dining rooms and out into the foyer. In the little reception area just inside the door a nightlight glowed.

*I guess I'll let old Pierre buy me a drink. And his bitch daughter too!* He walked to the bar, slipped behind it, feeling the coolness of the well-worn zinc bar top. Got down a bottle of Martel Napoléon. Poured a big crystal balloon glass half full. Swirled it around quickly. Took a long and satisfying pull. There. Thank you Mademoiselle Cochonne.—For nothing.

Yves finished the glass in one more swallow, poured again and drank again. And again. He could feel the fine amber fluid warming him as it slid down his throat. Warm it is, and there's a welcome to it almost like coming home. Only this welcome isn't like Armand's welcome. This one makes no judgments, gives no stern advice.

The glass was empty again. He filled it again, fuller this time, nearly to the brim. Sipped. Stepped out from behind the bar. Walked over to the portrait of Pierre.

Looked up at it, squinting. The night-light made Pierre look ghostly too. Well, he is a ghost, and I am a ghost, we're all ghosts together here. One happy family. And upstairs is a bitch ghost and she's probably fucking herself dizzy with the Claude ghost.

Suddenly Yves was struck by hunger. Realized he hadn't eaten a thing since breakfast. Well, Pierre, it looks like you're going to have to buy me supper as well as a drink. What do you say to that?

But Pierre said nothing. He stayed as he had always been in that picture, immaculate in his chef's whites, forever stirring the pot.

Yves looked down. Damn glass had gotten itself empty again. Must fix that. Back to the bar now. Fill it again. Bottle nearly empty now. More where that comes from. Mademoiselle Cochonne has cases and cases of the stuff.

Now, carrying the cognac glass very carefully, as though it were a live grenade, Yves made his way back to the kitchen. Set down the glass. Opened the refrigerator where the evening's leftovers would be. Found a banquet.

What have we here? Terrine de canard. Très bon! Yes, and cheese and some baguettes and here a nearly full bottle of Beaujolais. And we must have our last meal at Le Palais-Royal by candlelight.

He found a tall candle and stuck it in an empty wine bottle. Carried the works into the rear dining room and cleared a space at the round table for six near the tall window and sat down. Lit the candle in its improvised holder. Poured the wine, smiling at the effect. How pretty it is, the orange light glinting off the green silk draperies. Maybe we should use candles all the time.

Yves sat up with a jolt. There is no more we in this place, Yves. We is now she. Pig-bitch-Elise.

He tasted the wine. Ate some terrine. Broke off a piece of bread. Delicious. My own terrine. Pierre's, but mine too. The candle flame danced and made dramatic shadows on the walls and ceiling. If only the pig and her lover could see me now!

He poured more wine. How fine it is here. Le Palais really is the best restaurant in the world. And for all my brave talk to Armand, will I truly find another job so fast? And at what salary? And where?

He reached for his wineglass. Empty? Empty. And the bottle as well. How fast it goes. Just have to get another. Too bad the pig-bitch didn't give me a key to the cellar. Get the good stuff. Celebrate my departure with old Romney's Margaux. That'd teach 'em.

His feet didn't want to obey him. Yves stumbled on his way back to the kitchen, reached for the back of a chair, steadied himself. Made it across the kitchen—huge distance—to the refrigerator. No more Beaujolais. Half a bottle of . . . what? Sancerre. Good enough. Go with the cheese, white after red or not. Carefully now, walking on eggs, back to the dining room. *Aha!*

Cheese and Sancerre, Sancerre and cheese.

What if I threw myself on her mercy, said I didn't mean it, asked her to take me back?

He lifted the wineglass and looked deeply into the pale yellow wine. No answers there. But how fine it tasted, clear and fruity and cool. The bitch would laugh at me, make a worse fuss than today. Yesterday.

Yves bent to see the label on the wine he was drinking.

The letters swam, played tricks with his eyes. He put down the bottle. It was nearly empty like the other but it seemed so heavy now.

He picked up his glass and drank half the contents in one gulp. He wiped off the droplets that spilled out of the corner of his mouth. Ate a little cheese. Brie. Drank again. Heavier and heavier. Even the glass was heavy now. Well it should be. Today was a very heavy day.

There seemed to be a buzzing in his ears, a low droning noise, as if some insect might be trapped there.

Well, enough. Enough to eat, God knows enough to drink. Back to Armand. No. Back to the guest room. . . . No. That's finished too. He looked up, blinked, looked around the room. The room was waltzing, swaying, moving to unheard music. Picked up the bottle. Just one more glass. That's all there is anyway. Pour, pour, very carefully now, don't waste a drop.

But the glass was too heavy. Something was wrong with his arm. Rest the arm. And the other. Set down the glass. Reached for the candlestick. Missed. His head fell heavily onto his arms.

The tall candle in its slender bottle quivered, lurched and fell.

Its flame fluttered with the fall, then blazed as it caught the spilled wax on the linen cloth. The linen blackened, smoldered for a moment, then caught fire. A napkin blazed up. The flames crept along the tablecloth and down the skirt. Caught the delicate silk draperies. Up the draperies in a rush.

A soft whispering noise accompanied the flames' triumphant rise. The window was a wall of flame now. Acrid fumes filled the room.

# 14

ELISE SAT UPRIGHT, tense, sniffing. There was a bitter tinge in the air, a dark pungent smell that shouldn't be there.

"Claude?"

She shook him gently, still not really sure. He moved in his sleep, mumbled something she couldn't understand.

"Claude!"

He sat up. "Quelle . . ."

"I smell smoke, Claude!"

She felt him tense, straining. Sniffing the darkness. "Au feu!" he said at once. *Fire!*

For an instant Elise just sat there, paralyzed by fright. Then came the thought, This isn't happening. But it was. The smoke seemed more dense now. And in just these few seconds.

Claude shot out of bed, pulled on his trousers, fumbled for shoes.

The phone, must call the fire department. She groped for it, dialed 911. "Police emergency," said a woman's voice. It seemed a thousand miles away.

"Fire. There's a fire at Le Palais-Royal. One thirty-two East Sixty-fourth Street. Please hurry."

"Who is calling?"

"Elise Villeromain. I live here. But hurry! One thirty-two East Sixty-fourth Street."

"We're on our way, lady."

She hung up. Claude handed her her jeans and Elise wiggled into them, grabbing the sweatshirt he offered her. Shoes. Grabbed up her wallet.

"Hurry, chérie!"

The stairwell was thick with smoke. She pulled him back into the apartment.

"Wet towels!"

It took half a moment, then they were in the hallway again, groping their way downward. Now she could feel the heat. Her eyes stinging, one hand holding the damp towel over her nose and mouth, the other groping for Claude's back as he led the way, step by step. She was moving as fast as she dared in the searing fumes, dreading a fall, dreading even more that she might lose him.

She tried to remember things she'd heard about fires. How to move. Where to go. God, maybe we ought to be heading for the roof. But then if the fire moves up, the roof's a trap too.

It all felt like a trap, heat and dark and smoke. Lungs burning even with the towels.

She was sweating now, feeling the heat grow more intense as they fumbled their way down from the third floor to the second. Crossing the second floor landing she suddenly remembered Jean-Paul. Elise tugged at Claude's shirt and gasped the boy's name. The smoke was everywhere now, seeping into their lungs. They were both coughing, gasping, choking. She and Claude pounded on Jean-Paul's door.

The silence echoed.

Maybe he's dead already, she thought in sudden panic, and maybe we will be too. Suffocated. That's how people die in fires.

"Stand aside, chérie."

She heard the hoarseness in his voice, the edge of desperation, more than Claude's actual words, and found herself thinking, I've brought him to this. He should have stayed in his place in Forest Hills.

Claude ran at Jean-Paul's door and kicked it hard. Again.

God, he really is dead. And we will be too if we don't get out of here right now.

Claude hurled himself against the door a third time, kicking it violently. Something snapped, and the door swung inward. Claude recovered his balance and ran in. He was out again in seconds.

"Not there. Come."

The smoke was darker now, more dense. Elise felt it cauterizing her lungs. It hurt so much to breathe she almost stopped. Almost.

Every breath a victory. Every step down bringing them closer to—what?

Down and down. They went past the kitchen door and heard a muffled roaring punctuated by a terrible popping and crackling. She thought of the fire in their old iron pot-bellied stove in Vermont, how she'd loved sitting near it with Jared, hearing the wood hiss and crackle. Now it sounded like the overture to hell.

And I've brought Claude into this. What if he doesn't make it? Step by scorching step they inched downward. These stairs are a mile long. We've died and this is hell. Could hell be any hotter?

At the bottom was the service door, and beyond it, hope. A possibility of life, air. Claude got to it first, had it open in an instant that took forever. Pushed it outward and grabbed her as he half ran, half fell outside.

Into the air.

Elise was too deep in shock to feel any real relief. So we made it to the alley. Will we make it to the street?

But there was air, and for the moment that was all either of them could wish for. They just stood there in each other's arms, trembling. Breathing long deep luxurious breaths, choking still, coughing and sputtering and beyond words.

He's alive. I'm alive.

The world had been reduced to this: a sense of gratitude Elise felt must go on forever. Now, with his arms around her, she felt closer to him than ever before. Elise clung to him wordlessly as though he were the only hope in the night. As though if she let go for even one instant he might disappear into a cloud of smoke. Claude seemed to sense this and held her tight.

"Oh, Claude."

Just saying his name made her feel alive again. Saying his name made him real, too, not some part of this incredible nightmare of a fire.

Fire! We're standing here and Le Palais is in flames.

She looked up at him. She could see the flames reflected in Claude's face, an orange glimmering. In that instant they heard the first sirens. Far off but coming closer, banshee wails. They woke Elise and Claude from their trance. As if obeying some unspoken command they disentangled themselves and, still holding hands, walked slowly down the long narrow alley toward the street.

It was very dark here but not so dark as the stairwell had been. No windows faced the alley. They could smell smoke still but it wasn't the smothering, choking feeling they'd just escaped. At the end of the dark alley, a slice of brightness.

My God, the street's burning too.

It wasn't that. Claude guided her forward, taking care, looking out for hidden obstacles that might have fallen in the fire. When they made it to the street the dazzle shocked her. His arm around her waist, Claude led her across the street.

They stood together, watching what they'd just escaped.

Le Palais-Royal was blazing. Elise looked at it through some kind of a filter in her brain that gave her a small but blessed distance from the horror. At first it was like watching a movie. Her mind raced, bounced up against possibilities like some trapped animal.

The worst thing imaginable is happening and I can't imagine it. All her dreams were going up in flames. The invincible limestone facade of the building was only a framework now, an expensive setting for the orange-yellow-blue destruction within. There were other people in the street. Gaping. Elise paid them no attention. Her eyes were drawn to the restaurant and only to the restaurant.

The first fire truck came screaming down Sixty-fourth Street the wrong way, closely followed by another. The firemen swarmed, looking like monster insects in their black-and-bright-yellow slickers, their wide-brimmed hard hats. Tugging at hoses, shouldering long-handled axes, they ran up the front stairs.

It's a movie. It isn't real. Tomorrow I'll wake up and everything will be just fine again.

A long ladder snaking its way up from the red fire truck might have been something in a dream. A bad dream. Suddenly Elise's mind caught up with what her eyes were seeing.

Oh, no. No. Her lips formed the words but Elise couldn't speak.

*Oh, no!*

Her mind kept repeating those words, a mantra of terror. The men going into Le Palais with their axes. The end of my world. *No.*

Three firemen had paused at the threshold. One lifted his enormous long-handled axe. Elise tore loose from Claude and ran, not knowing that she ran.

"Stop!"

Amazingly, he stopped.

"Please. Don't break the door. I've got keys."

She opened it for him. The firemen raced inside, brushing past her as though she were invisible.

Welcome to Le Palais-Royal, boys, she thought. The roast pheasant may be a touch overdone but under the circumstances it's the best we can do. Elise shuddered then, startled at the touch of madness. She felt as though she'd opened the

258

doors of the restaurant not to its rescuers but to an invading army. Claude was at her side now, holding her hand, but all Elise could do was stare into the building.

She stood there like part of the limestone carving, not looking at Claude or at the crowd of people or the fourth fire truck as it came screaming up the street. Her eyes were drawn inside. Into Le Palais-Royal. A blur of orange fire and black shapes moving; shouted questions and commands.

The hose at her feet bucked like a live thing, writhing, twitching, obscene, engorged with water. She stared at it as though she'd never seen a hose before. Is there any way? Can they save at least part of it?

Standing there, feeling useless, she felt the heat again. Remorseless. I never thought before what fireman go through. Heroic. To do it every day, as though havoc like this is routine.

But how could the end of her world be someone's routine?

What would Daddy do now?

Daddy. The portrait!

She jerked her hand out of Claude's hand so explosively it startled him. Dashed into the foyer. The flames hadn't reached this part of the house. The firemen were all somewhere else. She walked straight into the foyer, almost afraid to look at the painting. Expecting it to be a ruin. But it wasn't. Her father looked past her into the middle distance, benevolent and calm and invincibly confident.

Maybe there is hope, after all.

Not looking left or right, ignoring the roaring fire and shouting voices, Elise reached up with both hands and lifted the portrait from its hook.

"Lady! Get the hell out of here!"

She didn't know where the voice was coming from. Didn't care. Lifting the big picture took all her energy, every last ounce of willpower. I am going to save Daddy's portrait if it's the last thing I do.

"Lady!"

Arms reached out of the billowing smoke and grabbed her.

"Elise!"

Claude's voice seemed to be coming from miles away. From another planet. Clutching the painting, she turned. The fireman who stood facing her now loomed out of the smoke, a giant in his rubber coat and huge wide-brimmed hat. An angry giant.

"Lady, who are you? What do you think you're doing?"

Elise smiled. He didn't seem to notice. "The painting," she explained. Elise held the painting in front of her like a shield. She didn't know she was crying. "It's mine. It's my father."

She walked past the fireman, past Claude, and out of the house. Feeling the weight of the portrait, welcoming the effort it took to lift it. At least I'm doing something. At least one thing is being rescued from all the horror.

Claude was right behind her now, offering to help. But Elise wouldn't—couldn't—relinquish the picture. It was a magical talisman now, her only protection against the monstrous thing that had happened here tonight.

She walked across the street. People parted in front of her, sensing she was not to be interfered with. On the far side of the street she set the picture down gently, leaning it against the side of a stretch Mercedes-Benz limousine, her eyes remaining fixed on Le Palais-Royal.

One of the firemen appeared, briefly, in the door. Said something Elise couldn't hear into a walkie-talkie, waited for an answer, said something more, wiped his forehead with a big smudged handkerchief. Elise sensed something important happening. She left Claude for a moment, walked across the street again, straining to hear. Afraid to ask. From inside the restaurant came a shout. Elise heard it all too clearly.

"Captain, we got a roast in here."

*A roast?*

It took only a second for the meaning of that to sink in. Elise fought the horror of it every inch of the way. Jean-Paul. It has to be Jean-Paul. He must have been in his room, under the bed or something, all the time.

Slowly, numbly, she walked back to Claude, put her arms around his neck, buried her face against his chest. For a moment she could only sob. Thinking of Jean-Paul, what a fine kid he'd been, how kind to her when she first came into the kitchen. Thinking that they might have saved him, somehow.

"Oh, Claude. Someone died in there. It has to be Jean-Paul."

"No."

"They just found him. I heard it."

"But, chérie, he was not in his room."

Elise could find no reply. She turned in his arms and simply stood there, Claude's arms warming her, but not enough to chase away the icy chill that had settled into her heart when the news had reached her: *We got a roast in here.*

If I live to be a hundred I'll never forget it. Or Jean-Paul either. Tears crept down her cheeks. She didn't even bother to wipe them away.

The fire seemed to have been brought under control now. Less orange was visible through the windows and even the oily billows of smoke looked to be thinning out. From inside came the glare and dazzle of the firemen's huge long black-handled flashlights. Their beams danced and flickered behind the half-broken windows, a light brighter and quicker than flames.

A shiny blue van drove up. ABC-TV NEWS was painted in crisp white letters on the van's side. The news crew came scampering out almost before the van stopped, quick and nimble as the firemen. A cameraman aimed his miniature video camera at the restaurant. A tall girl with immaculately coiffed red hair posed herself at the bottom of the stairs and spoke into a microphone. Elise shuddered.

*Ghouls!*

Again, she felt that eerie feeling of being distanced, of watching a bad movie. *Here they come to gloat over the ruin of my dream. Daddy's dream.* She sighed and filled her lungs with the cool night air and tried to force herself to think logically. It was a huge, maybe an impossible effort. *We've got to get out of here. Go to Kate. She'll take us in—I hope.*

But the energy had drained out of her. Elise felt as though she'd grown roots, that she might be found here in this exact spot months from now, gibbering, watching the wreckage.

All of a sudden the lady reporter was right in front of her, holding up the microphone as though it were some kind of magic wand. Elise recoiled. Claude was behind her, a bulwark of comfort. The reporter's voice was animated, as though she were telling a particularly interesting children's story.

"And here we have Elise Villeromain, whose father founded Le Palais-Royal. Miss Villeromain, can you tell our audience how it feels . . ."

Elise stared at the woman.

"No," she said softly. "I can't."

Then there was a commotion at the front of the restaurant. The reporter turned, scenting fresh prey. Two firemen were carrying out a stretcher. On it was something that looked like an enormous dark green plastic garbage bag.

*Captain, we got a roast in here.*

Elise turned from the scene. Burying her face against Claude's chest again. *Jean-Paul, what have I done to you?* She felt pain beyond pain. "Jean-Paul, Jean-Paul."

"Chérie," said Claude, "there was no more we could do." But his words dissolved in her grief.

The reporter was talking to the captain of the firemen now. Behind him the fire was out. Only the lingering smoke hung in the air, and the pungent stench of wet charcoal.

Elise ached from head to toe, dull, numbing pain. Her

eyes stung from smoke and tears, but the hurt inside her was worse. I thought Daddy's death was as bad as things could get. What is it they say about bad things coming by threes? First Daddy, then Jared, now this.

She looked at her watch. Two forty-five. It might have been any hour. Time had stopped for Elise. Her brain seemed to be crammed with sharp bright fragments. She had a vision of Reverend Romney, his blue eyes flashing anger, pointing an accusatory finger at her. Yes, and your sacred nineteen hundred Margaux is probably gone as well, Reverend, and what can I do about it but say I'm sorry and hope the insurance is all in order? Well, the wine cellar has a thick door, steel and insulation and more steel. Some way to test it.

She tried to focus on the cellar, clinging to that one small gleam of hope. Fire climbs. Maybe the wine, at least, is okay.

Claude's arms around her were comforting but Elise had a terrible feeling that maybe now she was beyond comfort, even beyond love.

Compulsively, as though by looking she could bring it back, she stared at the ruin that had been Le Palais-Royal. The creamy limestone facade was physically intact but desecrated by soot. Over every window great black smudges were streaked upwards where the smoke had come pouring out. It looked like a whore's heavy makeup. The elegant building had always pleased Elise. Now it seemed haunted, ghastly, an oversize skull, the black holes that had been windows staring lifelessly into the street.

Then there was a gentle touch on her arm and a familiar voice saying her name.

Kate. Elise blinked. She detached herself from Claude's arms and went to her stepmother. Kate was soft and warm and smelled of lilacs; for a moment she simply hugged the younger woman. Then, softly, she spoke.

"Oh, Elise. My poor darling. I came to get you, to bring you home. There's nothing more to be done here. Not tonight anyway. I saw it on television. Are you all right? And Claude?"

"We're fine, Kate. But something terrible happened. They found a body inside. It has to be Jean-Paul."

"Oh *no* . . . The poor child."

"We looked in his room—he wasn't there. Barely got out ourselves."

"Children, let's go home. You must stay with me as long as you like. There's all the room in the world."

Elise looked at Kate and smiled for the first time since the fire. Incredible. And after all the hard things I've done to her. After all the bad feelings. "You're sure?"

"Never surer. Elise, dear, it's your home."

Claude picked up the portrait and carried it in his right hand while he kept his left arm around Elise. Slowly, as though they were the last survivors of some defeated army, the three of them walked down the street, trying not to think about the ruin they were leaving behind.

Before they'd gotten halfway to the corner a tall pale figure came striding toward them.

Elise recognized him first and shouted his name. "Jean-Paul!"

At first she couldn't believe it. Her heart seemed to roar with the effort of holding all she felt. She broke away from Claude, ran to the astonished boy and kissed him. He grinned, blushing, and closed his mouth like a fish in an aquarium, saying nothing.

"Jean-Paul, we were so worried. We thought—we didn't know where you were. Someone died in there. We thought it was you." Elise looked up at him, at his long grave and slightly equine face, at the big dark eyes that were usually so ready to smile.

Jean-Paul looked at the restaurant, at Elise and Kate and Claude. Elise hugged him again, crying openly now, unable to contain her tears and not wanting to. "Oh Jean-Paul. Thank God it wasn't you."

He smiled. "I was at a movie."

She looked at him again and thought how lonely he must be. "You must come with us tonight, Jean-Paul. To Daddy's house."

The boy simply smiled, nodded, and joined the motley procession as it moved east toward Madison Avenue. Kate led the way, followed by Elise and Claude with the portrait of Pierre, with Jean-Paul making a sort of rear guard.

What a sight we must be, Elise thought through a haze of exhaustion. Every step seemed to be a special effort. She squeezed Claude's hand, looking at the portrait at his side. Daddy's coming home again, she thought, accepting the unreality as though it were the most natural thing in the world.

Daddy. Le Palais-Royal. They'd always been one and the same, and now they were both gone. Elise didn't let herself think that the restaurant might be gone forever now too. Just like Daddy.

They walked in silence. There seemed to be nothing more to say.

Finally they arrived, so tired that the mere effort of sorting out the guest rooms took the last dregs of their energy. Elise and Claude showered together, but the night's terrors had hit them too hard for there to be any real pleasure in it. They dragged themselves into the big double bed, kissed, and closed their eyes.

But Elise didn't sleep. The room swarmed with unanswered questions. Whose body can it be, if not Jean-Paul's? What's the state of Daddy's insurance? Even without seeing the wreckage she knew the interior must be nearly a total loss. It would be weeks or even months before they could fix it up again. Once more she thought of Reverend Romney. Of the Tastevin banquet and all it could have meant to the new Palais-Royal. But that was gone now too.

Tonight's fire had burned a great black hole in her future, a deep, deep pit into which all of her dreams were falling. . . . In the midst of this dream of falling and falling sleep finally crept up on her.

The next morning Elise got up early. Looked twice around the beautifully furnished guest room before it dawned on her where she was, what had happened. She shuddered, forced herself to dress. Went down to the kitchen to make coffee.

There sat Kate, stirring sugar into her morning tea. Elise was glad it was just the two of them. Impulsively, she bent and kissed her stepmother on the cheek.

"Kate, you were wonderful last night, and I didn't really thank you. I mean, it's beyond the call of duty, running a hostel for all us refugees."

Kate reached up to take Elise's hand and give it a squeeze. "No it isn't. I'd do a lot more than that for all of you. Especially for you. We're both Villeromains and we're all in this together. Even if you and I don't agree every minute of the day."

"We appreciate it, Kate. More than I can say."

Elise set water boiling, found the café filtre pot and filled it. She moved like a robot. Going through the motions. The memory of last night lingered painfully, a dull ache that seemed to run all through her, alternating hot and cold. Heat of anger, chill of fear. The litany came back to her: First Daddy. Then Jared. Now this. She felt as though she'd wandered into a Greek tragedy, that maybe some dread curse had been set upon her, on the whole house of Villeromain.

Kate sipped her tea, weighing words. "Elise, I know it's been rough on you, these last few weeks. My selling out to Dave and all that. But even if we have had our differences, if there's any way at all I can help you now, be sure that I will."

"I know that, Kate. At least I do now. And I know I've been acting—well, like a spoiled brat."

She poured herself some coffee, trying to sort out her feelings, trying to find just the right words to express them. Impossible.

"I mean," Elise went on, "why in the world should you

266

put up with my stupid whim of trying to run the restaurant? It was so important—still is—to me because somehow it's all tied up with my feelings about Daddy, and—well, about everything."

Kate heard the "everything" and knew instinctively that she must be included. "I do understand, Elise. Believe me. It can't be easy to have a stepmother dropped on you out of the blue."

Elise sat down. She looked at her stepmother and smiled. "It wasn't out of the blue. You and Daddy were fine about all of it. I was the rotten one, hiding out up there in Vermont, keeping Jared a secret until after we married. I knew Daddy would disapprove of him, and I thought you might too."

"Well, dear, it's very typical of parents to think nobody's quite good enough for their children. Jared—well I have to say he's a bit of an enigma to me. A very handsome one, though."

Elise laughed. Something I never thought I'd be able to do—laugh about Jared.

"He's an enigma to himself, too, Kate. That's part of the problem. The other part wasn't his fault at all. The other part was me."

"But you tried. Stuck up there in the wilderness all those years."

"Nobody had a gun at my head. I liked it. At first, anyway. And I loved him. He's quite a guy, is our Jared. But really—I see it now, even though I couldn't then—I was only running away from Daddy. And you. And the restaurant. I guess that's why the restaurant means so much to me now."

"It isn't a bad thing to want, Elise."

"Maybe not." She sipped the coffee, warm as hope. "But maybe I want things for all the wrong reasons. I'm not as sure as I was this time yesterday."

"Le Palais-Royal is worth wanting. I saw what your father poured into the place. Times I was jealous of it."

Elise reached out and covered Kate's hand with her own. "You were? So was I. All the time, in fact, starting when I was just a little girl. After my mother died it was all he had, really. He tried with me, but there just wasn't time."

"Poor Elise."

"You tried too, Kate, and I appreciate that. I'm sorry I was so rotten to you."

"Not rotten, dear. Just—elusive."

Elise sighed.

"Well, today's the day I face the future. Such as it is. God, but I dread phoning Reverend Romney, telling him it's all off. If he hasn't already had a seizure, reading about it in the paper. Thinking his nineteen hundred Margaux went up in smoke."

For a moment Kate said nothing. She drank a little tea and took a bite of toast.

"Elise, why don't you wait a bit before calling him? Why don't we all take a good look at the restaurant first? I've seen a few fires in my day, and often they're not as bad as they seem."

Elise smiled, a quick bitter smile. "The place was pretty well gutted, Kate. Anyone could see that."

"Well. Let's wait and see."

Elise looked at her stepmother, suddenly suspicious. Is she only buttering me up so I'll be more willing to sell out? But in her heart she knew Kate wasn't playing games. She wasn't that kind of person.

"It just couldn't have happened at a worse time," Elise said, tasting her coffee.

"In any crisis," said Kate quietly, "I often find myself wondering what Pierre would do. How he'd respond. And I think I know—so must you—what he'd do now."

Elise laughed.

"He'd probably find the inspiration for some new recipe in the ruins, Kate: charcoal-broiled something-or-other."

Kate smiled too. "Exactly."

"But I'm not Daddy."

"You are more his child than you may suspect. Your father had a stubborn streak—forgive me—very much like yours. And that's what made him excel. The determination. Nothing, but nothing, was going to stop Pierre Villeromain from being the best chef in the world. You've got to take your hat off to that, even if it isn't always the most comfortable thing to actually live with."

Elise looked at her stepmother and thought, Right you are, Kate. It couldn't have been all moonlight and champagne, being married to Daddy. Kate had been jealous of Le Palais sometimes too. Maybe that's why she was selling out.

"Well," said Elise after a little pause, "I'd better go rouse Claude. I've still got a few old things here to wear. But Claude is probably wiped out—Jean-Paul too. We'll have to do a little shopping or you'll think you're sheltering a convention of ragpickers." She got up, then paused. Another question had popped uninvited into her head.

"Kate, what will this fire do to your arrangement with Dave Hollander?"

"Good question. Nothing's been signed. Naturally, the deal was for the restaurant—for my share of it—as it was."

The words just hung there. *As it was.*

Elise felt as though she'd been kicked. She stood at the table repeating them slowly, as if she were learning a new language. "As it was."

But Kate smiled. "And as it will be, with even the smallest amount of luck. Your father was very careful about insurance, dear. Insurance poor, he used to call us. Simon naturally handles all that, and I don't know the details, but I'm sure there'll be enough to fix up Le Palais just the way it was—or better."

"Oh, Kate. I hope so."

Elise wanted to believe that so much that the very strength of her desire worked against her. Made her more afraid. She knew she'd count the minutes until they went to inspect the damage. And she wondered how she'd ever be able to face the place today.

Three hours later they left for Le Palais, Claude and Jean-Paul wearing brand new jeans and sports shirts and slightly incongruous overcoats that had belonged to Pierre. Elise wore scraps from her schoolgirl closet.

As they left Kate's house they passed Pierre's portrait. It stood where Claude had set it down the night before, propped casually against the wainscotting of the foyer. Elise glanced at it with a pang of sorrow. He's displaced, just as we are. Not sure where he'll be spending the rest of his life.

Even from the corner of Sixty-fourth and Madison they could see that Le Palais had become a morbid kind of tourist attraction. Pedestrians not passing by, but pausing, staring.

The building was worse than Elise remembered it. In the unsparing light of late morning every smudge and broken pane of glass was exposed. She wanted to turn on her heel and run. They came closer and a silence spread over them like a shroud.

Elise stopped just in front of the restaurant. She was holding Claude's hand and now she squeezed it. He put his arm around her but she felt little comfort in it. She felt cold, a deep chill that had nothing to do with the temperature. For the first time since she'd heard the news of her father's death, Elise found herself thinking, I'm glad he's gone, that he didn't have to see this. Because if he had, it might have killed him.

"Well," she said at last, "here we go."

The door was open and Elise immediately thought of looters. Not that there's likely to be much left to loot. But there was a team of inspectors from the fire department, a captain named DeCecco and two others. Elise introduced herself and the others, and DeCecco said, "Sure, Miss Villeromain, help yourself."

God help me help myself, she thought as they stepped into the foyer.

The stench hit her like a body blow, a mixture of smoke and damp and oil and charred wood. Elise fought back the

270

nausea that rose in her throat. Even though the flames hadn't reached the foyer it looked as though some battle had been fought here. The lectern lay on its side with the telephone a few feet away, the receiver out of its cradle and silent. Some of the glasses on the shelves behind the bar had been broken, and the rest were half filled with dirty water. On the bar was a nearly empty bottle of Martell Napoléon cognac, and next to it a crystal balloon glass with a quarter inch of the amber fluid still shimmering in it. Looking at the lectern Elise thought of Armand. Where can he be? He must have heard the news by now.

They forced themselves to walk into the main dining room. Elise looked, quickly shutting her eyes, as if that might make the ruin go away. She opened them again and thought for the second time that it was a blessing her father never had to see this.

Half the chairs and tables were gone, charred splinters now. Here and there in the black rubble she could see the glint of silver flatware. The antique silver-plated wall sconces Pierre had brought back from Paris were ruined, their delicately curved baroque arms bent and distorted, their shades of hand-gathered pale amber silk hanging in rags where they hadn't burned away altogether. She remembered how proud he'd been of finding a set of six, just enough for this room, and another set of four similar ones for the smaller back dining room. Maybe they can be fixed. Maybe. The silver sconces were only a fraction of the damage, but instead of furniture and accessories what Elise saw was the years of love and concentration it had taken to put together a decor that was fully the equal of the superb Palais-Royal cuisine.

The densely woven wool carpet squished underfoot, waterlogged, filthy with ground-in soot, oily smudges, dark scorch marks. She imagined the water seeping into the floorboards, warping, shorting out electric wires, eating away at the fine smooth plaster. In several places the ceiling, gouged open by the firemen's axes, looked as though it had been clawed by some huge vicious beast.

Elise felt herself trembling, shivering uncontrollably, even though the day outside was bright and she wore a warm coat. She relaxed a little at the welcome touch of Claude's embrace. He stood close and put his arms around her, and for that moment it seemed as though his strength was flowing into her. As though she could bear the disaster a little more easily now.

Kate had said very little during their sad tour, and Jean-Paul, nothing at all. Claude's touch was a comfort, but he was silent too. It's like the funeral all over again, everyone so filled with private sorrow that to speak at all is to risk breaking down completely, she thought in the brooding stillness.

They moved slowly through the ruin. Found the first of the two sets of padded service doors hanging off its hinges. Claude pushed open the second set of doors and held them for the others to pass through. Elise actually gasped out loud at the sight of the kitchen.

It seemed completely intact.

There were a few smoke stains and a little disorder and the inevitable oily water on the usually immaculate tile floor. But nothing had been destroyed. The flames hadn't made their way back here.

It was unbelievable after all the horror out front. Elise looked around carefully, deliberately. Every well-loved pot, every knife and wooden spoon, the huge black Vulcan ranges, the work island and the cutting boards and Claude's marble pastry counter—all there, all intact.

Suddenly she began to come alive again. The numbness she had felt out front slipped away. Maybe we aren't beaten, she thought. Maybe we really can put the pieces back together again, just the way Kate said we might.

Kate.

Elise turned to her stepmother and gave her a big hug. "You were right, Kate. It isn't a total disaster."

272

Kate managed a smile, but Elise could see the effort it cost her.

"Well, no. Not here surely. But the front—my goodness!"

Elise thought, thought hard and deep. "It can be fixed, though. As long as the insurance is up to it. But we won't be having the Tastevin banquet here, that's for sure."

"Surely the Reverend Romney will understand," said Claude.

Elise recoiled. Surprised and disappointed that he seemed to be accepting the loss of the banquet along with the loss of so much else. "He won't have much choice, will he, if we simply cancel on him? But maybe . . . maybe there is a way. Why couldn't we rent a place? All the good hotels have special private rooms, elegant suites just for entertaining. And with kitchens too. I'm sure the Pierre would help—or the Carlyle."

Kate said, "Dave has some influence there, Elise. We could ask him to help."

Elise repressed the quick, sharp reply that was forming on her tongue. Maybe Dave can help, she told herself sternly, and maybe I'd be an idiot not to use him. God knows, he's trying to use us. "It's a thought. What do you say, Claude?"

He smiled. "A good thought. This kitchen is probably usable as well, assuming the gas works. We could do most of the preparation here and then finish somewhere else." Claude paused, considering. When he spoke again it was softly. "But Elise, I wonder. I wonder if we're not fooling ourselves. Perhaps it can be done. But can it be done as your father would want it—entirely perfect?"

Elise looked at him, knowing what it must cost him to say those words. Knowing, too, that he was right. She tried a smile. "No one said it was going to be easy. In fact, it may be completely insane even to consider such a thing. But something in me has to try. I really hate the thought of my looking back on all this one day—maybe hating myself—and thinking, what might we have done, if only we'd tried a little harder? I realize it's crazy of me to expect anyone else to feel about Le Palais the way I feel. Must feel."

Elise was still reaching for the right words when Armand stumbled in. He looks like a ghost, she thought, and a shabby one at that. Armand, who's always the picture of elegance. Not this morning. He was pale, unshaven and wearing old clothes she'd never seen before. Clothes that looked as though he'd thrown them on without looking or caring. A faded windbreaker over a nondescript sweater and old corduroy trousers. She thought of him in the beautifully cut dinner jackets he usually wore. "Armand, what's wrong?"

He passed his hand over his eyes as though doing so might erase a terrible vision. His mouth trembled a little, and when he spoke his voice was ghostly, a pale reflection of his usual easy confidence. "Yves," he said, "it was Yves who died here last night."

"No!" But Elise instantly saw how it must have been. Of course. He had a key. Creeping back late at night to get his things, so he wouldn't have to face us—me. And with that thought a terrible suspicion arose. Elise brushed it aside but it wouldn't fade. Kept coming back and back. Could he have set the fire? Could even Yves do something that terrible? Something that might well have killed us all?

Armand leaned heavily against the dirty work counter. Elise thought again of the elegant, fastidious Armand she had always known. The very fact that he didn't seem to care anymore was a measure of his grief. Elise was more moved by this than by any words he might say. She went to him, put her hand on his shoulder.

"Armand—are you sure?"

"Oh, yes. I have just been at the morgue." He stopped talking, took a huge deep breath that was halfway between a sigh and a sob. "You see, he didn't come home last night. At all. After he said he was coming here. Then, when I heard about the fire . . ."

"You went to the police?"

"Yes. To the police. And they took me to . . . see him. Oh, mademoiselle. There is nothing left of—of Yves."

"Then—how can they be sure?"

"I am sure. You see, his watch. I had given it to him."

"Armand, I'm very sorry. Can I help? Is there anything at all I can do?" Armand looked at her, blinked. As though he's seeing me for the first time.

"Nothing, thank you, mademoiselle. You are very kind. I must of course tell his family. They will probably want the funeral over there, a little town south of Bordeaux. And I will see to that. There will be other details. It is all very sad."

Armand felt the firmness of the familiar work island supporting his back and he thought that but for it he might collapse. The sensation of being hollow had been with him for hours now. It was amazing to him that he could move at all, or speak. Or think. Thinking about Yves caused a burning, searing pain. Blinding. But not so blinding that Armand couldn't feel the guilt. *I wanted him gone and he is gone. Really, I murdered him. Poor Yves. And poor Armand.* He closed his eyes but the smell was still there. The sickening dead burnt smell. *Why did they make me look at him?* Trying not to remember only brought back the memory all the more vividly. He opened his eyes. The kitchen came back into focus. And Elise. Standing there so close. *She says she wants to help, and maybe she does. Partly it's her fault as well. If only she hadn't fired him, if only there had been some other way. If I'd tried a little harder, been more clever with him.*

Knowing the futility of dragging it all back did nothing to stop Armand. Over and over, a hundred times, a thousand times, he searched in his heart and in his brain for some consolation. There was none.

*I drove him away. He could sense I didn't want him any more, he said so last night.*

Last night? Was it only last night? It seemed to Armand

275

that his entire world had come crashing down in the most brutal way. Bad enough to end the relationship, even if everything else were perfect. Disastrous to lose Yves in this hideous, unnecessary manner. His big chance at buying the restaurant, as well, had gone up in smoke. Almost as if Yves had planned it.

Today, this same black and unforgettable day, just after coming back from the police morgue, Armand had sat for a moment in a trance of shock. Unable to move, to think, even to feel the depth of his pain. The phone rang. Automatically, like an idiot, he'd answered.

"Armand," said a familiar voice, "how are you?" Harry Pierrepont seemed to be phoning from another planet, some gilded citadel of wealth and privilege.

Armand mustered what bravado he could. "We are, of course, desolated, Mr. Pierrepont. Trying to make some sense of it all. The loss is huge."

"It's tragic, just tragic, Armand. I wanted to call you— I'd been hoping we could meet. I mean, before I'd even heard of the fire. Actually, it isn't really the fire I'm calling about, Armand. It's your proposal to buy Le Palais-Royal. As you know, I'd hoped to back you and Yves . . ." Pierrepont's voice trailed off into the opulent silence of his paneled office high above Wall Street.

Hoped, had he? Armand registered the easy phrasing with a kind of leaden acceptance. Of course. Why not some new disaster on top of the others? Armand felt the muscles of his throat working as he struggled to form a reply that wouldn't be a complete insult. But he could say nothing. The pause stretched on.

"Armand, are you there?"

"Oh yes, I am here. You were saying?"

"Well, it's very damn awkward, Armand, but I'm sure you'll understand. I mean, you have been reading about the oil glut and this OPEC nonsense and Yamani being sacked and, well, to make a long story short, Pierrepont Petroleum is facing some very rough times. Very rough indeed. Naturally, I won't insult your intelligence by pretending I'm bankrupt, or anything close to it. But we are a public company, Armand, and at a time like this, so I am advised, it simply wouldn't look very good for me to be underwriting something as—well, as frivolous as Le Palais-Royal. You see, Armand, we'll be closing refineries. Not just hundreds but thousands out of work. It'll only be a temporary thing, perhaps a year or two, and when the wind changes, you may be very sure—"

"Thank you, Mr. Pierrepont," said Armand softly. "If you will excuse me, there seems to be someone at the door."

"Of course, of course, don't give it another thought. We'll talk soon, Armand. And—I am sorry."

Armand hung up. The sound seemed to amplify itself. Like the closing of a vault, it echoed and reechoed in his heart. It was then that Armand decided he must go to the restaurant. At least the others didn't know of his dream. Perhaps, just perhaps, he could put it back together again. Someday.

Armand forced himself to look around the kitchen. Noticed Kate Villeromain, and Jean-Paul. And Claude.

"I think," Claude said almost causally, "that we could all use a cup of coffee."

"If they haven't turned off the gas," said Elise, relieved to have something practical to think about in the face of Armand's grief.

Claude washed a pot. The gas was working. Ten minutes later he was handing out steaming cups.

Armand was just able to sip a little of the coffee. He hadn't eaten at all, and it seemed as though he might never eat again. The memory of that stainless steel refrigerated drawer sliding out noiselessly with its hideous blackened cargo was enough to finish off any thoughts of food. Now and maybe forever.

But the hot coffee felt good all the same. Reviving. A

sign that there was life left in the world, life that must be lived.

For a moment no one said anything. Elise looked from face to face and wondered if this kitchen could ever again be what it had been. If she'd ever know the bustle, the warmth, the pure creative energy that animated the place when things were going well. It seemed years ago.

She took another sip of coffee, deciding to plunge right into the problem that worried her most: Claude's resistance to putting on the banquet. The doubts he had voiced just before Armand came in lingered in her mind. Now she looked at Armand, so very close to collapsing.

"Armand," she said quietly, "when you came in we were talking about the banquet; whether to try and put it on after all. Maybe rent a room in a hotel. I think we've got to decide about that today. And I'd like you to be part of that decision. But after all this, you know we'll understand if you don't feel like staying."

For a moment he said nothing. After all, he is in shock, she thought, deep shock. It isn't fair of me to expect him to make serious decisions right now.

"The banquet," he said as though he'd never heard the word before. "Of course." He looked at Elise, and at Claude and the rest of them, like a sleeper wakening. "I think it is best," he said slowly, "for me to work. To have things to do. You understand?"

"Sure we do, Armand. Just tell us if there's anything you need—anything at all."

"Thank you, mademoiselle." Something like a smile played on his lips. And once again Elise was reminded of the old Armand, the Armand of invincible charm and unflappable poise. He's taking it hard. Harder than I ever imagined Armand could take anything.

"What we were talking about," she said, taking him at his word and getting right back into it, "was the possibility of putting on the banquet somewhere else. In a suite in the

Carlyle, for instance. Claude thought we could actually use this kitchen for most of it, and just do the finish there."

"But it is in a week's time, the Tastevin banquet. Surely they won't expect us to—with the fire, with losing Yves—to carry on with it. It would be no disgrace to postpone it, non?"

"Better far," said Claude, "to do that than to rush into something and have it be . . . less than it should be."

Elise looked at Kate, who had been silent throughout this exchange. "Kate, what do you think? We've all got a stake in this, one way or another."

"Darling, I just don't know enough about it. My feeling is, it has to be done perfectly—as your father would have done it."

"Certainement," said Claude softly, almost to himself.

I can't let it all just slip away. We can do it. I know we can. Somehow. Elise took care to control her voice. This is no time to get angry. I need all my wits about me, and then some. "I think we owe it to Le Palais-Royal—to Yves's memory and my father's—at least to try."

There was a pause; then Kate spoke up. "It is important, Elise. Even I can see that. This sort of disaster might sink another restaurant. I agree with you: we've got to show the world that Le Palais-Royal is better than that."

Elise smiled for the first time that morning. But before she could say anything, Claude did.

"It will be very difficult, madame," he said to Kate. "Now there will be only Steve and Barry and me, and four dozen people to feed.

Elise felt a sense of betrayal coiling around her heart like a snake. "Claude," she said, too quickly, "you can do it— you could do it with your eyes closed." And as she spoke the words of encouragement, she wondered, does he really love me? Was he just amusing himself, catching me on the rebound? Maybe hoping somehow to get ahead?

Then he looked at her and Elise's doubts melted. "You

279

are a Villeromain to your toes, Elise. Of course it can be done. The question is, can it be done in the style of Le Palais-Royal?"

Elise took a deep breath.

"I'll bet my life on it. Maybe it'll take a miracle, but miracles are what Le Palais-Royal is all about."

"Well said, Elise!"

She turned, startled. Dave Hollander's voice resounded in the kitchen. "You bet it can still be done—and if there's anything I can do to help, I'll be delighted."

He walked across the room and took Kate's hand.

"Are you all right, Kate? I came the minute I heard."

Kate looked at him speculatively. He walked through this ruin like a knight in armor. Maybe he can save us from the dragon after all. She smiled, a gentle, noncommittal smile, fighting the silly, girlish flush she felt building. "Thanks for coming, Dave."

Elise watched this with a mixture of emotions, thinking. How easily he does it. Just steps right in and takes charge, never doubting. Never fearing. Or at least, never showing it. Will he walk over me this smoothly, once we're truly partners? She saw Dave's smile, the glow he induced in Kate's pale cheeks, and thought of the line from Shakespeare: "smiling damned villain." Perhaps she being unfair, but still Elise felt trapped. Cornered. Just when it looked like we might get Le Palais back together again, after all.

Easy, easy, she told herself. One step at a time. Let's first get through the banquet and then we'll see who's a villain. She looked at Dave, but didn't smile.

"It'll be tricky, Dave. We simply can't afford mistakes, This has to be the best meal these people have ever eaten—anywhere. And they're the most sophisticated palates in the world."

Dave smiled again, and again Elise wondered what might lurk behind the easy radiance of it.

"Cold feet, Elise?"

She felt the flush building in her cheeks, the heat rising

dangerously with her temper. But somehow she managed to smile back. You don't manipulate me quite that easily, buster. "We'll do the banquet. I don't know where, or how, but we'll do it. And we'll do it better than Le Palais has ever done anything." She paused, amazed at her own bravado. Breathless. Looked first at Dave and then at Claude, at Kate and Armand and Jean-Paul.

Dave was enjoying the exchange; Claude was just looking at her, his gaze steady, his expression unreadable. Claude, on whom everything now depended.

Kate broke the silence. "There are how many people expected at the banquet?"

"Forty-eight, if they've all accepted," said Armand. He seemed a little more in control now.

"Then I have an idea. Let's do it at home. At the Sixty-eighth Street house."

They all looked at her as though she'd spoken in Sanskrit.

Kate smiled. "It may sound crazy, but think. Think how much nicer it would be than having to rent someplace, not to mention cheaper. And there's plenty of room. Our kitchen—Pierre's kitchen—is well equipped. If we clear out the library and the front parlor, we could rent six round tables to seat eight each, three tables per room. That's not crowding. Have drinks in the foyer and the dining room and we've got it made."

Elise could see it as Kate spoke. Easy to rent tables and chairs. There might just be enough flatware and china left here—if not, that could be rented too. It'll be a scramble, but Kate's right. Nicer. Much nicer than someplace commercial.

"Kate, that's brilliant."

Kate beamed. "You don't think I've completely cast off my tether?"

"Never. Not you. Kate, we're going to do it. If we die trying we're going to make a banquet like no banquet has ever been made before!"

Kate looked at her, suddenly apprehensive. "Oh, Elise," she said, "I hope so. I really do."

# 15

ELISE WALKED UP Park Avenue to Saint Swithin's, uncomfortable in a dress she hadn't worn since college. The three new dresses she'd bought with Jared were at the cleaners, and the cleaners weren't promising they could remove the smoke stains or the smell. Another damn thing to do before the banquet. If there is a banquet after this meeting.

The *if* loomed over her. It was like standing on one rim of the Grand Canyon needing desperately to get to the other side, with nothing to help her but a fierce desire.

I'll do it somehow—even all alone, if I have to. She thought of Claude and all his doubts. And Armand. Who could say what kind of shape he'd be in this time next week?

As she approached Saint Swithin's, the familiar church scared her. Built in the 1920s, it was an expensive copy in gray stone of a small Gothic church, and the rectory that adjoined it was equally gray and Gothic and costly. And forbidding.

A big door knocker confronted her, a fierce bronze lion's head polished to a golden shine; she had to force herself to knock. A maid in uniform opened the door and escorted her into Romney's office.

She felt intimidated by the hush as the heavy walnut door closed silently behind her. Soft old Persian carpets muffled her footsteps. The mahogany paneling was inset with bookcases laden with books whose polished leather bindings gleamed dully with the gold imprinting of their titles. Elise surveyed the big shadowed room quickly as she approached Reverend Romney, sitting behind a huge old desk reading a large and scholarly-looking volume.

"Ah, Elise!" he said, rising and shaking her hand. "How good of you to come. Would you like some tea, my dear? Sherry?"

"Tea would be fine, thank you."

"Tea, then, Juanita."

Romney waved her into the leather-covered armchair that flanked his desk. She felt the walls closing in on her. It seemed difficult to breathe.

Romney beamed, but there was steel behind it. "You poor, poor child," he began gently. "So brave of you, Elise, to even think of going on with it. Do you really think it's wise? Or even possible?" The blue eyes regarded her, and there was no twinkle in them now.

Elise lowered her gaze to the desktop. She couldn't help but see a letter that lay open beside the book, a letter with *Le Cirque* engraved at the top.

A shudder went through her. Hell, if he's already talking to Le Cirque, maybe there's no hope. Maybe he's already made his commitment and this meeting is just a formality. She reflected for a moment and took a breath. He can't do this to me! To us.

Romney leaned forward expectantly.

"It's very important to us, Reverend. Keeping Le Palais-Royal going hasn't been easy since my father died, but we are doing it. Claude's a brilliant chef—but you know that. We had great hopes for the banquet. It was going to be our first really grand challenge—kind of the Olympics of cuisine, if you will.

"And now this—the fire, losing Yves . . . It's a disaster. But that, you see, is all the more reason why we have to go on with it. And we've made a plan, all of us together. I think you'll agree it's a good plan." I pray you will, she thought, hoping her words sounded more confident than she felt.

Romney's pink fingers toyed with the book; his plump hands looked almost candied. Elise thought of marzipan.

"Tell me about your plan, dear."

*As though he's talking to a half-wit child.*

"You may not have seen Le Palais yet, Reverend, but it's pretty well gutted. Luckily, as I told you on the phone, the wine cellar survived intact; so did the kitchen. We were considering renting a suite at some nice hotel, but then my stepmother offered her house—Daddy's house on Sixty-eighth Street. It'll be perfect. The kitchen there is fine, more than adequate. We can do some of the preparatory cooking at Le Palais, the finish at Sixty-eighth Street. It'll work out. I promise."

Elise paused for an instant, wondering if she was overselling. Promising too much. Wondering if Claude's doubts might not be justified after all. She rushed on.

"The fire has been a terrible setback—I won't deny that. That's why it's even more important now that we do this. We've got to show everyone we're not beaten, that in spite of everything we can still produce beautiful food, food my father would be proud of. And we can. I know it."

"My heart goes out to you, Elise."

*He's going to back out of it. Trying to let me down gently.*

The maid arrived with an elaborate tea service. Romney poured. Elise took a cup, astonished that her hand didn't tremble.

"I greatly admire your spirit, Elise. When first I heard of the fire and Yves's death, naturally I assumed our banquet was done for, as well. I did contact a few other places, just to keep the date, but nothing's been arranged as yet. Still, I wonder, is this the time for you to risk such a thing? If you fail, my dear, you'll fail in the most public manner possible."

Elise felt the bottom falling out from under her. "A restaurant isn't just real estate, Reverend Romney," she said, fighting to keep her voice even. "It's people. Yes, we lost Yves in that fire. But in another sense, Yves had left us even before that. I'd sacked him that day. Claude Montgeron is our chef de cuisine now, and we couldn't have a better one—or a more willing staff in the rest of the kitchen and out front. There's not a restaurant in town that will do better by les Chevaliers du Tastevin. I say that as my father's daughter."

Maybe it's cheap to invoke Daddy, but now's the time to pull out all the stops, so here we go, she thought, wondering if she'd forgotten any argument, if there was some promise beyond what she'd already promised.

He laughed.

Numbly Elise thought, I knew it. I've lost the banquet too.

"You certainly are your father's daughter, Elise. There's no denying that. I only wish he could see you now. I'll give you your chance, my dear, since it seems so important to you."

For a moment she just sat there, stunned by his response, not quite daring to be happy. I'll be happy, maybe, when the banquet's over. Not a minute before. But Elise smiled all the same. This is how someone on death row must feel when the last-minute reprieve comes through.

"Thank you, Reverend Romney," she finally said. "I do appreciate your going along with our plan."

"I see how much it means to you, my dear."

"It means everything to me." As she said those words Elise realized for the first time that they were the truth. Everything. If I can't bring this off, I don't deserve Le Palais-Royal. Or anything else. "You won't be disappointed, Reverend."

"I'm sure we won't be. Now do let me know about the details. Anything I can do to help, I'll be happy to do."

Elise got up and shook his hand and let herself out of the study.

The silence of the rectory seemed to smother her as she moved. Being out into the fresh air again was a relief. She filled her lungs with it, breathing like a diver who has just come up from a deep, deep dive.

He agreed just to be kind. He really doesn't believe we can make it happen.

But as she walked, the very fact of Romney's doubts increased her determination. Elise found herself walking faster, making plans, thinking. How in the world can I get Claude to feel the way I feel about all this? To make him want it the way I do?

Dave walked down the hallway to DeWitt Steele's office, trying to remember when the chairman had last invited him to lunch like this, calling late, sounding urgent. He wants something, that's obvious enough. But what? It was to be a working lunch.

Dave knocked on the door of DeWitt's private office and was bidden to enter. "How are you, DeWitt?"

DeWitt smiled but to Dave's eyes it looked like the effort of someone who was out of practice. "Concerned, David. That's why I asked you to drop by."

Dave sat down. "Concerned about what?" As usual, Dave noticed, Steele's immaculate desk contained only a few pieces of paper, mainly computer printouts. He's more at home with numbers than with people. Always has been.

Again, the attempted smile. "Stock's down three points. But you know that."

"I know it."

"Would you like something to drink, Dave?"

"No thanks. Tea with lunch, please."

Steele picked up his phone and gave the order. Put it down carefully. Looked at Dave.

"You're not going ahead with it, I hope."

Well, thought Dave, here we are. Gloves-off time.

"Going ahead with what?"

"Délices du Palais-Royal."

"Sure I am. I mean, we did agree to that at the board meeting."

"Dave, I'm not going to pretend I didn't have some doubts about the whole business. Timmy's presentation was very effective. So were the presentations for the Edsel."

Dave laughed, hoping it sounded easy.

"Do I detect a certain pessimism, DeWitt?"

"You detect a whole lot of caution. After this fire, is there even going to be a Palais-Royal?" He paused as a waiter in a white jacket and black trousers wheeled in a cart with tea, soft drinks, salads, and an impressive assortment of Sushi. The waiter asked if they needed anything else, then vanished. DeWitt continued. "I heard they were pretty well wiped out."

"They had a bad fire. Lost a chef. But they'll be back. That big Tastevin banquet will still be held. They'll get plenty of publicity on that—all the more because of the fire. Underdog stuff. And Kate Villeromain's all set to sell her half interest, and I think I'm getting closer to persuading her stepdaughter to sell, too. But even if only Kate goes for it, we can go right ahead."

DeWitt sighed, then stood up. He went to where Dave was sitting and placed a gentle hand on Dave's shoulder. "Dave, Dave," he said. "You know I've always been one of your biggest supporters around here."

Dave looked up at him, seething. He can't know how patronizing this all is. Or can he? But he refused to fight with DeWitt. Yet. On paper, in the corporate structure of Hollander Industries, DeWitt Steele outranked him. Even though, Dave told himself for the millionth time, without me there'd be no Hollander Industries. But what would happen if it really came to a showdown with the board of directors, and Dave and DeWitt were on opposite sides of the battle lines? Dave, so sure of himself in almost everything he did, couldn't even guess what the outcome might be. When he replied, Dave's voice was deliberate; calm, rational, and, he hoped to God, persuasive.

"You have, and I appreciate it. And I understand your having doubts about the gourmet project. But it'll work, DeWitt. I know it'll work. I can feel it. It's our best chance

287

to pull out of this—this plateau or whatever you want to call it."

"Dave, the board's getting antsy."

"They were fine at the meeting."

"Yes. They admire you, they were impressed by Timmy. But the reason we have a board is to play devil's advocate. And some of them are having second thoughts."

"And to hell with their second thoughts. They can second-think us right into the arms of Chapter Eleven." Dave stood up, fixing Steele with a look of quiet intensity. "We both know how we got where we are, DeWitt. You did it by the numbers, and I admire that. I did it by the seat of my pants, on sheer gut instinct, and that's what I'm operating on now. But it's instinct backed up by hard fact. People will always—*always*—go for the best of something. Whatever it is; a car, clothing, you name it. Especially food. Taco joints fold by the thousands, but places like Le Palais-Royal go on forever."

"Yes, you may be right—as long as the chef goes on."

"Come on, DeWitt. You were at my place last week. You tasted some of the stuff we've cooked up in the test kitchen. And you saw Claude Montgeron's reaction to it: he loved it."

"Sure, but who's Montgeron?"

"Only the new chef de cuisine of Le Palais-Royal. And a certifiable genius at that."

"Your opinion?"

"Pierre's as well. Pierre discovered the lad—at Le Tour d'Argent, no less."

"Your faith is a pure and beautiful thing, Dave. But we're talking millions and millions here."

"Four to five, to buy Le Palais. Maybe three more to launch Délices. In the black in a year, if all goes well."

"If."

"DeWitt, why are you going after me like this?"

Steele's eyes glinted with a chilly amusement. He likes to see me wriggle a little, thought Dave, likes to insert the old stiletto. But I'm not going to give him that pleasure.

"Because I like you. Because I do admire what you've

built here. Because I don't want to see you lose it all on one roll of the dice."

"What do I stand to lose besides eight or so million?"

"Your credibility, David. If this thing doesn't fly, the board is going to be after somebody's hide. I don't have to hire skywriters to tell you whose hide it will be."

"No," said Dave very quietly. "No, you definitely don't have to do that."

"Just a friendly warning, Dave."

"What exactly do you want, DeWitt? For me to drop the whole thing? For Hollander Industries to sit on its fat corporate hands until atrophy sets in? I really don't get it."

"I think—and some of the board seem to be coming around to my point of view—that in attempting to purchase this restaurant you're approaching irresponsibility. Dave, I know you've got a dream. And I know what Le Palais-Royal is—or was. But there have to be more ways than one to launch your gourmet line."

"Sure there are. But none of them have the cachet of Délices du Palais-Royal."

"Can you prove that?"

"You read Tim's proposal—he's got more backup than he needs. But there's an easier way." Dave paused. "Just take a stroll down Fifty-seventh Street after lunch. See what's happening at Burberrys and Louis Vuitton. At Bendel's and Tiffany's and the rest. Class sells, DeWitt, and in the world of food there isn't anything classier than Le Palais-Royal."

DeWitt strolled over to the waiting lunch cart. "I do hope you're right. Let's have some lunch, shall we?"

Dave considered the possibility of walking out right then and there; considered it, but didn't do it. "Anything you say, DeWitt."

Claude came back from Le Palais-Royal and let himself into Kate's house with the borrowed key, feeling like an interloper, even though Kate had gone out of her way to make him and Jean-Paul feel welcome. The magnificence of the place was almost scary. He stepped into the foyer, glanced at the little table where the mail was left on a silver tray. A letter from home! From Chateaubourg! Claude smiled. He'd know his father's script anywhere, astonishingly fine for such a rough-hewn man.

Claude picked up the thin envelope and carried it with him upstairs. Catching a glimpse of himself in the mirror, he decided he'd better shower first. I look like a chimney sweep, not a chef.

Five minutes later, glowing from the hot shower and from anticipation as well, Claude sat on the edge of the bed and carefully tore open the envelope. Read it thirstily. Frowned. Read it again, slowly now, letting the words sink in. It was a sunny afternoon but now the room seemed dim. Claude had a sense of distance, of unreality, sitting there and holding the thin airmail paper so tightly it wrinkled between his thumbs and forefingers.

Papa, being Papa, started with the good news: yes, Marie-Claire and the boy had arrived. Little François was thriving and Marie-Claire had made no attempt to prevent Papa's visits. All the same, she refused to discuss any conditions, any settlement or arrangement for Claude to visit.

So the old man had gone to his friend the magistrate. Thinking to apply a little leverage. Or at least to clarify the situation. But the situation was anything but clear.

Everything I feared, only very much worse, he concluded for the second time after rereading the letter. And still Claude held it, as if by setting down the paper he might sever this last fragile link between himself and the boy. His eyes roamed across the letter one more time and the hurt of it burned into his heart.

> . . . France is still France, cher Claude, and it is
> highly unlikely that the custody of one so young as
> François would be given to anyone but the mother,
> even if the mother is Marie-Claire. But the only way
> to know that for sure is to try. And to try you must

appear in person before the magistrate, who, as you may not remember, happens to be an old friend of mine, André Draquette. And there lies the urgency of my letter, cher Claude. Draquette retires at the end of the year—a little more than a month away. He urges you to come just as quickly as you can. And privately, very privately, he tells me that there might be the barest glimmer of a hope. Not to count on it, but a possibility. You are, after all, the abandoned party, and that does count for something. So consider this carefully and plan to come soon.

Always, your loving Papa.

The paper burned in his hand. His resentment was doubled by the sure knowledge that he had walked right into Marie-Claire's trap. *Nobody had a gun at my head. I said "I do" and I meant it. Idiot!*

It seemed beyond sadness. But every time Claude thought of his little boy the anger came flooding back, multiplied by his sense of helplessness. Draquette or no Draquette, he knew that the odds against his ever gaining custody of the boy were enormous.

He was still holding the letter when the door of the guest room burst open and Elise ran in, glowing, and hugged him hard. "Darling, I did it! He was almost going over to Le Cirque but I talked him out of it. Romney's letting us go ahead with the banquet. Isn't that wonderful?"

He looked at her, knowing how much of herself Elise had invested in this moment. *How in the world can I tell her I won't be here for her?* He put his arms around her, postponing the inevitable. "I am happy for you, Elise," he said quietly.

She pulled back a little, looking up quizzically. "You don't sound all that happy. Is something wrong?"

All he could do was to hand her his father's letter.

Elise took the fragile paper as though it was a warrant for her arrest. Read it slowly. Read it again. She handed it back to him, her face changed. Radiant with happiness when she came in, now Elise was all facts and action.

"No question, Claude, you must go there. But . . . can't it be after the banquet? I mean, it's less than a week now. And we simply can't do it without you."

Claude set the letter carefully on the bureau. I've got to make her understand. We're dealing with my baby's whole future, not just some damn social occasion. When he spoke Claude took great care to keep his voice even. Gentle.

"Elise, Elise. You must put yourself in my place. If I don't go—if I don't do everything I possibly can—then I must live with that all the rest of my life. And I would hate myself. I would not deserve the love of my son, then."

He turned from her. Claude could feel the tears coming to his eyes and he didn't try to stop them. He walked the three steps to the window. Waited.

The silence stretched out.

"You must go."

Her voice was flat, as though she were saying the words to herself in an empty room. As though the fact of his leaving had drained her. "Six days," she said. "That's all the time we have to pull the whole damn thing together somehow. Oh, Claude. Can't you wait six days? Call the magistrate, maybe? Is it really a legal requirement that you be there in person?"

"My father seems to think so. But perhaps not." He turned from the window, a little more in control of himself, but only a little. Walked to her. Reached out and cupped her chin in the fingers of one hand.

"Elise, Elise, you know how I feel about you. And about the restaurant. I can't help this."

But as he spoke, Claude wondered, Does she feel for me what I feel for her? Oh, yes, she likes me, this is not a frivolous girl. But with her tremendous need to have Le Palais-Royal succeed, will there ever truly be room for me? For any man?

Then he said what he had never said before: "I love you."

Her eyes seemed to grow ever larger, deeper, darker. For an instant he thought he had frightened her, that maybe this was too soon, that it had caught her off balance.

"Oh, Claude," she said very softly. "Claude."

She came closer and put her arms around him. For a time neither of them said anything more.

Elise broke the silence. He could feel her stir a little, as though a small convulsion had rippled all through her slim body.

"No one," she said, "ever promised it would be easy." In her voice was a softness Claude had never found there before. A longing. It was all of a sudden a little girl's voice, and Claude could sense a child's need in her. A need to be loved but also to be more than loved—to be taken care of.

And it is just now I must leave her.

"I can cancel that damn banquet, Claude," Elise went on, her voice softer and softer. "It's ruining everything for us, and no one will blame Le Palais, or me, or you. It's just that—"

"Don't say it, chérie. I will stay. Six days is not so long. I will call this magistrate, this Draquette. It may be that things can be started—papers prepared or whatever. Then, when the banquet is over, then I will go."

"Don't do this for me, Claude. I heard you very clearly, what you said before, and I understand. I know sometimes I sound as though I don't, as though there's nothing in my life but Le Palais-Royal. And these last weeks there hasn't been. Except for you."

"It isn't wrong to want something very badly, chérie." He took a breath so deep it was almost a sigh. "It's just that, sometimes, the world gives us more than one thing to want, all at the same time."

"I do want Le Palais. You know that. And this banquet— however stupid that may seem."

He laughed then, a soft and gentle sound, and held her close and wondered if six days really would make a difference. Surely François won't know, he told himself.

"Claude, my dear, dear Claude. I'll put you on the Con-corde the morning after the banquet. You'll be in Paris by noon, in Chateaubourg a few hours after that. Maybe your father could bring François to meet you."

He looked at her now, amazed that the wheels were al-ready turning—and then not so amazed. "When you want a thing, chérie, you want it very much."

"Yes. I guess I want it all—including you. But you know that. And I want to do right by Le Palais. Maybe that's wrong. To want so much."

And how can I answer her? It's the way she is.

"Happiness, Elise, is not a restaurant." He kissed her on the cheek, just as he might kiss a child who didn't quite understand. "Happiness is a thing that lives inside us. We can't will it or command it or make it do tricks. And that is why you must follow your heart, Elise, and I, mine. And right now mine calls me to Chateaubourg."

She moved in his arms but he held her tighter. I must, I must, must make her understand!

With a sadness that Claude thought more poignant than any words he had ever heard before, she said, "It was going to be such a beautiful banquet. It could have been. It could have worked. It could have been—the best ever."

For a moment he couldn't respond. Long ago, he thought, they would take a condemned man and tie one arm and one leg to one horse and the other arm and leg to another horse, and then they would whip those horses until, maddened, they galloped off in opposite directions. And here I am and the horses are about to be whipped and I may be torn limb from limb.

He thought of his son.

Elise stirred again in his arms.

Claude thought that right now, in this minute or the next one, his heart must shatter like dropped crystal. "But my darling, I will stay. I said that."

She looked up at him. "I know you did. And that made

me feel worse than ever. As though I'm wrecking your life with my damn banquet."

"I married Marie-Claire, Elise. I fathered the boy. I must take the consequences. And, really, you are right. Six days can't make that much difference. Not now. Not after she's done what she's done."

"I didn't want it to be this way, Claude. You know that."

"I know it." And he held her tighter, all the while thinking that it was too late already to call Papa. Tomorrow would be soon enough for that.

He felt the warmth of her, the closeness. And the fragility. She has bones as fine as a bird's bones, he thought, and her dreams soar like a lark in springtime. For the hundredth time since they'd been together, Claude wondered what he had done to deserve this astonishing girl-woman-lover-friend.

"Well, chérie," he said at last, "let us call Armand and get his thoughts. He asked to be included. And, after all, we have a banquet to prepare."

Kate opened the front door of her house and the sudden chill she felt had nothing to do with the weather. Dave stood there, grinning like a schoolboy, handsome as ever in his business suit, navy topcoat, black attaché case.

Kate looked at that case with special interest—interest touched with fear. She knew what must be in it. He has the contracts at last, he will have made the changes Simon Doughty suggested. All I'll have to do is sign and that will be that.

She offered her hand, feeling somehow awkward as she made the gesture. Feeling that there should be something more between them. Or less. Terrified that when she told him she was having second thoughts he'd be furious with her.

"Come in, David."

She took his coat and led him into the library. Tea was waiting. Kate sat on the love seat next to the birch fire. Dave sat, rather formally, in the Queen Anne armchair on her right. Kate poured tea for him, using the action to buy time, forming words in her mind and then rejecting them. I'm being a silly, indecisive female, she told herself sternly. She watched her hand as she poured, fascinated that it wasn't trembling.

Why, she asked herself, must everything be so damnably complicated? Before the fire I was all prepared to put as much space between Elise and myself as I could. Now, everything's changed somehow. Maybe it was the way she pulled my portrait of Pierre out of the fire. Whatever the reason, we're closer right now that we ever have been. I don't want to change that. Not even for millions of dollars. She's all I have, really.

"Well," said Dave, "here we are. Your Simon Doughty is one shrewd negotiator." He opened the black case and pulled out a crisp manila folder.

Kate watched it with deadly fascination, as though a cobra had come slithering out of the case. She felt Dave's eyes on her.

"Is something wrong, Kate?"

She took a thoughtful sip of tea before answering. He's done everything he said he would, she thought, right on schedule. Didn't mind about the fire. And he's been practically saintly about Elise. Dave's been a brick right through it all. And now I'm going to let him down and he'll hate me forever.

"Dave," she said, plunging into it, "I know how this is going to sound: it's going to sound crazy. But do I actually have to sign right this minute? The fact is . . . I'm having second thoughts."

Dave felt his heart stop; he remembered his lunch meeting with Steele. If Kate knew how much is riding on this, he thought, she wouldn't be talking this way. He looked at her for a moment before speaking, feeling like a tightrope walker. One false move could send him falling, falling, with no safety net below. He set down his teacup.

"Second thoughts? Kate, if you think my price isn't fair,

if someone else has gotten to you since we talked, just let me know. I'll try to meet any price."

Kate laughed.

Dave recoiled physically, as though she'd slapped him hard. Her laughter cut right into his heart. It was that cruel a sound, that unexpected. He waited, afraid of his emotions now.

"You businessmen! David Hollander, I am mortified you'd think I'm capable of that kind of game-playing."

Thank God, he thought.

Kate's laughter had come quick and sharp, but when she spoke, her voice was Kate's voice, gentle as English mist. The voice Dave knew he might come to love.

"Before the fire," she went on, "it was all different. More resolved. I really was getting fed up with Elise, with the way she was acting—the whole situation. But now, suddenly, we've gotten very close, Dave. For the first time, really. And—I hope you can understand this—Elise is important to me. She's all I have left of Pierre. And I do respect her for wanting to carry on Le Palais. She's so determined to bring off this banquet . . . I don't want to undermine her. Elise needs all the confidence she can get right now, Dave."

Kate paused, looked at Dave. He was simply watching her. Waiting. She took a breath.

"And that's why I wonder, would a week or so make that much difference? I mean, your project can go ahead just as well if I were to sign after the banquet, can't it?"

Now Dave began to feel slightly dizzy. As though there wasn't enough air in the room. "You can sign any time you like, Kate." He fought to keep his voice even, his tone easy. "As for Délices du Palais-Royal, it would be illegal, naturally, to use the name unless we have a clear right to it. Elise could sue us for doing that, and if she gets mad enough or desperate enough she just might."

Kate sipped her tea and found it bitter. "Well, Dave. It's

only that this seemed to be a chance for me to show her that—maybe—we can be friends in spite of everything."

He managed a smile. "I admire you for that. On the other hand, Kate, I admire you for just about everything."

She felt herself blushing like a teenager.

"There's nothing wrong about your wanting to help the girl," Dave went on. "It must be a terrible time for her. Forgive me if it seems to me you're being more fair to Elise than she might be to you if the tables were turned."

"Maybe. I always seem to be trying to do the right thing, and then it ends up being the wrong thing. Dave, you're the last person in the world I want to disappoint. I'm not backing out of my promise to sell you my share in Le Palais. I just don't want to do it right this minute. I want that girl to have every chance, and I must help her any way I can. Then, when it's all over—if the banquet is a success—maybe she'll feel a little more generous toward you. Toward both of us."

Kate paused, wondering whether her words would drive him away.

"If," she continued, "the banquet is a failure—and it could be—she won't be able to say I helped make her fail. Dave. Bear with me. Just until after next Sunday. I'll sign then—if you still want the restaurant."

"You think there's a chance I won't?"

"There's a lot riding on the banquet, Dave. If Elise devaluates the restaurant's reputation who can say? I don't want to offer you tarnished merchandise."

Astonishing himself, Dave laughed. "Pure gold doesn't tarnish, Kate. Maybe we ought to have a little more faith in Elise. And in Claude. I'd better be getting back to the office now. I'll take the contracts. And I'll come beating on your door right after the banquet."

She smiled. "Dave, are you in the Tastevin?"

"No. Never had the time—nor the palate."

"You have a fine palate, David. That dinner was splendid. But I was just thinking, since they've been kind enough to ask me, why don't you come too? As my guest. Believe me, I'll need moral support."

He stood up, feeling as though a vast weight had been lifted from his shoulders. She still wants to see me, he thought. She wouldn't issue an invitation like that if she were angry or disillusioned.

Kate rose with him as if drawn up on invisible strings. It hadn't gone so very badly after all.

"I wouldn't miss it for the world," he said, getting into his coat. "Sunday, then? What time?"

"Drinks at eight. Black tie."

"You'll let me know if there's anything I can do?"

"Of course."

Again, they shook hands. As formal, she thought, as an ambassador from Queen Victoria herself.

"Good-bye, Dave. I'm sorry for being so silly about this."

"You are anything but silly." he grinned, turned, and went lightly down the steps.

As she stood at the door, watching him walk away without looking back, Kate was struck by a fear so irrational it seemed silly.

She wondered if she would ever see him again.


The first thing Claude did the next morning was call his father. Even touching the receiver made François seem closer. He dialed direct and listened attentively to every click and whir of the line. Heard the phone ringing in his father's little cottage. Imagined the cozy room, part kitchen, part dining room, and part study. There'll be an applewood fire crackling in the hearth. Papa will be having his afternoon coffee, maybe a calvados by now.

The phone rang three times. With each ring Claude could feel the distance, mile by mile, and the further distance he'd be putting between himself and little François by delaying a week. He could almost feel the boy slipping away now; imagined a scene where he came up to the child, his arms open wide—and François walked right past him. Not recognizing this stranger who pretends to be his father. And Marie-Claire laughing.

Just after the third ring Papa picked up the phone.

"Papa?"

"Claude! How are you, boy? You got my letter?"

"Yes. And I am coming. But, Papa, there is something—it is difficult to get away immediately. If I come Monday next week, will that be too late?"

Claude waited for the answer, wondering if his father could possibly suspect how much hung on it.

"I am glad you are coming, Claude. The bitch grows fatter and more arrogant every day. Your boy is fine, though. I see him every day at least once. And—I have taken this liberty, so you must indulge an old man—I have asked my friend Draquette to initiate divorce and custody proceedings in which you sue the bitch on grounds of desertion and child-snatching. This is a ploy, Claude. Draquette doesn't really think it will work, but it will give you some new chips in the game, non? With which you will bargain. And the bargain will be François. Half custody perhaps, visiting privileges certainement."

Claude felt the relief coming over the wire as though it were some kind of magical transfusion. Felt the warmth building in his heart, felt the tight, tight knots in his gut coming slowly but certainly unraveled. "Thank you, cher Papa," was all he could manage.

"It gives me the most delicious pleasure, Claude," said his father with a small but quite audible chuckle, "to have a chance, any chance to get even a little revenge on that one."

"Who must be nameless?"

The old man laughed.

"On my tongue she is nameless. The bitch."

Claude smiled. François's future was in good hands.

"I'll call you again, Papa, when I know the flight times."

"Take care, mon petit. I watch her as the gyrfalcon

watches some fat little hedgehog. I hover, I circle—and then I strike!" He laughed.

"Until next week, then, Papa. And thank you."

"A privilege, boy. A great, great privilege. Justice will be done!"

"I hope so, Papa."

Claude put down the receiver and kissed Elise, who had been standing inches away.

"Now, Madame la Restauranteuse, we roll up our sleeves!"

Elise said nothing but the expression in her eyes was more than enough for Claude.

Half an hour later they were at the restaurant. Le Palais-Royal was bustling. Armand, still pale, still astonishing in his casual clothes, was supervising a crew of workmen. The air rang with hammering, vibrated with the whine of electric drills and handsaws, echoed with the shouts and laughter of the workmen sent in by the decorating firm that had done the place over to Pierre's specifications eight years ago.

Elise paused in the doorway. It was so good to hear laughter here again. Once again she thanked God for her father's prudence in matters of insurance. He even made them do an escalator clause, for inflation.

Five days since the fire. So much had happened. So much more was going to happen. *They claim they can get it back together again in a month. I'll believe that when I see it. But even so, it's a start. And by the time the banquet's over that month will be nearly half over.*

Her mind raced, visualizing the reopening.

*If there is a reopening. If we don't blow the whole thing with the banquet.* But her fears were a little tamer now that she knew Claude would be with her.

She turned to him and grinned. Le Palais was coming alive again, and for the first time since the fire she could walk into the place without feeling she'd just fallen down some bottomless well.

Her instructions to the decorators had been very simple: "Just make it as it was—exactly."

And Kate had agreed. "Do it your way, Elise," she had said. "It's your place now, or soon will be." Elise, knowing the papers weren't signed yet, hadn't consulted Dave Hollander at all.

"What I want," she'd said to Kate, "is for an old customer to be able to walk into the place and—if they hadn't heard of the fire—not know anything had happened."

Some of the old furnishings, she knew, would prove to be irreplaceable—things like the antique silver sconces from Paris. But the decorators were searching out something similar, and the insurance, blessedly, would cover it all.

Claude had spoken to Armand the previous afternoon. Now they got some coffee and began planning in detail. At first Elise let the men do most of the talking, pleased to see Armand coming back to life a little, making good suggestions, watching with interest as Claude made a rough sketch of the Sixty-eighth Street library and living room showing where the six tables would be and how the service would flow. Claude got out the menu they had created before the fire.

They were studying it to see if substitutions might be necessary when the kitchen door opened and a familiar voice said to nobody in particular, "I hope I'm not intruding."

Three heads turned to stare at Dave Hollander.

Dave looked back at them, meeting their inquiring glances. Intruding? Welcome as a skunk at a lawn party. A small flicker of amusement danced in his brain but Dave took care not to show it.

Elise spoke first. "Hi, Dave, how are you?"

"I'm well, thanks. I just wondered if there's any way I can help."

"Thanks, Dave," Elise replied. She even smiled. "I think we're at least beginning to get things under control. I talked Reverend Romney into letting us go ahead with the banquet—maybe Kate told you. It'll be a big step. We want to show the world we're back in business."

Her voice was level, reasonable, any trace of the annoyance Dave was sure she must feel perfectly under control. And good for her, he thought, recalling Kate's descriptions of the girl's attitude in the past. She must know I don't have any legal right to be here. Not quite yet, anyway.

"Bravo. And you're doing it at Kate's house."

"She was wonderful about offering. Now we're in a huge scramble, trying to match the few bits of china that survived. Armand's seeing if more can be flown in from Japan. Luckily the crystal is Baccarat and there is enough right here in town."

"And the cooking?" Dave spoke softly, intent on preserving the fragile truce between them.

"Well," said Elise quickly, "We're fine there, thank God. Claude'll be here, and our regular sauté and grill team—Barry and Steve—and all the rest. As many as we need. And all the waiters as well."

"I had an idea," Dave said then, deciding there was no point in not coming right out with it. "Suppose we fly in one of the famous chefs from France. Bocuse or Verge, for instance?"

Elise looked at him the way she might regard a rattlesnake. "Dave, that would have my father turning in his grave. We're doing this—breaking our necks to do it—to prove what the new Palais-Royal can do. We don't need help from some ringer from France."

"The Four Seasons does it from time to time."

"No doubt."

The chill in her voice could have frozen ice cream. Dave checked his anger. Concentrated on breathing slowly. Hell, maybe it wasn't such a hot idea after all. Maybe I'm letting it take on too much importance. Trying to load the dice a little. Still, he gave it one more try.

"Don't you think it might help to give an impression that

Le Palais-Royal can pull off anything? That the world's best chefs would give their right arms to do a star turn here?"

Elise smiled but didn't trouble to remove the scorn from it. "That's precisely what I don't like about it, Dave. The star-turn aspect of it. It's cheap."

Claude had said nothing at all during this exchange.

"It may not be such a bad idea, Elise," he said quietly now. "We chefs are not enemies, you know. In France we often drop by somebody else's restaurant and, well, improvise. Almost the way jazz musicians do after hours."

Dave had always respected Montgeron; now he admired him more. No ego trips here, anyway. But Elise is going to defend Le Palais-Royal the way mamma eagle defends her nest. And if I'm not careful she'll scratch out my eyes. To his surprise, Dave found himself admiring her for it.

"Of course," Dave went on, "it's just a crazy idea. I don't know what one of those guys would charge—or even if they're available. I just wanted to ask your opinion before making any kind of approach."

"Dave, that's very kind of you," said Elise, obviously struggling for control, "but it would cost more than I can afford. You know maybe better than I do what our cash situation is. All those taxes. We're going to do the banquet right—better than right—but we have to weigh every penny we spend. If it weren't for very good insurance, we'd be wiped out."

"I could persuade Hollander Industries to underwrite all costs, Elise."

She smiled. "You really don't ever give up, do you, Dave? Believe me; we can do it on our own."

Suddenly Dave found himself enjoying the fencing, and feeling a new respect for his opponent. If only she'd realize we don't have to be antagonists, that as a team we'd be unbeatable. Dave tried again. "Claude likes the idea. What about you, Armand?"

Armand reflected. When he spoke it was with something very close to his accustomed poise. "I agree with

304

Mademoiselle Elise. Tinsel. It is a superficial thing to do. And Le Palais-Royal is not a superficial restaurant."

Dave managed a smile.

"Outvoted—not that I really have any right to a vote around here. Well. I'd better get out of your hair. But really, if there's any way at all I can help, just let me know."

"Of course. Dave, it's kind of you to want to."

"Just don't help too much, eh? Believe me, Elise, I understand how you feel. The only thing I want is for Le Palais-Royal to make the most dramatic comeback since Pompeii emerged from its own ashes."

Her smile had a touch of warmth in it now. "Then we all want the same thing."

"Well, folks," Dave said, "I didn't mean to interrupt. I just wanted you all to know I'm here if you need me."

"So long, Dave," said Elise. "Thanks for dropping by."

Mexican standoff, thought Dave as he walked down the service stairs of Le Palais-Royal and let himself out into the alley. Maybe she can do it and maybe she can't. And what can I do in the meantime but pray?

There'll never be enough time. Elise felt the minutes ticking away, draining her. Their first project on Tuesday was transferring the Romney Margaux from Le Palais to the Sixty-eighth Street house. Armand had been adamant about that, so that the wine would have nearly a week to settle before the banquet. And there were the tables to be rented and the furniture to be moved and the tablecloths and napkins to be considered.

Kate was right to insist I be a part of it, dragging me from store to store until we found that wonderful fabric at Schumacher, the exact celadon green of the china, printed with those delicate chinoiserie plum branches. Perfect. Dear of Kate to go so far out of her way to help.

"But Kate, where will we ever find a seamstress?"

"Here I am, darling. I'll make them up. It's only eight big circles, for heaven's sake. And the napkins, of course."

Elise had simply stared at her stepmother.

Kate laughed. "I've made most of my own clothes for years, my dear," she said, "and not badly, either, if I do say so."

They'd carried the fabric back to Sixty-eighth Street themselves. Forty-two yards of the heavy Belgian linen was enough to stretch your arms permanently, Elise thought as they struggled out of the store with bulging shopping bags.

Kate's house looked like an army camp in wartime. The movers had come and taken all the biggest pieces of furniture out of the library and the living room. The dining room table was gone, and all the chairs. The space thus revealed seemed enormous to Elise. Seeing it this way for the first time, she was struck with a sense of foreboding.

It looks just the way it will when Kate sells it. For all her mixed feelings about her father's house and the woman who now lived here, a tremendous sense of regret came over Elise in that moment.

I grew up here. I laughed and cried in these rooms. And left them. And now I can't come back. Not really. Not ever again.

The banquet took on a new significance then. It's an ending, maybe a beginning as well. The last party in this house, at least as far as the Villeromains are concerned.

Pierre's portrait was still resting where they'd left it after the fire, leaning casually against the foyer wall. Elise looked at the painting and shuddered, not at all sure she could live up to that awesome standard.

The phone rang, jolting her out of that frightening reverie. It was Claude. On the line his voice seemed distant, and Elise realized how much she wanted him here, right next to her.

"Chérie, how soon will Kate's house be set up? We must have a complete run-through as soon as possible."

Elise looked at the chaos around her. Well, a run-through of the table settings won't help much, she thought. It's the coordination between the Palais-Royal kitchen and this one that really matters.

"We could try for Thursday evening—I think."

"You will check with Kate?"

"Of course. How many people do you need? As guests, I mean."

"Oh, eight will do. One table. We can't really do the filet de boeuf for fewer than that."

"I'll tell Kate. Shall I arrange for the van?"

"Mais oui."

Elise hung up the phone. More lists to write. More details to work out. Will Claude's convection oven really fit in Kate's kitchen? If not, good-bye soufflés. That had been Claude's idea. The convection oven was electric, unlike the big ranges, so they could just unplug it and—with luck—it might be moved anywhere. Elise had visions of blown fuses, crossed wires, sparks, flames, ruination.

From upstairs she could hear the reassuring humming of Kate's sewing machine.

The doorbell rang. The table and chair rental people delivering. She showed them where to place the tables, stark and all too utilitarian-looking they were. She touched one. Solid. The chairs, at least, were attractive, passable reproductions of country French. She signed the receipt and the men left.

It was beginning to look like the scene of a banquet. Elise prayed it wouldn't be the scene of a disaster.

She was standing in the library, considering the placement of the table nearest the fireplace, when Kate walked in carrying the first of the eight round tablecloths. Together they spread it on the nearest table.

Instantly the room was transformed. Elise began to see how the rooms would look, and suddenly it all seemed possible again—better than possible. Wonderful.

"Kate, it's lovely. I think we ought to use them in the restaurant too, when it's ready."

Kate smiled. "Let's get through Sunday first, my dear. But it does look rather nice, doesn't it?"

"It's perfectly beautiful. By the way, Claude called, about the run-through. Will Thursday be all right for you?"

"Anything's fine with me, dear."

"He wants eight people, Kate. Why don't you ask some friends?"

Kate paused, frowning. "Dare we? I guess it'll be fine if they're very good friends. Not exactly your regular dinner party, is it?"

"No, but it could be fun. It's just the only way to work out the timing, coordinate moving everything from Le Palais-Royal to here, work out the service, are the waiters tripping over each other—all that."

"Do you mind if I ask Dave?"

Do you mind if I poison him? Elise thought, but kept her mouth shut. "Of course not. He's been really kind about the whole disaster, considering how rotten I've been to him."

"Well, let me think who else I can ask at such short notice, Elise, and I will. And you're right: it will be fun."

"God willing."

Elise decided she could do no more at Kate's house so she walked back to Le Palais-Royal. The workmen repairing the place were going at it full blast now, and the sense of energy flowing through the ruined rooms was a vitalizing force in itself.

Elise felt that same sort of energy flowing fast and strong when she walked into the kitchen. There was an edge to it now, a special urgency. Steve and Barry were there, deep into discussions of logistics, consulting with Claude every five minutes as some new idea occurred to them. Elise could hear fragments of their talk as she moved about the busy room, reluctant to interrupt the flow of it.

". . . so we have the sauce for the oysters all made and just poach them for a minute at the Villeromain house," said Barry. "No big deal."

"Except a minute may be too long. Maybe we ought to steam the little bastards in their shells."

"And burn our hands getting 'em into the sauce?"

"Cancel the steamer."

"Can we get from here to there in the van in ten minutes?"

"Barring gridlock."

"Well, then, let's roast the filets here in the Vulcans. They've got to rest ten minutes or so anyway."

"Wrap 'em in foil."

"Pray for no gridlock."

Elise smiled to hear the confidence in their voices. She kept her imagined flat tires, smashups, stalled vans, and other disasters to herself.

"Soufflé base and raspberry puree made here, egg whites whipped and folded in there," said Claude, the general, behaving in typical Claude fashion like one of the team. It made her think of Yves, of the havoc he would have been causing if he were with them now. But any thought of Yves brought back all her guilt and sorrow, and it was redoubled because she hadn't liked him. No one deserves to die like that, but he certainly did deserve to be fired. Yet all the logic in the world made not a bit of difference. The guilt loomed, and Elise knew it would be with her forever.

There are going to be a lot of invisible guests at this banquet. Watching and judging me, just like the real ones. Daddy. Yves. Jared too—laughing, no doubt. Haunting me. Well, I did what I had to do, and if there are bad consequences I'll face them. But not now. Not till it's over.

When the chef's conference was over Elise helped Claude make more lists, checked with Armand about the availability of waiters—whom Armand had given permission to moonlight during the time before Le Palais was reopened—the details of linens, the required flowers, ashtrays, vases, wine coolers: it seemed endless. But it would end; Elise knew that with a terrifying certainty. It would end on Sunday at the Tastevin banquet. Despite the chaos and all her doubts, Elise felt good. It was working out. We've got a fighting chance, and that's all I ever asked for.

A messenger arrived from the travel agency. Claude's tickets for France. Round trip on the Concorde, departing Monday. Open return. Elise signed for them, controlling her astonishment at the cost. Some things you can't put a price on, she thought. But the words *open return* scared her, and even the look Claude gave her when she handed him the envelope didn't quite erase her doubts.

"Thank you, chérie," he said simply.

"It's for François," she told him in a voice that could barely be heard.

Everyone else in the bustling kitchen seemed to melt away in that moment. He took her hand and pressed it, saying no more. As if words might somehow be dangerous.

The phone rang. The phone was always ringing now, and Elise always felt she had to answer the damn thing. The florist. They weren't sure they could get enough white freesias for the banquet. Elise tried to be patient, to be diplomatic, listening to explanations and weighing alternatives. Feeling trapped. It isn't trivial, no matter what I think. Flowers count. It all counts.

The woman on the phone was being too polite. "Look, Miss Travis," Elise finally cut in, "do me a favor. Call Holland. If there's a way to get white freesias I'd like them. If they say no—well, we'll think of something."

Quick agreement. End of conversation.

Almost as soon as she hung up, the phone rang again.

"Damn!" She picked it up again and made an enormous effort to be professional. "Le Palais-Royal. Good afternoon."

It was Western Union. A gentle voice asking for Claude. Elise felt a shudder of pure panic. "I'll take it," she said, reaching for a pencil.

The woman didn't even try to pronounce the urgent French. Instead she spelled out the words. There were only eight of them but Elise felt her heart sink deeper and deeper

with every one: TON FILS GRAVEMENT MALADE. VENEZ
TOUT SUITE. MARIE-CLAIRE.

*François very ill. Come at once.*

"Thank you, Elise said, putting down the phone.

She walked across the kitchen, amazed that the floor
stayed just where it was, solid and unshaken. Feeling her
world coming to an end all the same.

Claude looked up from his pastry counter. Instinctively
he knew. "Chérie—what's wrong?"

Elise just shook her head. "Bad news. A cable for you."

She handed him the paper on which she'd copied down
the message. He read it and for a moment said nothing.
Sighed. Looked at Elise, whose eyes had never left his face.

"Well," said Claude in a hoarse whisper, "there can be no
question now, Elise. I must go to him."

"Of course. Let's go back to Kate's right now. You'll
have to pack. I'll see about flights—I can call from there."

Minutes later, breathless from running, they were in their
room at Kate's house, Claude throwing a few things into a
suitcase, Elise on the phone with the travel agent. It was
nearly three in the afternoon. Elise booked Claude on a
seven P.M. flight out of Kennedy. And once more said the
fearful words: "Open return."

She hung up and Claude picked up the phone and dialed
his father's number in Chateaubourg. No answer. He
waited, listening to the ringing, clinging to the tenuous connection across all that distance. Hung up, looked in his address book, and dialed another number. Marie-Claire's
parents' house. Again, no answer.

Claude felt the enormous weight of his helplessness. It
seemed about to crush him to a pulp. *If only I'd been there,
or had François with me, this might not have happened.*
Whatever "this" was.

Elise was busy again, calling a radio cab to come at four
thirty. "You have your passport?"

"Oui."

"Let's go downstairs, Claude. I'll make some sandwiches. You've got to eat. We didn't even stop for lunch today."

It was true, Claude was grateful, but he reacted like a zombie, moving in a kind of trance. His mind and his heart were already in Chateaubourg, trying to cope with the unknown menace. Imagining the worst: François under the knife, François crushed by a speeding car, François quivering with some nameless incurable disease.

He forced himself to eat. Elise opened a bottle of Bordeaux and Claude managed to drink a little, but it might as well have been kerosene for all he could taste of the velvety wine.

Elise said very little. If the banquet's ruined, it's ruined, she thought. What matters most is Claude. Getting him home just as fast as we can. Maybe it's not as bad as the cable said. Maybe Marie-Claire's panicking. It might even be a trick to get him back to her. But I can't suggest that.

"Would you like some coffee, Claude?"

He looked at her, reached out for her hand. "No, thank you."

A horn sounded twice. The taxi.

They crawled through rush hour traffic toward the Triborough Bridge.

Elise and Claude sat in the back seat, holding hands but saying little. There seemed to be nothing more to say except small talk, and neither of them felt up to that. Elise tried to think of comforting things to tell him but it all rang empty to her. Words just don't do it at a time like this. We've gone way past just words.

There was a sense of unreality in the taxi, as though they were trapped forever in some kind of a time capsule, removed from François's illness, from the wreck of Claude's marriage, and from all the cares that were engulfing Le Palais-Royal.

At the Air France ticket counter at JFK, Elise reached in her purse for her credit card.

"No, chérie. I cannot—"

312

"Of course you can. It isn't me, it's Le Palais-Royal. Daddy's card, anyway." She almost smiled. "It's the very least we can do."

As the lady behind the counter operated the seat-selecting computer, Elise handed Claude the envelope she had tucked into her purse as well.

"What's this?"

"Francs. Daddy always kept some around. They'll save you time at Charles de Gaulle. A car will be waiting, Claude. The driver will be looking out for you, but you should look for him as well. Usually they have a sign with your name on it. This way you won't waste a minute with rentals or anything."

The agent handed Claude his tickets and boarding pass.

"Open return, Mr. Montgeron?"

"Open return. Thank you."

They walked arm in arm to the gate. Elise felt as though she were walking in a dream. A bad dream. They stood in silence by the little rail that separated the boarding area from the main aisle. Air France called the flight. Elise put her arms around him. Looked up into his troubled dark eyes.

"Oh Claude. Good luck. I'll be praying for François every minute."

"Thank you, chére Elise. For everything."

He kissed her voraciously, and the heat and force of it almost shocked her. As though by the kiss he were trying to say the words he hadn't—couldn't—say to her. Then he turned, picked up the small suitcase and joined the line of passengers boarding the big jet.

Elise stood there paralyzed. The sense of her loss was rising up in her and she felt she might drown in it. Why, why do they always walk out on me?

She was still standing there ten minutes later when the 747 moved away from the boarding ramp. She made her way back through the terminal and got a cab. Managed to give Kate's address without actually crying. Closed her eyes. Forced herself into reality. There goes my last chance at pulling off the banquet.

313

# 16

KATE SAT IN the kitchen sipping tea and wondering where in the world Elise had got to. Not like her to vanish without calling, or leaving a note. Well it's probably something to do with the restaurant, some emergency or other, and she just didn't have time.

Then Kate heard the front door opening. Footsteps in the hall. She looked up and saw Elise. The girl looks as though she's seen a ghost—or is one. "Elise, what's wrong?"

Elise sat down. Closed her eyes. Opened them. Every little motion seemed to cost her an enormous effort. "Claude got a cable. His little boy's very ill. So I put him on a plane. I'm sorry, Kate. I just didn't think to leave you a note."

"Have you eaten?"

"Not really. But don't bother. I couldn't."

"It's not the end of the world, darling."

"That might be easier. Then I wouldn't have to make explanations—or face people at the restaurant."

"Elise Villeromain. You're not giving up now?"

Good old Kate. Damn the torpedoes, full steam ahead. I should have known. It's my world going down the drain, though, not hers. Easy enough to be gallant when you're a bystander.

She managed something close to a smile. "I'm not?"

Kate paused. She's so fragile right now. Tread softly, Kate.

"Elise, Elise, you're better than that. I know you depend on Claude. Rightly. But—this is something I'm learning myself, and it's painful. When someone we love and depend on is taken away from us, well, somehow we've got to go on. They'd want us to."

"Daddy would. I know that, Kate. Too well I know it. But it's just that every time I seem to be making a little progress with the restaurant, fate comes creeping up and lets me have it. Yves, the fire—now Claude."

"Let's see where we are. You've got the wine, the menu's fixed and approved, we have this house to give it in, you've got Steve and Barry—they're very competent are they not?"

"Better than that. But I don't think either of them can replace Claude's touch with the pastries, the barquettes and the dessert soufflés."

Kate's mind raced, but it didn't have to race very far before it alighted on Dave Hollander. "Elise, you remember Dave's dinner party?"

"Sure. Why?"

"That chef—I forget his name—but that was a really superb meal, don't you agree?"

"Oh, yes. I didn't want to be impressed, but I was. And so was Claude."

"Well that man works for Dave—in his business, I mean. I'll bet we can borrow him. May I call Dave and ask?"

"His name is Rideau. Gérard Rideau. And, Kate, if we could possibly get him I think it's a great idea."

Before Elise finished Kate was on her feet and dialing. Will Dave even want to speak to me, after I put him off about the contract? Kate remembered Dave's words, his reassurances. And she wanted to believe him. But still she wondered. Still there was a hint of doubt.

He picked up on the second ring. Briefly Kate filled him in.

In his apartment in the Carlyle Dave smiled. What an opportunity! "Kate, you bet Gérard'll help out. And anyone else Elise wants. I'll have him at Le Palais-Royal first thing tomorrow—well, say nine-thirty?"

Once again Kate felt the strength of him. The take-charge quality that she so admired. "Oh, Dave. Thank you. From both of us."

"Don't thank me, Kate. I'm part of this too."

You surely are, and so am I. For better or worse. "Well, we do appreciate it—very much," she said.

"You'll call me if there's anything else?"

"Of course. And, Dave—is there anyone you'd like to bring to the run-through on Thursday? We have two vacancies and I can't think of anyone who'd be just right."

"Timmy might like that. I'll get back to you."

"Thanks again, Dave."

"Don't thank me—Gérard will be thrilled."

Kate put down the receiver. How wonderfully competent he was. She turned to Elise.

"It's all set. Gérard Rideau will report to you at the restaurant tomorrow morning at nine-thirty. He's yours for as long as you need him, compliments of Hollander Industries."

Elise smiled through her resentment. Dave can snap his fingers, and master chefs come flying out of the wings, right on cue. "Kate," she said, "I know I've been horrible about Dave. But right now he looks like all the knights in all the fairy tales I ever read."

Kate got up and came to Elise and kissed her. "You know, it isn't really so black-versus-white."

Yes, thought Elise, it is. Once this man gets his greasy hands on Le Palais we'll probably begin seeing microwaves and frozen capital G gourmet entrées and all the rest. But all she could say was, "Maybe not."

"Are you sure you won't have a bit to eat now?" Kate asked again.

Elise shrugged.

"My stomach's been on a roller coaster all afternoon, Kate. Ever since Claude got that telegram. Maybe I'll raid the icebox later on, but don't worry about me."

"What's wrong with Claude's baby?"

"Didn't say. Sick unto death, was all."

"Poor Claude."

"It's tearing him up. He feels responsible, even though he clearly isn't."

"What a shame. Well. Maybe it isn't as bad as it seems."

"I hope not." And maybe it's worse. Maybe it's so bad he won't ever come back to me. But Elise couldn't give voice to these thoughts. Thinking them was painful enough. She wondered what Claude was thinking right now. Imagined the jet high over the ocean in darkness. At least maybe he can sleep a little.

Elise looked around the kitchen as though she'd never seen it before. Tried to force herself into imagining the banquet in full swing, the sounds and the smells of it, the bustle and the glory. Or the failure.

Kate sat with her for a while in companionable silence. Finally they cleared up the kitchen. Elise was on her way up to bed when Kate stopped her and led her into the library. Three of the six tablecloths were finished, finished and draped smoothly over the rental tables. One lamp was lit, and that on its dimmest setting. It was a moment before Elise noticed the real change.

There, over the fireplace that centered on the far wall of the library, where an old mirror usually hung, was Daddy's portrait. Pierre Villeromain gazed benevolently from behind the copper pot he was stirring, took in the library with its rented tables and lovely new cloths, looked past all that to the wide archway that separated the library from the parlor, where the three other tables were set up and waiting for their cloths.

The painting looked absolutely right there.

Elise touched Kate's arm. "He's home at last," was all she said. But that was enough.

They walked upstairs in silence, said good night and went into their bedrooms.

Elise undressed slowly, took a long hot shower, and put on a very old cotton flannel nightgown. She stood by the window for a moment before climbing into bed. At first she thought she was imagining the snowflakes. They were that tiny. Then, squinting, fixing her gaze on the nearest street-light, she saw that snow was indeed beginning to fall.

Snow reminded her of Vermont and Vermont reminded her of Jared. Funny how seldom I think of him now, when just a few weeks ago I thought of hardly anything else.

But it wasn't funny at all.

Outside, the tiny snowflakes had already dusted the street with a shimmer of whiteness. The cars huddled close to the curb were glazed with it: fine powdered-sugar snow. Just the kind Jared likes best, she thought, hugging herself against the chill.

She climbed into the big double bed and was immediately conscious of how empty it felt without Claude beside her.

It was daylight when the jet landed at Charles de Gaulle Airport outside of Paris.

Claude went through passport clearance and customs like a zombie, found the driver with his sign just as Elise said he would. The driver led him through the glittering maze, carrying the one suitcase, and to Claude it was all a bad dream. The car was a Mercedes, not a limousine but a big sedan, black as a hearse.

The morning traffic was in full swing now but the driver was skillful and mercifully silent. As though he sensed Claude's mood.

The Autoroute was a little less crowded. They sped west and slightly south, past the shoddy suburbs and the signs bearing their weight of France's vanished glory: Versailles. Chartres. Le Mans. Moving beyond the Île-de-France now, the land growing hilly. Laval. Vitré. And now a sign that read CHATEAUBOURG.

318

How many times have I come this way, and with what happy thoughts? Coming back on holiday from my first apprenticeship in Paris. Coming back to see Marie-Claire when I thought she was the most delicious woman in the world. Coming back to marry her. Coming back one more time to say au revoir just before we left for New York.

Had the town grown smaller and uglier in the four years he'd been away?

Claude made himself come awake now. Looked intently at the landscape. Where was the field that ought to be just there, on the hillside? All covered now with little houses that looked like counters in some child's game. Flimsy and all the same.

Hesitantly, Claude giving directions now, the Mercedes made its way through the narrow streets, skirting the center of town, edging out into the open land beyond.

Well, here at least it looks the same. But smaller. That must be New York working on me. Or maybe I've grown too.

Now they were on the gravel lane where Papa lived. Claude realized with a jolt that he had no idea what the arrangement was with this car, this driver. Surely he should tip the man. He reached for the envelope Elise had given him, opened it for the first time and blinked. Even without knowing how the franc was faring this week, Claude knew it must be thousands of dollars worth. Claude smiled. Knowing Elise, she probably hadn't counted the money either.

The big sedan pulled up to Papa's door.

Just as I remember it. At least this hasn't changed. An ancient house, soft gray stone, its massive wooden door weathered to nearly the same shade of gray, roof tiles mossy as ever. Something stirred in Claude's heart. And whatever happens, at least Papa will be here to stand by me. He gave the driver a generous tip and asked if the man would wait a few minutes. But of course.

Claude walked up the path to his father's door. Twenty

feet? It seemed much longer. Reached for the handle. Papa always kept his door open during the day, But the door was locked. Only then did Claude realize he didn't have his key. It's in the apartment at Le Palais. I never thought to take it. He knocked, on the unlikely chance that his father might be napping. Not Papa. Not at half past noon on a weekday. The thick old door seemed to amplify Claude's knocking into an ominous drumroll. The pounding echoed in the cottage, more loudly in Claude's heart. He turned and stood on the wide, low doorstep, blinking in the sunlight. The driver stood by the Mercedes, smoking. Expressionless.

On Papa's obscure little lane there were only three cottages. Claude looked at the other two and thought: Grandmère Boucheron: if anyone knows where he is it'll be that old busybody. Granny Boucheron, ancient and witchlike even when Claude was a child, did little but sit at her window all day, her eyes—tiny, bright and black, very like a bird's—taking in everything that happened in the little lane.

In two minutes Claude was knocking on her door. It opened a crack. The birdlike eyes peered out suspiciously.

"Madame Boucheron?"

"Claude! God save us, you're back!"

"I'm back. Madame Boucheron, perhaps you know where my father might be?"

The door opened wider. She was, Claude discovered to his astonishment, scarcely taller than a child. Under five feet, surely. And touchingly fragile, with a bird's bones as well.

"Oh, Claude, poor, poor Claude. He is . . . at the funeral. I couldn't go, or I'd be there."

Claude could only nod.

"At Sainte Thérèse?"

"Oui. Sainte Thérèse."

"Thank you, madame."

"Poor, poor Claude."

Claude turned and somehow got back to the car. Told the driver how to get to the Chapel of Sainte Thérèse. Buried his head in his hands and wept loudly, his breath coming now in great heaving sobs, the sounds he made scarcely human.

Gone, François is gone. I came too late. The bitch killed him somehow. The car moved slowly through town. A funeral procession of one.

The Chapel of Sainte Thérèse had been built several hundred years ago on a hillside on the far side of town from where Claude's father lived. It took some fifteen minutes to get there, and in those minutes Claude pulled himself together a little. I owe my boy this much, not to make a disgrace of myself at his funeral. He could feel his eyes burning from the tears, and his only handkerchief was a soggy lump.

The Mercedes pulled up behind several other cars outside the churchyard. Claude climbed out of the car, stumbled, managed to stand and walk. He could see over the low fence now. Saw the cluster of people at the far end of the burial ground. I'm not too late for this, at least. But it doesn't really matter. Nothing matters now.

Claude wanted to run but he could barely walk. And as he walked he remembered another funeral in this churchyard. A child's funeral, like this one.

I must have been seven. And what was her name? A girl from school, younger, no one I knew very well, but we all came to the funeral. He shuddered all over again, thinking of the small white coffin.

The people clustered around the open grave were all from Chateaubourg, all people Claude might have recognized on any other day. Any day when his eyes weren't misted with tears. Any day when his heart wasn't black with loss. He found his father, standing a little apart from the rest. Walked over and touched Papa's arm.

The old man started, as though Claude had touched him with a live wire. He turned. Saw Claude. A look such as Claude had never before seen on his father's face now came over it: something between pure astonishment and fear.

They embraced.

"But, dear boy, did you not get my telegram?" Papa whispered. Words were still being spoken at the graveside.

"Only the one from Marie-Claire."

Papa's face changed again. His eyes were looking upward, as though only heaven itself could provide an answer now. For the first time since Claude's marriage, Papa said her name, making it into a curse."

"Marie-Claire!"

"Papa?"

The old man could say no more. He took Claude by the arm and led him toward the grave.

At first Claude held back. Not sure he could face that pit. That tiny coffin. But Papa persisted and Papa had strength in his muscles as well as in his spirit. Claude felt himself being propelled toward the graveside as if on wheels. The small crowd seemed to part instinctively before them.

And there they were. At the edge of the grave, Claude hadn't the strength to look down into it. He looked, instead, across the hole, and there he saw Marie-Claire's mother, fat as her daughter, all in black and draped in black veiling. A great pyramid of black she was. Claude looked for Marie-Claire, thinking that it would be the hardest thing he'd ever have to do, to meet her here, now.

Papa touched Claude's arm. "Cher Claude. Look. See where her journey has brought her." Claude looked at his father as though he'd never before seen the old man. Blinked himself back to reality. Papa was pointing. Pointing down.

Hypnotized, Claude forced himself to look.

There in the bottom of the grave was a large casket of shiny brown wood, glittering with cheap gilt hardware. It took a moment before Claude made the connection between the size of the casket and the size of his son. But still the shock numbed his brain. He turned to his father. "Marie-Claire?"

"Marie-Claire."

Again Claude looked into the grave and in that instant he became so dizzy, his head such a rush of conflicting emotions, that he felt the strength draining out of him like water from a sink. The silence was absolute. He stood there without speaking for a moment. Then, slowly, as though he were moving underwater, he turned again to his father. "But—where is François?"

Papa smiled. "With your aunt in Le Mans. You will see him tomorrow."

Claude turned back to the grave. His eyes misted with tears, and the grave, the shoddy casket, and all the black-clad mourners seemed to shimmer, as if they might at any moment melt away. He crossed himself automatically, a gesture left over from childhood, and thought how lively his wife had been once, how full of hope, how eager to love him. So long ago it seemed like forever. Less than ten years, years that held a lifetime of dreams gone sour. But, Claude thought as the awareness of François, François alive, flooded his heart, I have the boy. He turned from the grave, took his father's arm, and walked slowly back to the car, unable to greet the other mourners or even to speak to Marie-Claire's parents, or to stay for the funeral service.

Back at the cottage, Claude, Papa and the driver—who by now seemed almost a member of the family—tasted Papa's tangy fermented apple cider. Claude felt so drained, so tired, that it was hard to conjure up any emotion. At last he said, "Papa, tell me the whole story."

"It's a long one. Marie-Claire's parents weren't exactly thrilled to have her back, even with François. More mouths to feed, and things haven't been going that well with the old man's gas station."

"I would have sent money."

"I know. Wasn't it I who told you not to? She was a bad apple, Claude. Well, after we spoke, my friend Draquette had papers drawn up: your suit for divorce on the grounds of desertion. She of course got wind of it. Inevitable in a town like this." He took a long drink of cider and refilled

323

everyone's glass. "Her back was up against the wall, and she knew it. As it happened, François had a cold. Just a cold, mind you, nothing to get alarmed about. I was seeing him every day. But it got worse, lots of coughing, a stuffy head. I insisted he see a doctor, and the doctor gave him a shot and some pills to take.

Claude shifted in his chair. "It got worse?"

Papa hesitated. "I hate to say this of anyone. Even her. She tried to make it worse. On the third day of his illness— a cold rainy day it was, too—I was up at our old farm, checking on the goats I keep there. Walking back late in the afternoon, who should I happen to meet but that bitch and the child. François was soaking wet and shivering. Well, of course I asked her what in God's name she thought she was up to. And I could tell by the fear in her eyes what the answer was even before she made up some silly excuse. There was no place in the world that boy should have been but home in bed. She knew it and so did I. She must have had some mad scheme to lure you over here for a reconciliation. Impossible to say, now, of course."

Claude felt as though he'd been stabbed from behind. All of his anger came back. Even in his darkest imaginings he hadn't thought Marie-Claire capable of anything like this.

"It could have been . . ."

"Murder. Exactly. Child-murder. She was so stupid— forgive me but she was—and so driven by her own crazy selfishness that I really don't think she knew what she was doing. What it could lead to. Of course, I took François that minute. Picked him up and ran—I can still run when I have to, don't think I can't. Brought him straight to the doctor's. Doctor put him right in a hot bath while I went to Marie-Claire's house for his clothes." Again, Papa paused.

"Interesting," he said at last. "Her mother made no protest at all when I came barging in there. Mad as a bull I was, as you can imagine. Took all his clothes, toys, everything. By the time I got back, François was out of the tub and smiling. Eating caramels. By some miracle of luck he hadn't caught on to what was happening. So I took him here and fed him and put him to bed. Next morning Marie-Claire still hadn't come home. By noon I heard about the telegram she sent you. Telling you the boy was dying or whatever."

Claude sat back and thought about how incredibly lucky he was to have this man for a father. François might really have died, but for him.

"How did she die, Papa?"

The old man shrugged. "That is between her and God. As you saw, she was buried in the churchyard. And maybe it was an accident. The gendarmes looked into it carefully, and there's no saying. She got drunk somehow. Seen in a few bistros, although none of the barmen will admit to giving her more than a glass of red wine. In the end, late that same night, she staggered out from some bushes and right into the path of an eight-wheeler transport truck. He tried to stop, of course, but it was raining and he couldn't. At least it was over quickly for her. The monster."

Claude sighed.

"Does François know?"

"Non. There seemed no point in it. I wanted to talk to you first."

Once more Claude felt a warm rush of love and gratitude toward his father. "Thank you, Papa. I'm glad I came."

His father smiled.

"I wired you not to come, but I guess you were already on your way."

"Monsieur Montgeron, I'll have to be getting back," said the driver, "or else call in and make another arrangement."

The man's words had the effect of jolting Claude back to another reality. He thought of Elise, Elise who had been so very good about his leaving, even though it must have been an unbearable blow to her. Of everything that was left to be done in the restaurant.

Claude turned to his father. "Papa—I want very much to see François. But I also have to get back to New York as soon as I can. Could I go now with the car, and stop in at Tante Georgette's on the way? Say hello to François and go on? Then, in a few weeks, if you can keep François in the meantime, I think I can make a more permanent home for him. I'd like to have him with me."

"In New York?"

"In New York."

Papa smiled. "I'll miss him, you know. As I also miss you."

Claude got up and embraced his father and kissed him on the cheek. "You will see him every summer. And you can come to see us in New York as well. I would be proud to have you dine at Le Palais-Royal, Papa. We both would."

"Both?"

Claude blushed.

"I guess I haven't had time to tell you. There is a woman. Someone wonderful."

"At the restaurant?"

Claude smiled.

"Very much at the restaurant, Papa. She owns it."

Papa frowned, took another drink of cider. "Very fancy."

"Very wonderful. You'll see."

Papa stood up, putting an arm around Claude's shoulders. Grinned. "So my son hasn't only been cutting out pastries over there. Good for you, lad. You deserve a fine woman."

At the door Claude kissed his father again. "Thank you, Papa."

"Bon voyage."


Wednesday dawned white. Five years in Vermont had given Elise an acute awareness of snow; the special silence of it, the muffling of sound, the muting of echoes. The snow outside colored the light in her room until the room itself seemed all soft and silvery. She opened her eyes, blinked, stretched luxuriously and remembered.

Claude wasn't beside her.

Damn! Just when everything was coming together. She

looked at the clock, tried to figure out the time difference. Has he landed yet? How's the child? Will he call?

She got up and went to the window. Last night's fine dusting of snow had built up to a few inches. *Maybe there'll be a real old-fashioned blizzard and nobody'll be able to come to the banquet. But the way my luck's been running all the members of the Tastevin are probably Olympic skiers.* She remembered one January night in Stowe when she and Jared had gone to a party on skis. Elise tried to recall just how it felt. *What kind of girl was I then? What was I thinking as we glided through the night? Not thinking at all, probably. Just reacting. Existing. Taking it minute by minute, laughing at Daddy's world. And now Daddy's world has caught up with me. And who's laughing now?*

Elise turned from the window and went into the bathroom. Washed and dressed and thought about all she had to do today. And do alone. Looking into her nearly empty closet reminded her of one more chore. Have a showdown with the laundry about those silk dresses or go back to Bonwit Teller and get more. She brought herself up with a jolt. *Claude's baby may be dying and I'm thinking about silk dresses.*

Standing at the top of the stairs, she held tight to the bannister, and thought, *Why didn't I chuck the whole damn banquet and go with him?*

Elise ate some toast and drank coffee in Kate's kitchen, listening to the eight o'clock news. Blizzards in the Rockies, a record freeze on the northern plains; more snow predicted for New York and vicinity.

*Well,* she thought, *I've got much more important things to worry about than a little snowstorm. Gérard Rideau, for example. How are Barry and Steve going to react to my bringing him in at the last minute?*

She looked at her watch, quickly finished her coffee and left the house.

Le Palais-Royal seemed to have been waiting for her. Armand was already there, and Barry, but Steve hadn't come in as yet. Elise told them about Claude's emergency and about bringing in Gérard Rideau.

Armand, as she expected, was agreeable. Barry surprised her; Barry had every right to be resentful. "I'm all for it, Elise. Anything that gets us through the banquet, anything that keeps Le Palais going strong—you bet I'm for it."

She looked at him and smiled, more relieved than she could have said. *He can't be much older than I. He could go anywhere after working for Daddy. He could leave me flat, and so could Steve.*

"Thanks, Barry. You understand it isn't any reflection on my confidence in you guys. We just need the extra hands."

Barry grinned.

"Elise, one day I'm going to be like Claude. But not right this minute. Nobody knows that better than I. That's why I try to work for the best people in the best places I can. That always meant Pierre Villeromain and Le Palais-Royal. Still does. Even with Pierre gone." Then, a little flustered, he turned away and found something to do on the other side of the kitchen.

*Oh, God, let it be true,* Elise thought as Gérard Rideau let himself into the kitchen.

"Gérard, I'm very glad you could come," she said, shaking his hand and taking him to meet Armand and Barry. The introductions were quick but cordial and in a few minutes they were sitting down to work out a plan for tomorrow's run-through.

"Choreography," said Armand, "will be everything. More difficult than merely preparing a meal here and serving it a few feet away."

Elise tried to remember the talks she'd had with Claude, his suggestions and her own. What could be done in the restaurant and what must be done at Kate's house.

"The movers are coming for the convection oven this afternoon," she said. "Let's pray it's still working when it gets to my stepmother's house."

More lists, duplicate battle plans to be checked and re-checked by phone. Gérard had some thoughts about that.

"If you'll call me here," he said, "about the timing of each course—just when they really do sit down, how quickly they eat the oysters, and so forth—we can coordinate better."

"I can do that," said Elise, feeling a little like a spy, imagining herself peering through keyholes at the unsuspecting Tastevin.

"I'll stay here," Gérard went on, "through the roasting of the filets. And we must have a few backups in case anything goes wrong with the timing."

He paused.

"They have to be absolutely à point."

"Yes, and backup soufflés as well," said Elise. "At least, that's what Claude had in mind."

"Naturally," Gérard murmured, as though Elise and everyone else in the world should have been born knowing about backup soufflés. But really, Gérard is being just great. He's a pro and we're damn lucky to have him helping out. She made a mental note to thank Dave properly the next time she saw him. Even if she choked doing it.

Somehow she got through the day without her thoughts of Claude driving her entirely crazy. Gérard was wonderful, blending right in as though he'd been a part of Le Palais-Royal all the time.

Elise had to repress a shudder the first time she saw Gérard working at Claude's pastry counter, glancing at his white-coated back—they were about the same size—and realizing it wasn't Claude. He really is a pro, she reminded herself, and pros can do anything. She remembered how Claude had saved the lobster soufflés on the day of the memorial luncheon.

Claude could be applying for a job at some great restaurant in Paris right this minute for all I know. Maybe he's decided America's no good for him—America and me and

Le Palais-Royal. If the baby dies, who knows what he'll think. What he'll do.

More than once during that long afternoon Elise looked at the phone and prayed for it to ring. Or nearly picked it up and dialed his father's number in Chateaubourg. But she didn't. When there's something to say he'll say it. The last thing Claude needs right now is pressure from me or anyone else.

A barrel of Olympia oysters arrived from Tony Barberini, the Palais-Royal's main fish supplier for several years. Elise stood by while Jean-Paul and Gérard opened it. A fine astringent whiff of salt air and fresh seaweed filled the corner by the seafood refrigerator. Gérard picked up an oyster knife and deftly opened one and handed it to Elise.

One tiny plump morsel no bigger than a dime. She ate it then and there, au naturel. The elusive sweetness mingled with a touch of brine. Magnificent.

"Perfect, Gérard. Have one. As if one could be enough!"

He tasted one and smiled. "One and a half dozen per portion will be about right. They are splendid. One never sees them in the East."

"They will at our banquet."

"Certainement. I will practice poaching them: a question of seconds, I'm sure. Not even one minute."

"Wonderful." But as Elise said it she prayed and prayed again that it would be. Claude, where are you?

The hours slipped by. Talks with the florist about the scarcity of really good freesias, with Reverend Romney just to reassure him—"Yes, Reverend, the Margaux looked fine, we transferred it to my father's house on Monday"—Elise felt that she was running on some kind of an automatic pilot now, and that scared her too. What if I've forgotten something? How can I expect Gérard to really know everything Claude does so easily?

The phone rang and rang but it was never him.

Finally there was nothing more to be done at Le Palais-Royal. Elise and Armand and Gérard and Barry and Steve together ran down the list, the menu and the battle plan for tomorrow night's dry run.

"Sauce Aurore?" Elise read aloud.

"Ready." Gérard was grave.

"Carrots, turnips, broccoli?"

"On hand," said Steve, "but we'll do the purees tomorrow, just before serving."

"Terrine de canard?"

"Done."

And so it went until they were all satisfied that everything that was possible to do in advance had been done. Still Elise worried.

They said their good nights. Elise and Jean-Paul walked together back to Kate's house. Companionably, at ease with each other, but both a little shy, saying little.

Kate had finished all the tablecloths and napkins. The table for tomorrow's run-through was completely set, but for flowers. The three stood together, admiring the effect. "Of course," said Kate thoughtfully, "It'll look much nicer when the flowers get here."

"Kate, it's fabulous. You've really made it work."

Kate smiled.

Claude took the steps three at a time. At the top stood his father's sister Georgette and a very happy François.

"Papa!"

If all the trumpets in heaven had been sounding they couldn't have felt better to Claude than his son's greeting. He swept the child up and squeezed him and felt the delicious wriggles of good health. Not a sniffle was left. Claude greeted his aunt and they went inside. He looked at the room, which he only dimly remembered, and tried to recall the last time he'd been here. Years and years. It was the sort of room in which nothing changes, but François's presence had transformed it all the same: his toys were everywhere, and Claude could detect his father's generous hand in the profusion of blocks and floppy animals and brightly colored balls. He'll be fine here until I can fetch him to New York.

Thinking of New York made Claude think of Elise and Le Palais-Royal and the banquet. Suddenly he regretted taking the extra day, sending the chauffeur and the car away. He looked at his watch and calculated the time difference. It's the middle of the night there. I'll send a telegram.

He composed a brief message and called it in. "And what would you most like to do this afternoon, cher petit?" he asked, turning to his son.

The small face looked up at him gravely and Claude thought that his heart might break. "Would you tell me a story? Mama never tells me stories."

Claude lifted François onto his lap.

"Once upon a time," he began, "in a land filled with wizards and dragons, there lived a beautiful princess named Elise."

"Papa, were the dragons very fierce?"

"Absolutely. Fire-breathing, long-fanged, bloodthirsty dragons. They smelled bad too."

An hour later, in New York, the Western Union overseas operator got Claude's telegram. Dialed the number on it. No answer. She then set the message aside to call again.

An hour after that, the operator dialed again. Still no answer. She yawned, promised herself she'd call again in a little while, then forgot about the whole thing.

Thursday passed like an express train. Elise hadn't a moment to wonder about Claude, but she wondered all the same. Wondered and worried.

She went to the laundry and found her dresses in fine shape. Brought them back to Kate's, helped Kate with the flowers, then went down to the restaurant to see what she could do there.

Their guests for the trial run had been invited for seven. At six-thirty Elise was still in the shower. You will be confident. You will cheer up. You will stop moping and fretting as though the damn world will end if a soufflé falls.

She smiled at herself in the shower and remembered the chef in France a few years back who had killed himself when the *Guide Michelin* pulled one of his stars. I know just how he felt.

She quickly dried her hair and brushed it, dressed, and applied the smallest possible amount of makeup. It's part of the job, she told herself. You're doing it for Le Palais-Royal. Which cheered her enough to dab on some perfume Daddy had given her years ago.

Elise surveyed the result of her dressing, her makeup, and her apprehension by taking a long and unsparing survey in the bedroom mirror. The face that launched a thousand bad restaurant reviews, she decided and stuck out her tongue at the reflection. As she left the guest room she looked at the phone, forcing herself one more time not to pick it up and call France.

Downstairs she found Armand and three waiters already at work. Checking everything and checking again. Barry was there too. Gérard and Steve and Jean-Paul were at Le Palais but would arrive with the filet course so that Gérard could finish the soufflés here.

At quarter to seven the phone rang. Elise jumped. She picked it up with a hand that was fractions away from trembling.

"Hello?"

"Elise? It's Gérard. I thought we ought to make the phone connection and just keep it open. I'll have someone near it here all night. Just yell if you want us."

"Good idea. I'll do the same here."

Kate's kitchen looked weird with the convection oven at a strange angle near the refrigerator and every surface covered with preparations for the run-through: trays for the hors d'oeuvres, the vegetable purees all made and warming on warming trays, the raspberry sauce for the dessert soufflé waiting to be warmed at the last minute so it wouldn't lose any of its freshness.

Kate came in, looking splendid in a deep burgundy velvet suit. "Nervous?" She asked, kissing Elise on the cheek.

"More like frantic. Does it show?"

"No, dear. You look fine. Better than fine."

The doorbell rang; Joan le Caille had come with the Millers—all old friends of Kate's—and soon they were happily sipping Laurent-Perrier in the cleared-out dining room. Dave arrived with Timmy. And I make seven, Kate thought, taking a glass of champagne but hardly tasting it.

She peeked into the kitchen and saw that Barry was in control and ready. Went back to Kate's guests and worked at making the talk flow easily. The time seemed to drag, but Elise could tell people were enjoying themselves. Armand whispered it might be time to sit down.

Elise went to the kitchen phone and alerted Gérard at Le Palais. Barry began poaching oysters.

Three minutes later Elise was at her seat between Tim Hollander and Sam Miller. The Montrachet had been poured; the candles were lit. Daddy's portrait looked past them from over the mantel. Elise felt her stomach winding up like some old-fashioned watch spring. Tighter and tighter, until it formed one hard cold steel lump.

She forced herself to sip the Montrachet, which was superb. Said a few cheerful words to Timmy and to Sam. Prayed that the oysters wouldn't be overcooked, that Gérard's puff pastry wouldn't taste like cardboard. That the roof wouldn't fall in, nor nuclear war break out.

A waiter came in with the Olympia oysters in their puff pastry boats. Elise looked at the presentation and thought, Yes, very nice, but if Claude had been doing these boats there'd be a little more spirit in the design. She broke into the delicate pastry and took a small forkful. Excellent, can't be faulted. Still, could the sauce have used a touch more lemon? Elise cursed herself for not being Claude, for not having Claude's palate, Claude's finesse.

She looked around the table.

Everyone seemed to be enjoying the dish. But they're all friends, they'll never say anything impolite. It's nice of them to come, but this isn't the real test.

Halfway through the first course Elise got up and went to the kitchen to tell Gérard how the timing was progressing. "Maybe ten more minutes and they'll be ready for the terrine."

"Très bon. When the terrines go into the dining room, we put the filets into the oven here."

"I'll let you know."

As she sat down again Elise found herself watching Dave. He always looks as though he has the lease to the whole world in his pocket, she thought with more than a twinge of envy. How does he do it?

A waiter began to clear away the oyster plates. Elise got up again and spoke to Gérard. This is a little silly, like planning a bank robbery or something, she decided as she set down the receiver. But it's absolutely vital. If we screw up on Sunday, people will talk. Ripples will spread. Justin Bosch will be there, and he'll think I've betrayed the Villeromain heritage. And he'll be right.

Her glass was still half full of Montrachet. Elise took just a taste. Excellent. Better than excellent. Now a waiter poured the Bordeaux that was standing in for the 1959 Margaux they'd be serving on Sunday. A more recent Margaux, 1971, and very good indeed.

If Romney's 1900 Margaux is vinegar, will he try to blame us?

She remembered some of Daddy's tales of the ceremonious openings of legendary vintages and how they were very often simply undrinkable. "There are bottles and cases of bottles, chére Elise, that only make the rounds of the auction houses. They sell for ever higher prices but no one dares to open even one bottle. It's a joke, a travesty of what wine ought to be about."

335

Maybe it's a joke, Daddy, but please let it not be at my expense.

The duck terrine was fine, every bit as good as Elise remembered it from her father's own hand. And the sauce as silky and subtle. Then why am I having these doubts? Why does it seem that something, some little touch, is missing?

The room was filled with candlelight and good talk and laughter. Kate's guests were obviously having a fine time. But for Elise something was lacking and irreplaceable.

Claude.

He's only been gone a day, and it seems like a year. Maybe I was beginning to take him for granted. Maybe I had to be reminded how much I need that man—and not only in the kitchen.

Elise heard the front door open. That'll be Gérard with the filets.

Again she excused herself from the table and went back to the kitchen. Elise the human yo-yo, she thought. But they understand—or at least, they ought to.

Gérard was setting one foil-wrapped filet on a carving board. "And two more," he said, "one slightly less done and the other much less done—to be popped in the oven in case they dawdle."

Elise smiled. Yes, he's perfectly competent, he's a big help, we probably couldn't do it without him. Claude, come back!

She went back to the dining room and played the guest again. There's nothing to do now but wait and pray she thought.

The filet came and it was splendid. Then the cheese course in honor of the 1900 Margaux, which was not being served tonight. But we have to make sure of the cheeses too, just like everything else. The Explorateur triple crème was ideally ripe, the Roquefort appropriately pungent, the New York State chevre, delicate and refreshing. Six cheeses in all. Elise tasted a crumb of each and found them in the best of condition.

I must act like the most severe of critics. I must judge this performance the same way we'll be judged on Sunday. She strained every critical faculty, her mind a jumble of remembered tastes. But always there was an underlying fear that she wasn't up to it, that there might be subtleties she was missing.

Claude, come back!

If only he were here beside me, tasting, judging. Elise made herself smile. The conversation rippled around her and she tried to be a part of it. To help make the evening a social success as well as a culinary one.

At last the soufflé was brought in, well puffed and fragrant. With a dancer's grace the waiter made a slit in the top with his serving spoon and poured in some of the raspberry puree, then served everyone a portion. The men began applauding and everyone joined in.

Elise went to the kitchen and brought Gérard, Barry, and Steve into the dining room. Congratulations all round.

Finally it was over. Cordials were passed after coffee, just as they would be on Sunday.

As their guests left, Elise stood with Kate at the front door, saying good-bye, exchanging handshakes and kisses and trying to overcome the feeling that the whole evening had been some kind of a dream. They keep telling me how fine it all was. Why can't I believe that myself?

She went back to the kitchen and thanked everyone, individually and collectively. "You guys were fantastic," she heard herself saying. "Now all we have to do is do it again on Sunday."

Feeling drained, Elise went up to her room.

At the Western Union office the night operator got a busy signal from the Villeromain number for the fifth time. Disgusted, she put down Claude's telegram. Let the next shift get that one.

It wasn't until the next morning that Elise discovered she'd left the phone off the hook all night.

# 17

CLAUDE WALKED THROUGH Charles de Gaulle Airport half in a trance. His heart churned painfully with a dozen confused emotions. But what he felt most was sadness for Marie-Claire. He kept remembering their early times together. What had become of all their love and laughter? She did it to herself. It didn't have to end the way it ended for her.

He felt relief, too, as though some great rock had been rolled away from the door of his prison. I'm free! Free as I've never been before. And then he felt like singing, dancing, shouting his freedom from one end of the great airport to the other.

What he did was buy a paper, check in, choose a seat, and walk to the boarding lounge. Scanning the paper, Claude realized what an exile he had become. Urgent headlines about people who meant nothing to him and issues he hadn't thought about for years. I am neither French nor American now, so what am I? And what can this mean for Elise?

He put down the paper, thinking about her. Can I bring her a child, just like that, fait accompli? Can she possibly accept that?

Maybe it's madness even to consider bringing him back to America. But how could I live with an ocean separating us? And Papa, good as he is, how long will he have the strength? No. Now it all depends on Elise, on whether she loves me that much. Will she still want me after the banquet? What do I mean to her, really? Am I just a warm body in her bed, a convenience? A pair of clever hands in her kitchen? Elise could have anyone. Me with no real education, a village boy from Chateaubourg, and she who has always had everything?

But then Claude thought of Elise the woman; how her smile could cut right across the busy kitchen and sing in his heart. How her dark eyes could say more with a glance than most women could put into a book. He remembered how she had relied on him in the days of Yves, with Yves likely to explode over any trivial thing, and Elise so unsure of herself, yet equally determined to make it work.

Claude remembered their first night together as though it had been last night.

The night of her birthday. The look on her face when she saw the famous gâteau Elise, and guessed who had made it and why. The touch of her hand when he'd given her Maman's old crystal vase. And the touch of her body all through the night.

Maybe, he thought, just maybe, there still can be a chance for us.

A voice came over the loudspeaker announcing Claude's flight. He stood up, left the newspaper on the seat, pulled out his boarding pass, and joined the line of passengers on flight 573 for New York.

Dave Hollander sat at his desk, toying with a cup of coffee. Tormenting himself with thoughts of Kate. He smiled through the pain of confusion. Was this what people called a mid-life crisis?

He tried to remember the last time he'd felt like this—nearly thirty years ago, and with Barbara. All the same, the feeling was unmistakable. It ran through him with a quickness and tingling that was more than electric, more than just desire.

Dave knew it was irrational. He knew that Kate probably wouldn't have given him a second glance if it weren't for her problems with the restaurant. Still and all, he wanted her, and Dave was used to getting what he wanted.

He asked himself what she must think about him, really. Probably thinks I'm pushy, trying to play on her grief to acquire Le Palais-Royal. Still, he knew there was something in their relationship that was—could be more than just professional. More than just an old friend of Pierre's trying to help his widow. He sighed. A snowball in hell had a better chance than he did with Kate Villeromain.

A knock on his door snapped Dave out of his reverie.

"Come in, DeWitt."

"How did you know it was me?"

"You always knock the same way: two loud quick ones."

"Dave, I've been hearing about this Tastevin affair."

"In food circles, it's big-league stuff."

"So I gather. And you're really betting the farm on it, aren't you?"

"That's putting it a little strongly, DeWitt. Sure, I'm counting on the reputation—the legend, really—of Le Palais-Royal to help the gourmet project take off. It can give us immediate credibility. If Elise and Claude can pull off this banquet, it'll be like winning the World Series with half the team in wheelchairs. I think they can do it."

DeWitt smiled the tailor-made smile. It still didn't fit. "I hear bets are being made—and taken."

"Then you hear more than I do, DeWitt. Hell, some people will bet on anything."

"Yes. Dave, the reason I dropped by is, if it comes to my having to defend you before the board, and it might, I'd like to be able to say I was at that banquet. Can it be arranged?"

Dave had to restrain himself from laughing. He just can't keep out of it, can he? Old DeWitt wants to be in on the kill. I'd better tell Elise to watch the back door. Make sure he isn't creeping around pouring rat poison in the hollandaise.

"I think I can work that, DeWitt. You really feel I'm going to need defending?"

"I think you just might, David. And . . . well, you know I've always been on your side."

Yeah, because it was easy to be on my side. I was winning. "I never doubted it, DeWitt. And I don't doubt it now."

"Thanks. I want to take every possible precaution, that's all."

"Sunday, eight P.M., the Villeromain house on East Sixty-eighth Street. Black tie. Unless you hear otherwise, you're on."

"You'll be there?"

"Oh, yes. The Villeromains were kind enough to ask me."

"I look forward to it."

"I'm sure you do."

DeWitt got up then, rubbing his hands together in a sort of parody of eagerness. Are you with me, DeWitt, or against me? Dave wondered. Which way will you jump if the board really gets on my ass?

"Yes," said DeWitt. "Well. It'll be interesting, won't it?"

"Very."

"Thanks for getting me in, Dave."

"Any time."

When Elise woke on Saturday her room was filled with fear and shadows. The air seemed thick, and for a moment it was hard to breathe. Something's wrong, disjointed, out of synch. Where's Claude? Why hasn't he gotten in touch? Her need for him was sharp and physical, a yearning more keen than hunger. And the fear rode with it, side by side. Fear for Claude's child, of losing Claude forever. Marie-Claire's full of tricks. One of them might just work—no matter what he said in New York.

She closed her eyes again and rolled over in bed. Too painful too think about. But not thinking was painful too.

Elise felt more alone now than she ever had. Abandoned. Cold under the warm quilt. *I won't get up just yet, because when I do, I'll have to think about everything. About Claude, the banquet, Hollander, Armand. About why I got myself into a crazy situation like this.*

She closed her eyes, but the worries stayed with her. The silence told Elise the snow had come again. For days now there had been storm warnings, but she had managed to put them out of her head. *What does the weather service know, anyway?* she'd told herself. *They're wrong as often as they're right.*

Now she lay thinking about all the damage a big snowstorm might do. *We gave the world's best banquet and nobody came. Swell. The final irony.*

Her mind raced, checking and rechecking their inventories. *We have the filets of beef, ducks for the terrine, the vegetables, raspberries for dessert. The puff pastry is made and waiting in the refrigerator. The oysters will come today and Gérard wants to make his own baguettes right here in Kate's house Sunday afternoon. God. That's tomorrow.*

Now she forced herself to climb out of the warm and comfortable bed. Forced herself not to think where Claude might be or what he might be doing. Forced herself to wash and dress and go downstairs to make coffee.

Neither Kate nor Jean-Paul were up yet. She could see out through the foyer to the front door. To the whiteness. Elise went to the door and looked out one of the narrow windows that flanked it on both sides. She tried to remember the weather forecast.

*There has to be seven, eight inches, and it's still coming down like it might never stop.*

The house was warm but Elise shivered. *Claude, where the hell are you?* As if just having him here would stop the snow. Or guarantee everything will go right with the banquet. She tried to smile. *If there's something to worry* about, trust me to find it. She went back to the kitchen and made coffee and put some bread in the toaster. Jean-Paul came in, scrubbed and smiling.

"Bonjour, Elise."

"Bonjour."

No forebodings for Jean-Paul. It felt good to see him bright-eyed and eager. But seeing Jean-Paul reminded her of Claude. Elise felt the blood coming to her face and wondered if it showed. *He couldn't help it. He had to go, and I had to help him.*

But logic did nothing to ease her sense of loss. *It's as though someone took a knife and cut away a great big piece of me—including my heart. He'll be back. I know he'll be back. And then everything will be all right.* Elise concentrated on making herself believe that. *Maybe, just maybe, there are such things as miracles.*

They made a quick breakfast and walked through the fluffy new snow to the restaurant. Barry and Steve and Rideau were already there, and bustling. It was a help to Elise to be in her father's kitchen again, despite the ruination in the rest of Le Palais. The kitchen had its own reality, a sense of good work in progress, a feeling that obstacles could be overcome.

She looked at the Tastevin menu that had arrived yesterday from the printer. There was an amusing Picasso drawing reproduced on the cover, a satyr with a cup of wine frolicking with an overripe nymph. And inside, beginning the splendid list of courses, "Les Huîtres de Olympia en Barquette, Sauce Aurore."

Something clicked inside her.

"Gérard, did the oysters come?"

"Not yet."

"Let's call Tony Barberini and check."

Gérard went into the office and dialed. Came back frowning. "He was just about to call us. Bad luck with the oysters, Elise. They've landed at LaGuardia but LaGuardia's snowed in. Tony's pickup man is stuck out in New Jersey someplace. But he does have some nice lobsters, so we can substitute those. Lobster medallions would go as well in the sauce, and they'll look fine in the barquettes.''

"Damn. We promised Romney Olympia oysters. I hate not delivering.''

"He'll understand. The weather's terrible.''

Elise just looked at him, repressing the sharp response that very nearly found its way out of her mouth. Gérard stood there imagining he was being helpful; calm, smiling, competent. And infuriating. If we fail tomorrow it won't be his dream that goes up in smoke. Or his future.

She thought of the oysters trapped out at the airport. Maddening. Thought of the van they'd rented to make the trip between here and Kate's house.

"Steve, where did you park the van?''

"Garage on Sixtieth, just west of Third.''

"Could I have the keys?''

"Here. But—you're not thinking of going out there?''

Try and stop me. She smiled. "You got it.''

"Elise. Let me come with you.''

"Thanks, Steve, but we need you guys here. I'm the dispensable one.''

"Hell you are.''

"Well, I'll go crazy anyway if I don't try. But I'm used to snow. Lived in Stowe for five years, don't forget.''

"If you're sure.''

"Never surer.''

Elise went into her father's office and dialed the Barberini number. "Elise, I don't know what to say, except I'm sorry,'' said Tony. "But the lobsters are swell. We'll call it even, even though the oysters are a lot more expensive.''

"Tony, that's fine. And if you could send someone up here with the lobsters, just in case, that's fine too. But I'm going to try and make a run to the airport. I called to be sure somebody'll be there to give them to me.''

"Elise, don't. It isn't worth it. The roads are murder.''

Elise smiled. That was all she needed to hear. "Thanks,

344

Tony. I'm sorry your truck is stuck or I'd be after you to get 'em. But as it is, I'm going to try."

"They're at the TWA cargo terminal at LaGuardia. I think someone's there. But let me check, Elise. I'll get right back to you."

"Thanks, Tony."

Elise put down the phone and tried to be rational about the stranded oysters. Gérard's right, lobster could be delicious, people wouldn't mind that. But the menu says oysters, and if we don't produce the oysters, they might say we're slipping, snowstorm or no snowstorm.

The minutes stretched out until the phone rang again. Tony. He'd gotten through to the TWA terminal, there was a man on duty. Gave Elise directions and further cautions. "The roads are nearly impassable, Elise. The police say don't drive unless it's an emergency."

"This is an emergency, Tony."

"You got snow tires? Chains? A strong back?"

"I will have. So I look for Dane Atkinson at the depot?"

"He knows all about it. Just sign the receipt."

"Tony, you're being very good about this. You will get us the lobsters, just in case?"

"They're on the IRT right this minute. Good luck, kid."

She smiled, remembering the first time Daddy had taken her down to Barberini's. I must have been seven or eight. Before mother died. Tony was the biggest man I'd ever seen, and with the biggest, warmest laugh. Opened a Belon oyster just for me. And I pretended to like it, just for him. Tony was practically family. But that didn't get the Olympia oysters into Le Palais-Royal.

She checked her purse to be sure she had some cash, put on her Vermont fleece-lined snow boots and got her down parka. She took a thermos of hot coffee and a snow shovel from the locker room and said her good-byes.

"Wish me luck."

Steve grinned. "You know you're crazy?"

"People in the restaurant business have to be a little crazy, Steve."

"Elise—don't go yet." It was Jean-Paul, all bundled up like an Arctic explorer. "I come with you. It is not good for you to go alone."

She looked at him, repressing the smile that came automatically on seeing his comical appearance. But it was more than amusing: Elise was touched and grateful too.

"Très bon, Jean-Paul. We will be two crazy people instead of one."

Five minutes later they were in the garage, persuading the attendant to put on chains. Twenty minutes after that the shiny blue van pulled out onto Third Avenue and headed for uptown.

The avenue had been plowed, but the snow was building up again. Elise tried to remember the route and decided the Triborough Bridge would be easier to negotiate. She turned right on Seventy-second street, then left on First Avenue. At least we don't have to worry about gridlock, she thought grimly, looking at the deserted avenue.

They got over the bridge without incident, paid the toll on the other side, and entered a landscape that might have been a moonscape—if the moon had blizzards.

The big Grand Central Parkway was a sheet of compressed, sanded, salted snow. One or two trailer trucks ground their way along in the slow lane, sounding as though the strain of it might burst their iron guts. Elise felt a shiver of fear. Somehow in the city the very proximity of buildings and people had been reassuring. But out here? Who would stop if we got into trouble?

Elise found she could barely make twenty miles an hour. It took the most intense concentration; even with the sand and the chains, the van had an alarming tendency to wander. Here and there, half hidden beneath the snow, were patches of glare ice.

They crawled through Queens, its factories bleak and empty, past cloverleaves that seemed to lead nowhere, past a forlorn green copper spike, the steeple of a church, and past a huge graveyard, whose thousands of monuments had been strangely transformed by the snow into soft-edged mounds.

It was a cold, empty landscape, and Elise felt cold and empty too, even though the cab of the van was comfortably warm. She knew the cold in her heart had nothing to do with the snow. It was about Claude, and why wasn't he at her side instead of Jean-Paul, and whether he could ever feel about her the way she now realized she felt about him. Where the hell is he?

They passed cars abandoned helter-skelter where they'd skidded. She wondered when, if ever, their owners would be back to reclaim them.

The van crept along. Elise felt as though time had stopped for her. Inching along, fighting for control of both the van and her turbulent emotions and trying all the while not to alarm Jean-Paul, she seemed to be moving through a world that had retreated into itself, into this bleak, endless white silence—possibly forever.

She had an image of the van as it might be seen from far above, a tiny blue speck creeping across the empty whiteness of Long Island as an ant might crawl along a sand dune. Dreamlike yet far too real, with the implicit danger in every turn of the van's wheels, the drive now consumed all of her. It was as though she, Jean-Paul, the van, the snow, and the distant, elusive oysters made up her entire universe.

Then the real world intruded with a jolt. Elise felt the van begin to slide sideways in an eerie drifting motion. But she guided the wheel expertly, looking up to see the half obscured sign she might easily have missed: LAGUARDIA AIRPORT. And the turnoff. As she turned the wheel, the van slid again, and her stomach seemed to lurch with it. But the years in Vermont hadn't been wasted, nor Jared's expert instruction. Elise steered with the skid, gently applied her foot to the accelerator and brought the unwieldy van back where she'd aimed it. The snow seemed deeper.

Finally she came to the main access road to the airport. The access roads were fairly clear; even though all flights had been suspended the night before, there were cars and trucks with business here. Watching closely, Elise still almost passed the turnoff to the cargo area.

Here there was no traffic. Chain link fence, gate open, no guard. The cinderblock warehouse had big blue metal double doors. Tight as a drum. Swell, she thought, we struggle through all this and nobody's home after all. But there was another door, human-size, to the left of the big ones, also blue metal. Elise pulled the van as close as she dared, staying on the plowed surface. And thank God it's level.

The door was open. Inside, at a desk, sat a tall young man with blond hair.

"Mr. Atkinson?"

He looked at her and laughed, but it was a deep, good-natured laugh. "Sorry, but I really didn't think you'd chance it. You have to be the oyster lady."

"Tony Barberini said it'd be all right if I picked them up."

"You bet it is. Two barrels. Just sign this and I'll help you load 'em."

Ten minutes later the two sturdy aluminum barrels were securely in the back of the van and Elise was slowly making her way out of the airport.

Not so bad—but we're not home yet, Elise thought, focusing on the road. They drove in silence for a few minutes, until Elise noticed a curious noise. A small metallic tingling sound as though a million tiny wires were whipping at the van.

Sleet. Elise felt her stomach lurch. Damn! It's bad enough in the snow. But this? The road'll be one big sheet of ice if it keeps up. Still she said nothing, not wanting to alarm Jean-Paul. And to hell with it. If I hadn't tried I never could have forgiven myself. At least I made the effort. At least we got out here. If our luck holds even a little we may still make it.

"Well, Jean-Paul, when you came to work at Le Palais, did you imagine you'd end up on an Arctic expedition?"

He grinned. "It is an adventure. Like in the movies."

Let's hope it has a happy ending, like in the movies. "That it is, for sure," said Elise.

The van slid sideways as Elise edged back onto the highway. Just a little drift to the left, but it gave her the feeling of being out of control, of being in the hands of the storm. Biting her lip and saying nothing, she guided the van forward and breathed a slow sigh of relief as it seemed to take hold now, slow but stable and going toward home. Far away, barely visible through the drumming sleet, Elise could glimpse the dark ragged silhouette of Manhattan. Usually she found it beautiful—today it looked threatening, a row of rotted teeth in a skull. She remembered too vividly the last time she'd been on this road: with Jared in a taxi, coming down for Daddy's funeral.

Can it have been only weeks ago?

Jared.

Maybe he was right after all. Maybe there is something wrong with New York, with all this striving. But no. Let Jared drop out if he wants to. I'm at least going to have one good try at it. And if I go down with the ship, down I go.

She pressed a little harder on the accelerator. The van speeded up a little, held steady. She didn't see the glare ice. The van suddenly began to drift sideways.

Her hands tightened on the wheel.

"Hang on, Jean-Paul!"

Not the brakes—do anything but brake. The van had a life of its own now, drifting in some crazy dream, slipping inexorably toward the shoulder. Elise held the wheel firmly, resisting the impulse to wrench it, trying to coax the van back on course. But the van kept sliding, sliding. She saw the shoulder coming closer, closer. Well there it goes. Now I've done it. Why did I have to speed up? Now I've wrecked the banquet, and God knows what it'll do to Jean-Paul and

349

me. Then, irrationally, as though he could have made a difference, Claude, where the hell are you? she thought wildly.

The van moved in slow motion, in a bad dream. Slid at an angle. Hit the snowbank left by the plow with a soft but ominous crunch. Burrowed into the big drift until the packed snow came up the windshield.

Silence.

"Jean-Paul? Are you all right?"

Fear. Even as she looked at him and saw that he was unhurt, pale and shaken but gamely smiling.

At once she tried reversing the van. Hopeless. The wheels spun and spun, digging deeper. She was just barely able to shove her door open. Jean-Paul clambered awkwardly after her, because his side was completely buried. She reached back and switched off the engine, taking the keys. Felt the stinging sleet on her face. *Damn!*

Elise stood at the side of the highway with Jean-Paul at her side, cursing her impetuousness. A car came along, a big shiny Cadillac.

She waved.

It went right by.

"Merde!" The Cadillac vanished into the sleet.

Nothing moved on the road for ten minutes. The sleet seemed to be letting up, but still it was more than enough to sting their cheeks and ice their eyelashes and chill them to the bone. "Elise, you wait in the van. No point in both of us freezing."

"Thanks, Jean-Paul. But I got you into this. Look. Here comes someone!"

She stepped out into the road and waved frantically.

The oncoming car swerved a little and for an instant Elise was sure it would join her van in the snowbank. But it wavered back on course and pulled to a shuddering halt. An ancient rusted-out Ford wagon. The man behind the wheel looked piratical: olive-skinned and bearded and wearing a dark red knitted cap pulled low over his bushy eyebrows. Elise was suddenly very glad she wasn't alone.

But when the man spoke he smiled, and when he smiled all of her piratelike first impressions vanished under the pure voltage of his warmth. "Lady, I can't tow you, but for sure I can give you a lift over the Triborough so's you can call."

"That would be wonderful. Could I ask you to take these barrels, too? They'll freeze out here, and they're very important. We'll be happy to pay."

"Where are you going?"

"East Sixty-eighth, between Madison and Park."

"You got a ride, lady."

The pirate and Jean-Paul carried the oyster barrels to the back of the wagon. The man's name was Fernando Perez and he was on his way to help out a brother who lived in New Jersey.

"His pipes froze," said Perez. "I'm a plumber."

Thirty minutes later Perez dropped them off at Kate's house, refusing all offers of money. Elise wrote down his name and address and formally shook hands. She felt like kissing him. "Mr. Perez, you don't know what this means to us. You really saved my life."

"No, lady, maybe we saved the oysters. Hell, you could of walked it if you had to. Take care now."

"Thanks again."

He left them on the sidewalk with their two aluminum barrels. Elise thought of the new Cadillac that had passed them by and of how wonderful Perez had been. And people are always saying how rotten New Yorkers are, how selfish and uncaring. Not my pirate. Fernando Perez is going to get a very nice present from Le Palais-Royal when all this is over, and she decided, thinking of the perfect gift. When Le Palais is back together again I'll invite him and his wife for dinner there. And serve them oysters!

She looked at the barrels of oysters and the *when* in her imagination suddenly became *if*. Maybe I'm just kidding myself, making all this fuss about the oysters. We can still blow it, oysters or no oysters. I can destroy Daddy's restaurant if the banquet isn't absolutely perfect.

Claude looked out of the window. Twenty-two thousand feet below, invisible under its gray intensity of snow and sleet, lay New York. Elise. Le Palais-Royal. The future.

Claude clenched his fists in outrage. The announcement had just been made: impossible to land at New York—they'd try Pittsburgh.

*Pittsburgh!*

Claude tried to remember where that might be. Somewhere west. His mind seemed to go blank with the pain of considering it—being separated from her even one more minute.

At least when I land I can call her. Assure her I'm alive, that François is well, that everything will be fine. That by some miracle I might even make it in time for the banquet. But even as he thought these thoughts Claude knew he was fooling himself. The real question he must face on landing had nothing to do with the banquet. My whole life is waiting down there—if she still wants me.

Elise and Jean-Paul wrestled the aluminum barrels up Kate's front steps and into the kitchen. The house was filled with flowers. Kate joined them, heard of their adventures. She laughed in relief, and Elise found herself laughing too. It all seemed so silly now, here in the warmth of Daddy's house. They went to look at the setting for tomorrow's banquet.

The rooms were transformed. Elise blinked, trying to force herself to remember that she'd grown up here.

Now all the phone calls to the florist, all of Kate's sewing, all of the improvisation and sweat had come together in one magical stroke. The six tables each had their centerpieces now: rustic baskets filled with white freesias and rubrum lillies and pale pink roses. Elise went to the first table and touched a flower, hardly able to imagine this was really happening. And there were more baskets: on the mantel, on the sideboard in the cleared-out dining room where drinks would be served, in the foyer.

"Kate, it's lovely. Thank you." Elise kissed her stepmother on the cheek.

"Not me, dear. Doris Travis."

"We know who sewed the tablecloths, Kate. And kept me from falling apart completely. And after I've been so rotten to you and Dave."

Kate blushed. "Shouldn't we check on those oysters?"

They went back to the kitchen and opened both barrels, tasting oysters from each. As the delicate, sweet and salty morsel filled her mouth with memories of the ocean, Elise felt more than just pleasure; she could feel the first faint glimmering of hope.

She called Le Palais and told Gérard the good news. He agreed they should pack the oysters in ice. They could be opened late tomorrow afternoon and poached at the very last moment.

She hung up and wondered for the millionth time where in the world Claude could be. Damn you, Claude! Part of Elise hated needing him this badly; part of her knew that if he didn't come back to her she might never again be able to love someone completely.

Thank God for the work.

There was so much to do, mountains of work. And Elise knew she had to do it herself, not because the others weren't reliable but because if she didn't see to every last tiny detail she might wake up screaming. She called a twenty-four-hour towing company and asked them to pick up the van. *That adds about three hundred dollars to the price of the oysters,* she thought, *but it's worth it.*

As she put down the receiver the afternoon's adventures came rushing back to her, unreal as some ancient movie seen late at night on television. *How could I have been that rash? We could easily have been killed.*

She still couldn't quite believe she'd done it.

Oysters are only a part of it, and a small part at that, Elise told herself grimly. They're only the first step. The banquet hasn't even begun yet and until it is there are a million things that can go wrong—and probably will.

Elise called Reverend Romney and filled him in on their progress. Asked him if he thought all the people on the guest list would make it in this blizzard.

"Oh, I think so, Elise. Of the forty-eight, forty live in town. One pair of Parisians I know is already at the Pierre. I haven't had any cancellations, but of course there may be some at the last minute."

They'll be here. They'll be here and judging me on every bite. And that's just the way I want it, for better or worse. She put down the receiver gently. Realized she hadn't eaten since breakfast. Made sandwiches for herself and Jean-Paul. They ate companionably, then Jean-Paul went back to the restaurant.

Elise looked at her watch. Three thirty already. "I'll come down later on, Jean-Paul," she said, knowing that there was really nothing for her to do there. Knowing too that to do anything would be preferable to staying here and worrying about Claude.

She went back into the parlor and the library and checked every place setting.

Flawless.

From over the mantel her father's portrait looked down at her and that made Elise feel a little better. As though he were really here, and helping.

The doorbell rang and she turned from the portrait and walked out into the foyer, still thinking of her father, wondering what new delivery this must be.

Elise's thoughts were far away when she opened the front door. There stood Jared, grinning, snow frosting the bronze-gold of his hair and eyebrows.

"Hi," he said as though the heart-wrenching weeks had been no more than a few minutes.

"Jared," was all Elise could muster by way of a greeting. She stood there, feeling like an idiot.

"You have seen through my disguise," he said. "Aren't you going to ask a fella in?"

"Of course. Have you eaten?"

He stepped past her, turned, and took her in his arms—and it all came back to her in one unstoppable rush. All the warmth, the magnetic passion, the pure heat and force and raw sexual confidence of Jared Carter.

Elise felt this like a physical shock, as though she had unknowingly touched a high voltage wire. Her arms went around him. She shuddered.

"Hi, again," he said.

Elise buried her face against his parka, closed her eyes and wished for the world to end.

"I came down here, Mrs. Carter, to invite you up to Stowe."

Mrs. Carter. Mrs. Jared Carter of Stowe, Vermont. It seemed a million years ago, something from another life, dimly remembered, neither mourned nor regretted. For a moment Elise had no words for him.

How often had she imagined this, or something like it, or seen herself going up to Vermont to beg his forgiveness? Now, in the foyer of her father's house, the fragrance of the banquet flowers faintly perfuming the air, the house itself spotless, silent and waiting, Elise knew for sure what she had never before been quite able to admit, even to the most secret and solitary corner of her heart.

Gently, she withdrew from his embrace. Stepped back a pace. Looked up into the glow and dazzle of his face, Jared's expression solemn now, yearning. Almost comical in the intensity of his desire. And very nearly irresistible.

"Jared, I can't. I'll always remember . . . what we had. I'll always love what we had. I don't want to change you—it was stupid of me to imagine I could." Then the words failed her. It felt as though anything she said now might choke her. And yet she knew she must speak.

"It's me who's changed, darling," she continued, "and that isn't your fault or mine. I didn't want it to happen, or plan it."

"No," he said. "You didn't." As he spoke, the expression of yearning on Jared's face became what Elise had never before seen there. It became something very much like fear. Then a quick rippling grin, a shrug, his hand reaching out, tentatively, to touch her cheek. "I loved you, Elise."

She blinked and he was gone. Quicksilver Jared. Elise stood in the foyer as though she had fallen under some fairy-tale enchantment.

Half of her wanted to run out into the snow after him; the other half was firmly rooted in the future.

She had no sense of time passing. Then the gentle chiming of an old French clock in the library reminded her of her promise to Jean-Paul.

Moving in a kind of trance, Elise pulled on her parka and walked out of the house and down the snowy street to the restaurant.

Gérard, Steve and Barry were in full swing now. The duck terrines had been baked and were cooling. The barquettes of puff pastry were all shaped and set out on baking sheets all ready for the convection oven.

Elise was just tasting the sauce aurore when the phone rang. She picked up hesitantly, wondering what new complication this might be. "Le Palais-Royal, good afternoon."

"Elise!"

He's alive, he's here, he sounds like he's in the next room! Claude's voice was all she needed to hear.

"Claude! How's the baby? Where are you? When are you coming back?"

"You didn't get my telegram?"

"No."

"Merde! Excuse me, but I sent it two days ago. The baby

356

is fine—I have much to tell you, Elise. But first I must get myself out of Pittsburgh."

"Pittsburgh?"

"The storm, you see. But we—another passenger and I— are renting a car, driving to New York. A matter of perhaps six hours, he says."

"Claude, stay right where you are. Don't even think of driving in this. It's a major blizzard. You could be—"

"Chère Elise. I must come to you."

"Oh, Claude. . . . Please be careful."

"For you, dear Elise, I will always be careful."

She held the receiver tightly, as though by letting go she might lose him forever. "I'll be waiting."

"I will be there."

"Claude . . ."

"Chérie, how is everything proceeding with the banquet? Are you going ahead with it?"

"Oh, yes—at least, we're trying."

"I must go now, darling."

"Claude . . . I love you."

"And I, you, Chérie." He hung up.

Gently, she put down the receiver. It's true, she told herself. I do love him. And if he hadn't gone away, if Jared hadn't come back like that, it might have taken me forever to realize it. She walked out of her father's office in a fine daze of happiness.

All around her the preparations for the banquet were in full swing and Elise knew it was urgent she pay attention to every detail. But something had changed inside her. Nothing about the restaurant was the same as it had been just a few minutes ago. He's here, she kept telling herself, only half believing it, he's here. On his way. And he loves me. She looked around the kitchen. Everything was as ready as it could be.

Elise walked home with Jean-Paul and even managed to keep up some sort of conversation. But her mind was in

Pittsburgh and on all the hundreds of miles of treacherous snow-covered roads between there and New York.

Please, God, let him be all right. Let him come back to me in one piece. Let us have a chance to make it work.


Dave paused for a moment at the bottom of the eleven steps that led up to Kate's front door. Suddenly, they loomed like some immense, unclimbable mountain.

Stupid of me to ask her out for dinner. I'm rushing it, hell, we were together Thursday, we'll be together at the banquet tomorrow night as well. Knowing it was rash, knowing Kate might think him pushy, too high-pressure, Dave had asked her all the same.

The astonishing thing was, she'd accepted.

Now, what? Dave took a deep breath and climbed the stairs.

Kate opened the door and asked him in.

"You have to tell me, Kate, if I'm getting to be a nuisance."

She looked at him. Smiled, feeling a too familiar shiver of anticipation. Gently, Kate, she told herself. He is just being kind, after all.

But Kate knew it was something more than kindness, more than Dave's very real interest in Le Palais-Royal. She knew that every moment she spent with this man was a moment to be cherished. And it frightened her terribly. Too soon. Too fraught with complications. Kate felt so fragile. Unready for any sort of commitment, let alone a new romance.

She looked around the foyer, then back at Dave. "You are anything but a nuisance, Dave. You're very kind to ask me out. I have the worst sort of stage fright, and it isn't even my show."

"The house looks beautiful."

"Can I get you a drink?"

"No, thanks. Our reservation is for seven."

Kate went to the closet, got her coat, and let him help her

on with it. As she was about to go out the door, Kate remembered that Elise wouldn't know where she was. She
went to the kitchen and left a note, hoping as she wrote it
that the girl wouldn't think she was being evasive—or,
worse, disloyal, going out with Dave Hollander.

They walked down the steps.

Our first real date, Kate thought. Not knowing where
he'd made their supper reservation, she found herself wondering what people would think if they saw her with him.
With a sudden, unexpected surge of confidence, Kate realized she didn't care.

Elise and Jean-Paul came home to an empty house. Elise
found Kate's note and read it, smiling. Kate and Dave?
Well, hamburgers or not, he was an attractive man.

She looked at her watch. Nearly seven. Glancing around
the kitchen, she found all in order. She turned to Jean-Paul.

"Jean-Paul," she said, "how would you like to be my
guest at dinner tonight? After our adventures today, I think
we deserve a little treat."

He grinned. "But of course. I am honored." Elise wondered if she had ever been that young.

They rechecked the oysters, then went upstairs to change.

An hour later they were sitting in a booth in a small Jap-
anese restaurant on Third Avenue. The snow had stopped;
the place was full. They drank warm sake, shared a first
course of sushi, then a fine clear soup followed by ethereally
light tempura shrimp. Elise made sure it was Jean-Paul's
night. She still hadn't quite gotten over the shock of thinking she'd lost him in the fire and then getting him back
again, alive and smiling.

They laughed a lot, ordered more sake, feeling a little like
schoolchildren on an unexpected holiday. He told her about
his plans for his father's restaurant near Beaune.

He raised the tiny sake cup. "You will come and visit me
at Le Coq d'Or, Elise? You and Claude—and of course
Madame Villeromain?

359

"I'd love it," she said, remembering. "Especially since I've been there once before—you were a tiny boy—with my father. Le Coq d'Or is one of the loveliest country restaurants in the world. I'm betting that with you in the kitchen, you'll get that third star."

He blushed, hardly daring to dream of the legendary third star rating in the all-powerful *Guide Michelin*. The waiter appeared with a menu for dessert.

"Red bean ice cream," said Jean-Paul in wonderment. "Who thought of that?"

"A genius. But, when you analyze it, it's not so different from my father's glacé des marrons, is it?"

He nodded.

"Speaking of Michelin stars."

Kate was in when they got back to the house. She invited Elise into her bedroom. "Darling," Kate said pensively, "what do you think of Dave Hollander—really. As a man, not as a business partner."

Elise paused. What was going on here? "Well. That's a heavy one, Kate. After. all the dirt I've done the poor guy, you might imagine I loathe him. Really, I don't. Actually, I'd never thought about him before all this. Is he making passes?"

Kate felt herself blushing. "Not exactly, and he'd better not. But . . . there is something. I keep wondering if I'm not a silly old widow-lady getting hot flashes. The truth is, I find him very attractive."

"And it's mutual?"

"I get that impression. Mind you—it's only an impression."

Elise smiled, thinking of Jared. Of how vastly her relationship with him had changed since Daddy's death. Maybe, she realized, it was Daddy who kept me with Jared. As an act of defiance.

"Well, Kate, I don't think I have very believable credentials as a romance counselor. Dave's fine. I always wrote him off as a type—Mister Corporate America, if you will.

But he's better than that. His dinner party was really special. You don't pull off an evening like that without a lot of taste—and a lot of thoughtful planning."

"Can I take it that you wouldn't be completely horrified if . . . something came of it?"

"Dear Kate. Ever since you came into Daddy's life, I've acted like a rotten, resentful brat. Don't ever think I'm not aware of the happiness you brought to Daddy. So anything that brings you happiness now, well, I'm all for it. Even if it turns out to be Dave Hollander."

Elise kissed her stepmother lightly on the forehead and went back to the guest room. Thought about waiting up for Claude. No, that's impossible, I'd be a wreck, and he may not even make it tonight. I'll need every grain of energy just to get through the banquet.

She shut off the light, climbed into bed, and closed her eyes. But her last thought before sleeping wasn't of Claude, it was of Kate. At least one thing's going right around here, whatever happens tomorrow. And Kate deserves it. Bless her.

Claude looked at the enormous man at the wheel of their rented Ford and thought, not for the first time, that good luck can come in strange packages. Lawrence Benjamin. "Call me L.B." Burlingame was not a man to be held back by blizzards, earthquakes, or hurricanes, and he supplied Claude with a seemingly endless fund of tales that illustrated his lifelong triumph over the conspiracies of nature. Well over six feet tall and with the build of a professional football player, which he had been, L.B. had a meeting to make in New York on Sunday and nothing was going to prevent him from being there.

Claude was grateful for the man's monologue, for his awe-inspiring enthusiasm for driving and his invincible conviction that they'd be in New York by early in the morning. L.B.'s stories gave Claude a welcome opportunity to sit back and think. The big car seemed to be floating through the storm. The highway was nearly empty and they traveled in a world whose furthest boundary was the end of the headlight's beam. Snowflakes moved at them and past them, and Claude remembered a film he had seen, a science fiction thing of spaceships gliding through galaxies of stars, billions of tiny bright pinpoints that reminded Claude of this, of the billions of snowflakes that now defined time and space.

She was fine on the telephone, sounded glad to hear my voice, and when she said she loved me it was as if an angel had sung out the news. But what will she feel when she hears of my plans for François?

L.B. Burlingame had just battled Hurricane Edna and was beginning to deal with an avalanche in Chamonix. Claude tried to listen, to make the appropriate expressions of wonder, but his heart was in the house on Sixty-eighth Street. And for all his eagerness to get there, he felt afraid.

Maybe she just isn't ready yet. For me. For the baby. How can I expect her to become an instant mother, with all that involves? As if running Le Palais weren't enough.

It took them three hours to reach Harrisburg. Outside of Harrisburg L.B. pulled into a big service station and restaurant and they had coffee and sandwiches. Claude had lost track of time but L.B. counted every minute.

"Three forty-five A.M." he said, checking the huge gold Rolex on his brawny wrist. "With any luck at all, we'll be in New York by seven thirty-eight."

The windshield wipers beat their way across the glass with a steady hypnotic rythm. To Claude it was as though they were saying Elise . . . Elise . . . Elise. He closed his eyes and prayed that she'd understand. That she'd still want him when he told her about François.

Kate lay in bed thinking—of Dave, of Elise. And especially of Pierre. The emptiness of her bed seemed endless around her. This bed she had shared so joyously with Pierre: it mocked the emptiness of her life now.

362

Don't fall into self-pity, Kate, she told herself sternly. You've got your health, decent looks, a talent for painting and, when it's all settled, a fine nest egg as well. Why did it all seem meaningless? Even Elise's response earlier on—her kindness about Dave—hadn't produced the effect Kate had hoped for.

Kate was vividly aware of the danger built in to her attraction for Dave. It might not be what it seemed to be. Dave might be attentive out of respect for Pierre's memory—or from a more mercenary motivation. She tried to imagine a life with Dave. And one without him. No luck on either score.

Well, she thought, rolling over for what might be the thousandth time, tomorrow will tell. After the banquet we'll all have a better idea of where we're going. The thought was a cold comfort.

Elise woke, blinked, and thought, Here it comes. Like a speeding freight train, and I'm tied to the tracks and my rescuer is nowhere to be seen. She shivered, hugged herself, imagining Claude dead in some snowdrift.

She pulled the blankets over her head, turned on her side and tried to force herself back to sleep. This day will be long enough as it is, she thought.

But the banquet would not leave her head.

She thought of Gérard and how helpful he'd been. Yes, we might almost just do it even without Claude. But Gérard isn't Claude. And again she had a feeling of abandonment, a dark chill in her soul that had nothing to do with logic.

She got up and took a long hot shower. Much better. Ten minutes later she was down in the kitchen for breakfast, dressed in jeans and an old sweatshirt. Ravenous. She made waffles, huge Belgian ones on Daddy's special waffle iron. They were just beginning to sputter and get crisp when Jean-Paul came down and joined her.

They ate like construction workers: waffles, maple syrup,

363

eggs, sausage, coffee. Eating as though she might never see another square meal, Elise began to feel better. Claude will be here soon. The banquet will be a smash hit. We'll all live happily ever after.

But no sooner had these cheerful thoughts formed themselves in her head than an old and too familiar inner voice said, You really are dumb, Elise, to imagine all that. What have you ever done to deserve such luck? How do you know he really loves you? Or that the soufflés won't fall tonight, or that the Margaux 1900 won't taste like battery acid or that the Tastevin won't send out for pizza?

She laughed out loud.

Jean-Paul looked at her quizzically.

"Don't worry, Jean-Paul, I haven't really flipped out. I was just thinking something funny. Stupid-funny."

"Many things are."

After breakfast they walked down to the restaurant. The snow had stopped at last but the streets were almost empty and for the most part unplowed. The silence was eerie. Gérard and Armand and Barry and Steve were all in the restaurant. They went over the battle plan one more time.

"We've got to assume," said Elise, "that Claude won't make it. So that leaves Gérard and Barry here with Jean-Paul, Steve and me at Sixty-eighth Street with Armand and the waiters."

"And I drive the van," said Barry.

"Yes, and you'd better check it out right now, to make sure it got towed back all right."

Armand spoke up then. Elise was pleased to see him looking a little more like the Armand of old: better color, more confident. Even capable of smiling now and then. "The wines are already at your house," he said. "The champagne and the Meursault are cooling and the red wines are resting upright to settle the sediment. It's just a matter of decanting the Margaux."

Elise looked from face to face. Everything that could be done had been done. Somehow, despite knowing that they were as ready as anyone could be, she hesitated to leave the kitchen of Le Palais-Royal, as though she might be breaking some spell. But there was no point in staying. "Well," she said, "let's get a little rest before the battle, all right?"

"We'll be over after lunch to open the oysters, Elise," said Steve.

"Great. I'll be there."

Kate was in the kitchen when Elise got home, sitting alone with a cup of tea.

"Hi," said Elise casually.

Kate looked up, smiled a rather wan smile. "Hi, yourself. Elise—did I sound batty last night? Ranting on about Dave?"

Elise laughed. "Hardly batty. And not ranting. As they keep saying on the West Coast, Kate, go with the flow."

"That," said Kate decisively, "is how one can end up sailing down the drain. I've always made a point of swimming against the damn flow. Rather like a salmon going upstream to spawn."

"He really is a nice man, Kate."

"Yes. He seems to be. It's just that he's—disconcerting. I'd so much hoped for a quiet life now. To paint. Maybe travel."

"No one can paint twenty-four hours a day, Kate. And traveling's a lot more fun with someone."

"Well, I'm probably imagining things, anyway. Maybe when I sign—if I sign—he'll simply vanish forever."

"Not likely."

The doorbell rang.

"I'll get it," Elise said, walking briskly out of the kitchen.

Claude stood there on the doorstep carrying her old suitcase, looking haggard, unshaven and terribly tried, but to Elise he was the most beautiful thing she'd seen in days. Maybe ever.

"Claude."

All she could say was his name and then he was in the house and his arms were around her and for a long, long moment neither of them said a word. Elise only knew she felt safe again, that her world was rightside up again, that no matter what happened tonight there was this. There was Claude.

"Come." She took his hand and picked up the suitcase and led him upstairs. "Tell me everything," she said when they were alone in the guest room.

"That," he said softly, holding her, "would take a very long time. The first thing is, I love you. The boy is safe— better than safe, he is fine. Well. Her telegram was a fraud."

Elise looked up at him. Whatever she had expected it wasn't this. "But—your wife?"

"Dead. Some call it an accident, but in fact, it was a kind of suicide, poor woman. Fell in front of a truck."

Elise took a breath. "Claude, how awful for you. And for François."

"It is over, chérie. I am here—with you. And that is all that matters now."

Elise felt the magic but she hardly dared to believe in it. She kissed him again and it didn't matter that his beard scratched her or that her mind was staggering from the shock of Marie-Claire's death. "Claude," she said, "I've missed you more than I ever dreamed I could miss anyone."

"And I, too."

She began unbuttoning his shirt and in a moment their clothes were a tangle on the floor and Claude and Elise entwined on the big green bed. Their lovemaking was at once gentle and urgent, a blessing and a release. Most of all it was a celebration. And when Elise could think at all, what she thought was Yes! This is what it's all about. This is real, this is my man and I love him.

Much later she said, "But you must be exhausted, Claude. Try to get some sleep."

"And the banquet?"

"Tonight. Dave Hollander's chef has been helping. You remember Gérard?"

"Très bien."

Claude did manage to sleep for a few hours. When he woke he showered, shaved, changed his rumpled clothes, greeted Kate, and went to Le Palais to help.

All through the afternoon they kept the phone connection open, just as they had done on the night of the run-through. Elise was enormously relieved to have Claude back and well and in love with her. But still she had fears about the banquet, and it seemed when she took one last look at the improvised dining room with her father's portrait hanging over the mantelpiece that she might disgrace him still.

Time crawled.

Finally it was five thirty, and she went up to dress. Took her burgundy silk dress from the closet and slipped it on, feeling a little like some athlete dressing for the big decisive game. I've never worn this dress anywhere but in Le Palais-Royal, and tonight Kate's house is Le Palais-Royal. For better or worse.

She looked at herself in the mirror; a pale stranger looked back. War paint is definitely in order, she decided, adding a blush of color to her cheeks, a slim line on her eyelids, a touch of pale ruby lipstick.

When she came downstairs at six the house was alive again, kitchen filled with Palais-Royal waiters immaculate in their black dinner jackets, laughing and joking as they always did.

"This is it, boys, the main event," she said, praying her voice was as light as she wanted it to be, that her stage fright was hidden. But just having them there made her feel better, and Steve too, arranging hors d'oeuvres on silver trays, getting ready to supply the waiters with champagne glasses. She asked Steve if she could help.

He looked up and smiled.

"You," he said with a courtly bow, "are the great lady of Le Palais-Royal tonight. Not to soil one's dainty fingers. Besides, we're in good shape—I think."

Kate came down then, splendid in green silk.

Elise kissed her.

367

"Kate, you look smashing. Really great."

"Thanks, dear. I feel like—I don't know what. I'd more confidence when I was fifteen, that's for sure."

"You will knock 'em dead."

"Just so long as they don't actually laugh." But Kate was pleased. Maybe tonight would tell her something after all. She reached out and took both Elise's hands in hers.

"Darling," Kate said simply, "I wish you the very best of luck."

They were cut off by the doorbell. Reverend Romney in an immaculately cut satin-lapeled dinner jacket and clerical collar. Worried about his Margaux.

"I shall decant it myself, Elise, if you don't mind."

Elise didn't mind.

The doorbell rang again; the evening had begun in earnest now. Dave Hollander, and with him that man Elise had met at his dinner party—Steele. With a smile to match his name. You could cut yourself on that smile, she thought, wondering why he was here. It was not a Tastevin sort of smile.

Soon the party was in full swing. Justin Bosch came in, kissed her, wished her luck. He pointed out another member, the restaurant critic of *Manhattan Magazine,* a friendly-looking woman who might not be so friendly in print.

Elise shuddered—and smiled. And smiled. But it was good to see the waiters gliding smoothly among the guests with trays of champagne flutes. The house looks wonderful she decided, and not just because it's ours. She could see that being in Pierre Villeromain's private house was having an effect on the guests. Thank God we didn't go for some suite in a hotel. And bless Kate for letting us have the place.

Harry Pierrepont came in, radiating good cheer and afflu-ence. Armand was there to greet him, smiling like the Ar-mand of old, the Armand before the fire.

Did Pierrepont whisper something secret into Armand's ear? Elise, across the room, couldn't tell.

More people. Sleek, perfectly dressed people. Men out-numbering the women maybe three to one. Elise forced herself to circulate, shaking hands and trading small talk and still managing to check the kitchen now and then. Redundantly, it turned out, because everything was working just the way they'd planned it.

So far.

The Laurent-Perrier Grand Siècle was flowing. In the kitchen, the puff pastry barquettes were crisping in the convection oven. The oysters awaited their brief poaching in the sauce.

Elise scanned the room. How would Armand do it? With style and charm. Elise herself felt about as charming as a wet hen. There, across the room, Dave Hollander was talking to Kate. *There* was style, and charm, and all the rest of it. Confidence as well. Instinctively Elise felt the familiar jab of resentment. That he should be here, and with Kate. That he should so effortlessly intrude on her dream.

But then she remembered that Dave had dreams of his own. And how helpful he'd been these last desperate weeks. How he'd given her Gérard and offered more—just about anything, really. In that moment, something changed in her heart. She took a deep breath and walked across the room, forcing herself to move slowly, to nod and smile and not to spill her barely tasted glass of champagne.

Both Kate and Dave paused in their conversation when she came up to them. Turned and smiled. Elise could feel the warmth of it. "Dave, I just want to thank you," she said softly, "and to let you know that, however tonight turns out, I think—I pray—that we can work together. I know I've been terrible—unreasonable, childish, all of that. And I'm sorry, truly."

Dave looked at her and the easy social smile left his face. "You have been terrific," he said. "You've been brave and tenacious, you've overcome incredible odds and done plenty of things they usually give medals for. You don't have to apologize to me, Elise. I'm one of your biggest fans."

Elise could feel the tears welling up. She managed a little smile, nodded her gratitude, touched Dave's hand and quickly turned away. Moved through the room in a daze. Made her way back to the kitchen, where everything was moving precisely and harmoniously toward the start of the banquet. She prayed that her father, wherever he was, might look down on all this and approve.

A little after eight Armand suggested to Kate that it might be time to seat the guests. For each guest there was a pale celadon green place card inscribed in dark green ink by the woman whose impeccable calligraphy adorned the menus at Le Palais-Royal.

There had been three cancellations. Reverend Romney urged Elise to dine with her guests,

"Thanks, Reverend, but I'd be too nervous." She smiled graciously and considered it an achievement. What, she wondered, can I possibly look like to all these sophisticated people? She knew, because she had checked and rechecked every tiny detail, that all of the banquet arrangements were perfectly in order. But that knowledge was only a small consolation. She felt danger lurking on every tray, in every glass, in the house's wiring and gas connections, in the functioning of the doorbell and the tires of the van.

The only possible salvation for her sanity was the inescapable fact that the great juggernaut was in motion now, gathering momentum, taking on rythmns of its own. Elise felt it in every nerve of her body as she strained to listen for things that might be going wrong in the kitchen, while she stood among the guests, projecting, she most devoutly prayed, the very image of confidence. Ha!

Waiters were going in with the Meursault now. Steve was on the kitchen phone speaking in low tones to Claude at Le Palais, coordinating the evening as though it were some crucial military operation.

Trays of Olympia oysters went by, the armada of puff pastry barquettes golden, the sauce Aurore glistening pinkly. Elise watched this and thought, The Tastevin will never know what they cost, those oysters. Steve was slicing the terrine de canard en croute, Jean-Paul garnishing the plates.

In the library DeWitt Steele sat at the same table as Dave and Kate. Took a bite of the oysters, said nothing, sampled the exquisite puff pastry and the silken sauce, looked up to find Dave's eyes on him. Just as quickly looked down. Took another bite.

I hope you choke on it, DeWitt. Dave turned to his left, to Kate. Is she different tonight, or am I imagining things? Kate was being charming—publicly charming. She gave Dave no sign at all about how she felt inside.

Elise looked at the group. The Chevaliers were a formidable collection of men and women whose knowledge of food and wine was world famous. There was wealth here to be sure, but something more as well: exquisite taste. Taste that could not be fooled. Please let them like the meal. Let the wines please them, and the service. Let us get through this night.

Elise went from the foyer into the kitchen, sat down for a moment and as quickly got up. Nervous as a cat—more nervous. Cats aren't, really. Ate one of the cheese straws that had been passed with the champagne.

Elise felt her mind racing as she imagined what the kitchen at Le Palais-Royal must be like just now. The split-second timing of the roast filets of beef, the continuous communication by telephone, the coordination with the kitchen here, the timing of the vegetable purees, the very slicing of the hot duck terrine, the warming of plates—thank God Daddy had been enough of a perfectionist to have a professional plate warmer installed in this kitchen—the complexity was breathtaking, and Elise's underlying nervousness was complicated by her equally pervasive sense of helplessness: a feeling that events were out of her control now.

Suppose Claude's jet lag catches up with him? What if he's simply too tired to concentrate the way a chef must concentrate? Will he get on with Gérard? With an uncontrollable shudder Elise recalled some of the scenes Yves had caused when his temper got out of hand. Maybe Gérard, pleasant though he'd always appeared, had secret depths of temperament.

Elise knew that if she didn't stop worrying she might literally go mad. All the same, she worried.

The waiters were going in with the duck terrine now, other waiters pouring the 1959 Margaux.

Elise walked over to the table where the cheeses were out and ready and had been for three hours. Not, she thought, that anyone's really going to bother with the cheeses when there's 1900 Margaux to be tasted. Still, the cheeses must be perfect.

Everything must be perfect.

Minutes passed. Claude and Barry came in, carrying between them a huge roasting dish that held eight filets of beef wrapped in foil. They carved, piping the vegetable purees through pastry bags into decorative shapes on the serving plates. Then the sauce, a sprinkle of parsley, a sprig of watercress.

The Reverend Romney came bustling in, followed by Armand, and proceeded to decant the 1900 Margaux. He opened each bottle with the care and precision of a brain surgeon, sniffed the cork, wiped the lip of the bottle with a cloth and held each bottle up to a candle flame while gently, gently pouring the wine through a crystal funnel into a crystal pitcher; rinsing the funnel for each bottle, a fresh crystal pitcher for each bottle.

Claude began whipping egg whites.

The crystal pitchers were placed on silver trays and carried into the dining rooms. Then the cheese trays.

There was an immediate hush throughout the house.

Elise stood in the doorway, watching. Afraid even to breathe: The moment all the Tastevin had been waiting for. Romney stood up. "Ladies and gentlemen, the 1900 Margaux."

Polite applause was heard even before the first glass had been poured. An historic occasion. Nobody could remember a time when so much of so precious a vintage had been poured.

The first glass was offered to Romney. The silence grew deep and purple as wine. He sniffed, frowned, sniffed again. Tasted. A very earthly kind of ecstasy suffused his face. Romney said nothing, but left the diners to form their own opinions.

In that moment the Chevaliers were as one with the gods of wine. They knew it and rejoiced in it.

"Magnificent, Romney," said Justin Bosch, speaking for all. "Utterly magnificent. Silky, I call it, a slight hint of cedar, which is as it should be, complex but gentle—and that finish. What a finish!"

Sounds like he's talking about a horse race, thought Elise, who hadn't been able to resist standing in the doorway and watching.

"Then you agree there may be something left?" Romney was suddenly coy, feigning nervousness. Elise was fascinated. She knew what an element of one-upsmanship there often was among wine lovers. Merely by owning the 1900 Margaux, Romney had achieved distinction. By serving it he had made himself an instant legend. And we're part of it, she thought: whenever they remember the Margaux, they'll remember where they had it. What they ate. Who was here.

The cheese trays, as Claude had predicted, went virtually untouched.

From the kitchen she detected a faint teasing aroma of raspberry. A little more relaxed now, Elise stayed in the doorway watching the Chevaliers du Tastevin as they romanced the ancient Bordeaux. Slowly they twirled their glasses, sniffing voluptuously, making the moment last. Making love to the wine.

Then a door opened behind her.

A waiter came in bearing a silver tray, and on the tray

were eight perfectly puffed raspberry soufflés, with the deep red raspberry puree that went with them.

There was more applause as the waiter walked into the dining room, Six other waiters following, one by one.

We did it, she thought. We really and truly did.

The air in the twin dining rooms was fragrant with the essence of raspberries, resonant with good cheer.

At Dave's table a waiter handed him an ivory-colored business card turned upside down. Written across the back of it were just two words: *You win*.

The card was DeWitt's.

Dave looked at Steele and nodded, just the barest hint of a nod, perhaps undetected by anyone else at the table. Steele smiled his razor smile.

He may not be finished with me yet, thought Dave, but he'll think twice before he comes on so strong about some new project that may not be exactly by the book or by the numbers as DeWitt sees them.

The relief that Dave felt was enormous but it wasn't the most important emotion in his heart. For that he looked to Kate.

She looked at him. No words were spoken, but something in her glance told Dave all he needed to know: that the glow in his heart might be reciprocated. That it wasn't some crazy adolescent dream, after all. It felt so right somehow.

Dave put his hand over hers and held it, and might have let out a war whoop of pure joy if Reverend Romney hadn't beat him to it with the clarion ringing of a silver spoon on a crystal wineglass, ancient signal that the toasts were about to begin.

"Kate Villeromain," he began, "and Elise Villeromain, fellow Chevaliers du Tastevin, odious as comparisons always must be, I am moved to declare this the finest banquet we've ever had."

"Hear! Hear!"

The voices came from every corner of the two dining rooms.

"We all know the difficult—tragic—circumstances that preceded this unforgettable meal. First the death of our beloved fellow Chevalier and former president, Pierre, whom we all consider the finest chef of his generation. Then, while his daughter was struggling bravely to carry on at Le Palais-Royal, another tragedy struck. The fire. The restaurant gutted. Another sort of young woman—another sort of restaurant—might simply have canceled. Not Elise."

At that moment Romney's eyes met hers and in his eyes Elise could see a radiance of pride.

"Elise," he went on, "is a true Villeromain. Tonight she has proven that beyond question. So I propose that the first toast be to her. To the new patronne of the best restaurant in the world. To Elise—with thanks."

Blushing and more than blushing, Elise looked down the length of the two rooms, past all the smiling, encouraging faces, past the beautiful flowers and the glowing candles. She was looking not at her guests but at Kate's painting of her father.

Daddy, help me. She looked left and right and wished for Claude.

Claude appeared at her side. Smiling. Handsome in his chef's whites, hardly showing the immense fatigue she knew he must feel after all he'd been through. When Romney had praised her Elise had felt the tears coming. Now she took Claude's hand and blinked them away.

She spoke softly, but in a voice that could be heard the length of the two rooms. "Thank you, Reverend Romney. If anyone ever got a finer compliment, I can't think what it could be. I hope that wherever he is tonight, my father heard those words. But I didn't create this banquet. Everyone at Le Palais-Royal had a hand in it. Including one great chef whom we borrowed: Géraud Rideau. But the inspiration was Claude's. May I present our new chef de cuisine, Claude Montgeron?"

More applause, cheers, ringing of spoons on glasses.

Elise went on, blushing fiercely now. "We're here tonight in my father's house by the invitation of a remarkable woman—his wife, Kate, whom I can never thank enough for her kindness—especially these last days, since the fire."

The clapping seemed to fill the room.

"Kate helped to make this evening special not just by lending us her house; she worked like a galley slave to make these lovely cloths and napkins herself, arranged for the flowers and more. It couldn't have happened without you, Kate."

Kate rose, flustered, bowed in acknowledgment of the cheers, but refused to speak.

Fresh champagne glasses were being handed around now, and trays of cordials as well. Elise and Claude each took a glass of champagne. He looked at her. Looked deeply into her eyes, and suddenly there were no Chevaliers du Tastevin, no Kate, not another soul in the house but the two of them.

He lifted his glass and touched it to the rim of hers. "Well, Chérie, you got what you wanted."

"What I want is you."

He put his other arm around her and held her close.

"And I, you."

That was all he said and all he needed to say.